THE DREAMERS

Rider McCall: A second-generation trainer who had watched his dad cheat death for a chance to run for the roses, he understood the power of dreams. It was just that his own seemed so damned fragile.

Colby Creighton: Pampered and beautiful, she became a plaything for disaster. But no matter how far she ran, she couldn't forget Rider McCall . . . or the dreams that wouldn't die.

THE DECEIVERS

Leland Creighton: Money, manipulation and a convenient marriage had made the senator the man he was today. His lust for power knew no bounds.

Jock McCall: A hardworking trainer whose pretty young wife's infidelity drove him to drink, he didn't yet realize his own capacity for revenge.

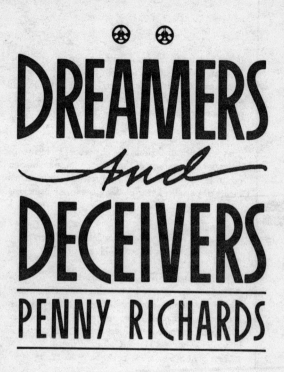

DREAMERS and DECEIVERS

PENNY RICHARDS

HarperPaperbacks
A Division of HarperCollinsPublishers

This is a work of fiction. The characters, incidents, and
dialogues are products of the author's imagination and are
not to be construed as real. Any resemblance to actual
events or persons, living or dead, is entirely coincidental.

HarperPaperbacks   *A Division of* HarperCollins*Publishers*
10 East 53rd Street, New York, N.Y. 10022

Copyright © 1991 by Penny Richards
All rights reserved. No part of this book may be used or
reproduced in any manner whatsoever without written
permission of the publisher, except in the case of brief
quotations embodied in critical articles and reviews. For
information address HarperCollins*Publishers*,
10 East 53rd Street, New York, N.Y. 10022.

Cover photography by Herman Estevez

First printing: October 1991

Printed in the United States of America

HarperPaperbacks and colophon are trademarks of
HarperCollins*Publishers*

10 9 8 7 6 5 4 3 2 1

DEDICATION

This book is dedicated to all the trainers, jockeys, grooms, hot walkers, pony girls and guys, blacksmiths, vets, and equine dentists—the hardworking people of the backside who put in seven days a week and without whom there would be no "sport of kings."

ACKNOWLEDGMENTS

Without the help of the following people, this book could not have been written. Many thanks.

Ken Richards—former trainer and the guy who ate a lot of fast food while this book was being written

JoVaughn Spraker—my connection

Jockeys Jerry Engle and Pat Day

Bill J. R. Wilson—the *Daily Racing Form*

Pat Powell—head starter, Louisiana Downs

Julia Williams—R.N.

Donna Addison—reference librarian, Garland County Library

Ray Stanfill—B.S., M.C.J.

Steve Asmussen—trainer

Rodney Butler—D.V.M.

AUTHOR'S NOTE

To the owners, trainers, and riders of horses running in any of the races mentioned in this book, I beg your indulgence and your pardon for the poetic license I've taken. My "tampering" with the conditions and outcomes of these races was necessary to the development and completion of this work of fiction.

PROLOGUE

"Oh, my God! Ohmigod!"

The words, escalating in volume and panic, parted the fog of unconsciousness hovering over Jackson ("Jock") McCall. He didn't want to be awake. Awake meant he could feel the pain that burned in his gut and pulsed through his body like hot waves in a fiery sea.

"Somebody! Somebody, please! Call an ambulance!" Over the frantic plea, Jock could hear the sound of feet pounding on the hard-packed dirt outside the tack room. Then silence. No. He could hear a whispered, feverish Hail Mary punctuated by an occasional sob of fear.

Through the racking waves of pain, Jock realized that the voice he heard belonged to his groom, Tomas Ramirez. He also realized it had been a long time since he'd been to mass.

He wanted to thank the kid, to laugh and tell him he was going to be fine, but another wave of agony and weakness washed over him. He couldn't speak or move. And he wasn't going to be fine. Dear God, he was sick, so sick . . . and afraid the doctors were right . . . afraid. . .

"What happened?" Another voice.

"I don't know. I just found him laying here in this—"

"Jesus, would you lookit the blood," yet another voice said. "Did he shoot himself?"

They were talking about him as if he weren't there, Jock thought as his tenuous grip on consciousness weakened. And maybe he wasn't going to be for long. *Holy Mary . . .*

"Has he got any family?"

"A son. In California, I think."

. . . pray for us sinners now and at the hour of our death. . . .

"Well, somebody sure as hell better call him."

Family. Vicky. Rider. He'd been so hard on them both. Too hard. Who did he think he was—God? *Help me. . . .*

From a distance, he could hear the sound of the approaching sirens. So far away. Too far. . . .

1

The forty-seven natural springs cloistered at the eastern gateway of the Ouachita Mountains were said to cure everything from arthritis to high blood pressure. Effective or not, the thermal waters had lured a steady influx of health seekers to the valley ever since Hernando de Soto scouted the area in 1541.

To reap the medicinal blessings of the Great Spirit, warring Indian tribes gathered at the neutral territory and laid down their arms long enough to bathe together in the steamy waters.

After its permanent settlement in 1807, Hot Springs became a mecca for tourists, especially Yankee tourists, anxious to try the curative waters and eager to escape the rigors of the northern winters.

From Reconstruction days until the sixties, the spa city was known for its gambling. It was the place to try a spin at the roulette wheel or a throw of the dice. By day, Central Avenue teemed with tourists; at night, the streets dazzled hotly with neon. Brazen, sassy, Hot Springs belonged to the hucksters and hookers, a come-on for the wealthy, the famous, and the infamous. There was a game for everyone who was game.

The heyday of the small Arkansas town came to an end with the help of a war hero who wanted the town cleaned up and a state police director determined to enforce the federal antigambling laws. One by one the celebrities stopped coming, and the casinos shut their doors.

Soon other doors had CLOSED signs on them. Even the bathhouses shut up one by one, leaving only two to serve the ailing. Like rats jumping a sinking ship, businesses deserted the downtown area and sprang up at the city's edge. There were various attempts to rejuvenate the downtown area, but despite the valiant efforts, Hot Springs succumbed to the slow-spreading disease afflicting downtowns across the country: progress.

Rider McCall was unaware of the changes or his surroundings. His mind was filled with thoughts of Jock.

It was hard to believe his dad was dying.

He'd been asleep when he got the phone call about Jock that morning, some Mexican kid named Ramirez speaking at Mach 2 told him that when he got to work at five he'd found Jock lying on the tack room floor.

"*Mucho* blood, Rider. You'll come, won't you?"

Rider had assured the kid that he'd come. And here he was.

How long had it been since he'd seen his dad, anyway? Four years? Five? Rider hadn't been back to see his dad since leaving Kentucky after his short stay eleven years before, but Jock had come to California to see him once. It had been disastrous, as every encounter between them was. They were oil and water, fire to ice, nitro on a bumpy ride. They'd never seen eye to eye, and from the wisdom gained in thirty-three years, Rider figured they never would.

So why had he taken the first flight out of L.A. to come and watch him die? Because regardless of the past, Jock was his father, and Rider owed him. Because blood was indeed thicker than water.

It only took about twenty minutes to cross town to the new, ultramodern hospital just south of the Hot Springs Country Club. Convenient for tennis elbow, Rider thought wryly.

He found a parking place and climbed out of the rental car. Dark clouds held the sunshine at bay, and a frosty wind whipped through the parking lot. Shivering, he turned up the collar of his jacket.

After spending the first twenty-two years of his life there, it hadn't taken him long to get used to the California sunshine again. Rider wasn't one for extremes. He liked the even temperatures of the West Coast.

Stepping into the hospital's sudden hush, he approached the front desk, which was staffed by a senior citizen with cotton-candy hair. She gave him a pleasant smile and directions to the second floor. Rider shared the elevator with an extremely pregnant girl and her husband. They were holding hands and looking at each other as if life couldn't get any better. Neither looked out of their teens. He felt old, suddenly. And more than a little lonely.

He left the elevator and, following a circuitous route, found the nurses' station, where a pretty blonde was filling out forms. A plastic pin on her uniform confirmed that she was Amy Chapman, R.N.

"Excuse me."

The R.N. looked up.

"I'm here to see Jackson McCall."

"Mr. McCall is in intensive care. Are you a relative?"

"I'm his son. I just flew in from California."

"Oh." She consulted a chart.

"What's wrong with him? The kid who called me didn't know much except that he'd lost a lot of blood."

She nodded. "He was brought in vomiting blood from a bleeding ulcer. Your father is an alcoholic, Mr. McCall." There was an apology in her eyes and voice.

"I know." The two words were heavy with the weight of an old pain. "Is he going to pull through?"

"That isn't for me to say," she hedged. "You'll need to talk to the doctor. Your father isn't in very good condition at the moment. We've given him blood, but he needs more. Unfortunately he's O negative, and, like all blood these days, it's hard to come by. We have a call in to the blood bank at Little Rock."

"I'm O negative," Rider said. He knew from an accident he'd been in at nineteen, during his short stint as a Hollywood stunt man. His first car chase had left him with a slight concussion, a gash on his thigh that had taken more than a hundred stitches to close, and a notice that he'd been replaced by someone with more experience. His dream to make it on the big screen had unraveled like the gauze used to dress his wounds.

"We'll have to test and cross-type you," the nurse said.

"No problem."

His slow smile almost sent Nurse Amy Chapman's professionalism backsliding. "You can go in for five minutes. I'll see if I can round up a lab technician."

"Thanks."

In a matter of minutes, an aide had ushered him to the intensive care unit and he was standing in the doorway looking at the man who had shaped his life.

Jock looked smaller, shrunken, somehow. There was a yellow cast to his skin. From the fluorescent lighting? Or from his ruined liver?

There were tubes everywhere: oxygen to his nose, a catheter draining into a bag attached to the side of the bed, an IV with a pint of blood dripping life through the needle taped to the back of his hand, and cables to the monitor that tracked the weak beat of his heart.

"You aren't supposed to be in here."

Rider's gaze moved from his father to a plump nurse with frizzled hair and a frown.

"I'm his son. Nurse Chapman said I could have five minutes. How is he?"

"He could be better, but we have the vomiting and bleeding under control for the moment." She shrugged. "He's holding his own. He came around a few minutes ago, asking for Vicky and mumbling something about a rider."

Rider swallowed hard, suppressing both grief and surprise. "I'm Rider. Vicky is—was—my mom. She's dead."

"Ah."

"Is it okay if I talk to him?"

The nurse nodded. "He may not answer. If he does, keep it brief."

Rider went to the bed. Emotion clotted in his throat and a familiar feeling of inadequacy washed over him. What could he say to this man to whom he'd never been good enough?

"Dad?" he said at last.

Nothing.

"It's me, Rider."

Jock's eyelids fluttered to half-mast, and the heaviness in Rider's chest lightened a little. He leaned over and looked into Jock's glazed brown eyes.

"You came."

If he hadn't been standing so close, Rider wouldn't have heard the words. He blinked back the stinging beneath his eyelids. For some reason he was having trouble breathing around the tight knot in his chest. "Of course I came. How're you feeling?"

Jock's lips twitched, as if they were trying to form a smile. "Bet-ter."

2

Jock's eyes closed again. Battling a sense of futility, Rider went back to his station against the wall and watched the slow rise and fall of his father's chest. It hurt to see Jock so still and frail when he'd always been so full of piss and vinegar.

It was hard to accept that he was about to die. Rider was glad he'd come back. After he had received the Ramirez kid's message, Rider had called Farley Pennington, Jock's old friend and Rider's boss these last few years. Despite the fact that he was busy getting another crop of yearlings ready to run, Farley urged Rider to leave on the next flight to Arkansas.

Farley and Jock went back a long way, and Farley had been a part of Rider's life for as long as he could remember. It was to "Uncle" Farley that he had turned when he and Jock had a falling-out, which was often. It wasn't that he hadn't tried to get along. As a kid, he'd knocked himself out trying to be what Jock wanted.

The mesmerizing *blip . . . blip . . . blip* of the monitor soothed Rider's troubled mind. One of his earliest memories suddenly surfaced. He could distinctly recall being lifted from his crib and bundled into a blanket. Though it was pitch dark, it was time for his parents to go to work. Vicky had been Jock's best groom, his helpmeet in the purest sense of the word. Rider remembered his mother holding him against her shoulder while Jock drove to the track. He could almost smell the scent of her Tabu, her small rebellion against the humdrum sameness of her days.

"It makes me feel good, Rider," she'd said. "It makes me feel pretty even when I'm knee deep in horse manure."

When they reached the track each morning, his dad would push two battered lawn chairs together in the tack room, and his mother would lay him down to sleep until the sounds and scents of the track woke him.

He'd grown up with doughnuts and Coke or chocolate milk for breakfast, while the aroma of fresh-perked coffee, the tarlike smell of Reducine, and the heady scent of manure and sweating horseflesh mingled in his nostrils. Even as a kid Rider had loved the smells, had got high on them.

Horse racing, he had learned early in life, was as addictive as drugs. Once hooked, you wanted more. Faster horses. Bigger stakes. Wealthier owners. The dreams never stopped, but they were cheap for the most part, and everyone, his mama said, was entitled to them.

Rider was hooked on the dream before he could talk. It was simple, really. He loved the horses because he knew Jock loved them, and he loved Jock. Vicky once told him that "horsey" was his second word. The first was "Daddy."

As a child, he never went where he wasn't supposed to, never touched anything he was told not to, always did what he was asked. He followed his dad around the barn, watching, listening, trying to absorb everything he could. He was sharp, willing to learn, and he knew he was learning from two of the best—Jock and Farley. He never interrupted; Jock hated rudeness. He was polite to his elders, helpful to everyone, and everyone thought he was the greatest.

Everyone but his dad.

Jock was the sunshine of Rider's life, and Jock treated him like shit.

No matter what he did, it wasn't right. How in the hell did he expect the mud to work when he didn't put it on thick enough? The leg wraps were too loose; they'd fall off. Or they were too tight; what was he trying to do, bandage bow the son of a bitch? He never rubbed the alcohol in long enough. The Reducine wasn't hot enough; it was too hot. He forgot to put the goddamn vitamins in the feed. Didn't he know he couldn't touch the tongue tie with freeze on his hands before a race? If the horse was tested, the chemical would show up as a foreign substance in a blood or urine test.

Jock never laid a hand on him. There was no need to. His verbal dressings-down were more than sufficient. But because there were times Rider caught a glimpse of emotion on his dad's face—regret for the harsh word; rare, reluctant approval when some other trainer praised his abilities; a hint of sorrow for no apparent reason—Rider never stopped trying.

By the time he was ten, Rider had figured out that something was eating his father from the inside out, and that something had to do with him. Sometimes when his mother tucked him in at night, he asked her why Jock was mad at him all the time. She would get all flustered and start fluffing the pillows and straightening the covers.

"He's just busy, sweetheart. He doesn't mean anything by it. You know we've got that big race on Saturday." The answers, crooned in his mother's soft Texas drawl, varied, but they were always a denial that anything was wrong: you had to take care of business in the cutthroat world they lived in; you couldn't afford to slack off; the horses deserved the best care possible; his dad was just trying to teach him right.

Rider would nod, as if accepting her explanations, but the truth was he didn't think his dad liked him. When he asked Farley if he knew why, his father's friend suggested gruffly that maybe Jock's problem was that he didn't like himself much. The remark didn't make much sense to Rider, but he tucked it away with all the excuses his mother offered.

By the time he hit his teens, he'd decided that maybe his dad just didn't like kids and hadn't wanted any. After all, they were Catholic, and he was an only child. Maybe Jock would rather have had Vicky all to himself. Though Rider never figured out what his particular sin was, he had eventually come to terms with the fact that he and his dad would never get along.

"Mr. McCall."

The voice drew Rider's thoughts from the past, and his fixed gaze moved from the man in the bed to the tired-looking nurse. "Ma'am?"

"Your five minutes are up, and the lab technician's looking for you."

Reality came back with a rush. Rider drew himself away from the wall and scrubbed a weary hand down his face. He'd been awake since three-seventeen A.M. California time, with nothing to eat but the cardboard sandwich they'd given him on the plane. He was starving and exhausted and depressed, not necessarily in that order.

"You look pretty rough," the nurse said. "After you get through in the lab, go get some rest."

"What if he . . . you need to get hold of me?"

"You can call and let us know where to reach you."

Rider nodded and let himself out of the unit where one overworked woman stood guard between his father and death. He didn't want Jock to die. Not until they could work out whatever it was that had kept them apart for so long.

After Rider donated his blood, he got a room at the Holiday Inn on Lake Hamilton and called the hospital to let them know where he was staying. Then he dialed Farley.

"Pennington."

"Farley? Rider. I wanted to let you know I got here okay."

"Good. How's the old man?"

"They're not sure he'll make it through the night."

Farley swore. "Well, if he comes around, tell the sorry son of a bitch I love him, will you?"

"Yeah. I'll keep you posted."

"Do that."

They said their good-byes. Then, ignoring his growling stomach, Rider crawled into the king-size bed. Eating would have to wait until morning. Before he drifted off, he realized he was glad he'd come to be with Jock these last hours. His dad's feelings had nothing to do with his own.

3

Jock's room was small, private, and had a win-dow overlooking the parking lot. That he was able to be moved into it was nothing less than a miracle. Defying the doctor's prognosis and confounding the hospital staff, he had recovered enough from his ordeal on Friday to watch ESPN and bitch about the soft food he was forced to eat.

"It can't be that bad," Rider said, watching Jock attack the mass of Jell-O quivering in a hospital-issue plastic bowl.

"Hell, if you get hungry enough, you'll eat anything that doesn't eat you first," was Jock's testy reply.

Rider couldn't help smiling. The liquor had taken its toll on his father's looks, and after his brush with death, he looked at least ten years older than his fifty-six years. But he was like a good horse: if he was eating, he'd be all right.

Jock wiped his mouth with a paper napkin and speared Rider's gaze. "How soon are they gonna let me outa here?"

"I don't know, but I wouldn't rush it." Rider planned on letting the doctor break the news that Jock was being sent somewhere to dry out for thirty days.

"I was pretty bad off, wasn't I?"

Rider nodded.

"Thanks for coming." There was a gruff awkwardness in Jock's voice.

"Sure." Caught off guard by the unaccustomed approval, Rider turned and looked out the window. An elderly couple was crossing the asphalt, arm in arm. The man opened the car door and helped the woman in. Again Rider felt an intense longing for his mother. He supposed it was facing the knowledge that he'd almost lost Jock, too—and still could, if he didn't get his act together.

"What day is it, anyway?"

"Monday."

"Monday! I can't believe I missed opening day."

"There's a first time for everything."

Jock scowled. "I guess. Anything exciting happen?"

"Not really. Springer Martindale's filly win the second race, and Danny Brewster tore them up as usual."

Like all racetrackers, Rider used the eccentric "win" instead of "won."

Jock grunted and sipped his milk. "You been to see the horses?"

His once impressive stable had dwindled over the years. He had eight horses in training—five of his own and three that belonged to a die-hard owner who had more luck making money than he did in buying a winner. Small though it was, the stable was Jock's life.

"I've been checking with Tomas to make sure things are going okay and to let him know how you're doing."

"You've been *checking* with Tomas? Do you mean you haven't been to the track yourself?"

Rider's stomach knotted in an old familiar way. He managed to bridle his emotions but not his sarcasm. "No, I haven't gone to the track. I've been sitting in a waiting room down the hall, reading six-month-old magazines and chain-smoking, waiting to see whether or not you were going to check out on me." He threw Jock a challenging look. "Somehow it seemed like the right thing to do."

Jock had the grace to blush. "I'm sorry."

Rider leaned one shoulder against the wall and stared at the floor. He didn't remember ever receiving an apology from his dad before.

"It's just that I'm worried about Jock's Dream."

Rider looked up. "Jock's Dream?"

Jock grinned. "A gray colt who's gonna make the name of Jackson McCall one to be reckoned with again."

"Yeah? How's he gonna do that?"

Jock wore a satisfied smile that hinted at the man he once was. "He's gonna win me the Derby."

"The Arkansas Derby?"

"The *Kentucky* Derby, son. Maybe the Triple Crown."

"Sure." Rider pushed himself away from the wall and plunged his hand into his breast pocket in search of a cigarette. "And Warner Brothers is gonna call and ask me to do the stunts for their next *Lethal Weapon* flick." He held up his Marlboros. "I'm gonna go grab a smoke."

He was halfway to the door when Jock's voice stopped him. "What's the matter? Don't you think I've got what it takes to train a horse for the Derby?"

Rider turned. "I think you have plenty of what it takes to get a horse to the Derby," he said honestly. "I just can't believe you think you have a horse who does."

"Believe what I'm telling you."

Rider looked doubtful. "Yeah?"

"Yeah."

"Okay," Rider said, putting his cigarettes away and sauntering toward the bed. He folded his arms over his chest. "I'm listening. Where did you get this wonder horse?"

Jock grinned. He looked like a kid who'd just found out there really was a Santa Claus. "From a Texas oil man who went bust. You oughta see him, Rider, he's—"

"What did you have to give for him?"

"Twelve thousand dollars, but he—"

"Ah, Jesus, Dad!" Rider said, throwing up his hands. "You actually think that a twelve-thousand-dollar colt stands a chance against horses whose stud fees are ten, twenty times that much?"

"Why do you think I named him Jock's Dream? Ever hear of lady luck, Rider? Well, the bitch finally decided to smile on me. He's a nice colt."

Rider leaned on the edge of the bed. His dad wasn't stupid. The horse must have some ability or Jock wouldn't be so high on him. But any fool knew it took more than a nice colt to compete in the Derby. "You're serious, aren't you? You really think you can go up against the big boys?"

"I really do. Or did."

"What's that supposed to mean?"

"It means that we both know they're gonna send me somewhere for at least thirty days."

Rider's mouth twisted into a half grin.

"And if they do, the colt's gonna lose a month of training he can't afford to lose."

"So hire somebody to train him for a month. You can afford that, can't you?"

"I guess," Jock said evasively, "but I don't want some jackleg trainer letting him rip down the track just because he can. He trains easy, and I want him brought along slow. I need someone I can trust, Rider. I need you."

Rider stared at his father, unable to believe what he'd just heard. A thank-you, an apology, and a back-door compliment, all in the span of five minutes. Maybe Jock's brush with death had finally opened his eyes.

"I appreciate the vote of confidence, but I have a life waiting for me back in California."

"Oh, yeah, I forgot," Jock said, pushing his tray away. "That girl—what's her name? Molly?"

"Her name is Holly, but that's not what I'm talking about. That's been over for months. I have a job and people who count on me."

"Surely helping me win the Derby is more important than those nags you train for Farley Pennington."

A muscle in Rider's jaw tightened. "I train for several people, Dad, not just Farley. And since when did you start bad-mouthing old friends?"

"I'm not."

"Sounds that way to me. Look, I know it may come as a surprise to you, but I have a pretty good thing going out there. I have a good reputation, and it's getting better. I'm not Charlie Whittingham, but the horses I train are running good for me. I'm consistently one of the top ten trainers at Santa Anita and Hollywood."

"You think I don't know that? Why the hell do you think I want you?"

Again Rider was surprised. He'd never expected

Jock to follow his career. Still, that didn't change things. "It would never work."

"Why not?"

"Ah, c'mon, Dad! I wouldn't be at the barn five minutes before you'd be all over my ass for something. Thanks, but no thanks." He started for the door.

"I wouldn't be there, remember? You'll have a whole month to do whatever you want."

"No."

"Okay, okay," Jock said placatingly. "Just do one thing for me before you give me your final answer."

Halfway out the door, Rider pivoted on the heel of one scuffed Roper. "I thought I just did."

"All I want you to do is go to the track in the morning and watch the colt work out of the gates. I guarantee you'll like him."

Rider heaved a deep sigh. "Okay. I'll watch him work, but it won't make me change my mind."

"See if Danny Brewster can get on him."

"Sure. Anything else?"

"No," Jock said, grinning with self-satisfaction.

"Great. See you later."

Rider made his escape before his dad conned him into anything else. As the door swished shut behind him, he heard Jock call, "By the way, Jock's Dream outworked the Creighton colt last fall."

Rider faltered in midstride. Outworked the Creighton colt? He pursed his lips in a silent whistle. Runaway Again had already earned over a hundred thousand dollars in his short career. Rider was impressed. Very impressed.

4

Jock closed his eyes and listened to Rider's footsteps fade down the hallway. He prayed the boy would take him up on his offer. Winning the race was his only chance to salvage his reputation, his stable, his very life. And having Rider prep the colt was his only chance to win.

Jock thought again about the increasingly frequent letters he'd been getting from the bank. Three pay horses didn't generate enough day money to keep his operation going and keep the colt's nominations to the big races current. He'd had to put up the farm in east Texas to get money to operate on. Though he had been paying interest all along, the bank, like so many small lending institutions, had bitten the dust, and the new owners wanted some indication of when he could "make arrangements to pay his loan."

The farm wasn't much—just a frame house, an old red barn, and eighty acres—but it was his last tie to Vicky. Her father had left it to them when he died, and it had always represented the only permanence in their nomadic life. He and Vicky had planned to retire there someday, and it was the one tangible thing he could leave to Rider.

But Vicky would never retire with him now, and if the colt didn't win the Derby, Rider wouldn't inherit so much as pine cone.

Dammit! Jock rubbed a hand over his whisker-stubbled face. The bank ought to know he was good for the money. Didn't he drop them a check when the horses ran in the money?

It was time he was honest with himself. The truth was, he had a little betting problem when he was hitting the bottle, and he'd thrown a lot of good money after bad at the windows.

Jock closed his eyes and tried to remember when everything had started to go wrong. Had his stable started going downhill because of his drinking, or had he started drinking because his stable was going downhill?

No matter now. He was alive. He'd cheated death, and he wasn't about to die before he stood in the winner's circle at Churchill Downs in May. He'd gladly let the doctors put him someplace for a month. There was a time when Jackson McCall had been a respected name on the racetrack. Jock's Dream was his chance to make it so again.

5

Lexington, Kentucky
October 1956

Jock rested his forearms along the top rail of the fence, one small section of the endless miles of white boards that crisscrossed the bluegrass state's fields and farms. He narrowed his eyes against the stinging October wind that chased wispy clouds across the blue sky—the first they'd seen in days—and let his gaze wander the hills of Hastings' Meadows Farm.

The pasture, brown now from plummeting temperatures, would be carpeted in the famous Kentucky bluegrass come spring. Now it was dotted with once sleek mares whose distended bellies swayed ponderously when they walked, distinguishing them from the yearlings frolicking in nearby paddocks.

Across the way was a forty-stall barn stabling the horses in training, and beyond that stood a brick breeding and foaling barn with all the newest equipment, including a direct phone line to the resident veterinarian.

He had arrived. In style. Here he was, just twenty-three years old, already hooked up to one of the oldest names in the Thoroughbred industry: Hastings.

At the turn of the century, Wilton Hastings, whose blue bloodlines could be traced back throughout England's colorful history, had packed up his family, two brood mares, and a steeplechase champion and come to Kentucky via New York. In a few short years he had become one of the state's most successful breeders, a fact as well known and undisputed as the outcome of the Revolutionary War.

Because of their connections with England's peerage and their considerable wealth, the Hastingses were recognized as bastions of society both in Kentucky and, albeit reluctantly, by the "real" society of the East Coast, unlike the nouveau riche, who were always trying to scale the invisible wall separating the two.

As was expected, Jerrod, the first son, followed in his father's footsteps, maintaining the high quality of horseflesh the family was known for and adding scads of money—the result of manufacturing crucial airplane parts during the Second World War—to the family coffers.

The only thing that didn't go well with the Hastings plan of building an American dynasty was Jerrod's inability to sire a male heir. God's refusal to answer his plea for a son, blessing him instead with three daughters, Ashley, Alexandra, and Audra, was something he never quite came to terms with.

It was Alexandra, the middle daughter and her father's favorite, who shared the family passion for the four-legged creatures whose existence was synonymous with the name of Hastings. And it was Alexandra's husband, Leland Creighton, Jock had managed to impress.

Without being cocky, Jock knew he was good at what he did. Conscientious, hardworking, and determined to be a good horseman, he had worked his way up through the racetrack ranks, from walking hots to grooming to an assistant trainer's position.

Since he'd married Vicky Roberts less than a year ago, his desire to train had given way to an even greater desire. He wanted to give Vicky a stable home life, wanted to plant some roots and security for the large family that, as strong Catholics, they both wanted.

Barely twenty years old, Vicky, quite simply, was the love of his life. Auburn-haired and green-eyed, she was a bundle of irrepressible energy who encouraged him to seek his heart's desire, to dare to be everything he wanted. Together they had planned and dreamed, and now those dreams were coming true.

Jock let the heady sweetness of his success wash through him. He was actually going to manage the three-hundred-acre Thoroughbred farm Alexandra Hastings's grandfather had built from the ground up. In waning health since a heart attack, Jerrod had given his darling "Alex" the place two years earlier, when she'd married Leland Creighton, one of Kentucky's native sons.

With his smooth good looks and thriving law practice, possessing everything that money and position could attain, Jock's new boss was touted by all Kentucky as a man to watch, a man whose star was on the rise. Leland, supposedly a descendant of Henry Clay, had political aspirations of his own, even though few of society's sons chose that avenue. Backed by "old" money, money made by the sweat and servitude of his family's slaves, there was little doubt that Leland, like Henry, would one day hold political office.

Jock didn't keep up with politics much, but he thought Leland Creighton looked the part of a politician as much as Alexandra looked the part of a politician's wife.

"What are you doing out here in the cold?"

Jock turned. The sound of Alexandra Creighton's voice coming on the heels of his thoughts caught him by surprise. She stood a few feet away, immaculately clad in jodhpurs and boots of soft brown leather, worn but polished to a high sheen. A tailored wool tweed coat with a velvet collar hit her midthigh, and a chocolate-and-mulberry-hued scarf was twined around her throat. Her pale blond hair, was, as usual, pulled back and tied at the nape of her neck in a George Washington. The wind had whipped bright color into her fair cheeks and freed several tendrils of hair, which kept blowing into eyes an incredible crystalline blue. Ice blue.

She was pretty, Jock thought. But not as pretty as Vicky.

He smiled politely. "I was just looking things over, Mrs. Creighton. Thinking how lucky I am to have landed this job."

"You may call me Alex, Jackson—or is it Jack?"

Jock nodded deferentially. "Actually, it's Jock."

"Jock, then," she said, plunging her gloved hands into her pockets. She inclined her head toward a cluster of outbuildings, which included the small red brick structure with forest green shutters that served as the office. "Let's go inside where we can talk."

"Sure." Jock fell into step beside her, their boots squishing over the soft ground as they left the pasture behind.

Jock allowed her to precede him up the narrow stone walkway, then reached out and held open the door. His mother had always taught him that good manners could take a person far. They'd never hurt him any.

Alexandra Creighton smiled her thanks, a swift automatic lift of her lips that failed to reach her eyes.

"Luck had nothing to do with your getting the job," she told him in the clipped, no-nonsense tone he was fast becoming used to. "You came with excellent references and a string of wins. You're qualified."

Jock closed the door on the cold. Warm air, and pleasure at knowing his hard work had paid off, swirled around him. He hoped he wasn't blushing like some country bumpkin. "I appreciate Mr. Creighton giving me the opportunity, anyway."

"I'm sure you'll do an excellent job. But just for the record, Mr. Creighton had very little to do with the decision to hire you. My husband's tastes run to more . . . exciting things than foaling mares. He's far more comfortable with business and politics. Life in the city."

"He seemed interested."

Alexandra flicked Jock a wry smile. "Oh, he likes playing the gentleman landowner when his friends come around, but his interest in the horses is strictly limited to how much money they bring in." A small sigh fluttered from her full lips. "But as long as it doesn't interfere with his own life, he's content to indulge me in my little pastime."

Jock was surprised. He wondered if the sarcasm he thought he heard in Alex Creighton's voice was real or imagined. He recalled tidbits from the gossip columns, hints of possible rifts in the Creighton marriage, though they acted like any reasonably happy married couple.

"It looks like he indulges you pretty well."

"My husband encourages me to have the best. He doesn't *pay* for it."

The bitterness wasn't imagined. Jock wondered what she had to be bitter about. "The best?"

"People and animals. He thinks you'll be an asset to Hastings' Meadows. I agree. But I'll be paying your wages, not my husband."

Jock shrugged.

"When will your wife be arriving?"

"Next week."

"You've seen the house?"

Part of Jock's wages was lodgings on the grounds. Though it was just two bedrooms, it was still the nicest house he'd seen in a while. A converted log hunting cabin, it boasted hardwood floors and a brick fireplace that covered an entire wall. It was decorated tastefully with traditional and antique furnishings.

"It's great. Vicky will love it."

Alex nodded, as if she'd known everything was fine. Jock found himself wondering if she'd been born with that aura of confidence or if it was an acquired trait or an affectation, like sipping tea with a pinky extended.

He watched her shrug out of her coat and lay it on the burgundy leather couch. She was slim, almost boyishly so. Her clothes looked comfortable and serviceable, and there was little doubt they'd been custom made of the finest fabrics, but they weren't new by a long shot. Just like the woman wearing them, and just like the money that had paid for them, they were made to last, and last beautifully.

In a sudden flash of insight, "to the manor born" took on meaning for Jock. The pencil-straight way Alex Creighton carried herself gave her that look of authority; years of wielding money and power had fostered her unmistakable aura of confidence. Alexandra Creighton had been born to her position in life, and it showed.

Moving with a long-legged stride that combined

that understated confidence with an easy grace, Alex crossed to the ebony-and-cherry desk beneath a horse racing aquatint by Samuel Howitt. She took a Gauloises from a box inlaid with jade and ivory and lifted the cigarette to her lips.

She perched on the edge of the desk, one booted foot swinging. "Have you been married long?"

"Ten months," Jock offered, automatically reaching for the Zippo in his jeans pocket. Alex was faster. She picked up the jade table lighter and in an instant was drawing fragrant smoke deep into her lungs.

Another brittle smile surfaced, and she blew a stream of smoke toward the ceiling. "Really? My husband and I celebrated our second wedding anniversary a few weeks ago with two hundred of our dearest friends."

Definite sarcasm.

"Does your wife smoke?" she asked abruptly.

"No."

"My husband does, but he hates that I do." That said, she took another drag on the cigarette. Waving aside a cloud of white haze, she asked, "If she did smoke, would you nag her to quit?"

Jock was beginning to get the feeling that life at the Creightons' wasn't as rosy as the world might think. "That would depend," he said truthfully.

"On what?"

"On why she was smoking in the first place."

To his surprise, Alex Creighton burst into laughter. The sound was girlish and liberated, nothing at all like the woman responsible for it. As the sound faded, she brushed her fingertips across her eyes. "You're a very insightful man, Jock. I like that. As a matter of fact, I like you. I think we're going to get along very well."

Jock shifted uncomfortably. He wasn't so sure.

Vicky arrived a week later. She was ecstatic over the house. Grinning, Jock watched as she ran from room to room, her happy laughter bouncing off the thick wooden walls. In the master bedroom, she spread her arms wide and fell back onto the forest green bedspread.

Jock followed her, bracing himself with his hands.

"It's wonderful!" she said, smiling up at him.

"*You're* wonderful," he countered, lowering his body on top of hers. Their lips met, softly at first, then harder, hungrier.

All laughter fled from their faces. "I missed you," he said.

"I missed you, too."

"I couldn't bear to live without you."

"You don't have to, goose. I'm certainly not going anywhere."

Vicky smiled up at him, but there was a familiar sadness in the depths of her eyes. That sadness meant she was thinking of her father, who'd walked out when she was six years old.

Jock rolled onto his back, pulling her over on top of him. With a gentle hand he brushed the wild tangle of auburn hair away from her face. "I'll never leave you, Vicky."

"Promise?" she asked in a tremulous voice.

"Promise."

She kissed him again and then, laughing, pushed herself up. "Show me the horses."

"Now?"

"Now. It'll be dark soon."

"Yeah," he said with a grin. "I'm counting on it."

"Sex fiend." She grabbed his hand and tugged. "Come on."

Grousing, Jock complied. Vicky donned her coat and boots and skipped across the frozen ground as he gave her a tour of the farm.

"It's gorgeous!" She gazed in awe at the huge Tudor-style house Wilton Hastings had built fifty-odd years before. The scene could have been taken from a picture postcard—the gently rolling land, the trees ablaze with riotous color, the low rock fences, the imposing edifice, all set against a salmon-and-mauve sunset. "Maybe we'll live in something like that someday."

"I wouldn't want to," Jock said. "Too big and impersonal for me. Just like the people who live in it."

Vicky cocked her head. "Maybe you're right." She looped her arm through his, and they started toward the barns. "So what are they like, your new bosses?"

"Boss."

She looked at him, a question in her eyes.

"Mrs. Creighton informed me that I work for her and she would be paying my wages, not her husband."

"I'm not sure I like you working for a woman," Vicky said with a scowl.

"Jealous?"

Her chin rose. "Maybe."

Jock draped an arm around her shoulders and drew her to his side. "You don't have a thing to worry about. But maybe I'd better watch you around Mr. Creighton."

She looked horrified. "You've got to be kidding. I'd be scared to death if he even spoke to me."

"I understand he had quite a reputation as a ladies' man before he married Alex."

"*Alex?*" Vicky said in mock anger. "She lets you call her *Alex*?"

"She asked me to," Jock said with pseudo-hauteur. "She thinks we'll get along very well."

Alex was right: they did get along. As an employer, she couldn't be beat. Nothing as he'd pictured a pampered woman of wealth to be, she was always polite, direct, and businesslike. Within a month Jock knew he'd made a good move. He intended to make himself the best farm manager Hastings' Meadows had ever had, and Alex didn't interfere with his work. She let him know what she expected and then let him do it his way, unlike employers who'd stood over him to make certain things were done "right."

She was sincere in her praise, fair with her criticism. And because she gave him her trust in every conceivable situation, Jock was conscious not to abuse it. He put in long hours, never asked his hands to do a job he wouldn't do himself, and he spent Alex Creighton's money as carefully as if it were his own. He was soon rewarded with a raise.

Since he and Alex were thrown together on a daily basis, he got to know her better than she ever would have dreamed.

He watched her ride her jumper over the course her grandfather had built on the east side of the property, urging the gelding into the jumps with a combination of gentleness and will.

He accepted her help in delivering a problem foal while the vet was away. Alex hadn't minded getting dirty during the delivery. He saw, and tried to ignore, the glimmer of tears in her eyes when, despite their efforts, they lost both the mare and the filly.

He compared the relaxed way she played in the yard with her two huge Airedales to the stiffness of her demeanor as, dressed in sable and silk, she left for various parties on her husband's arm.

Jock didn't see much of the famous Mr. Creighton, and he was glad their paths crossed infrequently. But every so often the young lawyer would stroll the gravel drives between the paddocks, his hands thrust into the pockets of his herringbone topcoat, his hair gleaming darkly in the sunshine, looking down his nose at the workers, looking exactly like what he was: a rich, spoiled son of a bitch. His attitude to Jock was condescending, and his attitude toward his wife was so sugary that Jock wanted to puke. He tried not to care, but he did.

It didn't take Jock long to conclude that Alex

Creighton was not happy, or to suspect that her husband was responsible for the emptiness in her eyes. If Leland cared as much for Alex as it appeared on the surface, why was she so miserable? And if she was so miserable married to him, why had she?

Sometimes when he knew she was down—usually after time spent with her husband—Jock wanted to ask her why she stayed with the bastard. But, of course, he didn't.

He liked her. He cared. But she was his boss, not his equal.

Besides, it really was none of his business.

6

Delmar. Hollywood Park. Santa Anita. Rider had done time at them all—and more. By the time he was four, he had learned that one track's backside was very much like any other. It made no difference if the oval was jammed up against a residential section of town or spread generously below the San Gabriel Mountains, one thing remained as unchangeable as sunrise and sunset: the routine.

Stepping into Jock's shed row and picking up the reins of his operation would be easy. Everyone, from the million-dollar trainers to the hot walkers, was prisoner to a routine as old and established as racing itself. Up before daylight, seven days a week, with no time off for good behavior.

Exercise boys and jockeys checked to see which horses walked, galloped, or worked, and how far. The young horses were like kindergartners. Each day they were indoctrinated to new and strange things they'd never encountered on the farm. One of their early lessons was "going with company," a simple matter of learning that being bumped and jostled by other horses was nothing to fear.

While the horses were on the track or being walked, either by hand or by a walking machine, grooms cleaned the stalls, filled up hay racks, and scoured feed tubs and water buckets. The animals were bathed, cooled out, and returned to their clean stalls, where their grooming was completed and physical problems taken care of—everything from body soreness to applying mud on the bottoms of their hooves and medicinal "sweat" to their legs to help ease inflammation and swelling.

Horses in training were shod at least once a month, to the tune of about sixty bucks per head, and if they were fortunate enough to have trainers who understood the importance of equine dental care, their teeth were worked on every three months. It was a killer routine that varied only slightly with the temperament of individual horses or trainers, the weather, or the feared but always anticipated accident or sickness.

It was a place where hard work and dreams could be undermined by greed and deceit, and its grinding routine was as familiar to Rider as his own body. Apart from his brief, disastrous stint in Hollywood, racing was all he knew. He both loved and hated it, and he suspected that would never change.

It was barely daylight when Rider turned into the Hot Springs track. The sun hadn't yet nosed over the horizon, but the starry night was giving way to a dawn as cold as it was clear. He stopped at the guard shack, showed them his California trainer's license, and drove through the gates.

From what Rider had heard, they'd made a lot of improvements. Though new stalls had replaced the silver-painted wood barns the old-timers had called Silver City, Rider didn't imagine the pecking order had changed. At any racetrack, the bigger, more influential stables were housed closest to the track itself. The smaller the outfit, the farther away it was stabled. Rider had never raced there, but he knew Silver City was reserved for the smallest outfits, those who were grateful to be given any stalls at all. The McCall barn was a long way from the track.

When he arrived, Tomas was tacking up a horse. The young Mexican groom looked up and smiled.

"Hi."

"Hi, Tomas. I'm Rider McCall. Jock's son."

The young man nodded. "You look much like your father. How's he doing?"

"It looks like he's going to be okay."

"Good."

"Who goes first?" Rider asked.

Tomas pointed to a nearby stall.

Rider unhooked the webbing stretched across the stall opening, stepped inside, and slapped the rangy gelding's shoulder to move him over. Curious, the bay nuzzled him and gave a blowing snort that sprayed Rider's down-filled coat with a combination of saliva and alfalfa. Rider swore and pushed the horse's head away. "Who's this?"

"Big Guy," Tomas said.

"He is that." The horse was tall and big-boned but too thin. "Can he run?"

Tomas shrugged philosophically. "He's pretty damned fast, but has lotsa bad luck. He's sick all the time, and he shin-bucked last year. We run him the other day, and he got into a trap coming for home. Then some sumbitch kick him on the way back to the barn."

Rider got the picture. It seemed the runners were always the hard-luck horses. A nag that couldn't outrun a fat man up a hill was seldom sick or hurt. And most two-year-olds that didn't get sore shins probably didn't have much speed.

"Hey, Tomas!" A young man in miniature rounded the corner of the barn. "Hi," he said, holding out his hand to Rider. "I'm Joe Lathrop."

Jockey or exercise boy? The name wasn't familiar, but the kid's handshake was firm and his attitude was confident. Rider liked that. "Rider McCall."

"I heard you were in town. How's Jock?"

"Better."

"That's good." Joe turned to Thomas. "What's Big Guy do today?"

"Just gallop a couple rounds," Tomas instructed, making a final adjustment to the girth.

"Let's go, then." Joe went to the horse's left side and bent his left leg at the knee. Tomas grasped the boy's ankle, hoisted him up, and led the horse outside. Joe ducked as they went through the doorway and shifted on the saddle to test the tightness of the girth. Then he adjusted the reins to his liking and knotted them.

"You coming, Mr. McCall?"

"Yeah." Rider shoved his bare hands into his pockets and fell into step beside the horse. He turned to Tomas, who was already tossing muck into a wheelbarrow. "Before you finish the stall, have Danny Brewster paged, will you? Dad wants me to work Jock's Dream this morning, and he wants Danny on him."

Tomas nodded.

"Boy, oh, boy," Joe said, "would I love the chance to see how fast that colt can go."

Rider's lips quirked. He'd divined a few things from Joe's statement. First, the horse could run enough to impress Joe Lathrop, for whatever that was worth. Second, Jock had been right to worry about some jackleg letting the colt rip. Third, the old man was pretty sharp in spite of everything. And last, Joe Lathrop had a lot of learning to do.

The trip to the track and back, which Big Guy

managed without mishap, was filled with familiar faces. Everyone seemed glad to see Rider, and everyone asked about Jock. Several people wanted to know if his illness would knock Jock's Dream out of the run for the roses. Rider couldn't deny that the questions piqued his own interest in the horse.

He was still thinking about the colt as he gave Big Guy a bath.

"Well, if it isn't Mr. California himself."

Rider kinked the hose and turned. The whiskey-rough drawl belonged to Danny Brewster, whose all-American face brandished a wide smile. As kids, he and Danny had been as close as brothers until Cliff Brewster's successful riding career had taken him and his family from the West Coast to the East.

Rider grinned back. "Well, if it isn't Danny Wayne Brewster, race rider extraordinaire."

They embraced briefly in typical, awkward, back-slapping male fashion.

"So how's it goin', old son?" Danny asked, tapping his whip against his dusty knee-high boots.

Rider grimaced. "Could be warmer."

"Sure could. How's your dad?"

"Well enough to start giving orders."

Danny laughed. "Jock was always good at that. So how's life out in the sand and surf?"

"Good," Rider said, relinquishing the gelding to the hot walker standing nearby. "I read in the *Form* that you're getting more than your share across the finish line these days."

Danny's dark eyes danced. "Velasquez and Pincay aren't exactly shaking in their boots, but I'm doing okay. Or would be if I could keep from getting hurt."

Rider grew serious. "You take too many chances, Danny. You always did."

"Sometimes you have to take chances to win."

Rider couldn't argue with that. Races were often won or lost on a split second's decision, about all the time there was to make a move into an unexpected opening in the pack. When a jockey got too scared or too complacent to make those gutsy moves, he stopped winning races.

"I hear you're doing okay in California."

"Lucas and Whittingham aren't shaking in their boots," Rider said, "but I'm doing all right."

They exchanged a smile.

"Nobody manage to drag you to the altar yet?"

Rider forced a smile and hedged. "I came close. I heard *you* tied the knot, though."

Danny's quicksilver smile made another appearance. "Yeah. I got married last year."

Rider's fleeting pang of jealousy passed in a heartbeat. "Sounds like you've got the world by the tail. A rising career and a former Miss Kentucky for a wife."

Danny looked disconcerted. "How'd you know that?"

"Word gets around, Danny boy. I suppose she's gorgeous."

"Too gorgeous."

"What's that supposed to mean?"

"She draws men like dogs draw fleas."

Rider laughed. "You have to take the good with the bad, Danny Wayne."

"I guess." Danny's whip tapped in a nervous cadence, and he checked his watch, suddenly all business. "I hate to rush, Rider, but I'm supposed to get on another horse in a little while. What can I do for you?"

The abrupt switch in mood took Rider by surprise. "Uh, Dad wants you to work Jock's Dream out of the gates."

"Sure. Is he still going to the Derby with him?"

"He wants to. He's asked me to stay and prep the colt, but, hell, Danny, I've got my own life, you know?"

"It might be time well spent, Rider. I've been on him a couple of times. He's a nice colt. Real nice."

"How nice?"

"Well, Jock never let me really blow him out, but he beat the Creighton colt's time down in Florida."

"So Dad said." Rider sought his friend's gaze. "Maybe it's time we found out for ourselves just how good he is."

Danny grinned, himself once more. "Suits the hell outa me."

Rider called to Tomas, who was negotiating a muck-filled wheelbarrow toward the manure bin.

"Yeah?"

"Tack up Jock's Dream for me, will you?"

The groom rolled his eyes and crossed himself. "Thank the good Father. I been walkin' that sorry sumbitch every day. He's higher than some dope head who jus' took a hit of some grade-A shit."

Danny and Rider laughed. Like any athlete in training, a horse accustomed to exercise and then forced to keep to its stall with only a placid thirty-minute walk to compensate got "high." The longer confined, the more excess energy it built up, and the more likely it was to injure itself in the stall.

At the moment the big three-year-old was standing at the door of his stall, his ears pricked, his intelligent gaze taking in the activity around him. He had a beautiful head, Rider thought, noticing the wide jaw and short ears.

Tomas unhooked the webbing, and Rider followed him inside, squatting down beside the colt. He was only marginally aware of the mingled odors of straw and manure and urine that wafted up to him. Even if he hadn't been inured to the scents, Rider, like a lot of horse people, was of the persuasion that horse manure smelled good.

As Big Guy had earlier, Jock's Dream nudged and nosed, checking out the unfamiliar human who had invaded his domain. Rider ignored the snuffling and nuzzling and cupped the colt's knees, feeling for heat. "Does he act like he's hurting anywhere?"

"No way, man."

Though he didn't see any bumps that might indicate the horse was shin bucked, Rider ran his thumbs down the horse's shins, pressing hard to detect possible soreness. Jock's Dream didn't flinch. There was no filling in his ankles, and the tendons running up the backs of his legs looked fine. His legs were cool and tight, apparently sound.

"Okay, let's tack him up."

Rider stood and joined Danny outside. "How is he in the gate?"

"Couldn't be better."

Another lesson a young horse learned when it came to the track was how to break from the starting gate. A novice horse was first led, then ridden, through the gates. When it accepted that step, it was asked to stand with the gates closed until it was comfortable being confined in the narrow, padded enclosure. Sometimes a frightened youngster balked, and it was up to the gate crew to load the animal however they could—usually by pushing, pulling, and cursing.

When the starter felt confident the horse wouldn't flip over or throw some other kind of fit, he opened the gates manually and let it break. From there the horse moved on to breaking with the bell and then graduated to working out of the gate. Only when the starter "okayed" the horse was it allowed to enter a race.

According to most horsemen, a good horse would stand in the gates indefinitely—a plus if there was a loading problem somewhere down the line. Unfortunately, with a long wait, both horse and jockey could lose that anticipatory edge and fail to break when the latch was sprung.

Then there were those that never learned their lesson well. If they acted up during a race, they were put on the starter's list and had to go back for more schooling, something a trainer couldn't afford if a certain race was targeted. With the Derby only three months away, Rider knew that everything in Jock's Dream's life had to go according to schedule.

Tomas led the steel gray three-year-old out of the stall.

"Jesus, he's a good-looking colt," Danny murmured.

There was no denying the animal was magnificent under tack or that Tomas had taken excellent care of him. The sheen of his coat and the dapples that shone through were testimony to health and good grooming. Jock's Dream wasn't as tall as Big Guy or as heavy-boned, but there was nothing feminine about him, either. The horse had class stamped all over him, from the regal carriage of his head to his perfect conformation. There was intelligence in his eyes and a spring to his gait.

Rider gave Danny a leg up. "Good-looking doesn't win money, Danny. The question is, can he run?"

"Oh, yeah," Danny said with a slow grin. "He can run."

Glad to be out of the stall, Jock's Dream bucked playfully and gave a shrill whinny. Danny laughed. Heads turned. Rider could almost feel the ripple of awareness as they passed. Evidently Jock's Dream was hot stuff, and Rider sensed that somehow even the colt knew it.

When they reached the gap, where the horses went onto the track, Danny reined Jock's Dream to a standstill. The colt stood quietly, watching the scene unfolding before him. A bay filly passed, going the wrong way, or "backtracking" on the outside rail in a slow, rocking gait called hobbyhorsing. Several horses galloped by. Down the straightaway, three colts who had broken off at the three-eighths pole came breezing to the wire. Jock's Dream watched as intently as the clockers who were making notes of the times of the works.

Rider watched the colt. A horse that would stand and watch what was going on without cutting up was usually pretty smart. "How long will he stand here?"

From his perch atop the colt, Danny looked down at Rider. The trio of horses and riders sped past, throwing clods of dirt and obscenities to the wind. "As long as I ask him to. How far do you want me to take him?"

"Breeze him three-quarters, out of the gate. I want to see how he breaks."

"And you want to see how fast he can go?"

"Let him do what he wants to without pushing him. Tomas says Dad wants to try to break his maiden by winning that fifty-thousand-dollar added race on the twenty-fourth. Let's see if he's anywhere near ready."

"Will do." Danny saluted Rider with his whip and stood in the stirrups. Clucking softly, he started backtracking to loosen up the colt.

The horse moved well, Rider thought, his muscles gathering and stretching with easy fluidity. Wanting to get a better look, Rider climbed the stairs of the clocker's stand and introduced himself to the two men who were already intent on the horse's progress.

Explaining that he needed to get a time on the work, Rider borrowed an extra pair of binoculars and concentrated on the colt's approach to the gate. They loaded him behind two other horses. As soon as the gate closed, they sprang the latch and he shot forward. Rider hit his stopwatch.

In three long strides Jock's Dream had left the other two at the gate. Rider heard the clocker swear and, glancing at him, saw the man shake his head in disbelief.

The colt was fast, and his stride was unbelievable. Danny lay close to his neck, almost a part of him. As they neared the stretch he urged the horse with nothing but a movement of his rein-filled hands. Jock's Dream seemed to shift into another gear, eating up the distance to the wire. The instant he crossed the finish line, Danny stood in the stirrups, and Rider stopped the watch.

Jock's Dream had run the three-quarters of a mile in an impressive one minute, eleven and three-fifths seconds.

Jock was right. The colt was nice.

7

"**Well, what did you think of the colt?**" Jock asked with a smugness that indicated he already knew the answer.

"You were right. He's a runner."

"What did he do?"

"Danny worked him three-quarters, out of the gate. He went in one-eleven and change."

"What change?" Jock wanted to know the exact time.

"Three-fifths."

Jock whistled. "What did Danny say? Did he have to go to the whip?"

Rider shook his head. "He hand rode him all the way and claims he never really asked him to run. He was impressed. So was the clocker."

"And what about you? Were you impressed?"

"How could I help but be?"

"Did he come back all right?"

"He seems fine. I'll check his legs at feed time."

Jock nodded in satisfaction. "And you'll stay and prep him for the Derby?"

Rider had known the question was coming, but

he still wasn't convinced he should give up his own life to chase Jock's rainbow. "Trying to win the Derby is a dream, Dad. The colt hasn't even run yet, much less win a race. We don't know what he'll do when he's faced with a field of horses, or how he'll behave in the paddock, or how he'll run with a crowd screaming in his ear."

"He's smart. He'll be fine. And breaking his maiden will be a piece of cake."

Rider looked doubtful.

"You're right, Rider. Winning the Derby is a dream. Hell, having a horse good enough to compete is a dream. But it's my dream, and this is my last chance."

Rider plowed his fingers through his hair and turned to the window. "I don't know."

"What's holding you back—other than you don't think we'll get along?"

Rider cast Jock a baleful look over his shoulder. "Don't you think that's enough?"

"No."

Never one to confide much in anyone, Rider certainly didn't plan to share his worries with the man who'd rejected him so thoroughly. He turned toward Jock and folded his arms across his chest. "Let's just say there are some people in Kentucky I'd rather not run into."

Jock seemed to know better than to probe. "I understand. I've been there. But time has a way of making things better."

"The old 'time heals all wounds' adage, huh?"

"I like to think of it as time wounding all heels."

Rider's grudging chuckle filled the room.

"Stay." The look in Jock's eyes was dead serious. "Stay, and I'll give you free run of the stable. Train the horses how you like. Run them where you want. Just take good care of the colt for me."

Jock had never asked for his help before. Rider could feel his resolve weakening. He felt ten years old again. Ten years old and hungry for approval. His chest rose in a deep sigh. "It'll be a disaster, Dad, and you know it."

"I promise to keep my mouth shut."

"The doctors would have to suture it shut to keep you from giving orders."

"Just ignore me, then."

"I will."

Jock's countenance brightened. "You will? Does that mean you'll stay?"

Rider nodded reluctantly. "Yeah. I'll stay. God knows why."

"You'll stay because you're no different from the rest of us," Jock said with a knowing grin. "Everybody likes to train a winner."

8

Rider spent the rest of the afternoon looking for a place to live. Staying in town to help Jock was one thing; living with him was something else.

By late afternoon he'd found a furnished trailer near the mall, and half an hour later he'd moved his suitcase in. Then he called Farley and broke the news that he was staying to help Jock until after the Derby. Farley gave him his blessing and the assurance that he could hold things together until Rider returned.

As he'd promised, Rider checked Jock's Dream's legs at feed time. They were cool, and Tomas told him the colt had eaten well. He had, in fact, "knocked the bottom out of his feed tub." Which was good. The work hadn't taken anything out of him.

Finished at the barn, Rider stopped off at the Kroger on Central Avenue and picked up a few groceries. Then he went to his new place and ate a solitary meal of Manwich and deli potato salad. Faced with a lonely night and no television, he slipped between the sheets and folded his hands behind his head, wondering, now that the deed was done, if he'd made the right decision.

It was funny how coming back resurrected memories he thought he'd buried forever. Seeing Danny had reminded him of so many things—old times, good times. People he'd forgotten. People he'd tried to forget.

Think about something else, McCall. Anything.

Danny's marriage. Yeah. Danny's marriage. That ought to do it. It was hard to imagine Danny married. He'd always been a rounder. Rider sighed, punched his pillow, and turned over. Everyone had to grow up sooner or later. He sure as hell had. He listened to the ticking clock and felt a rush of anger at the knowledge that his life was ticking away and he hadn't done any of the things he'd set out to do.

He might as well face it. He was jealous because Danny Brewster was married and he wasn't.

He could have been married, too, if he'd fallen for any woman but Colby. But life hadn't been so kind. It had denied him not only the love of his father, but the only woman he'd ever really loved.

Pushing himself up on one elbow, Rider reached for his cigarettes and shook one from the pack, trying not to notice how badly his hands were shaking. He flicked the lighter and drew the acrid smoke deep into his lungs. Now was one of those rare times he wished he were a drinking man. But he wasn't and never had been. Because of Jock.

Jesus, he thought, plowing a hand through his tousled hair. He shouldn't have agreed to stay. He knew better. Coming back would only stir up things best left alone. Farley said he could hold things to-gether in California, but Rider wondered if *he* could hold things together *here* until after the Derby.

Life was strange. He'd left eleven years ago be-cause he'd had no choice. No one, not even his dad, knew that it had been in Jock's best interest for him to do so. Now he had agreed to stay, for the same reason.

He hoped he'd made the right decision—for ev-eryone's sakes. He hoped the things that had hap-pened in the past would stay there. And he prayed that when he got to Kentucky, he wouldn't run into Colby. It had taken too long to purge the memories of Colby Creighton from his life the first time around. He wasn't sure he could do it again.

9

Danny stepped through the door of the ultra-
modern house he and Tracy had leased on Lake
Hamilton. The sounds of Whitesnake at full volume
assaulted his eardrums. Half a dozen boxes from
well-known department stores and boutiques he'd
never heard of lay strewn across the white suede
sofa; a black negligee, reminiscent of the one Tracy
had worn in *Playboy*, was draped over one arm. A
pair of lizard pumps looked as if they'd been walked
out of on the way to the bedroom.

The headache Danny had been fighting, aggravated by signs of Tracy's excessive spending,
throbbed more fiercely. He bypassed the living
room and headed for the kitchen. Reaching into a
cabinet, he took out a plastic bottle and unfastened
the childproof cap, shaking three Advil into his
hand. He longed for something stronger—a Perco-
dan for his headache, or at least an Elavil to lighten
his mood—but a recent stint at the Betty Ford Center had taught him that he couldn't have his pills
and success, too.

Dependent on several pills in the past, he had allowed antidepressants to become a friend after his marriage—just a little something to keep him from worrying himself sick over why a woman like Tracy would marry a man like him. She said she loved him, but he wasn't stupid—or blind—and he couldn't help wondering if the depth of her love wasn't directly connected to his ten-thousand-dollar-a-week paychecks.

Without the pills, there were nights he lay awake long after Tracy's incredible sexual appetite had been temporarily assuaged, nights sleep eluded him until it was time to go to the track, nights he wondered what would happen to his marriage if his career took an unexpected nosedive. Would his sexy bride love him so much if he couldn't keep her in the style to which she'd become accustomed?

It was a worry that never left him. Danny knew that success, like happiness, was a fragile thing. The bulk of his formidable string of wins hinged on his riding talent, but there were always unknown factors he couldn't control.

"Danny? Is that you?"

Tracy glided into the room on bare feet. Her pedicured toenails were painted shrimp pink, and matching lipstick glazed her ripe, model's lips. Her thick cream-colored hair was drawn back into a ponytail, and a white headband circled her brow. Perspiration beaded her upper lip, and damp tendrils of hair clung to her temples. The black spandex of her biker's pants molded her shapely thighs and tight rear with loving attention to detail. The absence of a panty line told him she wasn't wearing underwear. A damply clinging cropped Arkansas Razorback shirt highlighted her nipples. Danny wondered briefly where she'd gotten the shirt.

Her outfit and the film of perspiration were a testament to her daily, vigilant exercise program. Staying fit was almost a religious experience for Tracy, who worshiped at the altar of her body.

But then, so did he. Even though he hated the way men ogled her, Danny couldn't deny that he understood why. Even after more than a year of marriage, he felt himself growing hard just looking at her.

Her gaze, a stormy sea green, swept his body. She smiled. He started toward her. She backed away.

"How many did you win?"

Not "Hi, I'm glad you're home" or "Did you have a nice day?" The first words out of Tracy's mouth were always to ask how many races he had won. Danny stopped in his tracks, and his erection withered like a flower at first frost.

He wished she would show more attention to his interests, to his career in general, to *him*. He would have liked to share his excitement over the McCall colt. But Tracy's interests, like her conversations, were limited to money and shopping and sex. "Four," he said.

Squeezing her eyes closed, she gave a throaty squeal.

Danny realized with something of a shock that the look on her face was a replica of the one she wore when she climaxed.

She opened her eyes and gave him a slow, sexy smile. "I love you, Danny."

It was what he wanted, what he needed, to hear.

Tracy peeled off her T-shirt and dropped it to the floor. "And I want you." Her breasts were firm and full and as tempting as Eden's forbidden fruit.

"Do you?"

"I've been exercising, honey," she purred, "and you know how hot I get when I exercise. But I'm all sweaty. . . ." Her voice trailed away. She drew a deep breath, and her breasts quivered. She whipped off the headband and released the ponytail. Silky blond skeins tumbled around her golden shoulders. She wrinkled her nose. "I probably smell like a pig."

But Danny knew better. She'd smell like expensive perfume and hot, hungry woman. He felt his body rise to the challenge in her eyes.

Crossing the room, he pulled her close. Though he was tall for a jockey, Tracy was still a good head taller. Danny bent his head and took one tumescent nipple into his mouth as Whitesnake cranked out "Slide It In." A throaty laugh escaped Tracy.

Even as she pulled his shirt from his Levi's, Danny felt a frisson of unease scamper through him. But it was nothing he could put his finger on. And in a matter of seconds, he forgot all about it.

10

Rider was amazed at how quickly the month since he'd come to Arkansas had passed. The weather was typical—cold nights, balmy days. Crocus and daffodils were popping up in unexpected places, and the forsythia in the infield waved yellow-sprigged branches in the March winds. The dogwoods would bloom by the end of the month, and spring vacation would loose hundreds of kids on the unsuspecting city.

Jock's stable of eight wasn't hard to train, and Rider had soon picked up on the idiosyncrasies of each horse. Once Jock got out of rehab, he started putting in his two cents' worth, just as Rider had expected. He had to admit, though, that for the most part Jock's comments came in the form of suggestions, not demands, and they were tempered by a new respect for Rider's wishes and knowledge. The arrangement was working out better than he'd anticipated, and he hoped the truce would last beyond his brief stay in Hot Springs. He hoped it lasted until the running of the Derby.

Jock's Dream was a trainer's delight. Fit, healthy,

intelligent, and good-natured, he did what was expected of him and did it to the best of his ability. As Jock predicted, nothing bothered the colt, who had broken his maiden in an allowance race two weeks earlier. He was a winner now, and the win had gone a long way in restoring morale around the McCall shed row. Jock and Rider were now aiming for the Rebel Stakes, the first in a series of three races at Oaklawn, including the Arkansas Derby, that were stepping-stones to the big race at Churchill Downs the first weekend of May.

Though Jock's Dream had won his first competition handily, Rider knew it was foolish to think they could go all the way to Kentucky without any real competition. So he wasn't surprised to see a Hull & Smith van pull up and a striking bay colt come prancing down the ramp, looking around curiously, tossing his head, and whinnying to announce his arrival. Like wind rippling a field of grain, a murmur spread through the grooms and hot walkers, who stopped what they were doing to watch and comment on the newcomer.

"The Creighton colt . . ."

"Cass Creighton . . ."

"Another Derby hopeful . . ."

"Runaway Again . . ."

The colt Jock's Dream had outworked in Florida. Rider, who was on his way to the track kitchen, watched as a groom led the horse to his stall. The bay colt was certainly no slouch, in looks or breeding. Jock's Dream may have outworked him, but a work wasn't a race, and Runaway Again had already garnered his fair share of purse money. The two horses would be butting heads in every race between now and May. Whether Jock's Dream bested him or not would depend on lots of things—degree of fitness, talent, breeding, jockey, track conditions, and good old-fashioned heart, or any combination or lack of those vital elements.

Rider realized that the trainer's abilities would also have a great deal to do with the outcome of the races ahead. He had spent a lot of time the last few years pondering the apparent ease of Cass Creighton's phenomenal success as a trainer, while he worked his butt off with only modest rewards.

The difference, he'd decided, boiled down to one basic thing: money. Or owners who had money. Alexandra Creighton was able to buy the best horses in the country for her son to train. Rider had to take what he could and make it work within the system. And in the system, the rich got richer and the poor generally got screwed.

Rider wasn't bitter about his profession, but he had few illusions left. It had taken him a long time to come to terms with the harsh realities of the world, but if he was sometimes dissatisfied with what he was and where he was, he was at least happy with *who* he was. He was damned happy he wasn't a Creighton.

Still, just because Cass Creighton had taken his first bite of Pablum from the proverbial silver spoon, it would be the height of foolishness to underestimate his ability. Cass, too, had learned from the best.

With a cup of coffee and a couple of doughnuts in hand, Rider was talking to another trainer when the door of the track kitchen opened, ushering in a breath of chilly air.

A tall, dark-haired man stood in the doorway. A cashmere scarf was draped casually over his open lambskin flight jacket, and his classic khaki jodhpurs were tucked into the snug tops of cordovan riding boots. In a place where standard attire was worn jeans and cracked Ropers, most men affecting the unusual dress would have been laughed at. But the newcomer wasn't most men. He was Cass Creighton.

Cass's brown eyes panned the room as if looking for something or someone. His gaze swept past Rider and, when recognition dawned, moved back. They stared at each other across the room, across the span of a decade. The look in Cass's eyes changed from surprise to undiluted hatred.

Obviously Cass hadn't been able to forget, either. A spasm of fresh pain squeezed Rider's heart. Cass's feelings were justified. Rider knew that if some bastard had seduced and abandoned his sister without so much as a good-bye, he'd hate him, too.

For a long time Rider had hated himself for what he'd had to do. He'd loved Colby desperately and never would have hurt her if he'd had a choice, but at the time he hadn't been granted any.

Rider looked away, and Cass moved toward the counter. Bidding the trainer an abrupt good-bye, Rider made his escape, shaken by the intensity of his sorrow. He and Cass had once been the closest of friends. Remembering that closeness and how much it had meant to him made Cass's hatred now even harder to bear. Friends were supposed to be forever.

11

Lexington, Kentucky
March 1979

Rider was twenty-two the spring his family moved back to Kentucky and he met Cass Creighton.

Jock, who had built a solid name for himself in the twenty-two years he'd made California his home, had landed himself an honest-to-goodness filthy-rich owner. Lawrence Lopenski was a Hollywood mogul who always had a few select horses in training, and 1978 had been an excellent year for the movie producer, who laid claim to two multiple stakes winners and two box office hits—one of which had been nominated for three Academy Awards.

Lopenski was finally able to indulge in his dream and purchase his own Thoroughbred operation.

But Larry didn't want just any horse farm; his must be the crème de la crème of equine facilities. Ergo, it had to be smack dab in the middle of bluegrass country—not California. And because Jock McCall had done such a good job training his horses on the West Coast, Larry wanted him to take care of things in Kentucky. Lawrence Lopenski was ready for the big time, the big horse. A Derby winner. And he felt Jock McCall's skill could help him achieve that dream.

There were long, secretive talks between Rider's dad and mom. He sensed that Jock wanted what Larry Lopenski offered, but something was holding him back. Finally, after weeks of deliberation, Jock made the announcement that he and Vicky were moving back to Kentucky. If Rider wanted to come along, he was welcome.

Weighing his options wasn't hard. With his parents gone, there was nothing for him in California, not even a steady girlfriend. To please his mother, he'd tried college for a year, and though his grades were good, school wasn't for him. In an attempt to escape his dad and the call of the racetrack, Rider had used his connection with Larry to get a trial stint as a stunt man, a half-cocked idea that also ended in disaster.

His real reason for deciding to accompany his parents to Kentucky was his mother, who had discovered a lump in her breast the previous year. The doctors had removed the malignancy with a radical mastectomy, assuring Jock and Rider that they "got it all." A round of chemotherapy followed. It had been rough going, but Vicky now appeared to be in excellent health.

Rider had suffered when his mother was sick. Gentle where Jock was rough and blessed with a core of strength and good humor that enabled her to weather the worst of times with the best of attitudes, his mother had been Rider's inspiration and sole source of love. He couldn't imagine the world without her, and he knew he had to be nearby just in case she got sick again.

Besides, moving to Kentucky with them would enable him to see racing history in the making. He would witness the Derby firsthand. Rider chose to go. In spite of—because of?—his relationship with his dad, he wanted to be a trainer.

Jock was fond of saying that the horse business got in your blood. Rider thought it was true. He knew it was a life sentence, but one he'd been born to. Though the hours were horrendous and the rewards sometimes too few, the track was all he knew, and in spite of all the drawbacks, he loved the horses. And, like so many others, he was lured by the siren song of the big dream. Just one horse was all it took to garner a slice of immortality.

The Lopenski farm was outside Lexington, just down the road from Hastings' Meadows Farm, where Rider was told Jock had once worked. A legend in the Thoroughbred industry, Hastings' Meadows had bred two Kentucky Derby winners. Like most upstarts in the racing community, Larry

Lopenski had no patience for the years it took to breed a Derby hopeful—not when he had the money to buy one. His farm was primarily a training facility, a place to break and train the young horses he bought by the dozens, mostly colts that were headed for one destination.

Rider accompanied his parents to their new home, and Jock hired him as a groom. Rider gladly accepted responsibility for the four horses in his care and continued to absorb everything he could from his father. Jock in action was really something. He could watch a field of yearlings running and tell at a glance if one was going off—and if it was, what leg was giving it trouble. His ability to see a minuscule bump on a shin or a tendon was amazing. He could spot faulty conformation in an instant, and he had an uncanny way of picking out a runner from among horses that, for one reason or another, other buyers shied away from.

The first horse Jock ran for Larry Lopenski at Keeneland's April meet was a three-year-old filly Rider groomed. It was his job to help run the horse, to take care of all her needs prior to the race.

The filly had been having a little pain, and Jock had been training her on Butazolidin. They had stopped giving it a few days before the race, and Jock had instructed Rider to freeze her legs before the race so she could run without pain.

Fortunately the filly had no problem standing with her front legs in the knee-high plastic bucket filled with ice water and chemical "freeze." Some horses always tried to climb out of the tub.

While she stood in the stall, looking out at the activity across the way, Rider brushed her, combed out her mane and tail, and rubbed her down with an alcohol-soaked rag to make her shine. He picked her hooves and painted them with a conditioner, then rubbed her nostrils with a Vicks-like substance to help her breathe better.

He washed his hands so he wouldn't get any of the ointment on the tongue tie and stuck the strip of cloth in his pocket until the last minute. The filly tended to swallow her tongue when she ran, which made tying it down a necessity, and Jock would have a fit if the filly win the race and anything showed up in the saliva test.

The intercom system crackled, and the call to bring the horses to the paddock for the fifth race echoed throughout the backstretch. Rider got the filly out of the ice tub, took off the cold-water bandages, and put on the bridle. Unlike some horses, she didn't need a lot of special equipment—just a D-bit and the tongue tie. The horses were usually saddled under the trees, but because it was misting rain, Rider led the filly to the paddock, the number five place, which would be their position in the gate.

Jock, looking smart and fit—and a bit nervous—in new slacks and a tweed sport coat, was waiting for him. As was customary for owners and their friends, Lawrence Lopenski and his wife waited in the paddock with him.

Rider led the filly into the three-sided enclosure and turned her so that she faced the opening. He greeted Mr. and Mrs. Lopenski with a smile and a firm handshake.

"How do you like Kentucky?" Larry's tan and smile were pure Hollywood.

"So far, so good."

"How's the filly?"

"Never better."

"She looks cool and collected."

"She is." Rider knew that other people were checking out the filly, too. Railbirds—the equivalent of groupies—and veteran bettors flocked to the paddock to watch their favorite horse saddled for the race. It was a chance to see if the horse was calm or if he was so nervous and "high" that he washed out before the race. It gave the gamblers a chance to look at their favorite's legs and to see if they could pick up any last-minute tip.

The identifier came by with his clipboard, and Rider turned back the filly's upper lip so that the track official could check her tattoo against his list. Satisfied that the filly was who they said she was, he moved on.

"What do you think, Jock?" Larry asked.

Jingling the filly's bridle to keep her occupied, Rider listened intently for what Jock had to say about her chances.

A trainer's work wasn't over when he finished in the morning. If he was a good horseman and a savvy businessman, he came back to the races every afternoon to meet with his owners and watch horses run. A top trainer not only knew a horse's ability and limitations but had a working knowledge

of every other horse it was in competition with—
what kind of race they ran best, any physical problems, how they had run their last few races, even
what jockey got the most out of each horse. It was
that kind of knowledge that enabled the trainer to
gauge how his horse would compete and to make
an intelligent choice if he was looking for a horse
to claim.

There was no doubt in Rider's mind that Jock
knew exactly what kinds of fillies the Lopenski horse
was up against.

"She's training good," Jock said. "And she had a
good work the day before yesterday. I think we've
got a shot. The only horse I'm worried about is the
filly from Hastings' Meadows."

"Alex Creighton's horse?"

Jock's lips tightened. "Yeah."

"Who's training her?"

"Bledsoe."

Before Larry could comment, the valet assigned
to the five hole sauntered up, saddle in tow. "Hey,
Jock. How's it goin'?"

"Good, Rollo. You?"

"Not bad." Rollo put the saddle towel with the
number five on it high on the filly's back. He folded
it back and smoothed it before setting the minuscule saddle in place. Jock cinched the girth and
checked its tightness.

The valet wished them luck and left. Rider led his
horse out to the small ring in front of the spectators
and made a round or two while they waited for the
jockey to arrive. He caught a glimpse of the Creigh-

ton filly, which he had to admit was a flashy-looking thing, being led by a tall, dark-haired guy near Rider's age.

When he returned to the paddock, the jockey, wearing the red-and-purple diagonal-striped Lopenski silks, arrived.

"Hey, Julio," Larry said, shaking the jockey's hand, "how's it going?"

"Pretty good, Mr. Lopenski, pretty good." Julio shook hands all the way around. Then he planted his booted feet apart and crossed his arms across his chest. "What's the game plan?"

Jock kept his voice low so that it wouldn't carry beyond the immediate area. "Like I was telling Larry, I think our only real competition is Alex Creighton's horse. She's fast, but she drew an outside post. She's been off a while, and I'm hoping she needs a race." He looked directly at Julio. "Try to get an early lead, and we'll just see if she can catch us."

"No problem," Julio assured them as the call came to take the horses to the track. Jock checked the cinch one more time and gave Julio a leg up. Grasping the bridle, Rider led the horse to the freshly disked track, where he relinquished her to a pony girl sitting astride a powerful-looking quarter horse. It was the pony's job to keep the filly from acting up and going at a steady pace while it limbered up during the post parade.

His part done for the moment, Rider joined Jock and the Lopenskis, who were on their way to Larry's box seats. The producer and his wife went ahead, while Jock and Rider stopped to exchange a few comments with another trainer. They were just about to step into the aisle leading to the Lopenski box when Jock stopped in his tracks.

Rider dragged his attention from a pretty brunette who'd caught his eye to the couple standing directly in front of him. The woman was near his mother's age—early to mid-forties—tall, trim, and attractive. Her blond hair was brushed straight back from a smooth forehead and twisted into a chignon. The severity of the style enhanced the graceful length of her neck and drew attention to her pale blue eyes. The young man with her was the one Rider had seen leading the Creighton filly.

"Jock!" The warmth and pleasure in the woman's voice belied the initial impression of haughtiness.

"Hello, Alex."

Alex? Was this *the* Alexandra Creighton? The one Jock had worked for back when he was first married?

Before Rider could recover from the awe at being in the presence of one of the most renowned women in the Thoroughbred industry, he heard her say, "I heard you were coming back, but I didn't know if there was any truth to it until I read your name in the *Form.*"

"I'm running Larry Lopenski's place."

"That's fortunate for Mr. Lopenski but unfortunate for the rest of us."

"I beg your pardon?"

Alex Creighton's smile looked almost . . . wistful.

"You're an excellent trainer, Jock. You're going to make winning harder for the rest of us."

Jock looked decidedly uncomfortable. Which Rider thought was strange. His dad was used to rubbing elbows with the rich and famous. Why would Alex Creighton make him nervous?

"This must be your son." Alex Creighton transferred her attention and smile to Rider.

"Yes, ma'am," Rider said, holding out his hand and hoping it was the proper thing to do. "Rider McCall."

Her grip was firm, her palm unexpectedly rough. When Rider glanced down, he saw that her hand had short, unvarnished nails and a scratch across her thumb. Even though she was perfectly groomed, Alex Creighton was obviously not a pampered socialite.

"Jock, Rider, I'd like to introduce my son, Cass."

"Nice to meet you," Rider said.

Both Jock and Rider shook hands with the Creighton heir, son of one of Kentucky's most publicized politicians. Though both his hair and eyes were dark brown, there was no doubt Cass was his mother's son. He was tall and lanky and, if not for the aggressive thrust of his square chin and a hump—no doubt from being broken—in his otherwise patrician nose, he might have been considered pretty. His smile was his mother's. Warm and friendly.

Rider found himself responding to that smile with one of his own.

"What are you doing after the races?" Cass asked.

"After we beat your filly?"

Cass hooted with laughter. "No. After we beat yours."

Rider smiled. "I'm not doing anything."

"A friend of mine is having a party in town. Tell me where you live, and I'll drive by and pick you up."

The invitation came as a surprise. Cass Creighton, heir to a fortune, a senator's son, was going to take a trainer's kid to a friend's party? It was not only unexpected but unbelievable. Rider was as pleased as he was surprised. Twenty-two and a stranger in town, he could use a friend.

"I live at the Lopenski farm."

"Just down the road," Cass said. "Perfect. I'll be there at seven-thirty."

"Great!" Still smiling, Rider glanced at Jock, who was sharing a strange look with Alex Creighton. What was the matter with him, anyway? Did Jock think he'd disgrace himself in front of the rich folks by eating his peas with his knife or something? Surely he knew Vicky had taught him better than that.

As a matter of fact, Rider thought, his mom would be pleased. She was always telling him that he spent too much time with Jock's cronies and that he needed friends his own age. Maybe she was right. There was something about Cass Creighton that Rider liked instantly. Maybe it was Cass's easy attitude and the feeling that they could be competitors by day and friends by night. Whatever it was, he knew Cass felt it, too.

12

"We're running late."

Cass Creighton's statement was directed to his new bride's reflection in the mirror.

Bonnie Martindale Creighton, whose short, curvaceous body looked lush and lovely in a black lace teddy, cast him a withering look. "Tell me somethin' I don't know," she said in the Texas drawl he teased her about so unmercifully. "Damn!" She tacked on as she got mascara in her eye.

Cass couldn't help noticing the shortness in her voice. They'd arrived in Hot Springs that morning and were far from settled in, but they were going out to dinner with both sets of parents. The timing couldn't be worse, but Senator Leland Creighton had summoned his son and his wife to dinner. Their attendance was nonnegotiable.

Though Bonnie was usually unflappable, Cass knew she was tired from unpacking and on edge about the dinner meeting, not to mention that she felt terrible about leaving Colby alone in Kentucky to deal with three major accounts their interior design business had picked up the past week. And

Bonnie no longer bothered to hide the fact that his father scared her silly.

Cass went to her, tipped her chin up, and reached for a washcloth. He wiped the black half-moon from beneath her left eye with gentle strokes. "It's only dinner, and he's just a man."

"A man who doesn't like me very much," she told him.

"Why do you say that?"

Bonnie cast him an exasperated look, turned away, and picked up the mascara wand again. "I can tell. He thinks I'm trash or somethin'."

"Trash?" Cass laughed. "Your dad is one of the wealthiest men in Texas. How could anyone possibly think you're trash?"

"Our money isn't *old* enough." Bonnie traded the mascara wand for a plump blush brush, and used it to sweep peach tint onto her cheekbones.

"What's that supposed to mean?"

"You know what it means."

Unfortunately, Cass did. While the Martindales' bank account might compare with the Creightons', everyone knew it took at least three generations for a family's wealth to secure their position in society. Though his mother hadn't objected to Bonnie, his father hadn't bothered to hide his disdain that his son had married beneath him. Bonnie had learned quickly that Leland Creighton wasn't an easy man to please. He wasn't an easy man, period.

Never having seen eye to eye with his father, Cass had grown to manhood knowing that meant he didn't measure up. Fortunately he'd never aspired to fill Leland's size eleven shoes, much less to follow in his political footsteps. Like his mother and her father and her father's father, Cass loved the animals that had made the name Hastings famous in racing circles—a fact that made his father crazy. Wasn't it enough, Leland ranted on a regular basis, that they had one member of the family who grubbed around the stables?

Leland's disapproval had ceased to bother Cass by the time he reached adolescence. He wasn't sure whether he'd developed a cavalier attitude far advanced of his years that helped deflect all but the most piercing of Leland's comments, or whether he'd discovered that his father was a bastard not worth pleasing.

As he grew older Cass learned that not everyone was blessed with skin as thick as his. Bonnie was a fighter when she needed to be, but she wanted to please her new in-laws.

"If he says anything tacky to you, tell him to go to hell."

"Very cute, Cass." Bonnie went to the closet and reached for a chocolate-brown coat dress with brass buttons. "Here I am, tryin' to make the man like me, and you're suggestin' I swear at him."

"I'm suggesting you don't let him get to you. If you're right, and he doesn't like you, believe me, nothing you do in this lifetime will change his mind. Take it from one who knows—and doesn't give a damn. You'd be better off winning my mother over."

Bonnie looked crushed. "Doesn't she like me, either? She isn't still holdin' what happened between us all those years ago against me, is she?"

"Whoa! Calm down. It was just a figure of speech. Yes, she likes you. All I'm saying is that it makes more sense to cultivate your relationship with her. And, no, she doesn't hold what happened between us against you." A hard look crept into his eyes. "And speaking of that little incident, guess who I ran into at the track kitchen this morning."

Bonnie was buttoning her dress as she stepped into soft kid pumps. "You'll save us both a lot of time and energy if you just tell me, darlin'."

"Rider McCall."

Bonnie looked up. Cass had her undivided attention. "What's he doin' here?"

"Rumor has it that he came back to help Jock out."

"What's wrong with Jock?"

"He's a drunk. Apparently he had a bout with bleeding ulcers. They didn't think he'd pull through."

"But he did?"

"Yeah. They dried him out, and he's back at the track. But I guess Rider stayed on while Jock was in rehab to keep his horses in training."

"Oh."

"That's all you have to say?"

There was a challenge in Bonnie's amber-brown eyes. "What would you like me to say? You brought it up. When we got back together, I thought we agreed not to discuss Rider McCall."

"Because the son of a bitch cost me ten years with you."

"No, Cass," Bonnie said with cool logic. "Your stubbornness cost us the ten years."

"Fine." Cass raised his hands in defeat. It was always the same. They couldn't discuss Rider McCall without it turning into a free-for-all. "You'll go to your grave defending him."

"Someone has to when he isn't here to defend himself."

Cass sensed the subtle shift in the conversation. They weren't discussing the present; they were talking about eleven years ago. "He left, remember?"

Bonnie reached into the closet for her coat. "Let's go. We're late."

Cass let out his own breath in a slow hiss. She was changing—no, dropping—the subject. Which was smart. They *had* made an agreement not to discuss the past, yet he'd brought it up. Damn Rider McCall to a slow-burning hell.

"Good idea." He took the coat Bonnie held out and helped her into it. "Just one thing," he said as she scooped up her purse and started for the door.

Bonnie turned.

Cass shoved his hands into the pockets of his gray tweed jacket. "When Colby comes next week, don't mention that Rider's here."

Bonnie looked dumbfounded. "Don't you think you're too protective of her, Cass?"

"Maybe. But she's been through a lot, and you know as well as I do that she isn't very strong."

"She's stronger than any of you Creightons like

to believe. Or she would be, if you'd stop fightin' her battles for her."

"I know. But she's had a hard time bucking Dad over the split with Kent."

Bonnie shook her head slowly, a sad smile in her eyes, on her lips. "What's she gonna do one day if you're not there for her?"

"I will be."

Bonnie sighed again. The bond between Colby and Cass was strong. So strong a lesser woman might have been jealous of it. Yet as aggravating as it sometimes was, his loyalty was one of the things Bonnie loved him for. "I adore you, Cass Creighton. You're pigheaded, opinionated, a smart ass, and a real bastard at times, but—"

"But you put up with it because I'm so good in bed," he said, deadpan.

"So humble, too," Bonnie said dryly. She crooked her finger at him. "Come on, Cass-anova. Let's go before I have to put on my hip boots. It's gettin' a little deep in here."

13

The senator's party was ensconced in one of the six beautifully restored Victorian dining rooms at Alexander's, one of Little Rock's oldest and most popular restaurants. Having grown up with the same sort of splendor, neither Leland nor Alex was impressed, but Bonnie's mother found the elegance "sooo gorgeous."

It was a strange group, Cass thought as they talked over possible choices from the menu. As individuals, his parents themselves were poles apart. As a couple, they couldn't be more different from Bonnie's parents.

Leland was dressed for the evening in a dark-hued tartan-plaid sport jacket worn over gray flannel slacks. Cass supposed that the fact that he wasn't wearing his usual unrelenting black was his father's concession to the family get-together. Despite his somewhat casual attire, Leland had chosen clothing that—consciously or otherwise—still maintained his image of authority.

His mother, looking classy and chic, wore a pencil-thin navy skirt and a white linen blouse with a Carrickmacross lace collar that fell into a deep V. The heavy coil of her hair rested against the nape of her neck. With her still smooth complexion, Cass thought she looked much younger than fifty-three.

Together, his parents gave the impression of cool, understated confidence and authority.

In contrast, Bonnie's parents were more elaborately dressed. Cybill Martindale wore a teal Liz Claiborne pants and sweater outfit beneath a full-length fox coat, and her dark looks were as vivid as her outgoing personality. Bonnie's father, whose build and drooping mustache made him look like a cross between John Wayne and Yosemite Sam, wore tailored slacks, handmade boots, and a tan jacket of soft suede. Both Springer and Cybill sported an excess of gold and diamonds, and both boasted the quick Texas-style smile. It was obvious they were still crazy about each other.

Cass was quickly learning that, like the jewelry and the smiles, the Martindales possessed a wealth of love for those close to them. While it was wonderful that Bonnie had been raised with a surfeit of that emotion, there were times her closeness to her father caused him a moment's jealousy.

The two families represented new wealth and old money. Guts and grace. Trade and tradition. Bonnie was right. There was a difference. Only he wasn't so sure that the Martindales didn't have the real advantage.

"Did Runaway Again make the trip all right?"

Alex's question brought Cass's thoughts back to

the present. The waiter, armed with the orders, was walking away from the table. "He seems fine."

Ignoring Leland's frown, Alex drew a cigarette from her purse. "That's good. Do you think we have a shot at the Rebel?"

"I certainly do."

"What's this I hear about Jock McCall having a maiden he's taking to the Derby?" Leland interrupted. His voice was heavy with sarcasm.

"It's true. Only he's a winner now. He broke his maiden in an allowance race a couple of weeks ago," Cass said.

Leland snorted. "Surely no one in his right mind would seriously think a drunk like Jock McCall can take a horse all the way to the Kentucky Derby?"

Alex took the cigarette from between her lips and blew a stream of smoke Leland's way. She lifted her chin a fraction, her gaze meeting his. "Don't underestimate him. Jackson McCall was once a damned good trainer. I imagine he's more capable drunk than most are sober."

Unexpected laughter rumbled from Leland's wide chest. "You've always championed the man, Alex."

Cass didn't miss the coldness in his father's eyes. His dad hated for his mother to swear. And smoke. He wondered for the millionth time why they'd stayed together for over thirty-five years when it was obvious they despised each other.

"Maybe," she said. She favored Leland with a lift of her perfectly arched eyebrows and a pointed look. "But I happen to know that he got a raw deal from life."

Cass hardly noticed the narrowing of his father's eyes for the feeling of déjà vu that swept through him. They might be reliving his and Bonnie's earlier conversation about Rider.

"I agree, Alex," Cybill Martindale interjected, unaware of the growing tension. "He's always seemed like such a tragic sort of person to me. They say he just went to pieces after his wife died."

"Jock's all right," Springer added, "even if he does drink too much at times. I've always thought he was a top-notch trainer. It's a shame he didn't get better breaks the last few years."

A seasoned politician, Leland knew when he was outvoted. "Well, it's obvious you all believe he might be a serious contender. What do you think, Cass?"

Cass was thinking that he knew now where Bonnie came by her loyalty. He faced his father's bland gaze and tried to gauge his mood. Leland wasn't asking because he was interested in the outcome of the race. Cass suspected that the question was geared toward making the Martindales, who were racing fanatics, believe that he was as interested in the race as Alex was.

"I think that whether Jock McCall is talented or a drunk is immaterial, since rumor has it that Rider is training the horse for him."

"Rider?" Undisguised anguish darkened Alex's eyes. Leland's face suffused with angry color. Bonnie gave Cass a look designed to send him to an early grave.

"According to the grapevine, Rider came from

California to take care of things for Jock while he was in the hospital. I guess he decided to stay."

Alex threw Leland a panicked glance. He reached out and gave her hand a comforting pat. Cass realized it was the first time in years he'd seen his father touch his mother.

"I know that what happened between Rider and Colby makes it awkward to discuss him, but he's here, and we can't ignore the fact that it looks like he's here to stay—at least until May."

"You don't think he'll try to stir up any trouble, do you?" Alex asked with a frown.

"I'll kill the sorry son of a bitch if he does," Leland threatened.

"I don't know why you're all so down on Rider." As usual, Bonnie rose to his defense. "Somethin' happened. Somethin' we don't know about, or he never would have just up and left Colby like that."

Cass wanted to shake his pretty bride silly. Her leap-before-you-look attitude was one of the things he loved about her, but surely she had better sense than to deliberately taunt the tiger.

Leland pinned his new daughter-in-law with a hard look. "The bastard hurt my baby. That's all I need to know."

Bonnie turned deathly white. The Martindales, who knew Rider well enough to side with their daughter, looked shocked by Leland's attitude.

Stabbing out her cigarette with jerky movements, Alex stepped into the fray. The role of mediator was one she'd perfected through the years. "Well, it's all water under the bridge, isn't it? What do you think about their colt, Cass? Is he a threat?"

The invisible thread of tension binding the table's occupants slackened with the relative neutrality of her question. Cass could have kissed her. Once again his mother had smoothed over the awkwardness created by his father's temper.

"Everyone thinks Jock's Dream has what it takes. And we all know that Rider is no slouch as a trainer. We'll just have to wait and see. A lot can happen between now and the first weekend of May."

14

Leland Creighton turned to his side in the king-size bed he slept in, alone. Though he'd wooed sleep for hours, he couldn't get Jock McCall off his mind. Leland rued the cold, ruthless October day more than thirty years ago when he had urged Alex to hire McCall over the other applicants. At the time, the man had seemed like the obvious choice. His reputation was impeccable, his string of wins impressive. He was clean-cut and newly married. He had goals, ambition. Leland liked that. It meant he would do his best for Alex. And as long as Hastings' Meadows was the best, Leland was content.

Thirty years. He dragged a hand down his face. Where did the time go? It seemed like only yesterday that newspapers across the state had related with relish every minute detail of his wedding to Alexandra Hastings and just a few months ago that Cass and Colby had been born. But Cass had celebrated his thirty-third birthday in February, and Colby would be thirty-two in July.

Colby. His beautiful angel. His little blue-eyed princess. Leland could still remember her toddling to him on chubby legs, her black hair curling into a dark halo around her plump, snub-nosed face while she smiled that brilliant smile that showed off her two new front teeth.

Colby, running to him, her long legs exposed by the short skirt of her plaid jumper, the hallmark of the elite private girls' school she attended.

Colby. Growing up. Filling out. Becoming a woman.

Agitated as always when he thought of Colby, Leland rose and went quietly into the living room of the suite he shared with Alex. He didn't want to wake her and take a chance of renewing the conversation they had dropped with such haste at the restaurant. Talking about Colby's brief encounter with Rider McCall always left Leland feeling on edge, defensive.

He pushed back the heavy draperies and stared out at the calm, moon-mottled surface of Lake Hamilton. Why couldn't the past stay where it belonged? Why did it have to keep cropping up every few years, like one of those endless sequels to a tacky horror movie?

God, he was getting fanciful. He was tired, really tired. Leland glanced at the Rolex circling his wrist: 3:00 A.M. He went to the glass-topped coffee table and reached for the Kools lying there. His doctor had told him to stop smoking. Smoking hindered his constant battle to keep his blood pressure within an acceptable range. Most days he did pretty well controlling his urge to sample the forbidden, but sometimes he couldn't fight the craving gnawing inside him.

He drew the menthol-laden smoke deep into his lungs. Maybe, he reasoned, the taste of the tobacco would rid him of the bitter taste left by the name Rider McCall.

Rider McCall. Jock's spawn. The bastard who'd taken his little girl away from him. For the thousandth time Leland asked himself what someone as special as Colby had seen in a nobody like Rider McCall.

An errant memory of Vicky McCall flashed through his mind—Vicky laughing, skipping along beside him like a child, her bright hair gleaming in the sunshine. Grudgingly he realized that if the son were anything like his mother, Colby's attraction would have been easily justified.

Vicky. Leland spewed a stream of smoke toward the ceiling. If each man had a nemesis, or a Waterloo, he supposed his could be called Vicky.

Who would have thought that a brief fling with a naïve country bumpkin would prove to be the chink in his armor, the single act that had, in its own good time, set his world to crumbling beneath his feet?

15

Lexington, Kentucky
December 1956–March 1957

Leland wasn't looking forward to the evening. Alex was giving a party to introduce Jock McCall to the people he'd be dealing with as her farm manager. The guests, though he couldn't deny their generations-deep roots, weren't the usual crowd. There wasn't a single lawyer in attendance. No politicians. No one, in fact, who really mattered. Just the rich old coots Jerrod and Wilton had run with. Horse people. People who wore their ageless, custom-made clothing until it was threadbare. People who probably still had the first dollar they'd ever made—or inherited.

The party was hardly fifteen minutes old, and Leland was already bored senseless. There was the usual never-ending talk of studs and breeding and bloodlines. Derby contenders. Yearling sales. Leland stifled a discreet yawn. Didn't these folks realize there was a world outside a racing oval?

Knowing there was no way he could endure two hours of what he considered pure punishment, Leland excused himself and sneaked into his study for a snifter of brandy.

The fire in the grate was mesmerizing, and the brandy stretched to three, all drunk much too quickly. Never a heavy drinker—he liked to be able to think clearly—Leland was feeling a not unpleasant buzz from the alcohol. He straightened his shoulders and stepped through the doorway to the gallery, where the party plodded along.

The first thing he heard was feminine laughter. The light, bubbly sound tickled his curiosity, and he craned his neck to see who it was. It certainly wasn't Alex. If Alex ever laughed like that, it would be nothing short of a miracle.

Thrusting his hands into the pockets of his formal pants, Leland started across the room, stopping in his tracks at the sight that greeted him. His surprise had nothing to do with the magnificence of the twelve-foot Christmas tree decked with pearl ropes and satin ribbon. It had to do with black velvet and upswept hair and a bare, slender throat. Victoria McCall. Jock's wife.

Frederick Dunstan, as old as dirt and just as earthy, was telling a risqué story, using wild gestures and facial contortions that appeared to be the instigator of Vicky's laughter.

But Leland's attraction to Jock's wife didn't stop with the pleasing sound of her voice. What captured his attention was the animation of her face—the upward curve of her full lips, the dancing lights in her eyes, the way her nose wrinkled in amusement.

"Vibrant" was the word that slipped into his mind. Vicky McCall was uninhibited and more alive than any woman he'd ever encountered. Used to the more subdued women who traveled in his social circle, he found her vivacity an aphrodisiac.

He wanted her. Wanted to see if she was as full of life wrapped in satin sheets as she was draped in black velvet. She was forbidden, and he had always found the forbidden desirable.

He coveted Jackson McCall's bride. Coveted her and intended to have her. All he had to do was figure out how.

All in all, seducing Vicky was the easiest thing Leland ever did. It was certainly no big deal compared to the problems it caused. The hardest part was getting Jock out of the picture. Still, it took only a few well-placed phone calls and a little exchange of green, and Alex was suddenly without a full-time trainer to take care of the horses running in Florida.

Full of commiseration for her predicament, Leland suggested that the logical thing to do was have Jock, her farm manager, take over the horses— temporarily, of course. After all, he was a damned good trainer, and Alex was competent enough to keep things going at the farm for a while.

Assured that leaving Vicky to train Alex's running

stock was only a stopgap measure and that he would soon be back at Hastings' Meadows, Jock reluctantly agreed.

With Jock on the road for an unspecified period, Leland sat back, like a barn cat waiting for someone to spill a bucket of milk. As the weeks passed and Vicky got lonelier and lonelier, Leland saw to it that she had someone to confide in. He played the role of sympathetic listener for all it was worth. When she confessed that she was a little jealous of the time Jock spent with Alexandra, Leland was full of solicitation, allowing her the opportunity to give her jealousy full rein.

Innocent, trusting, Vicky was like warm wax in a sculptor's capable hands. Her loneliness and need for attention drew her inexorably nearer her destruction.

And all it took was three short months.

Leland prided himself that it could have been sooner, but he'd learned early in life that half the fun of conquest was the *quest*. He lured her with compliments and teasing and surprised her with simple, unexpected gifts of flowers and ribbons for her hair. When she became flustered or leery of his attention, he pulled back and let her think she'd wriggled out of harm's way. The day he finally snared her was memorable.

The jet stream had dipped across the country and loosened winter's grip. It was early March 1957, and the promise of spring was sweet in the air. The sap was truly rising, and desire hung heavily between Leland's thighs.

He asked Vicky to walk with him in the woods adjoining the farm. She demurred, but when Leland teased her about being afraid of a simple walk, she agreed. Pleased with her capitulation, he followed her through the trees, her quick smile and childlike enthusiasm making him want her all the more.

Months of denial had whetted his appetite. He told himself he was playing with fire, that Vicky's actions were innocent. But he knew she looked up to him. He was rich. He was in the public eye. And even though he knew she loved Jock, Leland also knew she was flattered by his attention. Rather than acting as a deterrent, the prospect of her protesting his advances fanned his libidinous fires.

When Vicky turned to ask him about a bird perched in a nearby tree, Leland reached for her, drawing her into a close embrace, smothering her mouth with his. She gave a startled gasp but didn't stop him. For a moment she allowed him to drink his fill. Her kiss was as innocent and exciting as her laughter. Eager to sample more of her sweetness, he slipped his hand beneath her shirt and captured her breast.

"Stop," she said, pushing at his chest.

Leland gripped her chin in his hand and forced her eyes to his. Excitement clamored through him, lending huskiness to his voice. "You want it, Vicky. You know you do."

"You said we were just going to walk." There were tears in her eyes and a quaver in her voice.

Leland's lips flattened to a thin line. "If you believed that, you're either stupid or a fool. You know this is where we've been headed for months."

"No," she said, but there was no conviction in her voice.

Holding her firmly, he kissed her again. Vicky wrenched her mouth free and struck out at him, her nails finding purchase in his left cheek.

Leland swore and released her. He lifted a hand to his stinging face and was surprised to see that it was smeared with blood. The bitch had made him bleed! Fury coursed through him. He looked up and saw her darting through the trees like a rabbit pursued by dogs.

She shouldn't have done that. She really shouldn't have done that. There was a loud ringing in his ears, and his heart pounded in his chest. Bitch. Hell, she wanted it, too. She'd led him on for months. He'd catch up with her and ask her what the hell she thought she was doing. Didn't she know who he was?

Let her go.

He shook his head to rid himself of the arguing voice inside him. He'd seen her type before. She claimed to love Jock, but deep down she was just like all the rest. Because of who and what he was, they all wanted to know what it would be like to screw him. She was playing hard to get—they all did—but Vicky had carried it too far. She shouldn't have scratched him. She really shouldn't have.

She's not worth it.

He started toward her in a fast lope. "Vicky!"

She turned toward his voice, stumbled, and

raced ahead. Leland quickened his pace. He could hear her sobbing, breathing heavily. Dammit, he'd give her something to cry about. Reaching out, he grabbed a fistful of her bright hair and spun her around.

"No!"

Don't do it.

The voice inside his head cautioned him, even as he struck her with an open-palmed slap that sent her reeling to her knees. He hauled her to her feet and slammed her against the trunk of an ancient oak, ignoring her cry of pain.

"Stop running, Vicky," he panted softly. "I always get what I want, one way or the other." Insinuating his hands between the fastenings of her shirt, he gave a hard jerk that sent the buttons flying. He grabbed the straps of her bra and peeled both garments down her arms, twisting the fabric and her arms behind her back.

"God, you're so beautiful . . . so sweet . . . and I want you so . . . much," he said thickly, oblivious to the tears sliding down the cheek that still bore the red print of his hand.

The rasp of descending zippers was blasphemous amid the cheerful chatter of the woods. She gasped as he dragged off her jeans, but this time the sound was rooted in fear, not pleasure. Green eyes clashed with blue. She shook her head. A plea? Denial? It didn't matter. She'd teased and taunted him for three long months, and he intended to have her.

Half lifting her, Leland bent his knees and thrust

himself inside her heat. His lips peeled back from his teeth in a grimace of satisfaction. Vicky shut her eyes and bit back a groan of pain.

She didn't fight, didn't cry out for help. She bit her lip, and the harshness of her sobs punctuated the ragged sound of his breathing. The frenetic pounding of his heart echoed inside his head, pulsing in time with the throbbing imminence of his release.

Close. Close. He pressed his lips to hers. She tasted of blood, but it didn't matter. With a final grinding movement, he emptied himself into her. She was sweet. So sweet. But he'd had to let her know who was the boss.

16

Alex heard the door of Leland's room close. She stiffened, breathing softly, listening. When she realized he wasn't going to wake her, she forced herself to relax.

So he couldn't sleep, either. No doubt he was thinking about the conversation they'd had at dinner and what Rider had done to Colby. Alex preferred not to think of that. Instead she let her mind drift back to her favorite times, her favorite memories. Memories of Jock McCall.

When he'd first come to work for her, she'd thought of him as nothing but a competent hand, someone who could help maintain the quality operation of Hastings's Meadows. She certainly never expected him to play an important role in her life. But somehow, during those long winter months, her respect for him grew, and she came to look forward to the times they were together as opportunities to gain a new and deeper perspective of the things going on around her. She discovered that Jock was a man of strong convictions and deep faith. He was quiet but gifted with a wry sense of humor that surfaced at the most unexpected moments. Being with him was easy, peaceful.

Unlike being with Leland. The moment her husband walked through the door, the muscles in her neck tensed and her nerves began to scream. Alex didn't need a counselor to tell her that her marriage was in trouble, that it had, in fact, been doomed from the beginning.

Though she'd suspected they were galaxies apart in values, she couldn't deny she was flattered when Leland Creighton, three years her senior, had shown an interest in her at the extravagant, fifty-thousand-dollar coming-out party her parents had thrown. Though the Creighton fortunes had been on the decline since the war, and despite the fact that Leland was a Harvard graduate and had political aspirations, her parents gave their approval to the match. The courtship was short, the engagement shorter. The June wedding was the event of the season.

The wedding night was a disaster.

Though he came to their marriage bed with a "reputation," Leland had no patience with her virginity. He was finished before the pain ebbed. Alex liked the kissing and touching part, but she wondered why her sorority sisters made such a big deal over the sex act itself. It hurt and it was messy.

Things didn't improve much during the first year of her marriage, but Alex never denied Leland her body. At rare times she sensed something pleasurable just within reach, but before she could grasp it, he rolled away, leaving her feeling empty and somehow betrayed.

Sex wasn't the only trouble spot in their marriage. Leland disapproved of her spending so much time with the horses and so little time socializing. She should buy more stylish clothes. She should laugh more and go to lunches and talk him up to his colleagues' wives. She should, by God, play the part of a successful attorney's wife.

Determined to do her best for her marriage, Alex went on shopping sprees. Leland never approved of what she bought. She liked tailored simplicity; he liked flounces and froufrou. When she argued that he was trying to make her look like a schoolgirl and that fluff wasn't her style, he retorted that she had no style. Like his other thoughtless comments, the barb hurt, and it chipped away another piece of her devotion to him.

But the Hastings dynasty hadn't been founded on

faintheartedness, and Alex persevered. She joined Junior League and headed various charitable endeavors. She went to countless lunches. She laughed at boring stories. She praised Leland's accomplishments. And she hated every moment of it. After more than a year, she began to decline all but the most pressing invitations. Leland's idea of the perfect wife wasn't hers.

It helped that he was away much of the time. By their second anniversary, she suspected he had taken a lover—or lovers—and was surprised to find that she didn't care. As long as he was discreet, she was content that he left her alone.

Then Leland committed the unpardonable sin with Vicky McCall. Alex always thought he had more class than to flaunt his affairs in front of her. She was wrong. His subtle but heated pursuit of Vicky was as tactless as it was obvious, at least to someone who knew him as well as Alex did. If Jock hadn't been away, he would have seen what was happening, too.

She watched her husband's pursuit of Vicky with a combination of anger and sorrow. Oh, she understood how Vicky had been taken in. After all, hadn't she herself fallen for that suave Creighton charm? Hadn't she been thrilled by the aura of authority Leland exuded? He was handsome. Charismatic. And he had manipulation honed to a fine art. Vicky McCall was easy prey for a man like Leland.

She didn't tell Jock her suspicions. She convinced herself that she didn't want him to find out about Vicky's deception because she didn't want him to leave her employ. That much was true, even if she wasn't being honest about her reasons. Alex told herself that even though Jock had been hired to manage the farm, her racing stock had never run better than they did beneath his caring hand. The truth was, she didn't tell him because she couldn't bear to face the truth. Jock had become more than a farm manager, more than a valued friend and partner. She was afraid she'd gone and done something extraordinarily stupid. She'd fallen in love with Jock McCall.

She had never let him know, and she'd told no one. Jock's love for Vicky had been as obvious as the advent of spring. Besides, Alex had known she could never leave Leland, even if Jock wanted her to. Marriage was sacred in the Hastings family. Once entered, it was not abandoned except by death. According to her mother, in polite circles not loving one's husband was no reason to leave him. Neither was an affair, which was nothing but a means to boost a man's flagging ego and prove his masculinity.

Family counted. Maintaining a stable environment for the children and putting up a good front was all-important. After all, men were men. They did what they wanted, when they wanted.

Women endured.

17

Jock's fingers curled around the letter resting in the pocket of his windbreaker. The raucous roar of the crowd was a backdrop for his troubled thoughts. He had memorized the letter, could recite every sentence in sequence, knew where every comma and period was. He wasn't familiar with all the legal jargon, but the gist of the letter was simple. The bank was going to take his land if he didn't come up with the money in ten days. How was he going to get more than a hundred and fifty thousand dollars in little more than a week?

Simple. If Jock's Dream didn't win today, he wasn't. Even if he did win, he would be far short of the bank's demands.

Buying the colt had put him in a bind, but it had been a smart move. His breeding was good. Not exceptional, but solid, marketable. But it was Jock's Dream's looks that had grabbed Jock from the first. He'd seen beyond the ribs and hipbones that stuck out because the horse had been sick. He had discounted the fact that the colt's hair looked dull and lifeless. Jock saw the conformation, the classic shape of the horse's head and the solid way he was put together.

Jock's Dream was a steal. Already in debt up to his eyebrows, Jock had borrowed more money to buy the horse, and he'd been going deeper into debt ever since. Overhead was high even on a stable as small as his, and keeping the colt nominated for all the big races was no easy thing. The payments rolled around as regular as the tides rolled in. But it was worth it. The colt was everything Jock knew he'd be, and success was only a few weeks away.

Trouble was, he didn't have a few weeks.

He'd borrowed money on the farm several times and always managed to pay it back. But this was different. This was a lot of money. Jock paced the crowded floor. If only his bank hadn't been swallowed by the bigger outfit now demanding payment. If only he could hold them off until May.

"If ifs and buts were candy and nuts, we'd all have a merry Christmas." Farley's favorite saying flickered through Jock's mind and brought a bittersweet smile to his lips. There were no ifs and buts. The letter didn't sound as if he stood a snowball's chance in hell of holding them off any longer.

Jock leaned against a steel support and stared unseeingly at the throng of people pushing their way to the windows and concession stands. On a bad day at Oaklawn the attendance still outnumbered the population.

"Hey, Jock! How's it goin'?"

Springer Martindale approached, his drooping mustache hiked up at the corners.

"Never better."

"Good. I heard you had a bout in the hospital."

Word got around. "Yeah. A damned bleeding ulcer, but everything's okay now."

"I'm glad to hear it," Springer said, and somehow Jock believed he was. "So, how's everything else? I see you've had a pretty good meet."

"I can't complain with the stock I've got."

"And the colt's doing okay?"

Jock glanced at Springer. He was talking about Jock's Dream. Word did get around. "Yeah, he's doing great," Jock said noncommittally.

"How do you like him today?"

"I think he'll win."

Springer smiled. "What about Runaway Again?"

"He's tough," Jock conceded with a grimace.

"For what it's worth, you've got the opposition stirred up."

"Yeah?" Jock said with a lift of his eyebrows. "How's that?"

"The Creightons know you've got a good horse, and they know Rider's back to help prep him."

Rider? Didn't they think Jackson McCall could train his own damn horse? Years of practice enabled Jock to hide his true feelings. "Rider's a good trainer, a real horseman. There aren't many of them around anymore."

"That's the truth. Everybody who owns a horse gets a trainer's license these days."

"Speaking of trainers, I hear you're letting Cass

Creighton train for you since your girl married into the family."

Springer shrugged. "Seemed politic, somehow."

"So how do you like being tied to the Creightons?"

"Hell, *I'm* not tied to them. My daughter is. She can't stand the senator—never could. But Alexandra is all right, and Cass worships the ground Bonnie walks on, so that's good enough for me."

"Cass used to be a good kid," Jock said reminiscently.

Springer looked up and saw Rider working his way through the crowd. "Here comes your boy, now."

Jock watched as Rider stopped to speak to someone, nodding and smiling around the short, hard drags he took of his cigarette. Jock couldn't help noticing the air of confidence he projected. It was a feeling he hardly recalled.

"Rider, you remember Springer Martindale."

"Sure. How're you doin', Mr. Martindale?" Rider extended his hand. "You're looking good."

"Getting older, but other than that, no complaints. How's California treating you?"

"Not bad. How's Bonnie?" Bonnie Martindale had been Colby's best friend, and she and Rider had hit it off from the first. There was something between them—a spark, a rapport that had nothing to do with romance or sex—that Rider had never felt for any other woman.

"Bonnie's fine. You knew she married Cass Creighton a few months back."

"I heard. It's about time they decided to tie the knot."

Springer laughed. "Tell me. After they broke up, I began to wonder if Bonnie'd ever find anyone else. I don't know what happened, but they started dating again a year or so ago, and they've been together ever since."

"That's great. Give her my love, will you?"

"You can probably give it to her yourself. She'll be here later."

"If I see her, I'll do that."

"So what do you think about the race?"

"I figure we got our work cut out for us," Rider said honestly.

"That's what Jock was saying."

Rider glanced at Jock. "As a matter of fact, I think I'll go get a form and check out the competition. Want me to get you something to drink, Dad? Coffee or a Coke?" Without the alcohol, Jock drank his fair share of caffeine.

"No, thanks."

Rider dropped his cigarette and ground it out beneath one of his eelskin boots. "It was good seeing you, Mr. Martindale."

"Same here." Springer looked at his watch, and Rider started off through the crowd. "I guess I'd better get going if I'm going to play the double. Do you mind playing part of it for me, Jock?"

"Be glad to."

"Great. I want two thousand across on my horse in the second." As he spoke, Springer pulled out a roll of money that would have choked the proverbial horse, peeling off six thousand dollars like leaves from a head of lettuce. It had been a long time since Jock had seen so much money.

"Make sure you wait until the last minute to play it," Springer cautioned.

Jock didn't have to be told. Springer didn't want to be seen betting an ungodly amount on his own horse, and he didn't want to bet too early and tip off the public. The odds would drop to nothing.

As Jock thrust the money into his pocket, his fingers brushed the crumpled letter. Springer must have tons of the stuff. By not keeping all his money tied up in oil, he had evaded ruin when the bottom dropped out of the nation's oil barrel. A wayward thought crept into his mind. If Springer could afford to lose this kind of money on a single race, he could afford to help an old buddy out of a bind, couldn't he?

Jock glanced around. The area teemed with humanity, yet it was almost as if he and Springer were alone. Should he show Springer the letter?

Rider stood at the concession stand talking, a serious look on his face. Jock owed him a lot for staying. He had to admit that things between him and the boy had been pretty good since he'd been released from rehab. Was it fair to ask for his help and then lose the chance of a lifetime over a few thousand dollars? Did Springer have enough gamble in him to go for the same deal he'd offered the bank? Dammit! He owed it to Rider to try to see this thing through. He owed it to him to win.

It wouldn't hurt to ask.

"Is something wrong?" Springer asked.

Before he could change his mind, Jock drew out the letter and thrust it at his friend.

Frowning, Springer took the proffered paper, his sharp gaze scanning back and forth as he read the words that were printed indelibly in Jock's mind. He whistled. "You got troubles, old son."

"No shit." Jock shifted his weight from one foot to the other. "I need to borrow the money from you, Springer. Just till after the Derby. If I win today, I won't need nearly so much."

"Come on, Jock, I didn't fall off a turnip truck yesterday. You don't have any guarantees you'll win today, much less the Derby."

"Maybe not. But you're a gambler. I'll put up my place in Texas, just like I did for the bank. And I'll pay you back with interest."

There was more than entreaty on Jock McCall's face. There was desperation. But Springer hadn't accrued his millions by making bad investments. "I might go for the deal," he said after a considerable pause, "if you're willing to gamble a little yourself."

"Sure." Jock shrugged. "What do you have in mind?"

"A little more collateral."

"I don't have anything else."

"You've got the colt."

Jock's face drained of color. "I can't do that."

"Why not, if you're so sure he'll win?"

18

As usual, the saddling of the feature race was an event. Bettors clung to the paddock rail, elbowing each other aside and craning their necks to scope out the saddling procedure taking place a level below them.

Rider waited in the enclosure with Jock, leaning against the wall with his arms crossed over his chest, while Jock paced the few feet inside the three-sided stall like a prisoner waiting for a reprieve. Rider wasn't talking. He couldn't. Instead, while they waited for the valet, he rehearsed what he wanted to tell Danny and tried not to dwell on the fact that he and Jock's Dream would be butting heads with Cass and Runaway Again. After losing the Southwest on the tenth, winning the Rebel was even more important. Winning would give credibility to Jock's Dream and to the McCall claim that he was the stuff Derby winners were made of.

Jock stopped his pacing abruptly. Rider looked up. Alexandra Creighton, looking chic and pale, stood a few feet away, staring past Jock to him. Rider was marginally aware of a stillness, a wariness, in his father. A feeling of déjà vu swept through him, and he almost expected to see Cass beside her. Instead his gaze collided with eyes a vivid sapphire blue.

Colby.

Recognition bolted through him. Before he could do more than grasp his own shock, Alex took her daughter's arm and propelled her toward the Creighton paddock. Even though he'd known he would run into Colby sooner or later, Rider was as unprepared for the sight of her as he was for the sea of emotions that buffeted him. A rush of joy. Confusion. Piercing sorrow. Regret.

She was the same, yet she wasn't. She was older, yet still as beautiful as she'd been at twenty. But the sassy impudence in her eyes was gone. And so was the laughter. His brief glimpse of her left him with the feeling that the changes he saw had little to do with the passing of time. How many of those changes were the result of his leaving her, that night so long ago, to face her father's wrath alone?

19

Alex was so intent on getting Colby away from Rider that she hardly noticed Jock. Though she'd expected to run into the younger McCall sooner or later, she'd prayed it would be later and that she would be alone. Facing Rider with Colby at her side was the substance of her worst nightmares and something she would have given her soul to avoid. Something Leland had told her to prevent at all costs. Protecting Colby was the only thing they had been in complete agreement about in thirty-six years.

Cass, on the one hand, had never shown much interest in pleasing Leland, perhaps because Alex had been careful to monitor their relationship. To her eternal thanks, her son's self-esteem was strong enough to deflect Leland's taunts of "sissy" and "mama's boy." Alex knew the emotional tug-of-war was potentially harmful to her Cass, but she was determined to shield him from Leland's mental manipulations and rages.

Despite the less than ideal circumstances of her conception, Colby had come into the world kicking, screaming, and healthy. She was beautiful, bright, and bubbly, and despite Alex's vow not to love her, she had. How could any mother not love a child whose favorite pastime was to cuddle up and listen to stories or songs? A child whose round face seemed forever wreathed in a gap-toothed smile? How could Alex not want to protect the child her body had nurtured from the man who had fathered her?

The problem was that when Colby was born, Leland had turned Alex's scheme around on her. Just as Cass indisputably was hers, Colby was Leland's from the moment he first took her in his arms. Unlike Cass, Colby craved her father's approval, and Leland reveled in the fact that she chose to spend time with him rather than Alex. As a child, she wanted him when she was hurt; as she grew older, she went to him with her problems. Alex believed Leland made such a fuss over Colby, made her so dependent on him, just to prove he could. She'd always felt Colby was a pawn in a game of get even.

He spoiled her outrageously and bought her anything she fancied. With time Alex realized Colby got what she wanted only if it was something Leland wanted her to have or something he convinced her she wanted. Though she'd been reared a pampered Creighton, Colby had a fair, generous nature and a streak of rebellion, no doubt inherited from the Hastingses, which surfaced when it was least expected.

Though it galled Leland, Alex knew that much of Colby's retaliation against his control when she was seventeen could be traced to the simple fact that she was growing up. Resenting parental authority was as natural as receiving her first kiss or lying about where she'd been. Leland tended to smother, and the older Colby got, the more she resented the never-ending questions about what she'd been doing and whom she'd been with.

Colby's first real clash with her father had occurred when she finished her required stint at Foxcroft and flatly refused a coming-out ball. If he wanted to spend money on her, he could send her to Chicago to study interior design. Alex feared Leland would have a heart attack. Creighton women didn't go into business. They graduated from Vassar, married someone with as much money as they had, joined the country club, and produced heirs to the family fortune.

It had been a major skirmish, but one that ended when Colby informed him with a smug smile that if he wouldn't pay for her interior design schooling, her mother would. Leland had no choice but to accept her decision. The victory had gone to Colby's head, and before long Leland had a full-fledged rebellion on his hands.

Alex had loved seeing Colby start an argument with her father or refuse to take everything he said as gospel. It was satisfying to see her take up for her brother and insist on visiting him when Leland had expressly forbidden it. It was gratifying to know that Cass, who'd had a serious falling-out with Leland over his decision to become a trainer, had been urging Colby to make the break, too.

Not that Colby's bid for independence had come to any good.

Alex suppressed an involuntary shiver and glanced at her daughter, who stood beside her in the paddock, waiting for Cass to saddle Runaway Again for the Rebel Stakes. Colby was pale, and there was a dazed look in her eyes. Alex wondered if she could get her back to the hotel without any further confrontations with Rider McCall.

It was unfortunate that when Colby had made the break with Leland, it had landed her in Forest Glade, the exclusive sanatorium where the elite of Kentucky hid away their embarrassments.

20

"There's no sense pretending it didn't happen, Mama."

Colby stood at the bedroom window of her mother's hotel suite and watched Alex brush olive-green shadow onto her eyelids.

"What?"

"You know what. Seeing Rider at the track."

"No," Alex agreed, hardly pausing, "I suppose there isn't."

"It's over. It was hell, but what happened between Rider and me is history."

Alex turned, a question in her eyes. "Is it?"

For a beat of her heart, Alex thought she saw an almost forgotten emotion in Colby's eyes, a softness, a look of pleasure. It vanished with her answer.

"How could you think otherwise?"

Alex lifted her slim shoulders in a shrug. "And you're . . . happy?"

Disillusionment lent an edge to Colby's voice. "Now, there's a word with many meanings."

"No jokes, Colby."

Covering the few steps to the chair where her Armani handbag lay, Colby reached inside and drew out a cheap plastic lighter and a pack of thin, feminine-looking cigarettes. "Let's just say I'm content. There's a certain satisfaction in finally 'getting one's shit together,' to quote my father the senator."

Alex knew Colby was referring to the way she'd stopped flitting from continent to continent and settled down to rebuild her life and pursue her longtime dream of having an interior design studio. There were times, both after Leland had committed her to Forest Glade and, more recently, before her decision to divorce Kent, that Alex had despaired of Colby's ever finding contentment.

"I'm proud of you."

Colby spewed a stream of smoke toward the ceiling. Her blue eyes sparkled with wry humor. "For what? Getting the first divorce in the history of two upstanding American families?"

"For having the courage to do whatever it took to make you happy, no matter whose principles and traditions got in the way. That takes a rare kind of bravery."

"Or lack of sensitivity."

"No one can accuse you of being insensitive. If anything, you care too much."

Colby dropped the guise of cynicism. "I didn't love Kent, Mama."

"I know."

"I don't think I ever did."

Neither felt it necessary to belabor the fact that it was Leland who had pushed for the marriage between his daughter and the eligible young lawyer.

"Don't punish yourself, sweetie. Kent wasn't unhappy."

"No." Colby brushed her hair away from her face. "He still calls at least once a week. Can you believe it? He waited three years for me to say yes, we had five and a half years of a disastrous marriage, and even after being divorced eighteen months, he still calls to see how I'm doing."

"Is that guilt I hear, Colby Creighton?"

The sternness she remembered from her childhood brought a slight smile to Colby's lips. "Maybe, just a little."

"Well, stop it. You can't force feelings that aren't there."

"That's what Cass says. But I shouldn't have

stayed married to Kent as long as I did. I never should have married him. It wasn't fair to either of us." She threw her hands into the air. "Listen to us! Why are we discussing this now? I didn't even talk to you about how I felt when I was going through the divorce."

"You could have."

"I know, but I'd used too many crutches for too long. I needed to put back the pieces by myself."

"And you have."

Colby stubbed out the half-smoked cigarette. Her laughter was shaky. "I'm getting there."

"What do you mean?"

"Well, I've ditched my husband, and I don't let Daddy run my life anymore. I don't depend on Valium and alcohol to make things bearable. Bonnie and I have a successful business. But no matter how far I've run, or who I shared a bed with, Mama, I still have the dreams."

21

I love you, Colby. I love you so much. . . ."

Rider was buried deep inside her. A soft spring breeze whispered through the trees and dried the perspiration slicking her body. Trembling with the aftershocks of her climax, Colby felt weaker than a newborn, as strong as her mother's prized stallion. Rider pressed a kiss to the small mole that rode the crest of her cheekbone just below her left eye. He trailed a series of kisses to her mouth, which he took with gentle nibbles, the tip of his tongue dipping inside, rekindling the wonderful need inside her.

Colby recognized the dream for what it was and didn't fight it. She enjoyed the first part. Sex had never been as good with anyone as it was with Rider.

Then, without warning, the wind turned angry, and the pleasure turned to pain. The bad part was coming—it always did. Fighting the pull of the dream-turned-nightmare, Colby forced herself awake, jerking into a sitting position. Breathing heavily, she threaded her fingers through her tangled hair and rested her elbows on her upraised knees. As usual, she was drenched with perspiration.

She peered through the darkness and tried to get her bearings. She was in a hotel room at the Arlington, and her pain wasn't real. It was only a by-product of the dream, which was always the same. One moment the sun shone through a canopy of trees and the wind kissed her naked body. The next instant there was darkness and pain, inside and out. Pain and betrayal.

She'd had the dream three nights in a row. When she'd first come home from Forest Glade, it had visited her nightly. Pete Whitten, the psychiatrist who treated her during her year's stay at the sanatorium, had assured her it was only her mind's way of trying to come to terms with Rider's desertion. Time and Pete's help had lessened the dream's frequency and dulled its terror. Time and filling her life with other things—things that pushed away the memories of the man she'd come face to face with that afternoon.

Until two years ago, she'd run from the truth of Rider's defection, running as fast and as far as her money could take her. She ran until she came to her senses and realized that she had let one man's rejection ruin her life. With Cass's help, she'd gathered the courage to seek a divorce from Kent, and from somewhere deep inside her, she'd found the strength to abandon her dependence on tranquilizers. It had meant being tough enough to face the truth about what happened between her and Rider and her father that day.

Rider.

He'd been as surprised by their unexpected encounter this afternoon as she. Colby could still see the pleasure that brightened his eyes before her mother dragged her away. If it weren't too silly, she could almost believe he was glad to see her. But was that any sillier than her own reaction to him? She'd felt two distinct emotions the instant their eyes met: the nebulous stirrings of something dark and malevolent, and an unaccountable feeling of joy and hope.

Joy. Now that was an emotion she hadn't felt for a long time. Satisfaction was as close to joy as she could manage, and that was a feeling she'd only lately become acquainted with. And hope? It was stupid to feel hope after so long, stupid to think anything had changed. "Joy" and "hope" were two words that just didn't go with Rider McCall.

Shivering, Colby got up, stripped off her jade silk gown, and made her way through the darkness to the bathroom. As usual after the dream, she wanted to take a bath, to cleanse herself of the lingering remnants of the nightmare, to rid herself of the memory of Rider making love to her.

Love? Rider hadn't loved her. He'd proved that. All he'd loved was her father's money. Colby swore and flipped on the bathroom light.

Even after eleven years, she remembered waking up in the sanatorium and realizing that she was clearheaded for the first time in weeks. The solemn expressions on the faces of her father and Pete Whitten were etched into her memory, as was the knifelike pain she felt when Pete told her why she was there—that she'd gone to pieces when she'd seen Rider McCall accept a twenty-thousand-dollar check in exchange for his promise to get out of her life forever.

22

May 1979

The closer the plane cruised to Lexington, the gladder Colby was that she'd let Bonnie talk her into spending Derby weekend with her and Cass. Despite her father's insistence that she stay clear of her brother, Colby was looking forward to spending some time with him and meeting his new friend.

Cass was teaching her that there was a certain amount of satisfaction in making her own decisions. She liked the heady feeling of power she got when she went against her father's wishes—something she'd experienced for the first time two years before, when she'd refused to go to Vassar and moved to Chicago with Bonnie instead.

Though Colby and Bonnie had known each other for years, they hadn't been close friends right off, because of the distance between their home states and the gulf separating them socially. But when Bonnie, who was already registered, learned that Colby wanted to attend the Chicago School of Interior Design, she suggested they share an apartment. Once the dust settled after her first major fight with her father, that's exactly what Colby had done.

The arrangement turned out to be a great idea. She and Bonnie were as compatible as peanut butter and jelly, and when Bonnie and Cass realized that their casual acquaintance had evolved into something more, Colby was delighted. If Cass's goofy smiles were anything to go by, Colby expected Bonnie's name to change from Martindale to Creighton as soon as she finished school at the end of summer.

Her friend and her brother were so much in love they were almost sickening to be around, but spending weekends watching them paw each other was better than going home and listening to her dad nag her about marrying Kent Carlisle. Colby hated fighting with her father, but the very idea that he thought he could tell her whom she should marry made her blood boil.

She was closer to him than Cass had ever been. Cass always seemed hell-bent on doing exactly the opposite of whatever Leland wanted. Their battles had raged for as long as she could remember, and they intensified in volume and bitterness as Cass got older.

Things had really blown up three years before, when Cass decided to take up horse training instead of attending law school. Her mother was delighted, but her father had raged for days. Colby had been forbidden to mention her brother's name in his presence, forbidden to communicate with him, forbidden to see him.

At first she had complied, but after a few weeks she'd broken down and called Cass from the anonymity of a pay phone, so the monthly phone bill wouldn't give her away. She'd visited him, too, under the guise of spending the weekend with friends. She'd prayed her father wouldn't find out.

When Cass had discovered her deception, he was disgusted with Leland's demands and her cowardice for not taking a stand. She was eighteen years old, he'd argued, and it was time she started thinking for herself.

Convincing her wasn't hard. Colby had already begun to chafe under her father's strict guidelines. Cass was right. It was time to start making her own decisions.

When she finished boarding school the following year, she launched a major campaign to break away from Leland. She told him to hell with what people would think, she wanted to pursue a career. She wanted to make her own mistakes and see what life and the world had to offer. Mostly—though she didn't tell him so—she wanted out from under his heavy thumb.

If she'd thought living out of state would help, she was wrong. Leland made frequent trips to Chicago to see how she was doing and to try to "talk some sense into her." He tried to influence her in every area of her life, including whom she should or should not associate with.

Which brought her newest problem—the pressure to marry Kent Carlisle. She would get her interior design certificate in a few months, and it would be time to start in a new direction. For Cass and Bonnie that direction was probably marriage, but Colby couldn't picture herself married—at least not to Kent. It wasn't that she didn't like him. He was nice enough and terribly good looking, and as a nephew by marriage of the New York Lyonses, he was certainly eligible. The trouble was, there were no sparks when he kissed her, and if she never saw him again, she wouldn't lose any sleep over it.

Whenever they argued about Kent—which was frequently—her dad listened to her objections with that maddening, indulgent smile of his and calmly shot down every objection she made. It was hard to believe she used to think that smile attractive—probably because she knew when he wore it she had his full attention. Lately she'd found herself wanting to slap it off his face.

Just as the smile irritated her, so did his constant touching. He still wanted her to sit on his lap when they talked, and he still expected the hugs and kisses that were part of their lifelong ritual of father-daughter talks. All that had been fine when she was a child, but the demands made her uncomfortable as an adult. Being Daddy's darling was one thing at ten, another at twenty.

So with Cass's encouragement, she was still engaged in a full-fledged, ongoing, two-year rebellion against her father, which included seeing her brother when and where she wanted. Accepting a date with his friend, another racetracker, was an added touch of defiance.

As the plane eased toward the tarmac, Colby felt her anticipation climb. Cass said Rider McCall was the best, and she trusted her brother implicitly. It was going to be a wonderful weekend.

It was the worst date of her life. Cass and Bonnie were slow dancing to a song on the radio, and Rider McCall was slouched on a chair, a bottle of beer dangling from his fingertips, his watchful gaze tracking Colby's every move. He'd had a few too many beers, and so had she. But she'd needed something to help make the evening bearable.

What she'd seen of her brother's new friend, Colby liked. Like Cass, he seemed steady and strong and acted older than his twenty-two years. Unfortunately he wasn't much of a talker, and Colby suspected that her chatter was getting on his nerves. She'd regaled him with stories about boarding school and living in Chicago. She'd even gone through her repertoire of slightly obscene jokes. Colby knew that any impression she might have made was the wrong kind. Still, she hadn't been able to control her runaway mouth.

But there was no conversation now. She couldn't think of a single thing to say, and Cass and Bonnie had disappeared into the kitchen. Great. Mr. McCall was certainly no help.

Desperate to find some common ground, Colby asked him about the movie they'd seen earlier, even though *The Main Event,* with Streisand and O'Neal, wasn't her kind of story at all.

"It was okay."

At last, an opinion of sorts. One she could even agree with. "I know what you mean. Personally, I like movies and books with strong heroines." As if he gave a damn what she liked. "Like Scarlett in *Gone with the Wind.* That's my kind of woman."

"She was a bitch."

For a moment Colby couldn't answer. "What?" she asked when she'd managed to overcome her surprise.

Rider carried the bottle to his lips and tipped his head back. His Adam's apple crawled in his throat as he quaffed a healthy mouthful of Budweiser. Then he pinned her with a level gaze. "She was a bitch."

This time he managed to ignite the Hastings temper. Colby had had all she wanted of carrying the conversation—and the date. At the moment she didn't give a tinker's damn if Rider McCall liked her or not. "She was not!"

"She was a spoiled brat who did whatever she

had to do to get her way. But then, I can see how a spoiled little rich girl like you could relate to her."

Spoiled little rich girl? The insufferable bastard! Colby leaped up from the chair and started across the room. She was almost to the door when Rider spun her around and slammed her against the wall, resting his palms on either side of her head. They were so close she could feel his thighs brush against hers.

His brown eyes caressed her face and lingered on her lips. He smelled like beer and some masculine cologne that reminded her of windswept fields. "What's the matter?" he taunted. "Did I hit a nerve?"

"You've *got* a nerve."

One corner of his mouth lifted. "Maybe."

"Scarlett O'Hara was a survivor. And you have no idea if I'm spoiled or not."

"I've heard plenty about you from Cass." Rider reached out and fingered the ruby-and-diamond pendant she was wearing, a birthday gift from her father. His hand was warm and heavy against the hollow of her throat. "The real thing, I suppose?"

Unable to speak, she nodded. When he reached behind her and pulled out the neck of her shirt to read the label, she was too shocked to do anything more than focus on a pearl snap of his western shirt. The heat of his body intensified the heady scent of him. The room was too hot suddenly. Her head swam. Too much beer.

"Rubies. Diamonds. Designer shirt and jeans. Boots that cost three hundred dollars if they cost a penny."

The mocking voice brought her head up. Her voice quivered with hurt. "Did anyone ever tell you that you're a real bastard?"

He didn't answer. Instead he stared at her for a moment and then slowly, carefully, lowered the necklace back to its resting place. He stepped away from her and raked a hand through his red-brown hair. "I'm bushed," he said. "I'm going home."

He left her standing there, a glimmer of tears in her eyes. The apartment felt strangely empty with him gone. So did she. She wondered why his taunts had hurt so much. Why should Rider McCall's approval be so important?

Colby made it a point to stay away from him the rest of the weekend, certain he never wanted to see her again. But the next time Bonnie asked her to go back to Kentucky, she agreed. Like a lemming lured to an untimely end in the sea, she had run willingly toward her own destruction.

23

"**What's the matter with you?**" **Rider de-**manded.

Jock, squatting in the stall, was rubbing alcohol onto a filly's legs. "Nothing. Why?"

"You've been down in the mouth ever since yesterday."

Jock poured another palmful of alcohol, slapped it against the horse's leg, and began to rub it in briskly. He couldn't tell Rider he was sick that Danny's careless riding the day before had cost them more than a race. Typical frickin' McCall luck, Jock thought. Danny'd always been a bit of a maverick rider.

For some reason known only to God and maybe Danny, Jock's Dream hadn't gotten out of the gate the way he should have, and when Danny tried to make up the precious seconds, he'd bumped another horse going down the backstretch. The maligned jockey had made an objection, and when the stewards reviewed the tape, they'd moved Jock's Dream off the board and put Runaway Again in first place. To make matters worse, they'd given Danny days, and he wouldn't be able to ride the rest of the meet, including the Arkansas Derby.

Jesus, he owed Springer a shitload of money, but better Springer than the bank. Thank God they'd been paid off with a Martindale Oil check weeks ago, and ever since he'd made the deal with Springer, Jock had counted on winning a chunk and whittling down the amount he owed. But he couldn't worry about that right now. Right now he had to steer Rider's questions away from yesterday's loss.

"You haven't exactly been a candidate for Dale Carnegie yourself," Jock snapped.

"Look, if you blame me for what happened—"

"I don't blame you, dammit!" Jock exploded, recapping the alcohol and tossing it back into the box of grooming tools.

"Then why won't you talk about it?"

"Talk's cheap. It's over. We lost the race."

"Danny says the horse next to him swerved over in front of Jock's Dream. I wasn't there, Dad. What do you want? Do you want me to go ask the colt if it's true? What?"

"I wanted to win the race."

"Dammit, so did I! I'm not staying here for my health, you know."

"Well, if you don't want to stay, you know where the airport is." As soon as the words were out, Jock wished he could call them back. He and Rider just stood there, staring at each other, recalling all the other times their tempers had pushed them apart and wondering where they went from here.

"I left once. I can do it again," Rider said at last. There was no anger in his voice, only resignation.

For the first time, Jock wondered if Rider had left because he'd been so hard on him. For the first time, it seemed imperative that he know the truth.

"Why did you leave?" he asked, the lost race temporarily forgotten.

Rider didn't answer for a moment. "At the time, it seemed like the best thing for everyone," he said at last.

The cryptic statement answered Jock's question. Rider had left soon after Vicky's death. Jock knew he hadn't been the easiest person to live with. He'd been mean and ornery and full of anger at God and the world. His anger had been festering since that fateful spring of 1957 when Leland Creighton had upset his carefully planned world. Vicky, Alex, and Rider—had all borne the brunt of that anger.

Jock had known for a long time that he brought a lot of his misery on himself and those he was closest to. It was hard dealing with the guilt of how much he'd hurt them and how sorry he was for all the lost time and the wasted years.

"Well, it's not the best thing for everyone now," he said. It was the closest he could get to an apology.

"You're the one who suggested it."

"I didn't mean it. I'm just upset about the race. I don't blame you," he added hastily. "If anyone's at fault for losing, it's Danny. He's been riding like shit the last few weeks."

Rider nodded, accepting Jock's pseudoapology.

"Okay. So who do you want to put on the filly Tuesday?"

"Hathaway, if we can get him."

"I'll check with his agent and see."

Rider walked away, and Jock let out a relieved breath. He could offer Rider no excuse for his moodiness today, not without telling him about the deal with Springer.

There was no real excuse for the way he'd treated Rider all his life, and Jock didn't offer one. All he knew was that with his heart torn and bleeding and all his dreams shattered like a piece of Alex's fancy Waterford crystal, lashing out was the only way he'd been able to deal with the pain.

Pain that was rooted in Vicky's infidelity.

24

Lexington, Kentucky
March 1957

Ever since Vicky had called and said she was
flying to Florida to spend a few days with him, Jock
had been in a frenzy of anticipation. He was so excited about seeing her that he'd spent the better
part of an hour at the airport, as if his being there
waiting might bring in the plane sooner.

He saw her as soon as she stepped through the
doorway. She looked pale and tired. Frightened. He
smiled. She'd never flown before. She really must
be missing him to come by herself on the spur of
the moment. He knew he'd missed her like hell.

She saw him then and, with a little cry, catapulted
into his embrace. Jock crushed her to him and felt
her arms close around his neck. He buried his face
in her hair and breathed in the clean scent of Halo
shampoo. It seemed longer than three months
since he'd seen her. It seemed like an eternity.
Peace, that rare commodity in the cutthroat world
he existed in, ebbed through him.

Finally he set her away from him and took her face between his palms. She was crying. He felt his own throat tighten. Leaning down, he blotted the dampness from her cheeks with gentle kisses. She moaned and clasped his wrists, as if she needed to touch him.

"I've missed you so much." Her voice trembled.

Jock was having trouble controlling his own voice. "I know, sweetheart, I know. But it won't be much longer until I ship back to Kentucky."

Vicky bit her bottom lip, and her eyes filled again. She nodded.

He smiled. "Let's get your bag and go to my apartment. There's a nice big bed waiting for us."

Her gaze slid from his. She nodded again and tried to match his smile.

The bed was soft. Vicky's body was softer. In the aftermath of their lovemaking, with Vicky sleeping fitfully beside him, Jock tried to take stock of their situation. She looked tired, and there were dark circles beneath her eyes. She claimed not to rest well without him, and he knew his own lonely bed wasn't conducive to sleep.

Even now, with her lying next to him in the darkness, he found rest elusive. His mind teemed with thoughts, few of them pleasant. Though he'd wanted Vicky, and he knew she wanted him, their lovemaking had seemed strained. It had taken a long time for him to feel she was ready for him, and even then there'd been more desperation than joy in their union.

She stirred in his arms. Jock wanted her to wake up so they could talk. He missed their lively exchanges and hearing her voice her opinions. God, he just missed her. He had to have a talk with Alex Creighton. Soon. She had to find someone to take his place at the track. Being away from Vicky was like trying to live without oxygen. And he was suffocating.

He smoothed Vicky's bright hair and pressed a kiss to her temple. She opened her eyes, and he smiled at her. She smiled back, and then she shivered and looked away.

"What's the matter?"

Vicky shook her head and drew away from him. She sat up and pulled the sheet over her breasts. A glimmer of tears shone in her eyes.

At a loss, he just lay there, wondering what to do, how to reach her, fearing that during his absence the dreaded had happened. Dear God, had she come to tell him she'd found someone else? He reached out and turned on the bedside lamp.

"Talk to me, sweetheart," he said, smoothing his palm over her tousled hair.

There was no denying the misery in her eyes. "I love you, Jock. I really love you."

The fear that she'd found someone else changed, mutated into an even worse fear. Something was wrong with her. "What's wrong, Vicky?"

She bit her lip and groaned, as if she were in agony. Jock thought he would die from the unknown. He grabbed her arm to force her to look at him. She gasped and flinched, and his gaze dropped to her arm. Several purplish bruises stained her skin, almost as if other fingers had bitten into her soft flesh.

"For God's sake, Vicky, what's the matter? What happened?" he asked, releasing her.

She threw back her head and ground the heels of her hands into her eyes. Still, tears trickled into her temples. "He . . . raped . . . me."

The words grated into the stillness of the room and through Jock's nerves like the high-pitched howling of a dog. The pain was like taking a blow to the stomach by Floyd Patterson. For an instant he couldn't breathe, and the room turned dark and danced around him. Nausea and despair churned inside him.

He felt Vicky's hand on his arm. His first inclination was to pull away. Instead he tried to put himself in her place. To feel what she was feeling. Rape. Jesus. If he was hurting, it had to be minimal to what she was going through. "Are you—all right?"

"I am, now that I'm with you."

"You told the police?"

"No." She sounded apologetic.

"Why?"

"I just . . . couldn't."

"When?" Jock knew he was asking the stupid, mundane questions to keep from asking the most important one. Who?

"Yesterday."

"Yesterday? Jesus!" Yesterday, another man had touched her, had forced himself on her and filled her sweet body—the body that belonged to him.

Jock felt like throwing up. Dear God. How could he live with that? How could he ever make love to her without thinking about it? *Could* he ever make love to her again? He swallowed hard and cleared his throat. Even looking at her hurt.

"Hold me, Jock," she whimpered.

He drew a ragged breath. He wanted to cry himself. To cry and scream and curse the God who would allow this to happen to someone as sweet and pure as Vicky. He smoothed his callused palms over the bruises on her arms, offering her what comfort he could.

"Where did it happen?" he asked at last when her crying had abated.

"In the woods . . . at the farm."

"In the woods? What in the hell were you doing in the woods?"

"We were just . . . going for a walk. He seemed . . . okay, and I . . ."

Jock's mind was racing. Who was "he"? One of the hands?

"He, who?"

She wouldn't look at him.

"Dammit, Vicky, who was it?"

Her eyes were tortured. "Leland," she whispered.

Jock blinked. "Creighton?"

She nodded.

"Creighton?" His pain gave over to unreasoning fury. "What in the hell were you doing in the woods with Leland Creighton, Victoria? You know what kind of reputation he has!"

"He didn't seem . . . that way. He's been nice to me since you've been gone."

"*Nice!* And you fell for it? Shit, Vicky, Leland Creighton hasn't been *nice* since his momma squeezed him out of the womb."

"He was! He brought me flowers and talked to me and—"

"Brought you—" Incoherent with rage, Jock leaped from the bed. "He brought you flowers? And you took them?" he asked in a voice so deadly quiet, it frightened her.

She nodded again.

"The bastard brought you flowers, and you went with him into the woods. Suddenly, I'm not sure we're talking about rape at all, Vicky."

"What are you saying?" Vicky murmured through bloodless lips. There was panic in her voice. And fear.

"I'm saying that Leland Creighton didn't rape you, he seduced you."

"No!"

"Come on, Vicky. You knew his reputation. Why would you go anywhere with him?"

She shrugged helplessly. "I was so lonely, Jock."

"Lonely? Horny, you mean?"

Her gasp sliced through the tension in the room. Vicky flung herself off the bed, suddenly as angry as he. She tossed her head and flung her copper hair over her shoulder, managing to look as dignified as if she wore a business suit instead of her nakedness.

"Maybe he did seduce me! I don't even know anymore. I was lonely, Jock. Can't you understand that? So I went for a walk with him. I laughed at his jokes. I don't know, maybe I even flirted with him. He kissed me, and God help me, I let him. But that's all I was willing to do."

Her shoulders drooped and her bravado and anger gave way to tears of contrition. "I'm not making excuses. I know I shouldn't have gone with him, but I guess I was flattered that someone as important as Leland Creighton would even look at me."

Jock swore and turned away. He gripped the dressing table until his knuckles grew white. "I get lonely, too, Vicky, but I haven't started taking women for walks in the woods."

Vicky went to him and touched his shoulder. He jerked free, and she stepped back. "I know. You're the most honorable man I've ever known." Her voice cracked.

He didn't respond. "I know I'm not innocent of wrong," she continued. "My actions may have led him on, but after he kissed me, I came to my senses. I ran away, but he came after me."

Still he didn't speak. She struggled for self-control. "I guess in your eyes I'm guilty, but if I am, I'm guilty of vanity and maybe stupidity, but not infidelity."

Jock turned to face her, his eyes cold. "You wanted another man and what he could give you, even if it was only for a moment. And as far as I'm concerned, even if nothing had happened between you, the fact that you thought about screwing him is the same as doing it."

Silence filled the room. Tears sped down her cheeks. She nodded, accepting his censure, and shrugged in futility. "So where do we go from here?"

"I swear to God, I don't know."

"I suppose," she said in a quavering voice, "that forgiving and forgetting is out of the question."

Forgive? His faith told him that he should. It was his duty. But forget? "I'll never forget."

Her sharp intake of breath cut his heart to ribbons. If he'd hoped to hurt her, he'd succeeded.

"What do you want me to do, then? File for divorce? Or do you prefer to have that honor?"

"Divorce?" The word sounded hollow, empty. Like his heart. "We can't get a divorce. We're Catholic."

"We wouldn't be the first."

"We would be in the McCall family."

Her eyes filled with fresh tears. "Then what? What do you want me to do? I love you. I want to do whatever will make you happy."

Jock felt the sting of emotion burning beneath his own eyelids. "Then turn back the clock," he said in a harsh whisper. "Turn it back to yesterday morning."

Twin tears slipped down her cheeks. "I only wish I could. I guess you'll want me to go home now."

"No! Go to Texas to visit your mother for a while. I don't want you staying at the farm until I can go back."

She dashed the tears from her cheeks. "Wh-what are you going to do?"

What was he going to do? He wanted to find Creighton and smash his perfect nose into a bloody pulp. He wanted to kick him in the balls or, better yet, castrate the son of a bitch. Maybe he ought to press charges. . . .

Ah, hell. Making a formal accusation against Leland Creighton would be useless. Vicky would be the one who got hurt. And then there was Alex to consider. Should she have to pay a public price for her husband's sins?

"There's no sense confronting Creighton or pressing charges," he said with a bitter twist of his lips. "It would be your word against his, and the bastard has enough money to buy his way out of a treason charge. I'll give my notice as soon as I can, but I owe it to Alex to stay until after the Derby."

"What do we do then?"

"I don't know," he said, looking at her with barren eyes. "I guess we can try to pick up the pieces and move on."

It was small comfort. But the best he could offer.

That night Jock got roaring, stinking drunk.

Vicky left the next day.

Weeks passed, and his life was hardly bearable without her, just as he knew it would be with her. Then, just before he was to run the Hastings' Meadows entry in the Derby, Vicky called from her mother's and told him she was pregnant.

The joy he'd once hoped to feel was lost in a jumble of other emotions. "How far along are you?"

There was a slight pause. "Almost two months."

It had been two months since Vicky told him about Leland. Jock hadn't been home for a month before the . . . incident, and he hadn't slept with her since. There was no doubt when she'd conceived. The only question was, who had fathered Vicky's child? He or Leland Creighton?

25

Rider dragged the curry comb through the colt's tail, pulling out the tangles and bits of straw. The monotonous stroking kept time with the name throbbing in his mind: *Colby. Colby. Colby.* He tried to deny himself the memories of her by filling his days with endless mundane tasks. But his nights were a different matter. He couldn't control his dreams, and in them he and Colby were young and happy and in love. He always woke to the heartlessness of reality and the knowledge that he was no longer so young—or in love—and that happiness was a relative feeling at best.

Since seeing Colby in the paddock nearly a month ago, he'd once again tried to come to grips with the past. Funny, how love and friendships came along when they were least expected. And sad to think that both could end the same way.

When he had first met Cass, Rider was surprised that two such different people could forge so strong a bond. He'd expected snobbery from the senator's son but hadn't found it. The Creighton wealth and name hadn't spoiled Cass, and despite the differences in their personalities and backgrounds, they'd grown close.

His friendship with Cass had been a secret from Jock, who'd made it clear that Rider was to stay clear of the Creightons. Alex was all right, he conceded, but she was a Hastings. Creightons were users, takers, and Cass Creighton was no different. When the opportunity arose, he'd not be able to deny his blood. To Rider's surprise, his mother, who was usually open-minded and more than fair, had added her objections to the friendship.

For the first time Rider could remember, he'd lied to them both. And, unwilling to tell Cass that Jock hated Leland, he said his parents were against the friendship because they thought he was out of his element. Cass hadn't understood the reasoning, but he'd understood that it was important to Rider not to broadcast their friendship.

Actually, they'd understood a lot about each other. Both held the title of shed row foreman, and both hoped to make assistant trainer soon. Like most racetrackers, they could be rivals during a race, but when the results flashed up on the tote board, they were able to set that rivalry aside. Competition was their business, but they'd both learned

early on that top trainers and their fleeting moments of glory could slip away as easily as a rich
owner defecting or a horse shattering a leg. Friends
were forever.

At night, long after the shed row had been raked
clean and the horses bedded down, Rider and Cass
shared their dreams and goals. Rider confessed his
fears for his mother's health and haltingly told of
his struggle and failure to win Jock's affection.

In turn, Cass confided that his parents hated each
other and that he suspected his mother of having
affairs. He knew Leland wasn't as innocent as he
would like his constituents to believe, but so far no
one had caught him in the act. Rider was appalled
by Cass's blasé attitude.

"You don't mind?" he'd asked.

Cass grinned. "Life's short, McCall. My father
doesn't make my mom happy. Never has."

"Why doesn't she divorce him?"

"Creightons don't get divorces, they cause
them."

And Rider listened while Cass raved about his
younger sister, Colby, the free spirit. She was bubbly. Funny. And a bit wild. Rider decided right off
that he didn't want anything to do with Little Miss
Rich Girl. She would intimidate him. He wouldn't
know what to say. But at Cass's prodding, he
agreed to double-date with him and Bonnie Martindale when the two roommates flew down from Chicago for the weekend. And even though that first
encounter was a disaster, he had continued to see
her every time she came to town.

26

Lexington, Kentucky
June 1979

Anyone who wanted a hot hamburger and a cold beer could find them at the Pink Hippo, just beyond the jaundice-yellow-and-hot-pink neon lights emblazoned across the entrance. Inside, a battery of condiments occupied one side of the Formica-topped tables that were often pushed aside when the patrons felt the urge to dance. Low-voltage lighting illuminated the foot rail of the bar and hid all but the worst cracks in the red vinyl booths. An ancient Wurlitzer cranked out current hits at a decibel level almost high enough to drown out the staccato pings from the pinball machines and the crack of colliding wooden balls that filtered from the game room at the back.

The Pink Hippo was loud, wild, and a favorite of Lexington's younger set, including Cass and Rider, who were nursing a couple of beers while waiting for Colby and Bonnie to arrive.

After their first visit in May, when he'd acted like

a real jerk, the two girls had been down every other weekend. The product of a working-class family, Rider didn't see how they could afford it, so he asked Cass outright.

Cass took a deep draft of beer while considering the question. "I imagine she's putting her plane fare on the credit card Dad gave her."

"She's charging her tickets?"

"Yeah. No sweat until he starts checking out the bill to see how she's spending his money. Which he'll do, eventually—not because he can't afford it, but because he likes to tell her what to do." Cass wore a gleeful smile. "And when the son of a bitch does find out she's using the sacred Creighton money to visit her black-sheep brother, the feces, as they say, will hit the old fan." He belched indiscreetly. " 'Scuse me."

"What'll he do?" Rider asked.

Cass raised the glass to his lips once more. "If she doesn't agree to walk the straight and narrow, I imagine he'll take the card away."

Rider was surprised to feel a bit of regret. He was getting used to Cass's little sister. "So she won't be able to come with Bonnie anymore?"

"Bothers you, does it?" Cass asked with a sly smile.

Despite his resolve to appear detached, Rider felt his face grow hot. But then, his resolve hadn't been too swift lately. He'd made up his mind not to like Colby Creighton, yet every time she came he found himself more and more attracted to her. He thought he'd hidden his feelings, but obviously Cass knew him too well.

"It doesn't *bother* me," he said with an admirable facade of cool. "I just don't understand the workings of the ultrarich family." Feigning earnestness, he leaned across the table. "It fascinates me, you know? Sorta like that sick fascination we have for reptiles?"

"Sick, huh? That's the Creightons all right." Cass seemed to focus on something across the room, but Rider had the impression that his friend was really looking inward, at something private and dark. "That's why I love Bonnie. She's so damned normal."

When Cass, who was seldom serious, got that solemn look on his face, Rider grew uneasy. "Bonnie's good for you."

A sudden smile banished the shadows in Cass's brown eyes. "And whether you know it or not, Colby is good for you. She brings you out of yourself." He took a swig of beer and shook his head. "It's truly amazing, y'know. You've actually been known to speak a whole sentence when she's around. Sarcastically, of course, but at least she can rile you out of your shell. Hell, sometimes you even laugh."

"Yeah? Well, that could be because she knows more dirty jokes than most of the grooms on the backside."

"She does that." Cass grinned again. "Don't worry about it, McCall. If Dad cuts her off, Mom'll pick up the slack."

"Your mom'll give her another card?"

"Sure. Especially if she knows it'll piss Dad off."

Rider shook his head. "Man, I just don't get your family."

"Me either." Cass lifted his mug aloft at a passing waitress. "Another *cerveza, por favor.*"

The woman, barely drinking age herself, stopped at their table and shifted her weight to one hip. "This isn't my table."

Cass ran his hand up over the smooth black fabric that fit snugly over her thigh. "So make an exception."

Her smile was slow and inviting. "And what'll you give me if I do?"

"What do you want?"

"Three guesses, bubba. First two don't count."

"You'd better cool it," Rider drawled sarcastically, "I see a mean-looking little redhead coming through the door."

The waitress slipped away, and Cass looked over his shoulder. Bonnie, petite and cute in tight jeans and a silk shirt unbuttoned enough to show the swell of her generous breasts, was just entering the smoke-filled room. Colby followed close behind.

Bonnie leaned over and planted a wet kiss squarely on Cass's mouth. "Flirtin' with the help again, darlin'?" she cooed, slipping into the booth next to him.

"Hell, sweetheart, I gotta keep in practice."

"Right. What did she want?"

"My body."

Bonnie's elbow connected with his ribs. "And

you'd be only too glad to accommodate her, I'm sure."

"Ah, sweetheart, you know better than that."

"Maybe we'd better make ourselves scarce."

Colby's voice drew Rider's gaze upward over her crisp white slacks, past the sapphire-blue summer sweater scooped low over her breasts, to her matching blue eyes. She was the prettiest thing he'd ever seen, and he hated himself for thinking so.

"Don't leave on our account," Cass said.

"Good idea, Colby," Bonnie said simultaneously.

"Okay. I get the picture." Wearing a grim smile that matched his feelings, Rider rose and took Colby's arm. The last thing he needed was to be alone with Cass's little sister. It was hard trying to think of anything to say to her. Cass was right. When he did speak to Colby, it was usually cutting and sarcastic. He couldn't seem to help himself. The truth was, her pampered prettiness and quick tongue intimidated the hell out of him.

"Where are you going?" Cass asked.

Colby dangled a key from her pink-polished fingertips. "To your place. See you later." She threaded her way through the tables to the door, Rider reluctantly on her heels.

Outside, the summer heat hit him like a slap in the face. It was getting dark, and thunderheads were gathering to the west.

"What's the matter?"

He glanced at her sharply. "Nothing. Why?"

"You looked like you just took a big bite of a green persimmon."

"That bad, huh?"

"That bad," she said with a nod.

"It looks like it's going to come a toad floater, and we have a horse in tomorrow that can't run a lick in the mud."

"I'm sorry."

"You can't win 'em all," he quipped.

"But you'd like to."

"Wouldn't you?"

She shrugged. "I don't know. I like racing okay, but it isn't the be-all and end-all of my existence the way it is for Mama and Cass."

Rider took her arm to help her across the busy street. "I thought Bonnie was the most important thing to Cass."

"Oh, she is, but he'd wither away if he couldn't get up every morning and mess with those stupid animals. Just the way you would."

"I'm not that crazy about it."

She smiled, a supremely confident smile. "Yes, you are."

Rider saw the conviction in her eyes. Maybe she was right.

They reached his beat-up Ford pickup, and he unlocked the door for her. The combined scents of Numotizine and horse manure assaulted him. Great. Just the thing to impress a girl like Colby Creighton. He shoved aside a pile of racing forms and leg wraps so that she'd have a place to sit and prayed there was nothing on the seats that would ruin her slacks.

When he turned she was standing close behind him, almost as if she expected him to scoot across the seat. Surprised and a little off-balance, he took her upper arms in his hands to steady them both. He immediately wished he hadn't. Some sweet perfume began a subtle assault on his senses, and his hormones revved into overdrive. As if she were too hot to handle, he let his hands fall to his sides. It was a toss-up as to what he wanted most: to get the hell away from her or to see if those red lips tasted as good as they looked.

With her eyes locked on his, she stepped away. "I'm sorry."

She didn't look sorry. She looked sexy and ready for anything.

"No problem." He beat it to the other side of the truck. She could damn well shut her own door. By the time he pulled into traffic, he had his feelings under control, sort of. "I'm sorry the truck is such a mess."

"It's all right. I'm used to it."

He looked askance at her. "You, Little Miss Ritz?"

"Little Miss Ritz grew up on a horse farm, remember?"

The beast that took control of his tongue the moment Colby came into view spoke up. "So you like the smell of horse shit, huh?"

"Yeah, I do. Don't you?"

He took his eyes off the traffic long enough to see

whether or not she was putting him on. "You're serious?"

She shrugged. "Maybe I'm crazy. Mama says it's the best smell in the world, and I think she may be right." Colby laughed. "Must be in the Hastings genes."

He couldn't help smiling.

"You know, Rider, you ought to do that more often."

"What?"

"Smile."

Rider told himself not to get excited. Girls like Colby had flirting finessed to a fine art. "Life's a pretty serious matter."

"Yeah, it is."

"I thought girls like you only worried about what color to paint their nails." He gave his attention back to the traffic, but he was aware of her staring at him.

"Don't you ever get tired of it?" she asked at last.

He glanced over at her. "Tired of what?"

"Baiting me."

She was angry. No, not angry. Weary.

"All you ever do is put me down or ignore me. It's getting old, Rider. Particularly since I don't know what I've done to make you hate me so."

He thought about that. She was right. It occurred to him suddenly that he was treating her exactly the way his dad treated him. Why?

"I don't hate you."

"Then why do you do it?"

"Maybe because I don't know how to act around

a girl who can fly away to wherever she wants whenever she gets the urge."

"The money bothers you?"

"I don't know. Maybe." He sighed. "Yeah, dammit. The money bothers me."

"But you're friends with Cass, and he has money."

"That's different."

"How?"

"It just is. Cass doesn't run around in designer jeans and ruby-and-diamond necklaces."

"I hope not."

Her sudden smile vanished. "You may not believe this, but money can be as big a burden as it is a blessing."

"Yeah? Well, it's a burden I'd like to carry around a while."

"I'm serious. Just because my family is in the *Social Register* and my father's a senator doesn't mean I'm different from any other girl. If I cut myself shaving my legs, I bleed, and I have feelings that get hurt as easily as the next person's. You don't know what it's like to wonder if you're being asked out because the guy likes you or because your family has a wad in the bank."

Rider had never thought of money as an obstacle, and he'd sure never thought Colby Creighton would be so sensitive about it. "I thought that was the reason for coming-out parties—so you rich girls can find someone with as much money as you have, so you don't have to worry about ulterior motives."

"There you go again."

"I'm sorry."

"No, you're not."

"I am. Really."

Something in his eyes must have convinced her. She smiled reluctantly. "Of course, I haven't had to worry about how *you* feel about me. Your feelings are crystal clear."

"You know what they say. The best defense is a good offense. A guy like me has no business getting involved with a girl like you."

"And what does that mean?"

"That even if I did want to . . . date you, it could never come to any good. Girls whose families are in the *Social Register* don't end up with racetrackers."

"What's wrong with racetrackers?"

"Nothing's wrong with most of them, but you and I are from two different worlds. You know your dad would have a shit fit if he found out we were dating. It's just a whole lot easier not to start anything."

"My father does not tell me who to date."

"Is that right?"

"Yes, it is." A soft sigh escaped her lips. "I'm not talking about forever, Rider. I'm talking about a movie now and then, a few laughs. Some good times. I'd—" Wild roses bloomed in her cheeks." I'd really like . . . to spend more time with you."

"And what happens when you move on to another guy and rip out my heart?"

She looked at him thoughtfully for a moment. "For me to rip out your heart, you'd have to care."

Rider looked at her again. His eyes were serious. "Maybe that's what I'm scared of."

She smiled, and so did he. The moment was a turning point in their relationship that neither of them ever forgot.

27

On April twenty-second, the stables packed up their equipment and loaded it and the horses onto the lumbering vans that would take them to Kentucky. The one hundred and sixteenth run for the roses was just two weeks away. The Arkansas meet had been a disappointment to both Rider and Jock, since Jock's Dream was unable to do better than a fifth in the Arkansas Derby.

They'd been lucky to get Luis Mendoza to fly in for the race, but even with the hot new Puerto Rican rider on board, Jock's Dream didn't perform as they'd expected. Luis was regretful, and since he'd never been on the horse before, Rider and Jock could forgive him for rating the colt a bit too long. It wasn't uncommon for a jockey who was unfamiliar with a horse to miscalculate and wait too long to make a big run. If there was any consolation in not winning, it was that Runaway Again had gotten into trouble in the turn and hadn't even made the board.

The meet was over. It was time to move on.

"I want to ride Mendoza in the Derby," Jock said just outside Little Rock.

Rider's attention shifted from the interstate to his dad. "What?"

"I know he didn't do all that great yesterday, but he's sharp. He'll be okay next time out."

"Jesus, Dad, you can't do that to Danny. He's brought the colt this far. You can't just turn your back on him."

"Danny cost us the Rebel. And several other races, too, if I'm not mistaken. His riding sucks lately. Don't tell me you haven't noticed."

Rider couldn't deny that Danny had made a few moves that hadn't set well at the time. Still, he was a friend. "Everyone has off days."

"Yeah, well, Danny's having off nights, if I don't miss my guess."

"What are you talking about?"

"That blond bitch he's married to is leading him around by the dick, that's what I'm talking about."

"Tracy?"

"Hell, everyone on the backside knows she'll let anyone with an itch do it to her. And if Danny doesn't know, he's bound to have some strong suspicions."

"I can't believe that."

"Believe it," Jock said wearily. "She's nothing but a common road whore. She's just got prettier packaging than most."

Rider was skeptical, though Jock's explanation cleared up a lot of things—like Danny's nervousness and his unwillingness to talk about Tracy.

"Well, I still think it's a shitty deal to turn Danny around this way. He's almost family."

There was a determined look on Jock's face. "Family's family. Business is business. I've got to win that race."

Rider swore, but deep down he knew Jock was right. If a horse wasn't winning, it was common practice to change everything—equipment, feed, blacksmith, dentist, and especially the jockey—to try to capture the elusive winning position. Knowing Jock was right didn't make accepting his decision any easier. How would he tell Danny?"

"I'll tell him," Jock said as if reading Rider's mind.

"Be my guest."

The trip stretched on. They swapped driving and stopped to eat. The moment they drove over the Kentucky line, Jock turned solemn. Attuned to his moods, even after so many years apart, Rider noticed. "What's wrong?"

"I was thinking about your mother. Kentucky always brings a lot of memories."

"I was thinking about her earlier," Rider confessed. "I guess it's the time of year."

It had been a perfect May day when they'd learned that the cancer cells the California doctors had assured them were eradicated had returned, angry and vengeful, determined this time to finish what they had started. Jock didn't like to think of how Vicky had suffered in the end, and though he swore not to let them, the memories swarmed through his mind.

They'd been happy. Even though he'd been hard on her the year or so following the incident with Leland Creighton, Jock felt that when the priest had given Vicky the last rites, she was content with their life together.

It was their strong commitment to their marriage that helped them through those rough years, the promises made on their knees before man and God that kept them together. That and the love they felt for each other despite their mistakes. He never brought up the past. Neither did Vicky. But she was aware of his fears. He'd seen the worry reflected in her eyes, and if he drank too much on occasion, she let it pass. It had taken time, but gradually a new trust had developed between them. Still, not a day passed that he hadn't wondered if the boy Vicky had given birth to was his or Leland Creighton's.

Jock glanced over at Rider, who was lost in his own thoughts as he drove. He'd always been a good kid. He had his mother's looks and her desire to do everything right. There wasn't really a sign of Creighton in the boy. God knew he'd tried hard enough to work it out of him, just as he'd tried his hardest to care for him. But somehow he never could quite get past the doubts.

Those doubts had driven him to succeed when he and Vicky had left Kentucky and gone to California. Though he'd never admit it, he had needed to prove to Vicky that he could give her all the com-

forts she wanted—all the things Leland Creighton
might have given her.

Maybe, he'd thought a thousand times, he was
offering a silent apology for his own indiscretion,
the stolen weekend he'd spent with Alex Creighton,
the only time in his life he'd deliberately used
someone.

28

Lexington, Kentucky
May 1957

As she'd done for years, Alex spent the week
of the Derby at Windwood, the ninety-year-old
manor house and adjoining acreage that the Hastingses had kept open year-round for as long as she
could remember. The ten bedrooms provided
ample space for family members who were likely
to drop into town from time to time, especially during racing season. It was much more pleasant making the twenty-minute drive to the track than
enduring the trip from Lexington every day.

When she'd shown up at daybreak on Monday

morning to watch the horses, Jock had been surprised. He was pleased by her praise for his efforts, and he realized after a few minutes that he'd missed her dry wit. After the first morning, he found himself looking forward to her daily arrival.

"Tell me the truth," she said on Tuesday, her long-legged stride keeping pace with his as they headed back to the barn, "do you think Hasty Pudding has a chance Saturday?"

"If he didn't, he wouldn't be running, would he?"

"I guess not. What about Bold Ruler and Iron Liege?"

"They'll be tough. So will Round Table and Federal Hill."

She flashed him that sort-of smile. "We've got our work cut out for us, then."

Jock stopped in his tracks. He'd never noticed how the bow in her upper lip was more pointed than round, and he'd forgotten how unusual her ice-blue eyes really were.

"What are you looking at?" she asked, self-consciously raising a hand to her hair.

"Nothing." Jock started off at a fast clip, embarrassed and ashamed of his thoughts. It was the first time since he'd met Vicky that he'd been conscious of another woman's looks. Vicky. He had to remember Vicky.

But Vicky had betrayed him. With Alex's husband. He quickly pushed the hurtful thought away.

To his dismay, however, once his awareness of Alex manifested itself, it continued to grow. On Wednesday she invited him to Windwood for dinner. Even knowing that to do so was dangerous, he found himself accepting. Alex, dressed to the nines, played the part of hostess with supreme confidence and then, still wearing a dress that cost more than he made in a month, went outside to romp with the beagles that had free run of the place.

He was back on Thursday evening when she took a call from Leland. Even from the next room he could hear her side of the conversation through the partly open door.

"I have no intention of driving back to Lexington to attend the Bancrofts' Derby party so that you can get smashed and attack me," Jock heard her say. Then, after a moment, she added, "Did it ever occur to you that my lack of response might have something to do with your technique?"

She laughed, but there was no humor in the sound. "Frigid *and* a common bitch? Actually, Counselor, I think it would be fair to say that I'm the sum total of what being your wife for more than two years has made me." There was another pause. Then, very coldly, she said, "Screw you," and hung up the phone.

Jock stood in the middle of the parlor, unable to believe what he'd just heard. He was wondering if he should slip out and save Alex the embarrassment of facing him, when the door swung open.

She stood in the aperture, pale and trembling, her eyes awash with tears she refused to let fall. At that moment Jock realized that her air of supreme confidence was nothing but a veneer to hide her vulnerability. He suspected that Alexandra Hastings

Creighton could write a book about hurt and battered pride. Without considering the repercussions
of his actions, he crossed the room and drew her
close.

"I'm not frigid, Jock. I'm not." Her eyes begged
him to believe her. Then, as if to prove her point,
she burrowed closer and, standing on tiptoe,
pressed her mouth to his.

The moment he tasted her softness and warmth,
Jock realized just how vulnerable he was, too. She
pulled away and looked at him, waiting for him to
make the next move. Desire hit him squarely between the thighs. He wanted to keep kissing her.
Wanted to feel those strong horsewoman's legs
gripping his waist.

God help them, she wanted it, too. It was in her
eyes, in the breathless, waiting quality holding her
still in his arms. He was a married man, a man who
loved his wife. But loving Vicky didn't stop him from
wanting another woman. This woman.

Vicky. Sanity returned as her name played
through his mind. He released Alex and turned
away toward the window, so she wouldn't feel how
hard he'd grown.

"I'm sorry," she whispered, horror in her voice.

He spoke over his shoulder. "There's nothing to
be sorry for. You were upset."

Something between a bitter laugh and a sob escaped her. "My husband is very good at upsetting
me. I sometimes think that's his sole reason for ex-
isting."

Jock rounded on her. "Why do you stay with the bastard?"

She gave him that brittle smile of hers. "Because I'm a Hastings. And Hastingses don't quit."

"It isn't fair for you to spend your life with him and be miserable."

"No one ever guaranteed life would be fair, did they, Jock?"

He thought of Vicky and what she'd done to him in spite of the love he felt for her. "No. I guess they didn't."

"So we just go on about life and make the best we can of it."

He understood what she meant. That's what he was doing. But getting along the best he could wasn't what he wanted. He wanted happiness. At the moment, he'd settle for a reasonable facsimile. "I'd better go."

She nodded. "It's getting late."

Jock was exhausted, but he couldn't sleep. He was confused by the pain of Vicky's betrayal and the heady feeling of worth brought on by Alex's need. He tried to think of Vicky. But Vicky had hurt him, betrayed his trust, and trampled their marriage vows in the dust. Just before his alarm went off, he fell into an uneasy sleep. His last conscious thought was that maybe he was crazy for not taking what Alexandra Creighton offered.

It was feed time the following afternoon when Alex finally made an appearance. She didn't look as if she'd rested well the night before, either. Jock wished he could change things for her. Make her happy. But hell, he couldn't even control his own happiness. "Hi," he said.

"Hi."

"I'm . . . sorry about last night. I had no right to say anything about your husband or your marriage."

"I wasn't offended."

"It's just that I . . . care about you."

She nodded. Then she straightened her shoulders, visibly gathering herself, and went to Hasty Pudding's stall. "How is he?"

"He's fine. No problems. He's at his peak, so we just have to wait and see how the race goes."

"Actually," she told him, doing her best to smile, "the waiting is driving me crazy. I don't suppose you'd like to kill a few hours with me?"

If he said yes, he knew he'd be asking for trouble.

"I'm so hungry I'm almost sick," she continued. "I haven't eaten in almost twenty-four hours."

Not since the dinner they'd shared. Knowing he was pushing the limits of his control, Jock said, "I could use something myself. How does a big, greasy cheeseburger with onions sound?"

Alex smiled. "Heavenly."

"My treat."

"Sounds even better."

The diner Jock took her to was a favorite of his. The burgers were huge and wonderful, the fries crisp, and the chocolate shakes so thick Alex resorted to using a spoon.

When she'd finished every bite, she dabbed her

mouth with a paper napkin and sat back with a sigh of repletion. "That was better than delicious. How did you find this place?"

"Racetrackers are like truckers. They know all the good places to eat."

"I appreciate your taking time to feed me."

"My pleasure." He picked up the check.

On the way to the parking lot, Jock was congratulating himself on the fact that they'd made it through the meal with no undercurrents of awareness, when Alex said, "I understand Vicky's been away for a while."

"Uh, yeah. She's at her mother's. She got . . . homesick."

"Is she coming in for the race?"

"No." He glanced at Alex. "I guess your whole family will be here?"

She nodded. "The whole clan. Windwood's full, so I made arrangements to stay in town tonight," she said innocently. "I'm at the Hilton. Why don't you come over for a drink?"

His eyes met hers. "I don't know. . . ."

"It's early yet. I won't keep you up too late."

No one had ever accused Jock McCall of being a saint, and he knew that if he went, he'd stay the night. "Sure," he said, throwing caution to the wind, "why not?"

When they reached the hotel, Alex headed straight to her room. She had a suite, of course, all decorated in sunshine colors and natural wood. It was too contemporary for his taste, but it really didn't matter. He wasn't there to judge the decor.

Alex went to the bar and peered inside. "What would you like?" she asked over her shoulder. "I've got whiskey, tequila, rum—"

The carpet had deadened the sound of his footsteps, and when his hands clamped on her waist, she whirled to face him. His hands slid to her hips.

"I didn't come for a drink, Alex."

"I know." She reached up and laid her palm against his cheek, rough with a day's worth of whiskers. "I want you, Jock," she told him in that forthright way of hers. "I've wanted you for a very long time."

Her confession filled him with a certain satisfaction. "You have?"

"I don't think I've ever truly wanted a man before."

The words were a balm to his shattered masculinity. He bent his head and kissed her, his open mouth meeting hers, his hands going to her breasts.

It was strange touching someone besides Vicky. Strange and exciting. Her kisses were quick, feverish, and her mouth clung to his in blatant hunger.

"Slow down," he murmured, his fingers freeing the buttons of her blouse. "We've got all night."

"It won't be nearly long enough," she said, leading him to the bed.

Jock pinned her to the mattress with his weight. Between long, drugging kisses, they rid each other of their clothes. She was almost boyishly slim, and her breasts were small, firm and tasted like ambrosia. Her body was sleek and hard from physical activity, and, as he'd known they would be, her legs were strong and clinging.

Jock found out that Alex Creighton was far from cool and controlled, and she was definitely not frigid. She was filled with dormant passion and a hidden fire that blazed beneath his touch. He showered her with praise, and he was surprised at how easily he could bring her to readiness again and again. He had no way of knowing that his gentleness and consideration for her pleasure touched a part of her that Leland didn't even know existed.

They took all night. And Alex was right. It wasn't long enough.

He left before dawn, kissing her and telling her that he'd see her at the track.

Then he pushed both Alex and Vicky from his mind and concentrated on running the colt. It was the day he'd been waiting for. The day every trainer in the country longed to be a part of. There was no time for personal feelings.

The race turned out to be one of the most unusual in the eighty-three-year history of the Derby. Hartack, aboard Iron Liege, and Shoemaker, riding Gallant Man, were battling down the stretch when Shoemaker stood up at the sixteenth pole, mistaking it for the finish line. When he realized his mistake and took to the whip, it was too late; Iron Liege squeaked under the wire, first by a nose.

Hasty Pudding shattered a hock going down the backstretch and never finished the race. Alex's disappointment over losing was second to her agony at having to destroy the Hastings' Meadows future sire.

She didn't say anything. She just stood beside her father and watched as the vet administered the lethal injection that would end the colt's pain. Like so many other dreams, this one had succumbed to the vagaries of the racing world.

The races were long over and the crowd had thinned when Alex stopped by the barn before driving back to Lexington. Jock saw the sorrow in her eyes. Her week of freedom was over, and Jock was just about to start a life sentence.

"I'm sorry about Hasty," he said. "I know it hurt to put him down."

She shrugged, but he could see the pain in her eyes. "It's part of the business. You always hope it won't happen to you, but deep down you know your turn will come around sooner or later."

Jock couldn't help feeling that she was talking about more than racing. "That's a healthy attitude."

"It wouldn't help to have a bad one." She put her hand on his arm, and Jock almost jumped with guilt. "I want you to know that I appreciate everything you did for the horse. I know he had the best of care."

"Thanks."

She tried to smile. "Maybe we'll have better luck next year."

Jock thrust his hands into the pockets of his sport coat and took a deep breath. "I won't be here next year, Alex."

Her pretty face went slack with shock.

"I've been planning to give you my notice for several weeks."

"Why?"

Her voice was a whisper, and it was hard for Jock to face the confusion in her eyes. "Because Vicky can't live at the farm anymore."

Alex didn't speak for a long moment. Instead she pulled one of her inevitable Gauloises from her Dior handbag and tapped it on her palm. "He's been bothering her, hasn't he?"

Jock's gaze jerked to hers. "You know?"

Alex's mouth—a slash of scarlet color—twisted into a mockery of a smile. "I know my husband. I saw it coming."

"Then there's no use dragging the ugly mess out in the open."

Her slim shoulders lifted in a weary shrug. "Not really. It isn't the first time it's happened, and it certainly won't be the last."

The finality of the statement made Jock realize that he had been too wrapped up in his own pain to consider that Leland's affairs might hurt Alex, even if only her pride. He drew his Zippo from his pocket and flipped the top.

"I love her." It was the only excuse he had.

"I know." Alex bent her head and placed the tip of the cigarette in the flame. For a second or two he could see nothing but the round crown and floppy brim of her white straw hat. In contrast with the stylish picture she presented to the world, her nails, polished with something clear and shiny, were far too short to be fashionable.

She raised her head and blew a stream of bluish smoke skyward. "What about me?"

Jock noticed that her movements were jerky, awkward. Her words were clipped, the way she'd sounded when he first met her. His heart beat in a painful cadence. It was the second most distressing confrontation of his life.

"I'll miss you," he said, and meant it. "It's been a real pleasure working for you and . . . last night was . . . wonderful. You're a very special lady, Alexandra Creighton."

Her eyes gleamed with gathering moisture. "What if I . . . asked you to stay?"

"You know I can't."

Her mouth quirked in her hallmark humorless smile. "No, I suppose not. Is there . . . anything I can do?"

He shrugged. "Maybe a letter of recommendation."

She looked shattered. He hadn't meant to sound flip. He wanted to tell her he hated leaving, hated what had happened. Hated hurting her. "Jesus, Alex," he said, his voice intense, "you know I'd never hurt you intentionally."

"No?"

The single word was an accusation. Hadn't he done just that? Hadn't he taken her the night before, knowing that it had everything to do with lust and retribution and nothing to do with love? Hot color rushed to his face.

She reached out, as if intending to touch him, thought better of it, and drew away. Instead she straightened her shoulders and clutched her handbag to her breasts. "Thank you for . . . everything."

Torn between sorrow and gut-deep embarrassment, he looked away.

"I'll have it for you in the morning."

"What?"

"The letter of recommendation."

He'd already forgotten. Somehow a letter seemed unimportant when three lives lay trampled in the Kentucky dust. "I'll never forget you, Alex."

"Me either."

Head high, she turned and walked out of the shed row, the heels of her navy-and-white spectator pumps making small holes in the hard-packed dirt. Each one was like a pinprick to his heart. Revenge wasn't so sweet after all.

He realized that sleeping with Alex had been prompted by more than revenge. It was mixed up somehow with male pride and his need to prove to himself that he was still attractive and desirable. It had a lot to do with that elusive thing called manhood. No, revenge didn't taste as sweet as he expected. It tasted like bitterweed.

A week later he was out of her life. He packed up his and Vicky's belongings, stopped by her mother's to pick her up, and headed for California. He didn't see Alexandra Creighton again until the spring more than twenty years later when he and Rider ran into her and Cass at the track.

But he'd kept his word. He'd never forgotten her.

29

Sunshine streamed through the window. Sweat poured from Danny's face as his body pummeled Tracy's. He groaned with his release and collapsed against her. Then, breathing heavily, he raised himself to his elbows and looked at his wife's beautiful face. Her lower lip trembled, and a fine sheen of tears glazed her eyes.

"I'm sorry," she whispered.

Danny's heart fell. *She* was sorry, apologizing because she hadn't come. So why did *he* feel like such a miserable failure?

Because you're supposed to be good enough, experienced enough, to satisfy her, asshole.

He moved away from her warmth and leaned against the headboard. Resting his elbows on his raised knees, he buried his face in his hands.

"It's just that I'm worried about money. . . ."

Danny's muscles tensed. The recurrent feeling that he was on a head-on course with some indefinable disaster flitted through him. He turned to look at the body a good percentage of the U.S. male population had lusted over. Anger nudged his uneasiness aside. "Why would you worry about money?"

She shrugged, and her perfectly shaped C-cup breasts bobbed with the movement. "Thirty days is a long time to go without riding, and now that Jock doesn't want you to ride in the Derby . . ." Her voice trailed away, and she shrugged again. "It's a lot of money we'll be missing out on."

Danny's lips twisted. Unbelievable. She was so worried about not having money that it had affected her performance in bed. Or was it *his* performance it affected?

At that moment he truly hated her. Maybe love was blind, but his illusions had dissipated more and more over the last few months. Tracy was that rare creature, a true hedonist. She lived strictly for herself, for her own gratification and pleasure. And what usually gave her pleasure and fulfillment was extravagant, excessive spending. And sex. She got a hell of a lot of pleasure from sex.

But if sex was Tracy's pleasure, it was also her power. Danny worried about other men every hour he was away from her. Men who were more successful. Had more money. Men who were better endowed physically.

Even despising her as he did at that moment, he understood that there were things inside a person, things that had to do with self-esteem, that demanded some means of satisfaction. He didn't know what Tracy's were, but his were the devils that told him he was less a man because of his size, even though he was tall for a jockey. Controlling a fifteen-hundred-pound animal, feeling that raw power between his thighs, knowing that his skill could enhance that animal's performance, went a long way toward satisfying his own personal demons. It was the same euphoria he felt as he rode Tracy toward her climax, her screams of "Yes, Danny, yes, oh, yes!" reminiscent of a crowd cheering him to victory.

But there hadn't been any cheering today. Or for the last week, for that matter.

Screw it. Screw her.

"You're mad."

He looked at her, hating himself. "No, I'm not."

"Yes, you are." She took his hand and moved it to the moist juncture of her thighs. "I don't want you to be mad at me, Danny."

He felt his anger diminish as his hardness grew. He hated that little girl voice of hers, hated himself for his weakness where Tracy was concerned, hated knowing that she could manipulate him through his own sexuality.

She leaned over and kissed him, filling his mouth with her tongue. Then she straddled him and guided him into her.

"I just want to make you happy," she cooed. "We'll manage somehow."

He groaned in defeat. Hating the way things were didn't change them. As she squirmed against him, Danny's demons roused from their brief rest and started their banshee tauntings.

30

"Rider's here," Bonnie said with all the non-chalance she could muster, knowing she was going against the Creighton family's wishes by telling Colby.

"So I hear."

Frowning, Bonnie looked up. "Who told you?"

"Cass."

"*Cass* told you?"

"Uh-huh." Colby brushed seafoam green onto the watercolor rendering of a wealthy client's pro-posed new bedroom with controlled, steady strokes. "I guess he thought he ought to prepare me so I wouldn't have the shock I did at Oaklawn."

Bonnie sank onto a nearby chair. "Oaklawn? What happened at Oaklawn?"

"Mama and I saw him in the paddock the day of the Rebel."

"You saw Rider in Hot Springs?"

Colby met her sister-in-law's concerned gaze. "Face it, Bonnie, I was bound to run into him sooner or later."

"And?"

"And what?"

"Lordy, Colby," Bonnie drawled, "you do know how to drive a person to distraction."

Colby's smile was unrepentant.

"How did he look? What did he say?"

"He looked . . . tired. He didn't say anything. I think he was as surprised as I was." Colby rose and went to the window that overlooked a busy Lexington street. She crossed her arms and leaned against the window frame, staring down at the slow-moving traffic. She sighed. "It's funny. I know I'm supposed to hate him for what he did to me, and when I think about it, I get really furious. But for a second, I didn't even think about the bad part. I was just glad to see him."

"That's natural, I think," Bonnie said. "After all, you loved him very much."

"Yeah," Colby said wistfully. "I loved him. Too bad he didn't feel the same."

"I don't believe that for one minute. Why, Rider was crazy about you."

Colby turned away from the window. "He was crazier about Daddy's money."

"There had to be a reason for him to do what he did."

"There was. Twenty thousand of them."

"I still think there was more to what went on than met the eye. I know Rider. He just wouldn't go off and leave you like that. Not with you . . ."

"Pregnant?" Colby said, finishing the sentence.

"I wasn't gonna bring that up."

"Why not? It's certainly no secret—not in the family, anyway. Actually, it might help if we all talked about it more often instead of pretending it never happened. Why can't my parents just face the fact that I made a mistake and got pregnant by someone they didn't approve of? I'm not unique. It happens all the time."

"I don't think it's your mistake they object to talkin' about. I think they don't want to discuss anythin' that might remind you how much Rider's leavin' hurt you."

"Would it surprise everyone to know that I think about him and what happened quite a lot? And it did hurt, Bonnie. Obviously it more than hurt, since it took me a year at Forest Glade to get over it. I just don't understand why my parents can't see that Rider's taking the money was the best thing in the long run. It's taken me eleven years to realize it was a blessing in disguise."

"What are you talkin' about?"

"Thank God we saw his true colors before he found out about the baby. The only thing worse than having him desert me would be if he'd stayed out of some sort of pseudonoble sense of duty and drained us dollar by dollar."

"Drain you? Rider would never have ever done that. And I think you know it. He loved you, Colby, and I think he'd die if he knew you aborted his child." The moment the words were out, Bonnie wished she could call them back.

There was a suspicious glimmer in Colby's eyes. "I do regret that. More than anyone knows."

Bonnie gave Colby a fierce hug. "I shouldn't have brought it up. I wasn't thinkin'."

"It's okay." She tried to smile. "I wasn't in any frame of mind to fight Daddy over it."

"Look, darlin', you've got to stop beatin' yourself up about that. Once your daddy gets somethin' in his mind, he's a hard man to buck."

"Tell me something I don't know."

"How about somethin' like I believe with all my heart that Rider got as raw a deal as you did."

Colby gave a weary shake of her head. "Cass is right. You'll defend Rider McCall to the bitter end."

"No offense, but I'd have to be a little wary of any deal your daddy had his finger in."

Colby saw the conviction in her friend's eyes. Bonnie did believe Rider was somehow innocent. Colby recalled the flash of happiness she fancied she'd seen in his eyes at Oaklawn and wished with all her heart that Bonnie was right. The time with Rider had been the best time of her life.

31

Lexington, Kentucky
June 1979

Colby sat at the edge of a pond on the outer
fringes of Hastings' Meadows Farm, a cane pole in
hand. Rider was several yards away, slumped
against a tree. He wasn't running any horses that
afternoon and had convinced Jock to give him
some time off. He must have needed the rest. From
where she sat, it looked as if he were doing less
fishing than sleeping.

The pond was a good place for it. Far enough
away from the farm's activity to give a sense of pri-
vacy, it sat in a field of green with just a smattering
of trees to shade the glimmering surface. The only
company they were apt to have were the mares and
foals that sauntered to the water's edge for an occasional drink.

She hadn't been caught charging her airfare yet,
and she'd flown down, ostensibly to visit her
mother, because her father had gone to California
for the weekend. Ever since the night two weeks be-

fore when she and Rider had talked, things had gotten better between them. Not only had she run up her charge cards, she'd also run up her phone bill, calling him long distance. Rider called her, too, usually when he was upset about his mother, who was getting worse by the day.

Colby shook her head, banishing the unhappy thoughts. She wanted to bake in the summer sun and revel in the fact that she was with Rider, who was teaching her, of all things, how to fish. A sappy smile claimed her lips. Lord, who ever would have thought it? She was in love, wonderfully, totally, in love, and she thought that even though he was fighting it, Rider was falling for her, too.

Her happy gaze drank in the sight of him slumped against the trunk of a tree whose roots were perilously near the water's edge. A St. Louis Cardinals cap shielded his eyes, which she suspected were closed, since he hadn't moved in twenty minutes. The soft cotton of a black pocket T-shirt molded itself over the hard contours of his chest. Wash-worn Levi's sheathed his legs, and he'd traded his disreputable boots for a pair of just as shabby sneakers.

As Colby watched, Rider's red-and-white bobber disappeared beneath the water.

She leaped to her feet. "You've got one!"

Hearing her voice, Rider grabbed his pole and gave a hard jerk, setting the hook in the unsuspecting fish and hauling it out of the pond's placid waters.

Colby squealed and raced around the bank, her

spanking new Keds slipping in the grass that sparkled with moisture from the unpredicted flash-in-the-pan shower that had dumped a half inch of rain earlier.

"What kind is it?" she asked. Before he could answer, the fish flopped onto her shoes. Colby squealed and jumped sideways. Her foot slipped on the grassy slope. She gave another shriek as she started to fall.

Rider grabbed the bottom of her T-shirt and gave a hard jerk that sent her sprawling forward. Dazed, she realized she lay smack dab on top of Rider, who wasn't moving a muscle. Her heart was racing like crazy, and she was having trouble breathing.

As Colby flattened her palms against the grass and levered herself upward, Rider's eyelashes lifted in lazy increments. There was something in his eyes she'd been hoping to see for weeks. Something that made her heart race.

She could feel the warmth of him through his shirt and the hardness of his body beneath hers. He reached up and brushed a lock of hair from her eyes. "Are you okay?"

His voice sounded normal. Struggling to achieve that same status, she nodded. "Are you?"

"I'm fine."

Colby knew she needed to put some space between them. When she braced a hand on his chest to push herself up, her palm encountered something hard in the pocket of his T-shirt. Rider winced.

"I'm sorry. What is it?"

She thought he blushed. "It's nothing. I had something for you, but it's corny and cheap and—"

"A present?" she cried in surprise. "You bought me a present?" She started to slip her hand into his pocket, but his fingers closed around her wrist.

"I didn't buy you a present. I made you one." He sounded embarrassed. "I dabble with designing jewelry sometimes, turquoise and silver mostly, but this is—"

"You made something for me, and I want to see it." She folded her arms across his upper chest and rested her chin on them. Their faces were mere inches apart. She could see the darker rays of color in his brown eyes, as well as the insecurity. "Please."

He closed his eyes. Her fingers worked into his pocket.

"I'm warning you, it's nothing."

Colby drew the object out. It was a heavy necklace of white, irregular rectangles polished to a shine. Each had its own unique pattern of bumps and darker whorls. Caps, she thought, recognizing the "baby teeth" immediately. Interspersed between each flat piece were the pointed wolf teeth that resembled canine teeth. It looked like a necklace a pagan island princess might wear as she leaped into a burning volcano. Colby traced her fingertip across one rectangle. The necklace was beautiful, if for no other reason than because Rider had made it for her.

"It's horse teeth," she said in wonder. "Caps and wolf teeth."

"At least you can be sure no one in your circle of friends will have anything like it. Jesus, I can't believe I really gave you that piece of—"

Colby put her hand over his mouth. She could feel the warm gusts of his breath against her palm and suppressed a shiver. "Will you be quiet? I love it." She uncovered his mouth and slipped the necklace over her head. "I know a trainer's wife who had a necklace of camel's teeth that everyone went crazy over." She straightened her shoulders. "What do you think?"

Rider regarded his gift against the thrust of her breasts, along with the ruby-and-diamond necklace her father had given her. "I think the contrast about sums everything up."

"What are you talking about?"

Rider gathered both necklaces in his open palm. "That's the difference between you and me. You're third-generation society. I'm second-generation racetrack. You're a diamond kind of girl. I'm a rhinestone sort of guy. We're champagne and beer, Colby. Chanel and horse sh—"

Colby stopped him with her mouth. For a moment, her action surprised them both. Then, very slowly, she raised her head to look at him. His brown eyes had turned a dark, unreadable black.

"What do you think you're doing?" he asked at last.

"Shutting you up."

"Why?"

"Because I don't want to hear it." She tried to get up, but Rider jerked her back down and rolled her over, pinning her to the damp ground with his body.

"It's only the truth, Colby, and you know it."

"It doesn't have to be. We both come from families of gamblers. Don't you believe in us enough to gamble a little on our future?"

"There is no us. We have no future."

"I want us to," she said. Her blue eyes were filled with earnest entreaty.

"You don't know what you're saying." Frustration lent harshness to his voice.

"I'm saying that I'm falling in love with you. And if you really want to hurt me, you'll tell me to get up and out of your life."

Disbelief held him still, and his eyes searched hers for the truth.

She tugged his T-shirt free of his jeans and slipped her palms over the taut skin beneath. Rider stopped breathing.

"But if you care for me," she continued, her fingers working beneath the denim waistband, "even a little bit, you won't let me leave here without making love to me."

Rider was strong, but he wasn't that strong. He bent to kiss her, and the moment he did, he was lost beyond redemption. In a matter of minutes their clothing littered the ground. She laughed at his awkward attempts to peel off her jeans and watched in awe as he rid himself of his.

His hands skimmed her nakedness, as if he were afraid she'd vanish at the slightest touch. He adored every inch of her. Colby's mouth explored the hardness of his body in innocent wonder, from the flat nipples hiding in the whorls of dark chest hair to the strong thighs that tangled with hers.

She felt loved and needed. Whole. Complete. It was more than sex. It was an extension of the love she felt for him and prayed he felt for her. When Rider eased his fullness into the tight tunnel of her virgin softness, the aching emptiness in Colby's heart was filled. She gave a soft sob of wonder and held him closer. Faster. Faster. Neck and neck they raced for the finish line, and when Colby's back arched to take his final thrust, she knew she was his. Now and forever.

"Why didn't you tell me you were a virgin?"

Colby, wearing only her necklaces, took his cigarette from him and drew in a deep draft of the acrid smoke. When she'd stopped coughing, she asked, "Would it have mattered?"

"I could have been more careful."

"You were wonderful. You *are* wonderful. *It* was wonderful." She laughed and placed the Marlboro between his lips. "Besides, would you have believed me?"

"Probably not," he admitted around the cigarette. Colby laughed and nestled close to his side. "We're gonna be covered with chiggers."

"A small price," she said, running her hand over the hair that covered his chest and trickled down his hard stomach.

Rider caught her wrist. "That'll get you in trouble."

"Promises, promises," she grumbled.

"I'm serious. We need to go. It's almost feed time."

She sighed and rose. "You know," she said, tossing him his shorts, "I think I like learning how to fish."

Rider snatched the underwear from the air. Grinned. "I sorta like teaching you, myself."

"And you're wrong, you know."

"About what?"

"We're not champagne and beer. We're catfish and hushpuppies."

32

"Come, on, Colby. It's only lunch. I'm not asking you to reconcile with the man."

Colby tried to ignore the pounding in her head and concentrate on what her father was saying. Confronting him was enough to give anyone a headache. "Maybe not, but it's what you're after."

Leland smiled his famous smile and placed a manicured hand over his chest. "Ah. Pierced to the heart."

Looking at him across her desk, it was easy to see why the world at large found her father attractive. Though he'd thickened somewhat the last few years, he was far from overweight, and what few creases scored his face softened the hard gleam in his eyes. The streak of white through the center of his black hair only added an extra dollop of distinction to the overall picture he strove to maintain: that of the consummate politician. Still, there was something about him that Colby found increasingly unattractive—probably the ruthlessness and manipulative manner the cosmopolitan veneer concealed.

"You don't have a heart, Daddy."

Leland's grin slipped a notch. "Your mother will be disappointed. The Martindales will be there, and she was hoping we could have a real family get-together."

"Bullshit. *You'll* be disappointed because one of your schemes has gone awry. Face it, Daddy. I'm not going to remarry Kent, and the Creightons aren't exactly the Brady bunch."

Leland's lips tightened, though he'd long ago given up trying to stop Colby's cursing.

"Now, sweetheart," he soothed in his best promise-'em-anything voice, "you know as well as I do that all families have problems now and then."

"We don't have problems. We're the ultimate dysfunctional family. You screw anything in skirts. You and Mama could give a damn less about each other. You didn't speak to your only son for three years, and your daughter is the biggest disappointment of the century. Not only did I get knocked up by a lowly racetracker, I've had an abortion and the first divorce in the history of the Creighton family."

"Colby—"

"Maybe," she continued, recklessly ignoring the warning in his voice, "I should have thanked Rider when I saw him at Oaklawn. At least what he did to me got you and Cass back on speaking terms." Her smile was genuine Diamelle. "Which proves there's truth in the old adage that trouble brings a family closer."

"You saw Rider McCall?" As usual, Leland zeroed in on the one thing Colby wished she hadn't mentioned.

She dropped the sarcasm. "I figured Mama told you."

"She didn't," Leland said, "but I might have known."

"Might have known what?"

He lifted his broad shoulders in a shrug. "Knowing you saw Rider McCall explains a lot of things."

There was an air of resignation in his manner. A warning signal flashed through Colby's mind. Her father was never resigned to situations that weren't to his liking. She wondered what was coming next. "Like what?"

"Your actions. You've been on edge lately."

Had she? The pounding in her head increased. It was exhausting trying to keep up with her father, much less stay one step ahead of him.

"You're not yourself, Colby. Let us help you. Let Pete help you get through this. . . ." Leland's soft,

lilting voice surfaced from someplace in the past, during her time at Forest Glade.

"I should have recognized this belligerent attitude you've had the last few weeks. You're acting the way you did when you were sneaking around seeing McCall."

"You've been behaving terribly, Colby. And I will not have it, do you understand?"

"What belligerent attitude?" she asked, trying to shake off the troublesome memories.

"Refusing to attend a simple luncheon, for one thing."

"That constitutes a belligerent attitude?"

"A dutiful daughter would want to please her parents."

The hard look in his eyes belied the softness in his voice. Colby felt herself losing the control she'd struggled so hard to gain. He was doing it to her again.

What do I do now, Cass? What do I do?

"Spit in his eye, babe. The son of a bitch can't stand it when someone gigs him back."

"I tried being a dutiful daughter, Daddy," she said, holding on to the memory of Cass's advice. "I wasn't very good at it."

"If you weren't so selfish, you might improve," he observed. "You might try putting other people's wishes ahead of your own for a change."

She lifted a hand to her temple, and her gaze swept the elegant Art Deco appointments of her office at Creighton Interiors. Old arguments whirled inside her head, melding with the equally ancient guilt he was so adept at resurrecting. She had to stop her father's insidious infiltration of her new confidence, her newly created world.

"All right! I'll go to your damned lunch. But I will not go back to Kent. I don't love him. I never did. And I'm not about to stay tied to someone I don't love the way Mama has."

Leland's face darkened, and Colby felt a bit of strength return.

"Your mother's and my marriage is none of your concern."

"And my marriage, or the dissolving of it, is none of yours."

Watching his anger change to woe was like watching a chameleon change colors.

"Is it wrong for me to want to see you happily married? Is it wrong for me to want a grandson to dandle on my knee?"

"You had a grandson, Daddy," she reminded him in a voice so brittle it cracked. "But you made me get rid of him."

There was no sign of remorse on Leland's face. "I'm not talking about some whelp of Rider McCall's. I'm talking about someone worthy of carrying on the Creighton genes."

Colby laughed. "What's so great about the Creighton genes? It seems to me the world might be better off if the Creightons died out."

Leland shook his head. "I can't believe you're so bitter, so ungrateful. I was taking care of you the best way I knew how. Whatever happened to my daughter? The one who used to sit on my knee and do anything to please me?"

Colby's flush of jubilation faded. Before she could answer, he turned and started for the door.

"Come on, baby. Do what Daddy says. That's the way. Good girl."

For a moment her anger and determination faltered.

"You will do as I say, Colby Antoinette. And you will do it now. This instant."

"Daddy?"

He turned.

"That Colby died. You smothered her."

A look of exquisite sorrow crossed Leland's features. "You really ought to talk to Pete, sweetheart. Seeing Rider McCall has you all fucked up again."

33

"Why didn't you tell me Colby ran into Rider McCall in Hot Springs?" Leland asked Alex that night at dinner.

Alex laid down her fork, clasped her hands in her lap, and raised her limpid gaze to his. "I didn't think it was important."

"You didn't think it was important?"

"We were on our way to the paddock the day of the Rebel, and he looked our way. They didn't even speak. It was nothing." Alex neglected to mention how upset she'd been over the encounter.

"Well, it certainly affected Colby."

"I haven't noticed her acting any differently."

"Trust me, she is."

Alex laughed. "I'd sooner trust the Devil. What's Colby done that you think is so terrible?"

"When I first asked her, she refused to join us Wednesday for lunch."

"Before or after she found out Kent would be there?"

Leland stabbed at his coq au vin.

"She isn't going to go back to him, so you may as well forget whatever little plan you have in mind."

Leland pointed his fork, which held a bite of chicken, at Alex. "Kent loves Colby."

"Does he love her, or does he say he does because you're his biggest supporter in his congressional race?"

Leland ignored the taunt. "He's miserable without her."

"And she's miserable with him. Leave her alone. She's happy."

"She doesn't know what will make her happy."

"And you do?" Alex shook her head. "You have no idea what goes on in her head, and furthermore, you don't care. Why don't you try being honest with yourself just once. You want things your way, and that's all that matters."

"Are you implying that I manipulate people?"

"Implying? No. It's a fact that you've tried to choreograph Colby's life to suit your plans, from which schools she attended to whom she dated."

"Are we back to Rider McCall, then?" Leland snapped. "You were happy enough to let me take care of things when you found out he'd left her pregnant."

"I don't want to talk about it."

"McCall was scum."

Alex gave him a considering look. "That's a strange attitude, since his mother was good enough for you to sleep with."

Leland's silverware clattered onto his plate. "You shut your fucking mouth."

"Sorry. Not this time. What's the matter, Senator? Didn't you think I knew that it was your screwing around that lost me the best farm manager I ever had, maybe the best man I ever had the good fortune to know?" She rose and, dropping her napkin to the table, turned to leave the room.

"And you knew him well, I imagine." Leland's voice stopped her halfway across the room.

Alex pivoted on the heel of one alligator pump. "Jock McCall was a valued employee who happened to love his wife very much."

"Answer me, damn you," he commanded, his eyes glittering with reptilian intensity. "Did you or did you not sleep with the bastard to get back at me?"

Alex's laughter was soft and mocking. "I don't kiss and tell. Besides, if I had slept with Jock McCall, I would have done it because he was attractive, not because I wanted to get back at you."

Leland's nostrils flared. "You common whore."

She smiled the smile that had become so familiar to Jock. "You used to call me a frigid bitch. Which is it?" She turned and started for the door.

"Where the hell are you going?"

She looked at him over her shoulder, innocence personified. "Why, I'm going to call the Martindales and make all the arrangements for our little family luncheon."

Before he could answer, she slipped through the door. Trembling, she leaned against it.

Dammit! Had seeing Rider really upset Colby as

much as Leland had implied? Dear God, she couldn't go through all that again, she just couldn't.

Alex sighed. Even after eleven years, it was inconceivable to her that Jock's son was capable of hurting someone the way Rider had Colby. He and Cass had come to the house when Leland wasn't there, and being around Rider was a pleasure. He was so much like Jock that it was unsettling at times. Alex almost found herself wishing Rider and Colby would get together, and when Cass let it slip they were seeing each other, she was secretly pleased.

But Leland had been furious and determined to end the relationship. He had plans for Colby, plans that included marriage to Kent Carlisle. Alex had been unable to sway him, and when Leland received a tip that Colby was seen leaving a track hangout with Rider, he'd followed.

He'd caught them making love, and the two men had fought. Colby had gone berserk. So berserk that after Leland had given Rider a check to get out of Colby's life, he had had to take her straight to Forest Glade, where she had been heavily sedated. When they learned she was pregnant, Alex had been forced to agree with Leland's insistence that they terminate the pregnancy.

It had taken almost a year of psychiatric help before Colby was well enough to be released, and though they gradually explained to her what had happened, and her reaction, she had no actual recollection of anything after Leland's arrival. The mind was a strange and wonderful thing, Pete Whitten said. It could sweep damaging memories into some dark recess. Colby had banished the hurtful recollection of her lover taking the payoff and hidden the memory of the abortion in some faraway corner. The only thing it couldn't banish were the dreams. Those, Pete had assured them, were her mind's way of dealing with the pain of Rider's defection.

Those first years after she'd come home from the hospital were terrible for Alex. A stranger with Colby's body had come home in her daughter's place. Once headstrong, vivacious, and fun-loving, Colby was quiet, unsure of herself, even fragile.

It had taken her daughter years of counseling and years of depending on pills and alcohol to get over the fact that Rider had cared more for money than for her. Malleable, even vague, she let Leland take charge of her life again. When she agreed to marry Kent Carlisle, she was once more her daddy's darling. Unable to reach her daughter, Alex longed for the old Colby's spit and fire.

Then, a couple of years ago, Colby seemed to wake up. She stopped seeing Pete, and when she expressed dissatisfaction with what she had become, Cass took her in hand and started helping her put her life back together. The first thing she did was move out of Kent's house and into an apartment. The second thing she did was file for divorce. The third, and most satisfying, thing she did was buy into Bonnie Martindale's interior design business.

As might have been expected, Cass's intervention put a strain on his already uneasy relationship with his father, but when everyone commented on how improved Colby was, there was little Leland could do or say.

Alex didn't think Colby was happy—not yet—but she did think that her troubled daughter was satisfied with the course her life had taken. She and Bonnie were successful in their business, and Colby was starting to date again, starting to sound like the young, carefree Colby.

As much as Alex had loved Jock, and as hard as it was to believe Rider had done what he had, her first allegiance was to her daughter, and she intended to see to it that nothing halted Colby's progress back into the world of the living.

Alex pushed herself away from the door and started toward the phone. Why, why had the fates been so unkind as to bring Rider and Colby face to face after all this time? Fleetingly she recalled the look on Rider's face that day in the paddock. There had been surprise in his eyes and a glimmer of joy, which was odd now that she thought of it. Joy was an emotion that didn't fit the picture at all.

34

Leland finished every bite of his dinner. He was long past the point when arguing with his bitch of a wife upset him, if it ever had. He knew she'd slept with Jock McCall, but he'd never been able to prove it. After all this time, what did it matter, anyway?

Alex had never loved him, nor he her, but he had married up, and it was a good match, from several standpoints. Though they hadn't objected to his marriage to Alex, the Hastingses had shown him in dozens of little ways that he wasn't quite good enough for their daughter. The right people didn't see law as an acceptable career, and politics even less so. Politicians might be public servants, but they were servants nonetheless.

Leland tossed back the dregs of his Chablis. Screw the Hastingses! Screw Alex. She had denied him the love of his son and kept it all for herself, but no one was going to take his Colby away from him.

She'd rebelled once, and the fiasco with McCall was the outcome. But she'd come to her senses, and for a while she was content to let him and Kent take care of her. Then she'd made another turn-around. She'd divorced Kent and gone into busi-ness with that mouthy twit Cass had married.

It was as if Colby had to try it on her own every few years, and he didn't understand why. He had given her everything she could possibly need or want. He had granted her every wish. Couldn't she see he was only trying to take care of her?

Leland stared across the dining room and rubbed his bottom lip with his finger. Whether she realized it or not, seeing Rider McCall had a lot to do with her refusal to join the family and Kent for lunch. It had no doubt stirred up memories Leland hoped she'd left at Forest Glade.

It seemed the past was catching up to them in spite of everything, but there was no way he was going to let Rider McCall or the memory of him mess up Colby's life the way he had before. When Leland had first traced the exorbitant amounts on Colby's credit card to airplane tickets to Kentucky, he'd been furious. It was a toss-up as to whose ass he had wanted to kick more—Cass's or Rider's.

The argument, like every argument he'd ever had with Colby, was indelibly etched into his mind. . . .

"I want that charge card, Colby. You've abused my generosity and gone against my express wishes about seeing your brother."

Calmly Colby reached into her purse and pulled out the card. She met his gaze without so much as the quiver of an eyelash. "I'm sure Mama will give me another one."

Leland's nostrils flared. "You ask your mother for a card and I'll—"

"What? Forbid me to see *her*? I'm twenty years old, Daddy. An adult. You can't tell me what to do or who to see."

"Dammit, Colby, I'm doing this for your own good."

Her eyes were arctic blue and just as cold. "You're doing it because you can't face the fact that I'm growing up and have a mind of my own. I'm not your little girl anymore, Daddy. You can't keep me in line with presents and promises, and I'm—"

Blood pounded in Leland's head. The sound of Colby's voice receded, and her image blurred before his eyes. It was Alex's taunts he heard, Alex's face that wavered in front of him. Or was it Vicky McCall's? Who did she think she was, anyway? He was sick of her smart mouth, sick of her. . . .

The sound of his palm striking flesh brought things back into focus. Colby stood before him, her hand on her reddening cheek. The sound of her shocked gasp still lingered in the room, rivaling the disbelief in her eyes.

She wasn't being such a smart-ass now. She was surprised and afraid, just the way she'd been as a child. He had turned things around, despite her cocky attitude. Leland pressed his advantage.

"Don't you raise your voice to me, young lady. You will do as I say, or I can, and will, make your life a living hell. Do you understand?"

Wide-eyed, Colby nodded.

"If you want to lower yourself by spending time

with your no-account brother, that's one thing, but
I will not have you screwing around with Jock
McCall's bastard."

Colby cringed.

"Oh, I know you've been seeing him. But it's got
to stop. You're a Creighton. Creightons marry their
equals. They produce children who will keep the
line going. I sure as hell don't intend for yours to
be sired by some racetrack scum, especially Rider
McCall. Do I make myself clear?"

"Yes." She swallowed. Tears swam in her eyes,
but she held her head high. "May I go now?"

For a moment his resolve wavered. For a moment he wanted to give his little girl whatever it was
that she thought would make her happy. Impul-
sively he held the credit card back out to her.
"Here," he said gruffly. "Keep it."

Colby's eyes were filled with numbness and cold.
"I don't want anything from you," she said, and
bolted from the room.

Leland sank down onto his leather chair with a
heavy sigh. Why couldn't she see that he was only
trying to protect her? Why couldn't she see that he
loved her, that he couldn't bear to think of Rider
McCall putting his filthy hands on her? It would be
hard enough allowing Kent Carlisle that privilege.

She was angry with him now, and hurt, but she'd
come around. She always did. Leland wiped his
perspiring brow. He hadn't handled things well. He
could see that now. From now on he would have
to stay cool.

She had agreed to his demand that she not see

McCall, but he knew his headstrong daughter better than that. He would have her followed, and if she went against his wishes, he'd take care of things. . . .

Just as he'd take care of this thing with McCall now. Colby was all he had, all he'd ever had. Though they weren't seeing eye to eye at the moment, she was his and always had been. The current rift in their relationship was more of a nuisance than a real problem.

It was time to play it cool again. He didn't want to alienate her any more than he already had. She was the only one who had ever loved him unconditionally, and it hurt too much to be at odds with her.

Leland stared at the place Alex had vacated. She was no help. She was glad that Colby had "had the strength to do what it took to make her happy" and thrilled that Colby was "getting her life together." What bullshit! Alex was just glad he'd lost his control over Colby. Well, that was only temporary. It would change. He wasn't about to let the likes of Rider McCall screw up his plans for Colby this time. He'd taken care of the McCalls before, and he could damn well do it again.

35

"Do you think I'm acting funny?" Colby asked
Cass the evening of her argument with Leland.

Cass looked up from the soup he was stirring. "Funny as in 'ha ha' or funny as in strange?"

Colby stabbed out a Virginia Slims with quick, jerky movements. "Funny as in strange."

"Other than taking up chain smoking since I saw you yesterday, not particularly. Why?"

"Daddy came to the studio today while Bonnie was gone. I let it slip that I'd seen Rider in Hot Springs."

"And?"

"He said that explained the way I'd been acting."

"What the hell does that mean?"

She shrugged. "I don't know. I imagine it has something to do with him asking me to join the family at the track for lunch tomorrow, and my saying no when I found out Kent would be there." She smiled wryly. "Of course, after he got through putting me through the old guilt wringer, I accepted."

"Don't let him mess you up, Cole," Cass said. "You've come too far."

"I know, but he starts talking, and he implies all this stuff, and the next thing I know I'm so mixed up I don't know if he's right or not. I can almost physically feel him trying to pull me back."

"He's slicker'n owl shit. You're just gonna have to be on guard every minute you're with him."

"I know. But it scares me. I don't like to be alone with him anymore."

"Then don't."

She nodded. "Will you and Bonnie be there tomorrow?"

"You bet. So will Bonnie's parents and Mom. Dad can't get too obnoxious with her there to keep him in line."

"True." She stared across the room for a moment.

"What?" Cass asked.

When she looked at him, there was worry in her eyes. "He said I ought to think about making an appointment with Pete Whitten. He thinks seeing Rider has me all messed up again."

"What do you think?"

"I admit that I've been doing a lot of thinking about him."

"And?"

"And it still hurts. It hurts as bad now as it did when I woke up in Forest Glade and Pete and Daddy told me he was gone. But I haven't started drinking, and I haven't taken any pills."

"Do *you* think you should see Pete?"

Colby looked lost, helpless. More like the girl who

had come home from the sanatorium and less like the successful woman she'd become. "I don't know," she said at last. "Maybe it wouldn't hurt to give him a call."

36

"What do you think?" Cass asked Bonnie when Colby had gone.

"I think your father is a sorry bastard."

"That goes without saying. I'm talking about Colby. Do you think she's . . . on the edge again?"

Bonnie shook her head. "I know all this has upset her, but I think she's pretty strong. She's come a long way this past year."

Cass's eyes held a faraway look. "He really did a number on her."

"Who? Your dad or Rider?"

"Both, I guess, but I was talking about Rider."

Bonnie sat down beside him. "Tell me about it. Don't yell at me. Just make me understand, and I'll leave it alone, I promise."

Cass nodded and drew a deep breath. "You'd have to understand just how close Rider and I were.

We were like brothers, and I trusted him with the sister I loved. You didn't see Colby sitting in that chair by the window, day after day, her hair all stringy and her face as white as a sheet. You didn't see that dead look in her eyes."

He swallowed back the emotion that thickened his voice. "And you didn't see her when she was finally well enough to come home." He snorted in bitterness. "Jesus, what a joke. She wasn't well. It wasn't even Colby who came home. It was someone masquerading as my sister. She'd dropped twenty pounds. She never smiled, never laughed. There was no sparkle in her eyes, nothing. If my dad said frog, she jumped. I felt like"—he made a gesture of futility—"if I, you know, even touched her, she'd fly into a jillion pieces."

He gripped Bonnie's hand tighter. "I felt as if she'd died, Bonnie. I felt as if my sister had died. And all because she believed Rider loved for herself, not because she was a megabucks Creighton."

For once Bonnie didn't try to defend Rider. She just held on to her husband and tried to absorb his pain.

Cass tried to smile, but it was a sad effort. "I guess that theory was shot to hell when he took the money. It was like he took everything she'd given him—all her love, everything—and sold out for twenty thousand fucking dollars."

Bonnie squeezed his hand tighter.

"He was my friend, dammit!" Cass said, old hurt and old anger throbbing in his voice. "Why did he have to do that to Colby?"

His devil-ridden eyes searched Bonnie's for an answer she didn't have. But she knew that the agony he felt was as much for the loss of a friend as it was for the loss of a sister.

37

Colby wished she hadn't come. Making an ap-pointment with Pete Whitten seemed tantamount to admitting she was falling apart again. Losing it. And she wasn't—was she? Coming here was a crutch, like the booze and the pills, and she'd sworn never to use those crutches again.

"So, Colby," he said with a cheerful smile. "What's bothering you? Your mother told me you were doing great."

"I am. It's just . . ." She paused, groping for the right words. She didn't want to make more of things than she should. "I saw Rider in Hot Springs."

Pete nodded. "And you felt angry at him all over again. That's understandable."

"No."

"No?"

"I didn't feel angry. Not at first, anyway. I was . . . glad to see him." She shrugged. "It's crazy, I know."

Pete blinked. Then he smoothed the few strands of hair combed carefully across his tanned scalp and leaned back in his leather chair. He laced his fingers together and folded his hands across his pot belly. "No, not crazy. It's a normal reaction, considering that you once loved the man. You blocked out his betrayal, so it's natural that your first impression of him would be the memory of the good times."

It made sense to Colby.

"So now that you've had time to think about it, how do you feel?"

"I'm a nervous wreck," she admitted with a shaky laugh. "I haven't been sleeping well, and when I do, I've been dreaming a lot."

"Same old dream?"

"Yes, only now it's more intense somehow. I feel that if I just tried a little harder, I could remember everything."

Pete steepled his fingers and rested the tips against his lips. "Hm. I wouldn't try to push it, if I were you. You're doing so well, it would almost be a shame to bring all that ugly mess out into the open again."

She nodded. Just knowing what had happened was bad enough. Remembering it in minute detail would be devastating.

"Is he in town yet?"

"Yes."

"Do you think he'll try to contact you?" The phone

on Pete's desk buzzed before Colby could answer. "Excuse me," he said, lifting the receiver. "Yes, Doris? Of course. Put him on."

"Pete? Is she there?" Leland Creighton's voice was soft, so it wouldn't carry into the room.

"Yes."

"How does she seem?"

Pete smiled at Colby, who, politely, was trying to appear uninterested in the conversation. "From what you told me, much as I expected."

"Is she still hung up on the son of a bitch?"

"It appears that it's a distinct possibility."

"Shit."

"Precisely."

"Well, see what you think, and do whatever you need to. And if that means putting her back in, you do it. Understand?"

Pete nodded in resignation. "Yes, but I'm sure that won't be necessary."

"Look, Pete, if your conscience gets to bothering you, just remember you owe me."

"Don't worry," Pete said with a wan smile. "I'll take care of it for you."

"Make sure you do."

Leland slammed down his receiver, and Pete winced. He recradled his own earpiece and stared across the room for a moment.

"Pete?"

He rallied and looked at Colby questioningly.

"Are you okay?"

He urged a smile to his bloodless lips. She was such a pretty woman, he thought. Not as attractive to him as she'd been as a young girl—she'd lost that innocent look—but lovely just the same. It was no wonder Leland felt about her the way he did. If she were *his* daughter, he'd want to keep her close, too. "I'm fine, thank you."

He shuffled the papers on the desk and cleared his throat. "I apologize for the interruption. Now, where were we?"

"Trying to figure out if I'm loony or not."

"Of course you aren't."

Colby smiled. "You wondered if I thought Rider would try to get in touch with me, and I don't. I am afraid I'm going to run into him again."

"And if you do?"

She drew in a deep breath. "A part of me says I'm strong enough to handle it, but I just don't know. Daddy says I'm already regressing—reverting back to the way I was when Rider and I were dating."

"What do you think?"

She shook her head. "He wants me to go back to Kent, and I have no intention of doing that. I think I'm trying to keep my father from controlling my life, and he doesn't like it."

Pete's lips tightened. "Few people like someone else telling them what to do." He reached for a prescription pad. "I think you're handling this very well, Colby. The anxieties you're feeling are normal, but I can give you something to ease you through the bad days." He scribbled something on the pad. "I am worried about your not sleeping. You lead a busy life and need your rest, so I'm also going to prescribe a little tablet to help you sleep."

"I don't want anything I'm going to get hooked on."

"Of course you don't," he told her, ripping the pages from the tablet and holding them out to her. "As soon as the Derby is over, things will settle back down, and you'll be as good as new."

38

Tracy stood at the bathroom mirror and dabbed at her bleeding mouth with a wet wash-cloth. If the bruise showed, Danny would have a fit. They hadn't been getting along so hot as it was. The shit would really hit the fan if he ever caught her screwing around on him, and she couldn't afford that. Not yet, anyway.

She'd met Danny when she'd gone with a girl-friend to Santa Anita. She had been looking for hunks and a good time, and she'd met him through a friend of a friend. She thought Danny was so cute, and he led such an exciting life, not to mention that he made loads of money. Lucky for her, he'd fallen for her—hard and fast, the way he did everything.

When he asked her to marry him within the

month, she agreed. She certainly didn't have any better offers. Despite her stint as Miss Kentucky and her *Playboy* spread, her stay in Hollywood was taking her nowhere but from one bed to another. Marrying Danny was a step up. If she couldn't blaze her own trail to glory, she'd ride along on his coattails. Besides, he was absolutely the cutest thing, and he could do the cleverest things with his tongue.

The only problem was that she just wasn't cut out for monogamy, and Danny was getting suspicious. She tried to be careful, but she could tell he knew something was going on, which was why his riding had been off at Oaklawn. Things were better now that he was riding again, but she was really afraid that what happened during the Rebel would happen again. She'd have to watch herself. Danny just couldn't keep it all together when he stayed wound up so tight.

Masculine hands slid around Tracy from behind, closing over her breasts and kneading them gently. Blue eyes met hers in the mirror.

Her lower lip slipped into a pout. "You hurt me," she whined, pushing his hands away. "I told you no rough stuff."

"I'm sorry."

"Sorry doesn't get it, thank you very much."

"Does this?" A diamond-and-emerald necklace was draped around her slim throat. The circle of gems blazed in the overhead light.

She lifted the necklace and rubbed the smooth stones against her lips. Her eyes climbed to his in the reflection. Her smile was slow and sassy. "It helps."

39

The lunch was going better than Colby ex-
pected. Her father was acting almost human, and
Kent was polite and attentive without smothering
her. Though Bonnie's parents had looked a bit non-
plussed when Leland introduced Kent as Colby's
ex-husband, they'd rallied, and along with Bonnie
and Cass they were doing an admirable job of
keeping the conversation running. For once her father appeared not to mind that the talk was cen-
tered on horses, specifically the upcoming Derby.

The track was fast, their horses were expected to
do well, and a quick check of the program had al-
layed Colby's fear of accidentally bumping into
Rider. The McCalls weren't running any horses that
afternoon, thank God. She could sit back, sip Coke
and lime, and let the little pill Pete Whitten had pre-
scribed do its thing.

She had no intention of letting her life get out of
control again. Still, the medication helped take the
edge off her worry and allowed her to divorce herself from the hypocrisy around her while appearing
attentive. She felt like one of those children born

with no immunities who were put into plastic bubbles. The bubble might keep them from participating in the world, but it also kept anything from hurting them. It was a nice, secure feeling.

"What do ya'll think about the McCalls puttin' Luis Mendoza on Jock's Dream?" Bonnie's mother asked after lunch. Colby's bubble developed a slow leak.

"Mendoza?" Alex said with a frown. "Danny Brewster is supposed to ride Jock's Dream."

"I know, but Springer heard differently in the kitchen yesterday, didn't you, darlin'?"

"Sure did, but then, there are always rumors."

"Have you heard anything, Cass?" Alex asked.

"There's always talk." Cass raised his glass of beer. "They're saying Danny's lost his edge."

"Because of one inquiry?"

"I'm just repeating the gossip, Mom. I didn't start it."

"If it is true, how in the hell did somebody like Jock McCall get someone as hot as Mendoza?" Colby's father interjected.

Cass shook his head. "Who knows? Maybe Rider convinced him. Jock's Dream is a runner, and he's had some strange things happen during his races. Maybe Mendoza thinks he can get the horse to do what Danny couldn't."

Springer leaned back in his chair. "I imagine Jock is trying to pull any rabbit he can out of his hat. He needs to win real bad."

"Why's that?" Alex pushed aside her dessert dish and leaned forward. Leland frowned. Colby, who'd drawn her last breath of euphoria when Cass mentioned Rider, wished she could leave. She didn't want to hear about the McCalls.

"He cornered me one day at Oaklawn, after he got out of the hospital, and asked if I'd buy his note from some bank in Texas. He got himself into a helluva financial bind, borrowing on some farm he owns near Mt. Pleasant to keep his stable going."

"If he hadn't drunk himself half to death, he wouldn't be in such a bind."

"It wasn't just the drinking," Springer said. "I heard he visited the windows pretty regularly, too."

"I know all about the gambling," Leland said, rubbing his lower lip thoughtfully. "So what kind of deal did he want to make?"

"He said he'd put up the same collateral he had for the bank. His farm." Springer answered Leland's snort of disbelief with a slow smile. "I told him I really didn't need the farm, but I'd go for the deal with a little added collateral."

"The son of a bitch doesn't have anything else."

Springer gave a half smile. "Oh, yes, he does. He's got something pretty damned valuable."

"What?" Leland asked.

"The colt," Cass said, topping off his glass of Miller.

"The colt?"

"Yeah, Dad, the colt. Jock's Dream is sound. He's just a hard-luck horse. With any kind of break, he has a lot of good races in him. If he pans out later on in the year, he ought to be worth something as a sire, even if he doesn't win the Derby."

Obviously, not being a horseman, her father hadn't thought of the colt's potential. Suppressing a smile, Colby glanced at him. He was looking at her mother, and there was a gleam in his eyes she couldn't grasp.

Colby felt Kent's hand on her knee, and her thoughts took an instant turn.

"So, are you going to bet the next race?" he asked as the conversation flowed on around them.

He really was an attractive man. Blond, tan, fit. And excruciatingly boring. His hand slid higher. Colby was reminded of all the nights she'd lain in their big bed while he made love to her. It was years after they married before she could reciprocate at all, and even when she had, she knew there should be more, there should be . . . *Oh, God, Colby, I can't stand it, it's so good!* fireworks . . .

"I like having you teach me to fish."

and laughter. . . .

"I sorta like it myself."

"Catfish and hushpuppies."

"What?"

Colby turned a blank gaze to Kent. He was frowning. "I beg your pardon?" she said.

"You said something about catfish and hushpuppies. Are you still hungry?"

She put her palm against her throbbing forehead. She had to get out of there. Fast. "No, no, they just sounded good, that's all."

"Maybe you'll let me take you out tomorrow night and we'll get you some."

"Oh, Kent, I don't know. . . ."

"Just think about it."

"Okay," she said with a feeble smile. "I'll think about it." She groped for her purse and stood.

Every eye at the table turned toward her. "Where are you going?" her mother asked.

"I've got a bitch of a headache." She gave a vague wave. "Cigarette smoke, I guess. I've got to get out of here."

Bonnie and Cass exchanged worried looks. "Are you okay, sis? Do you want me to drive you?"

"No, thanks. I'll be fine. I just need to go lie down a while."

"I'll call you later," Alex offered.

"Sure," Colby said. "Do that."

40

Cascio's, a small cafe near the track that was run by two Italian brothers, served the best fettuccine Alfredo and spumoni in town. Like the Pink Hippo, it was well attended by people from the track.

Rider had seen in the *Form* that the Creightons had several horses in that afternoon, and experience warned him that Alex would be attending. If she came, there was a chance Colby would come, too. He was thankful none of his horses had drawn in; he wouldn't have to attend the races at all. No sense tempting fate. Instead he'd hung around the barn until the lunch crowd cleared out of Cascio's so he could sit back and indulge in some ice cream and paranoia, undisturbed by anything but his troubled thoughts.

The big race was getting closer, and every day he spent in Louisville he expected to look up and see Colby or, worse, her father. Besides his personal problems, he worried that something would happen to the colt. When he heard another horse was sick, he feared Jock's Dream would be next to come down with the ailment. He worried about Jock, and if he could stay on the wagon.

"How's it goin', California?"

Rider looked up from his lunch. Danny stood at the table, his red-rimmed eyes bleak and tired. Rider added another worry to his list: how Jock's decision not to ride Danny in the Derby was affecting the jockey. Whenever Rider saw his old friend at the track, he seemed less like the Danny he had grown up with and more like a stranger.

"Things could be worse," Rider said. "How about you?"

"Could be better."

Rider grinned. "Have a seat." Danny did. "Lunch?"

Danny shook his head. "No, thanks. I had a late breakfast."

"I'll buy you an ice cream, then."

"Just some coffee, thanks."

Rider ordered the coffee and watched Danny stir in two spoons of sugar. If the far-off look in his eyes was any indication, his thoughts were miles away. What the hell. There was no time like the present to set things straight.

"Look, Danny, I know you're upset about Dad taking you off Jock's Dream. Personally, I think it sucks."

Danny tapped his spoon against the rim of his cup. "It's his horse, his decision. Hell, I don't blame him. I rode like shit at Oaklawn."

"You haven't had any trouble getting mounts since you got here, have you?"

"No. Why?"

"You aren't riding today."

"Actually, I've had a bitch of a headache. I had to have Tracy take me to the emergency room last night."

"Jesus. What did they say?"

"Vascular. They gave me a shot and said I'd be better. I am."

"How is Tracy?"

For a second, the calmness of Danny's countenance shattered. He shifted in the booth and started tapping his spoon against the table. "She's fine. She was a little worried about money while I was off."

How could Danny have money problems, even if he had been off a month? The first thing that entered Rider's mind was drugs, but he couldn't picture Danny doing dope.

"Is everything okay, Danny Wayne?"

"Everything's fine. But a Derby win would have been a great way to come back after being off."

"Yeah, it would have." And if everything's fine, I'm Mel Gibson, Rider thought.

He wondered if Jock was right about Danny's flirty bride. Was Tracy the cause of his headaches and his money problems? "I don't mean to pry, but if you ever want to talk, I'm here."

Danny didn't say anything for a long time. "Everything's fine," he repeated.

The bell on the cafe door jingled, and Rider glanced up. For a moment he thought he was hallucinating or that the sun was creating an optical illusion. It couldn't be Colby standing there in the sunlight, uncertainty clouding her eyes.

For the span of a strangled breath, they stared at each other. More than the width of the room separated them. They were separated by years of grief and the pain of betrayal. Regret was a crushing ache in his chest. Tears stung his eyes. What should he do? What should he say? Before he could decide, she turned and pushed open the door, escaping to the street.

Getting to his feet, Rider wove his way through the maze of tables to the door. It had rained in the night, and the spring air was clean and damp and filled with the promise of life. He drew a deep breath and glanced in both directions.

Colby was hurrying down the sidewalk, her heels clicking on the cement. He caught up with her in a dozen running steps. Reaching out, he grabbed her arm and hauled her around. She felt thin and fragile.

"Colby, I—"

Her eyes blazed up at him with blue fire. Her lips curled in contempt. She struck at him with her free hand. "Let go of me, you son of a bitch."

Rider let her go, but she didn't walk away. Instead she looked up at him with furious, accusing eyes. Her breasts heaved with anger. Her lower lip trembled. Her teeth sank into its softness before she straightened her shoulders and turned away, deliberately shutting him out—the way he had shut her out eleven years before.

41

Rider watched Big Guy cross the finish line.
The horse had finally beaten the law of averages
and managed to win a race in spite of chronic bad
luck.

Rider started for the winner's circle on automatic
pilot. There was no particular joy in the win; it was
just something he'd needed to do, another goal at-
tained. He was tired of the horses, tired of the
seven-days-a-week routine and the same old people. He was suddenly track sour and sick to death
of the monotony of his life. He was thirty-three
years old, and all he had to show for it was a new
truck and a better-than-average string of wins. Still,
dammit, the wins were testimony that there was no
other life he was better suited to.

The truth was, the restlessness had grown steadily stronger since he'd run into Colby two days before. He felt confined, like a horse that hadn't been
tracked in a month. In limbo. As if he were waiting
for something to happen.

The past two days had been hell. He saw Colby's
face in every crowd, and every husky female voice

he heard reminded him of hers. The recollection of her anger ate at him. The memory of what he'd given up threatened to destroy him all over again, just as it had more than a decade ago.

It had taken him months to regain a semblance of sanity, and years before he was able to think of Colby without wanting to rip out Leland Creighton's black heart for making him choose between the woman he loved and the father whose love he craved.

For a while he'd really gone a little crazy. He'd drunk too much, smoked too much grass, and slept with more women than he could remember. In an instance of temporary insanity, he'd even married one of the girls, a feisty little thing with a permanent pout who worked on the backside. When he'd sobered up and realized what he'd done, he knew it was time to get a grip. He'd made his decision, chosen his path. He had to walk it. Screwing up what was left of his life wouldn't change things.

He'd gotten a quickie Reno divorce and, with Farley's help, started rebuilding his world. It hadn't been easy. There'd been times he missed Colby so much he knew he'd made the wrong choice. Jock had never given a hoot in hell about him. So why did he even keep trying?

The one time Jock had come out to California to visit him, Rider had braced himself. No way was he going to let his old man get the best of him; no way was he going to let himself be set up for a fall. Surprisingly, Jock hadn't put him down at all, but the visit was a disaster just the same. Seeing Jock drinking himself into an early grave had been a bitter reminder to Rider that he had thrown away the only happiness he'd ever known for a man who just didn't give a shit.

42

Lexington, Kentucky
June 1979

Clods of umber earth fell onto the casket. The hollow thuds echoed through the empty corridors of Rider's heart. She was gone. His dearest friend, his confidante, his only shelter, had died of the disease the doctors had been so sure they had eradicated. She'd died after a month of excruciating pain.

Clinging to their hands, Vicky had told Jock and Rider to be good to each other and, smiling a radiant smile, had simply closed her eyes and drawn a final shuddering breath.

Jock had stumbled from the room and gone to the nearest bar. He hadn't been completely sober since. To Rider, the pain of losing his mother vied with the agony he knew his dad was suffering. Jock had been hard on her, but Rider was as sure that his dad had loved his mom as he was that he himself had somehow failed to earn that love.

Sobs fought their way up his throat, but he refused to give in to them. Instead he lifted glazed, unseeing eyes to the rolling hills dotted with tombstones, their plastic flowers fading in the summer sun.

The ancient priest's voice droned on, a monotonous chant Rider knew by heart. The words were designed to comfort and uplift, but they did neither. His mother was gone, and Rider was more alone than he could ever remember.

"I'm sorry, son."

He turned and saw a trainer whose name he couldn't recall. He nodded and looked around in surprise. The graveside service was over, and people were clustering around him and Jock, offering watery smiles of encouragement and well-intended words of hope and consolation. Rider saw Alex Creighton offer Jock her hand. Instead of taking it, he pulled Colby's mother into a tight embrace and started to sob.

Barely able to control his own tears, Rider pushed through the crowd of friends and acquaintances to his truck. Tugging at his tie, he started the engine and whipped the Ford around the hearse. He'd refused to ride in the family car with Jock. Somehow he'd known he would need to escape.

Though it was only two in the afternoon, Rider drove straight to the Pink Hippo and ordered a beer. One didn't faze the pain. When Colby arrived at five, he was still drinking. He looked up when she slipped into the seat across from him. There was sorrow and empathy in her eyes. And love. "Hi."

He lifted the bottle to his mouth. "Hi."

"I'm sorry I didn't make it in time for the funeral. I had that job interview and couldn't make the right plane connections."

Now that she'd graduated, Rider knew how important this particular interview was to her. She'd been dreaming of going to work for the exclusive interior design outfit ever since he'd first met her. "It's okay. It wasn't much fun, and there was nothing you could do. Did you get the job?"

"They said they'd let me know in a few days."

"I'll keep my fingers crossed."

"Thanks." She reached over the table and held out her hand.

Rider laced his fingers through hers.

"Are you okay?"

He nodded but his eyes swam with tears. "I miss her already, you know?"

"Yeah. I think I do. How's your dad taking it?"

"He's drinking like they're going to bring back Prohibition tomorrow."

"It looks like you're doing a pretty good job of that yourself."

Rider looked at the bottles littering the table. He hadn't let the barmaid take them away. He supposed he wanted to count them, to see just how much liquid forgetfulness it took to ease the pain. "I guess I am."

"Drinking won't help, Rider."

"No?"

"It hasn't yet, has it?"

He looked surprised to realize she was right. "No."

"Come on, then. Let's get out of here."

"She died with a smile on her face." Rider lay with his head resting in Colby's lap. She had held him while he cried. Gradually his tears had dried, and a comfort he'd despaired of ever feeling crept over him.

The dwindling evening sun cast dancing shadows across the pond where he and Colby had made love the first time three weeks before.

"She was probably looking forward to not hurting anymore."

Pushing himself upward, Rider placed his palms in the grass on either side of her. "Thanks."

"For what?"

"For knowing what to say. For coming back."

"I never would have let you go through this alone. Surely you know that."

"I know." He drew a deep breath. "This may not be the best time to say this, but I want to marry you, Colby."

"What?"

"Don't look so shocked. You must have known it would come to this. I know your family will have a fit, and your dad will probably cut you out of his will, but I promise I'll do my damnedest to make you happy."

Colby's eyes filled with tears. "You do make me happy, and my father be damned."

"That's easy to say. I want you to think about it. Really think about it. I can't give you diamonds or fancy clothes and fast cars."

Colby put her arms around his neck and, closing her eyes in contentment, pressed her forehead against his. "I don't want diamonds and cars and fancy clothes. I want someone to love me just the way I am."

"I do."

She held him tighter. "I'm so afraid of losing you." The words were a fierce whisper.

"Never," he promised, threading his fingers through her hair. "I will love you, Colby Antoinette Creighton, longer than forever."

"Show me," she whispered.

They made love slowly, sweetly, in celebration of life. Touching each other, tasting each other, chanting each other's names, they defied death. The setting sun gilded them; the summer breeze cooled the fevered heat of their young bodies and crooned a prelude to the evening. They made love, and then they made plans. Love gave them the courage to tackle the world. The shortsightedness of youth was their only weakness.

The indisputable setting of the sun and the sudden onslaught of mosquitoes forced them to get dressed. Colby stepped into her panties and reached for her bra. Rider, wearing nothing but his suit pants, hooked it for her, teasing her with soft, openmouthed kisses to her neck and shoulders.

"What in the sweet hell do you think you're doing?"

Colby's head whipped around at her father's furious question. "Nothing, now." The defiance in her voice belied the fear in her eyes. "We're done."

Leland Creighton swooped down on them like the angel of death, fury and something else, something Rider couldn't put his finger on, blazing from his eyes. He took an instinctive step forward, putting Colby a pace behind him.

"You slut!" Leland grated, reaching for her.

Rider gave Leland a hard shove. "Leave her alone."

Leland pinned him with a hard look, and Rider felt the full force of the senator's hatred. The man was frickin' looney toons, Rider realized a moment before Leland's fist connected with his jaw.

Colby screamed. Rider staggered beneath the blow. Pain exploded through his jaw, and he felt the warm trickle of blood ooze down his chin. He shook his head to clear it and lunged at Colby's father. It was like running into a slab of beef. Leland Creighton was heavier by forty pounds and wild with anger. Rider took a blow to his stomach that sent him sprawling.

Rolling to his knees, he squinted up through a haze of pain and saw that Colby was striking at her father with both fists. Leland grabbed her wrists and shook her like a terrier with a rat. Dark hair flew around her pale face, and the fury in her eyes mutated to fear. As Rider tried to struggle to his feet, Leland drew back an arm and sent a heavy-handed blow to her cheek. The force of it sent her stumbling sideways into a nearby tree. Her head struck the trunk, and with a groan she slithered to the grass.

"Colby!" Surging to his feet, Rider started toward her, but Leland tripped him up and sent him tumbling to the ground. A leather-shod foot caught him in the stomach. Rider clutched his middle and doubled over in agony. "Leave her alone," he croaked.

Creighton's voice seemed to come from a deep, dark well. "Now, that's what I call good advice. As a matter of fact, it's so good that if I were you, I'd take it myself."

Rider clenched his teeth against the the pain. "Colby and I . . . are getting . . . married."

Leland hauled Rider to his feet and thrust his face close. "Not as long as I'm alive."

"Yeah? Well . . . maybe that . . . can be arranged, too," Rider gasped with forced bravado.

Creighton laughed. "You've got a lot of your mama's fight. I like that. Come on over here, boy. We've got a little business to take care of."

Half dragging him, he led Rider to his truck and slammed him against it. Too spent to move, Rider leaned against the fender and watched Colby's father reach into the breast pocket of his black suit and draw out a checkbook and gold pen.

He smiled benignly. "Here's what we're going to do. I'm going to write you a check for ten thousand dollars, and you're going to take it and get as far away from Kentucky and my daughter as it will take you."

Rider spat a mouthful of blood toward Leland's imported shoes. "Screw . . . you."

The smile broadened. "Don't be difficult, McCall. I can make things very hard for you. And for your father. I've done it before; I can do it again."

Even through his pain, Rider recognized the threat to Jock. "What are you talking about?"

"I'm talking about Jock's career, boy. He's doing so well right now, it would be a shame to see it all go down the tubes, now, wouldn't it?"

Rider couldn't believe what he was hearing.

"Horses can have accidents," Leland continued in a conversational tone. "So can jockeys. And it really is a shame the way some owners just yank an entire stable out from under a guy."

Rider got the picture. "You bastard."

"I like to think of it as protecting my family."

"You'd ruin . . . my father . . . just because I want to marry Colby?"

"I'd ruin *my* father to keep Colby from tying up with the likes of you. So what's it going to be, boy? Are you going to get the hell out of our lives, or is your dad's training operation going to undergo a sudden reversal?"

"You bastard," Rider repeated, turning to walk away.

Leland grabbed Rider's shirt, jerking him back. "Tell you what I'm going to do," he said thoughtfully, scribbling in the checkbook. "I'm going to sweeten the pot. I'm going to up the ante to say . . . twenty thousand dollars. And if you don't do as I tell you, I'm going to go straight to the sheriff's department and tell them what I found here. Unfortunately, I didn't arrive in time. You were crazy drunk, and you'd already raped my little girl." He made a sweeping gesture toward Colby, who was moaning softly. "Why, you were so drunk, you got a little mean and roughed her up a bit."

Disbelief exploded in Rider's mind. There seemed to be no limits to the lengths Leland Creighton would go. "Colby won't let you get away with this."

"Oh, I think I can handle my own daughter, don't you, McCall?"

The confidence in Colby's father's cold blue eyes told Rider that he could deliver on the threats. And he would do it with relish. He had the money, the power, and the connections to see Rider rot in prison over trumped-up rape and assault charges. He'd already demonstrated how effectively he could silence Colby. There was Jock to think about, too. His dad was devastated by his mother's recent death. His horses were all he had left. If Creighton took that from him, Jock wouldn't have anything to live for.

Rider felt like a rat in a maze. His anguished gaze sought Colby's long-limbed body sprawled against the base of the tree. How could he leave her? How could he just walk out of her life after all the plans and promises he'd made? How could he live without her? But if this was the price she had to pay for loving him, sweet Jesus, what else could he do? "All right," he said. "I'll do whatever you say."

"A very wise decision." Leland ripped the check

from the checkbook. "Spend it well, and maybe you can make something of yourself yet.

Ignoring the proffered check, Rider cast a last tear-glazed look at Colby. Then he brushed past Leland and wrenched open the Ford's door. He cranked the engine and shoved the truck into reverse. As he let off the clutch, a slip of folded paper fluttered through the open window and landed on the dusty floorboard.

He gunned the truck all the way to the highway. He didn't have to pick up the buff-colored square to know it was the check.

His payoff for deserting the only person in the world who loved him.

43

"Did anyone ever tell you that you got a shitty attitude?"

Rider looked up from the girth he was tightening and met Jock's gaze over the filly's back. "A time or two, why?"

"Hell, you're like a bear with a sore paw lately. What's the problem?"

Rider knew he'd been acting like a jerk the past few days, and just because he couldn't get Colby off his mind was no reason to make everyone he came into contact with miserable.

"No problem," he said, lowering the stirrup. "I'm just a little edgy about the race, that's all."

"Edgy? Jesus, son, you're wound as tight as an eight-day clock. Why don't you take the day off and go to the movies?"

"I don't like the movies."

"Hell, go get drunk, or laid or something. You're drivin' me to frickin' drink."

Rider grinned. "We can't have that, so I'd better get the hell out of here."

"Please," Jock said with a sweeping gesture.

"Actually," Rider said, "I've been wanting to talk to you, to tell you that you look great, and"—he paused and shrugged—"I'm really proud of you. I knew you could do it."

"You gotta have goals, son. That's what gives you strength. Goals. Don't ever forget it."

"No, sir."

"And my goal is to run that Creighton horse into the ground." He slapped Rider on the back. "We're gonna win this one, Rider. I can feel it in my bones."

Jock's enthusiasm was catching. It was good to see his dad regaining his health and self-esteem. Good to hear him laugh.

"It's probably just arthritis," he said solemnly.

Jock narrowed his eyes. "Not only do you have a shitty attitude, you're a smart-ass."

"It runs in the family," he said in mock seriousness.

Jock grinned.

44

Alone in her bedroom, Alex sat down at the chintz-covered window seat that overlooked the flagstone terrace. Afternoon shadows striped the yard and English gardens, offering the imported Japanese goldfish a brief respite from the sun. Drawing up her bare feet, she clasped her knees to her chest.

Colby was losing it. She knew her daughter well, and the fact that she'd gone to see Pete Whitten was in itself enough to trigger concern. Colby wasn't sleeping well and had left the track with a headache on Wednesday. She was a grown woman, a far cry from the fragile girl they'd brought home from Forest Glade. Still, coming face to face with her past had obviously shaken her.

Alex wished Colby would talk to her more. Their relationship had improved since Leland was no longer the center of her daughter's world, but Alex wished they were closer, that they spent more time together. Maybe she'd call and see if Colby wanted to drive out to Windwood for dinner.

Rising, Alex went to the telephone on the polished surface of the *Régence* secretary.

Leland's voice filtered through her partially opened door.

Damn! She hadn't expected him home. If he didn't have plans, he would expect her to dine with him. Her husband didn't like eating alone, and dining *en famille* was one of the few things he still required of her, one of the few things she was willing to do to keep up appearances. She crossed the hall to his study. When she heard him mention the name McCall, she paused, her fingertips on the doorknob.

"It's a helluva deal, Springer," he said. "A tidy profit."

Springer? Alex stepped closer to the door. What kind of deal could Leland be making with Springer Martindale?

"We're both interested in making money. Besides, I wouldn't have any objections to adding a horse like that to our stable, if he's as good as everyone seems to think."

What horse could Leland possibly be interested in, and why?

"Okay. I'll express you a check first thing tomorrow. . . . Right. Good-bye."

Alex heard Leland cradle the receiver. Careful to avoid the floorboards that squeaked, she retraced her steps to her room. Back on the window seat, she lit a cigarette and frowned at the lengthening shadows while she tried to make sense of the fragmented conversation she'd heard. Something to do with the McCalls, a horse, and profit. What did it all mean?

Then she remembered. *"Jock McCall . . . He cornered me one day at Oaklawn . . . asked if I'd buy his note from some bank in Texas . . . added collateral . . . something pretty damned valuable . . . the colt . . . Jock's Dream."*

Alex ground out the cigarette in a heavy crystal ashtray. Of course! Leland must be buying the paper from Springer. But why? He'd never cared a damn about any horse, and certainly Jock's Dream was no better than a hundred others he might have purchased through the years.

Another unexpected memory crept through her mind—Leland saying that he knew all about Jock's gambling problems. How? And more important, why?

She remembered his asking her the other day whether or not she had slept with Jock. The possibility that Leland had made it a point to keep tabs on Jock McCall for thirty years out of some perverted jealousy was unbelievable. But not impossible. Leland lived to be in control; this sort of vendetta wouldn't be beyond him.

Alex's stomach churned. If Jock's Dream lost the race—and she was sure Leland could make that a probability—he could go to Jock and demand either the money or the farm and the horse.

Alex rose and began pacing the room. What

could she do? She had no proof, only suspicions based on overhearing one side of a phone call. She had to get the facts straight before she confronted Leland with her suspicions. But deep in her heart, she knew the truth. She could almost see the gloating smile on Leland's face as he thrust the knife deeper into Jock McCall and gave it one last, painful turn.

45

Leland looked down at the papers in his hand. Overnight mail was wonderful. He'd wired Springer the money the evening before, and the paper on Jock's note had just arrived. He held Jackson McCall's destruction in his hands.

Leland smiled, imagining the look on Alex's face when he showed her the papers to Jock's Dream—just a small reminder to let her know he hadn't forgotten that she'd screwed her farm manager. He would never forget. As long as he was living, he'd see to it that the McCalls, all of them, got exactly what they deserved.

Which reminded him. He needed to call Solly and have him pay Danny Brewster a little visit. With Tracy's insatiable appetite for more and better things, Danny just might be glad to see him.

46

Danny stepped out of the jocks' room and started for his silver Mercedes, a spring in his step and his smile more like the old Danny's than it had been in a long time. He'd had a good day—four wins. Things had been better with Tracy since they'd come to Louisville and he was riding again. It was sort of like starting over. The demons had, for now, stopped their howling.

He was punching in the alarm numbers on his car door when he heard a reedy voice say, "Hiya, Danny. How's it goin'?"

Danny turned. A slender accountant type stood behind him. The man had a big nose and a balding head that looked as if he'd just left the temple and forgotten to take off his skullcap.

"Things are going great. What can I do for you?"

The man held out his hand. Danny couldn't have

explained his reluctance to accept it if he'd tried. The man's handshake was as flaccid as his voice. "My name is Solly Tobias. I have a little business proposition for you."

The words triggered an inner alarm. The hair on the back of Danny's neck stood at attention. For all his store-bought style, Solly Tobias did not look like a representative from the Better Business Bureau—unless it was being run by Don Corleone. Danny strove to act unimpressed while his mind worked overtime to try to figure out what the hell was going on.

"I'm not interested in any business propositions, thanks. I have a stockbroker who takes care of all that." He lifted the door handle. Solly Tobias's hand shot out and slammed the door shut.

"I really think you ought to hear me out, Danny." There was a controlled, cajoling tone to his voice. "There are people out there who really care about your situation."

"My situation? What situation?"

A smile slid across Solly's face, but his dark eyes remained as flat as his voice. "Why, the trouble you've been having with your wife, of course."

"I'm not having any—"

"Spare it, Brewster. We know how much your wife likes spending money, and we know that in the past, the drop in your take-home pay has caused a few problems in your happy home."

Danny was so stunned that Solly Tobias was privy to that kind of information that he couldn't even begin to hide his surprise. "How do you know that?"

Solly gave a dismissive wave. "It's not important. The important thing is that a friend would like to help you out of a bind."

The meaning of Solly's visit began to make sense. Danny started getting angry. "Who is this friend?"

"He prefers to remain anonymous, if you know what I mean."

"I think I do, yeah."

"That's good. It's very simple, really. All you have to do is ride a horse in the Derby."

"Since your friend knows everything else, how come he doesn't know I don't have a mount in the Derby? The McCalls took me off their horse."

"My friend knows that. But he wanted me to ask you if you'd be interested in riding the colt in the event that Mendoza couldn't ride."

Danny's heart began to gallop at Solly's unspoken insinuation. His stomach knotted. He could imagine what Solly and his friend might dream up to keep Luis from riding. Danny tried not to let his apprehension show. "I'm not interested, thanks. I make it a rule not to take advantage of my friends' misfortunes."

Solly raised thin eyebrows. "That's too bad. There was quite a lot of money involved."

"What does your friend have against Luis Mendoza?"

"Not a thing. He just wants to make sure the McCalls don't get any part of that purse."

Someone had it in for Rider and Jock. Who? "Let

me get this straight. If I ride Jock's Dream, you want me to do whatever I need to to lose the race?"

"That about sums it up," Solly said with a nod.

"The McCalls are my friends. Besides, I'll get a shitload of money if I win."

"And if you lose, you don't get shit. Think of this as a little insurance, Danny. It's no secret that your riding has been off lately. If you blow this one, no one will be the wiser."

The slur against his riding ability was strangely painful. A slur against his manhood. The demons stirred. "I will. If anyone finds out, it'll ruin my future as a jock."

"Whadda you care? You'll have enough money to start over, doing whatever you want."

Danny couldn't believe what he was hearing. It sounded like a bad script for a B movie. "Thanks, but no thanks."

"It's too bad other people aren't so noble."

"What are you talking about?"

"I'm talking about your wife, Danny."

The bottom dropped out of Danny's world.

"Instead of standing by her man the way she should, your Tracy is out looking for some action, if you know what I mean."

Danny eased back against the car door. He had suspected she was seeing someone from time to time, but as long as he'd had no proof, he could live with it—and himself. And he really thought things were different since they'd arrived in Kentucky. Danny tried to tell himself that Tobias was just a dork who knew which strings to pull. But he'd also known about Tracy's dissatisfaction over the money. If he knew something that personal, could he be lying about this?

"A million plus would go a long way toward keeping her happy, now, wouldn't it?"

A long way, Danny acknowledged. But he still wasn't a cheat. "Why does your friend want to help save my marriage?"

"He doesn't. He just wants the McCalls to lose."

Danny's mind raced through the names of people who had horses in Saturday's race. Offhand, he couldn't think of anyone who hated Jock to the extent that they were willing to pay over a million dollars to make sure he lost a race. "What does he have against the McCalls?"

Solly smiled his oily smile. "He didn't say."

"Well, whatever his beef is, he'll have to find another jock, because my answer is no."

47

"Nice race."

Rider, who had just come from having his picture taken in the winner's circle, turned toward the feminine voice. Bonnie Martindale—Bonnie Creighton, now—stood a few feet away. Smartly dressed in a peach linen suit, she looked fresh and pretty, just the way he remembered her. He realized with a pang that he'd missed her. His first inclination was to give her a big hug, but the memory of Cass's hate-filled look at Hot Springs brought a stiff smile to his lips instead.

"Hello, Bonnie."

"Hello, Bonnie?" she echoed with a lift of her eyebrows. "Is that any way to greet an old friend?"

He thought of all the mental turmoil he'd been through since he'd agreed to help Jock and the beating his emotions had taken when he'd seen Cass and Colby. He didn't want things stirred up any more than they already were.

"It is if the old friend is married to Cass Creighton."

The fire Rider remembered flashed in her eyes. "Cass be damned!"

"Probably."

She laughed and gave him a brief hug, surrounding him in femininity and the scent of White Linen. Rider was acutely aware that it had been a long time since he'd held a woman who cared. He and Holly had called it quits months ago, and trying to build a relationship with someone new required more energy than he could dredge up. But he'd missed the softness of a woman in his life; he needed it.

Smiling, he set her away from him. "You haven't changed, Bonnie. You're as pretty as ever."

"Thank you," she said with a smile. "You don't look half-bad yourself. The cowboy image suits you."

Rider shifted from one booted foot to the other and fumbled for the Marlboros in his shirt pocket.

"I heard you were back helpin' Jock."

"Yeah," he said, striking a match from Cascio's. "Temporarily."

"How is he?"

"Good. Planning to beat the Creightons in the Derby."

Bonnie's eyes held a wistful gleam. "Nothin' changes, does it? I remember how you and Cass used to butt heads two or three races a day and then go out and party together at night."

"You're wrong," Rider said gravely. "Things do change. So do people." He took a deep drag off the cigarette and hooked his thumbs in the pockets of his jeans. Smoke spiraled up between them like a gossamer wall. "As a matter of fact, your husband probably wouldn't like it if he knew you were talking to me."

The light in Bonnie's eyes dimmed. "Probably not."

"And that doesn't bother you?"

"The Creightons, including Cass, do not dictate my actions."

He shook his head. "Same old Bonnie. I'm glad you and Cass finally got together."

Bonnie smiled. "Thanks. So what have you been up to?"

"Not much. Different racetracks, same old thing. How about you?"

"Gettin' used to being married. Gettin' to know Cass all over again."

The reminder that his friends hadn't married years before, as he'd expected, made Rider ask, "What happened, anyway? I figured the two of you would have half-grown kids by now."

"You happened," Bonnie said, never one to beat around the bush.

"Me?"

"You. When you left without a word, Cass was . . . upset with you, to say the least."

A spasm of pain crossed Rider's features. "I imagine he was." He forced himself to meet the accusation in Bonnie's eyes without flinching. "How is she?" he asked, needing to know the answer as much as he feared it.

Bonnie didn't have to ask who "she" was. "Fine, now, I think."

"Now? What do you mean?"

"Don't you get any gossip in California, McCall?"

"What kind of gossip?"

Bonnie shook her head in answer to her own question. "No, you wouldn't. The Creightons cover their tracks pretty well."

"Cover their tracks? What are you talking about?"

"When you left, they had to put Colby in Forest Glade." Bonnie's eyes said she was sorry to be the one to tell him.

"Forest Glade?" Rider frowned and ground out his cigarette as he tried to place the name. He looked up sharply. "Isn't that a psychiatric hospital?"

"Yes."

He grasped a metal support. "What happened?"

"You'd know that better than I. Leland said she was hysterical, crazy with grief because you wanted the money he offered instead of her."

Rider's head spun. The noise of the crowd receded to a low roar in his ears. Colby in a psychiatric hospital? Because of him? No. Because of Leland. Bitterness lent an edge to his voice. "Leland said that, did he? I suppose everyone believed it?"

"Not even you can deny you dumped her and disappeared. I was the only one who believed you had a reason none of us knew about."

"And that's what caused the trouble between you and Cass?" Rider said in disbelief.

"That was it," she admitted.

"No wonder Cass hates my guts."

"To put it mildly."

"I don't suppose it would help if I said I was sorry."

Bonnie put her hand on his arm. "I've never blamed you for breaking up me and Cass. I blame Cass. You were his best friend. He should have had more faith in you. He should have at least tried to find out your side of the story."

"I imagine Leland was pretty convincing."

"Just seein' Colby was pretty convincing."

"Colby?"

"She was in bad shape, Rider. They kept her sedated for weeks, and after they made her have the abortion, she just—"

Rider's body jerked as if he'd been shot. His fingers closed around Bonnie's upper arm. "What did you say?"

"Oh, God," Bonnie whispered as she looked into his white face. "You didn't know."

Dazed, Rider released his hold on Bonnie's arm and turned away, staggered by the weight of the news. Colby, pregnant with his child. Had she known? Why hadn't she told him?

"They didn't find out until she'd been in the hospital a couple of weeks," Bonnie said as if she could read his mind. "The abortion was Leland's idea, but—"

"Why doesn't that surprise me?" was Rider's caustic interruption. His child was dead, and all because of Leland Creighton. It was unbelievable that something like this had happened without a breath of it reaching him. Bonnie was right. The old guard closed ranks when they wanted to protect their own. Rider doubted if anyone outside the Creighton family knew the truth.

"Are you all right?"

"Yeah. I'm fine."

"You don't look fine."

"Give me a decade or two. It isn't every day a man finds out that he could have had a ten-year-old child."

48

Rider lay with one arm behind his head, staring up at the ceiling and lighting each Marlboro from the butt of the last. His mind replayed his meeting with Bonnie over and over and over again.

Hurting so much he wasn't sure he could stand it, he had left Bonnie standing in the middle of the packed grandstand and headed for the barn, where he gave Jock some lame excuse about picking up some jeans at the laundry and left the track.

It had been all he could do to keep from going straight to Colby's business and telling her exactly what he thought of her killing their baby. The only thing stopping him were fragments of Bonnie's conversation that drifted in and out of his mind like flotsam washed up and back by the tide. *"She was hysterical . . . it was Leland's idea . . . crazy with grief . . . Leland's idea . . ."*

He knew it wasn't fair to blame Colby, when Leland had instigated the abortion, but on some level he did. He squeezed his eyes shut. Thinking about the baby hurt. Would his and Colby's child have been an ornery little boy with reddish brown hair and blue eyes or a little girl with Colby's sweet smile and bouncy curls? Rider raised himself to one elbow and crushed out his cigarette. Girl or boy, the child would have been ten years old. The age to play catch, or take fishing.

Rider felt gritty tears burning beneath his eyelids. Dammit, he *wanted* that child, wanted that unique part of him that could never be replicated exactly the same again. Ten years. Jesus, the last ten years had been a long, lonely lifetime. He had wanted, and needed, someone to love, someone to love him back unconditionally. Only a child could do that, as he knew all too well. The last ten years could have been completely different, if not for one man—Leland Creighton, the power-hungry senator who had the money and the connections to do whatever he damn well pleased. The bastard could probably get away with murder.

49

"**What the hell do you mean, you told Rider** about Colby?"

Bonnie clasped her trembling hands together. She and Cass had argued about Rider many times, but she'd never seen him so angry.

She shrugged. "We were just talkin', darlin', and I let it slip about the abortion."

"Dammit, Bonnie, you know I told you never to breathe a word of that to anyone!"

"For God's sake, Cass, I didn't do it on purpose. I just didn't think."

"You never think."

"Well, I beg your pardon. Maybe it has somethin' to do with a clear conscience, but I'm afraid I'm not the kind of person who goes around weighin' every word that comes out of my mouth the way you Creightons do."

"Maybe you ought to try it. But then maybe you told Rider about Colby because you saw an opportunity to make my dad look bad."

The unfairness of the accusation, from Cass of all people, ignited Bonnie's own short fuse. "Oh, Leland doesn't need me for that. He's pretty good at doing that all by himself!"

"Okay, Bonnie. It's no secret that you can't stand my father. Does that mean you have to help Rider McCall ruin the family?"

"Ruin the family? That was done years ago, darlin'," Bonnie drawled with saccharine sweetness. "And neither Rider McCall nor I had anythin' to do with it."

Cass stared down at her, a muscle in his jaw jumping. "You stay away from him," he said, pointing a finger at her. "Do you understand?"

The color drained from Bonnie's face, but she raised her chin to a defiant angle. "No one tells me who I can and can't associate with, Cass. Not even you."

"Then you won't stop seeing him?"

"I won't turn my back on a friend."

"Friend? Hell, the way you carry on about him, I'm not so sure he isn't more than a friend."

"Just exactly what are you implyin'?"

"You know what I'm implying, Bonnie Jean."

Bonnie reached up and slapped him as hard as she could. It was a toss-up as to who was the most shocked—she or Cass. Giving a low cry of rage and disappointment, she turned and stalked across the room.

She was almost to the door when Cass whirled her around and shoved her against the wall. The print of her hand stood out against the healthy tan of his cheek. He lowered his head and took her mouth in a punishing kiss. A response wasn't mandatory, or even possible, considering Bonnie's fury.

When he finally released her, he was breathing heavily. The pain in his eyes was almost her undoing. He'd seen so much fighting growing up, and she knew he hated it. So did she. But she hadn't done anything wrong, and she wasn't going to let him pull a Leland Creighton act on her.

"I'm your husband, Bonnie," he said as if that were the answer to everything.

She looked him straight in the eye. "Well, that can certainly be remedied."

50

Rider thumbed through the telephone directory until he found the name he was looking for. His tears had dried, and the pain in his heart was subsiding in direct proportion to his rising anger. Midnight was way too late to call anyone, but he didn't give a damn. He had to talk to Colby. He wanted to know how she could let Leland talk her into destroying a child conceived in love.

He punched in the numbers. The phone rang once. Twice. A third time. Someone picked up.

"Hello?"

Rider almost slammed down his own receiver. Low-pitched and sultry with sleep, Colby's voice held the same breathless quality it was reduced to when they made love. It had always sent tremors rippling through him, and tonight was no different. He cursed himself for feeling anything.

"Hello?" she said again. This time she sounded more awake—and wary. "Who is this?"

He couldn't answer. There was so much to say. A decade's worth of apologies, explanations—and recriminations. *Dammit, Colby! It was our baby. How could you?*

"Look, if this is some kind of crank—"

"Colby."

The sound of him speaking her name stopped her in midsentence. He thought he heard a sharp intake of breath.

"It's me."

Something between a moan and a sob filtered through the line. He collapsed against the pillows and threw his free arm over his eyes, fighting his own emotions. "I saw Bonnie today. . . ."

He heard a soft gasp.

"She told me everything." He took her silence as consent and forged ahead. "She told me about the—"

"I don't have anything to say to you," Colby interrupted. "I don't want to see or talk to you again. Ever."

"Colby—"

"Don't call back, Rider," she said, her voice rising. "Don't ever call again."

51

Colby barely had her breathing under control when the phone rang again. She swiped the tears from her cheeks and stared at its squat silhouette, wishing it would stop. Finally, on the fifth ring, she hit the button of her answering machine. She didn't want to hear Rider's accusations, but she couldn't ignore what he had to say.

She listened to her outgoing message and was surprised and relieved to hear her brother's voice, not Rider's, after the beep.

"Colby? Where in hell are you? If you're there, pick up the damn phone."

Hearing the urgency in his voice, she did. "Cass? What's the matter? Is it Mama?"

"Nothing's wrong with Mom. I just wanted to call and warn you."

"Warn me?" she asked, sitting up straighter. "About what?"

"Rider McCall."

A frisson of unease tripped down her spine. "What about Rider?"

"Bonnie saw him at the track today and let it slip about the abortion."

"Oh, God . . ."

"Now don't go to pieces on me," he soothed. "Bonnie said he was pretty upset. It was bound to be a shock for him, but I really don't expect him to do anything after all this time."

"He's already called," Colby said dully.

"What?"

"He called me a few minutes ago, but I wouldn't talk to him."

"Shit! Look, babe, you stay put. I'm coming over."

"No, Cass, I'll be fine. I told him not to call again, that I didn't want to have anything to do with him."

"Good for you, but I'm coming over anyway."

"Cass—"

Cass gave a bitter laugh. "Look, sis. I'm coming for me, not you."

"What are you talking about?"

He sighed. "Bonnie and I had another fight about Rider, and I think I went too far this time."

52

Colby studied her image in the mirror that hung in her private bathroom at Creighton Interiors. Weariness had etched fine lines around blue eyes cloudy with despair. The world she had struggled so hard to build was getting shakier by the day, by the minute.

Cass had arrived just after twelve-thirty, and they'd stayed up talking until two. Even after she'd gone to bed she hadn't slept a wink.

She couldn't believe Cass and Bonnie had quarreled so bitterly over Rider McCall, especially since Bonnie had never kept her belief in him a secret. She also couldn't believe the brother she adored had behaved like such a jerk. She didn't blame Bonnie for threatening to leave him.

The outer door buzzed. Bonnie was on a job, but their assistant, Tony, would take care of whoever it was. She needed to see about putting some color on her face and taking one of Pete's wonderful little tablets.

"A customer asking to see you, Colby," Tony said from the doorway.

She sighed and put down her blush brush. "Tell 'em I'll be there in a minute."

She gave herself one final look, tugged the boxy jacket over her narrow skirt, and frowned at her reflection. She'd have to do. Donning her most professional demeanor, she stepped into her world.

Creighton Interiors was situated in downtown Louisville. Its facade and interior were primarily Art Deco, though other styles and periods were represented. Strategic placement incorporated carefully selected pieces into a pleasing whole. Original Erté designs and celluloid-framed mirrors hung against white walls above massive Boston ferns. Three of Giuseppe Armani's *Fair Lady* figurines resided in all their models' elegance and allure on black marble pedestals of staggered heights.

As she crossed the teal carpet toward the customer, Colby realized how proud she was of Creighton Interiors. Devoting herself to the business had been her salvation from her dependencies—all her dependencies, including her father's domination.

The man stood with his back to her, his weight on one leg and his thumbs hooked in the pockets of his slacks. Sunlight slanted through the windows, finding the red highlights in his brown hair. Her heart began to race, and it hurt to breathe. From the back, the man looked like Rider. Colby forced herself to stay calm. After all, she'd mistaken a lot of men for Rider in the past.

With the carpet shrouding her footsteps, he couldn't have heard her, but he turned, and all her fantasies, all her dreams, all her nightmares, melded into one reality. It was Rider. An older, angry, disillusioned Rider. She'd been too upset to notice the changes in him the day he'd followed her out of Cascio's.

As she looked into his bleak brown eyes, she realized that he hadn't slept much the night before, either. She felt like crying suddenly, though she couldn't have said why. A part of her longed to rub the frown from between his eyebrows and tell him she understood his anger and pain. Another part wanted to run and hide from the heartache she knew he brought with him.

A half dozen steps from him, she stopped. He studied her with unnerving intensity.

"Hello, Colby," he said at last.

Clasping her hands together, she forced herself to meet his gaze without letting her ambivalence show. "What are you doing here? I told you I didn't want to talk to you."

She could see him struggle to keep his anger in check. "I know. But I thought it was high time we cleared the air."

"I don't think that's necessary. Things are perfectly clear to me." She turned and started to walk away. She had taken no more than two steps when she felt his hand on her upper arm, but gently. The unexpected tenderness was at odds with the coldness in his eyes.

"We're going to talk. The only choice you have is whether you want to do it in front of your help."

Freeing her arm, she started across the room. Rider followed. Inside her office, he closed the door, cloistering them in the expensively appointed room. Colby rounded her desk and sat down, placing the solid expanse of wood between them.

Rider took the chair across from her and looked around. "Nice."

"You didn't come here to comment on my decorating skills," she said with a coolness so reminiscent of her mother it was frightening. "Let's just get this over with."

Rider nodded. "Fine. Why didn't you tell me you were pregnant?"

Colby gasped. No one talked about the baby. No one. The subject was taboo.

"I don't talk about the . . . baby. Not even to you." She prayed he couldn't hear the slight quaver in her voice.

"Why not?"

She blinked. "Why not?" Wasn't it obvious? "Because it hurts too much, that's why."

He leaned forward. "You don't know what hurt is, lady. How would you like to find out eleven years after the fact that the woman you loved had aborted your baby? That's hurt."

Colby stood so quickly that her chair rolled into the wall. She was shaking. "Don't talk about the baby!" she cried, her own anger sending her around the desk. "And don't you dare talk to me about hurt. How would you like to find out that the person who said he loved you took twenty thousand dollars to get out of your life?"

He should have seen it coming. Leland wouldn't have missed that trick for anything.

"What's the matter, Rider?" she taunted. "Don't you remember? My father told me all about how he offered you ten thousand dollars to leave me alone, and how you wanted more."

Rider was suddenly bone weary, worn out by his misdirected anger. Leland was the villain in this piece, not Colby. "Is that what he said?"

"That, and a whole lot more."

"And it didn't bother you that he offered that money deliberately to break us up?"

Colby looked the slightest bit uncomfortable. "At first," she admitted. "But he was only doing it for my own good. He was trying to protect me."

"Protect you? From what?"

"From you. Daddy said he had you pegged as a fortune hunter from the first, and he was right, wasn't he? All the 'I love you's were just part of the plan. All you really wanted was the money."

After everything else, Rider supposed he shouldn't be surprised that she believed money was all he cared about. But he was. Surprised and hurt. "I never lied to you. Not about that or anything else."

The calm statement knocked the props out from under her anger. Mute, she stared into his steady brown eyes. She wanted to believe him and hated herself for wanting it. She'd never had many defenses against Rider; it didn't look as if that had changed.

She placed her palms on the desk and leaned toward him. "Why did you come back?" she asked in a harsh whisper. "It's been hard putting my life back together. I don't need this. Not now."

"Believe me, I don't need it, either. I just wanted to know how you could let your father talk you into getting rid of my baby when you knew how much I loved you."

"*Our* baby," she ground out between clenched teeth. Raw pain shadowed her eyes. "And if that's how you treat someone you love, then I couldn't stand for you to hate me." A renegade tear slipped down her cheek, and she brushed it away. "When you left, it felt as if someone had ripped out my heart. You betrayed me and everything I felt for you."

"If anyone betrayed you, it was your father, not me. And that's the truth."

"Truth?" Her mouth was a bitter twist. "I don't know if I'd even recognize the truth anymore."

Wordlessly Rider reached into his shirt pocket and drew out a slip of paper. Unfolding it, he held it out for her inspection. "Do you recognize that?"

Colby stared down at the creased, dog-eared paper, unable to believe what she was seeing. Oh, yes. She would recognize her father's scrawl anywhere. It was a check made out to Rider McCall for twenty thousand dollars, dating from June 1979.

It had never been cashed.

53

Rider didn't make it to the barn until almost noon.

"Where the hell have you been?" Jock asked.

"I was here bright and early," Rider hedged. He had no intention of telling Jock he'd gone to see a Creighton—not three days before the Derby. "I told Tomas to tell you I had to run some errands."

"He did. Said you were all duded up."

Rider didn't want to deal with this. Not with his mind still reeling over his meeting with Colby. Trembling with shock after he'd shown her the check, she had asked him to leave, and he had. Things had been unsettled for over ten years. Clearing up the misunderstandings could wait until after the Derby. It would have to. God knew he had enough on his mind with the race only three days away.

Telling himself he wouldn't worry about Colby for now was easier said than done. But he owed it to Jock and to himself to concentrate on winning the race. And he owed it to Leland Creighton. Especially now.

Ignoring Jock's comment about being dressed up, he asked, "So what's the problem?"

"The Richard boys stopped by this morning."

Jock gave the name the Cajun pronunciation, "Reshard." The Richard brothers were equine dentists from Louisiana who worked on some of the best Thoroughbreds and quarter horses in the country. They were considered to be two of the best in the field.

"I asked them to check out the colt," Rider said.

"Hell, boy, I just had the whole stable worked on in Hot Springs."

"I know, but that guy didn't use a mouth spec, and I don't think he got those points in the back."

Jock snorted. "That's exactly what they said. They claimed Jock's Dream had a couple of caps that needed pulling, too."

"If they said he had caps, he had caps."

Besides needing their teeth floated—filed—periodically to keep the sharp edges rounded off, horses, like children, had baby teeth—or caps—which they lost as three-year-olds. Loose caps could cause several problems, including fighting the bit, blowing turns, and losing weight due to improperly chewed and digested feed. A good dentist could change a horse's whole way of going . . . could actually change his attitude.

"They charged us forty frickin' dollars."

"Look, Dad, when I agreed to help you, you said you wouldn't interfere. You are. I wanted his teeth looked at, and that's that. Besides, what's forty dollars at this point? The colt will probably go like a charm when we work him tomorrow."

"I hope so," Jock said glumly.

"What the hell's the matter with you?" Rider snapped. "You've been moping around for days."

"Nothing's the matter with me. I'm just getting antsy about the race."

"I thought you were so sure we were going to win this one. What's the matter? Is the great Jock McCall nervous?"

Jock narrowed his eyes at his son. "It happens to the best of us."

Dammit, Rider thought, what was he doing ragging Jock? Just because Colby had him tied in knots, he shouldn't take out his frustrations on his dad. He knew how important the race was to Jock. There was more at stake than winning a big purse and national recognition. For Jock, winning the race went hand in hand with regaining his rightful place in the racing industry.

Rider wanted it for Jock as much as Jock did. It was a tense time, and the next couple of days would be worse. He ought to be glad the pressure hadn't sent his dad tumbling off the wagon.

He reached out and squeezed his father's shoulder. "Look, Dad, the colt's a runner. He's good right now. We've given him the best care possible, and we've got a top jock on him. There's nothing else we can do except try to get him to the gate without any mishaps. From there on out, it's up to him and Luis."

"I know," Jock growled, "I know."

"Then stop worrying."

Jock nodded and tried to smile. "Maybe I ought to pray instead."

"It sure as hell couldn't hurt."

54

When Danny got home from the track, the apartment was empty. He'd hoped Tracy would be there so he could take her to lunch before he had to go back for the afternoon's races.

He went toward the kitchen to check the refrigerator for a note. He was halfway there when the telephone rang, making him jump. He reached for the receiver.

"Hello."

"Danny?"

"Speaking."

"This is Solly. How's it goin'?"

A shiver of apprehension shimmied down Danny's spine. He thought he'd made his feelings clear to Solly Tobias. "Look, I told you I wasn't interested in your friend's deal."

"Oh, you did, Danny, but we thought you might have changed your mind now that you've had a few days to think about it."

"I haven't changed my mind."

"What's the matter? Wasn't it enough money? My friend thought his offer was more than generous."

"It has nothing to do with the money. I'm just not interested."

"Now, that's too bad, for Tracy's sake."

For Tracy's sake? Danny heard the unspoken threat in Solly Tobias's voice. "Is that a threat, you son of a bitch?"

Solly replied, "Of course it isn't a threat. I don't make threats, Danny. I make suggestions."

"How do you know so much about Tracy?"

"Everybody knows about Tracy. She's got nice tits, your wife. A nice ass, too."

Danny's stomach began to churn, and the demons raised their heads. "You shut your filthy mouth."

Solly's laughter was like oil on water. "Hey, nothing personal. Just common knowledge. You know, from *Playboy*."

But the seed was planted. Was it just from *Playboy*?

"Leave Tracy out of this."

"I would, Danny, but I know she'd want you to do this for her. I know she likes nice things. Look," Solly said conversationally, "I got an idea. Why don't you ask her to show you her new diamond-and-emerald necklace?"

"What diamond-and-emerald necklace?"

But the only answer Danny got was the phone buzzing in his ear.

55

Rider was just stepping out of the shower when he heard his doorbell ring. He was tired and disgusted—with himself mostly, for coming down so hard on Colby that morning. He didn't need any visitors. All he wanted to do was get something to eat and crawl into bed, where he hoped to get more rest than he had the night before. Sleep and forgetfulness were top priorities for the evening.

Scraping his wet hair away from his face with his fingers, he wrapped a large towel around his middle and went to the door, leaving a trail of damp footprints on the carpet. Debating whether or not he should even acknowledge he was at home, he looked through the peephole.

Colby stood on the doorstep, turning away and about to head back toward her car.

Jesus. He fumbled with the dead bolt and opened

the door. Colby whirled at the sound. She looked wary, almost sorry he'd answered her summons.

"Hi," he said, unable to fabricate a coherent sentence.

Colby took a step closer. There was none of the morning's anger in her eyes. She was calm, collected. "I didn't think you were home."

"I didn't hear the doorbell for the shower running."

"Oh."

"What can I do for you?" he asked.

Colby gave a helpless shrug. "I realized I'd sent you away without giving you much of a chance to explain. Seeing the check and finding out that my father had lied to me took me by surprise. Although, knowing him as well as I do, I can't imagine why."

Rider just stood there, offering nothing, making no demands.

"I've been thinking about it all day." She laughed. "Actually, I haven't been able to think of much else. I realized that if he lied to me about the money and your leaving, then maybe I ought to hear your side of the story. And I decided that maybe you were right. Maybe I should—" Her voice broke. "Maybe we can talk about the . . . baby."

Rider felt his throat tighten. He stepped out of the doorway. "Come on in. I'll get dressed and we'll go get something to eat."

The cafe, near his apartment, was small and unpretentious and served the closest thing to home cooking that Rider had found in his migrations from track to track.

"Sorry it isn't fancier," he said as she slid into the vinyl booth across from him.

"It's fine."

A waitress brought them water, took their order, and disappeared into the netherlands of the kitchen. Colby just sat there, folding and refolding her napkin into a fan. Obviously, Rider thought, she didn't know where to start, but someone had to.

He lit a cigarette and took the plunge. "Why didn't you tell me about the baby?"

She focused on her napkin. "My periods were always pretty erratic, and I didn't want to say anything until I was sure. I was afraid to tell you at all." She looked up and tried to smile. "I didn't want you to think I was trying to trap you into marriage. Did Bonnie tell you they took me to Forest Glade?"

"Yeah." Meeting her eyes was difficult.

"I'd been there a while before they found out."

"How long were you there?"

"A year, give or take a few weeks."

"A year!" He swore.

"They told everyone I was seeing Europe." She threaded her fingers through her hair and pulled it away from her face, resting her elbows on the table as if supporting the heavy weight of the memories. "They tell me I was pretty bad off. Screaming and crying and carrying on. But I really don't remember much. They kept me sedated at first, and then I just . . . blocked it all out."

Rider closed his eyes, wishing he could do the same.

"I saw the psychiatrist every day, and they put me on a lot of drugs." She grimaced. "But that's another story."

"Bonnie said the abortion was your father's idea."

"It was, but everyone assured me later that I couldn't have taken the strain of the pregnancy, mentally or physically."

Strain of pregnancy? Having a baby was supposed to be a joy, not a strain, wasn't it? Rider ground the pads of his fingers into his burning eyes. He shook his head. "If I'd known, nothing in this world your father threatened me with could have made me leave you. I would have wanted our baby, Colby. Surely you know that."

Colby pressed her trembling lips together and swiped at her nose with a napkin.

Sensing he should ease off a little, he asked, "What happened after you got out?"

"Nothing much. I stayed close to home. Sat and stared a lot." She gave a poor imitation of laughter. "After three years or so, I married Kent."

"I heard about it. Your dad always did want you to marry Carlisle."

"Well, I finally did."

"And?"

"And . . . I didn't love him. I tried. I guess we both tried, but it just wasn't working. We split up over a year and a half ago."

"I heard that, too.

"Did you hear the rest of the ugly story?"

Rider frowned. What else could possibly have happened? "No."

"While I was married to Kent, I had what the media refer to as a substance-abuse problem. Vodka and Valium, mostly." When Rider offered no comment, she continued. "Then, about three years ago, Cass took me to some hotshot psychiatrist he'd heard of in New York. We rented a place away from the world for a while, and when he brought me back, I was clean and dry. I've been clean ever since. That's when I got in touch with Bonnie, and we decided to go into business together. It's been hard, but for the first time in more than ten years, I have a real life."

"And then I came back."

Colby's smile was bittersweet. "Yeah. You came back. But I'm handling it. I've been to see Pete, and—"

"Pete?"

"My shrink. He's given me some pills, and I—"

"Jesus, Colby! Don't start all that shit again. Not because of me."

"I won't. Really. He only gave me a few, and now that we've talked, I think . . . things will be easier."

Rider's eyes were bleak. "I never meant to come back and screw everything up."

"I know."

He stubbed out his Marlboro in the flimsy metal ashtray. "Jesus, what a mess."

So much pain. So much misery. And all because of one man. Rider was sick of being Leland Creighton's scapegoat. Maybe it was time to tell his side of the story and get the poison out of his system.

"What is it?" she asked, seeing the indecision on his face.

"I didn't want to leave you," he said roughly, "but I had to."

"Why?"

Rider lit another cigarette and stared across the cafe, his mind focused on a place in the past. Then he glanced at Colby. "Do you remember when he slapped you?"

"Yes," she said, closing her eyes against the memory.

"You fell against a tree. You must have bumped your head, because you just lay there. He wouldn't let me go to you. That's when he offered me the ten thousand dollars to get out of your life and stay out. I told him no way, so he added an extra incentive. He told me he'd ruin my father's training operation if I didn't do as he said."

"Oh, Rider . . ." Colby shook her head in disbelief.

He took a short, hard drag off the cigarette and expelled the smoke ceilingward. "The scary part was that I knew he was capable of it. We'd just buried my mom, and Dad was already crazy with grief. I knew he couldn't take anything else right then."

"No."

"I didn't know what to do," he said. "I loved you both. Then he told me he was upping the payoff to twenty thousand, and that if I didn't take it, he'd go to the police and tell them I'd raped you."

"He *what*?" Colby's face lost all its color.

"Yeah." Rider's lips made a brief, upward quirk. "Nice guy, huh? What could I do? It would have been my word against his. Who's going believe a kid from the backside over a senator? He had the clout to make the charges stick, and he'd probably have pressed for the maximum sentence. With his connections, he'd have gotten it."

Colby blinked back tears. "I'd have told them the truth. I wouldn't have let them charge you with rape!"

Rider shook his head. "I'd already seen what your father could do to shut you up, and it scared me shitless. I think the worst part was having to leave you there, on the ground."

She gave him a watery smile and offered him her hand across the table. As if more than a decade hadn't passed since the last time, he automatically laced his fingers through hers.

"So you did what he said."

"I jumped in that old Ford truck and cut out as fast as I could. Not very noble of me, maybe, but I was young and stupid and scared a lot easier then than I do now. Your father must have tossed the check in the window as I drove off."

"But you didn't cash it," she said, and the bit of joy he saw in her eyes was enough to brighten the gloomiest day.

"No. I didn't cash it. I left, but I did it for you and for my dad, not for money. He never bought me, Colby. Twenty thousand couldn't buy a fraction of what I felt for you."

56

When Alex joined Leland and Cass for dinner in Windwood's elegant dining room, the first thing she noticed was her daughter-in-law's absence.

"Where's Bonnie?"

Cass rose and pulled out her chair. "I couldn't say. Bonnie and I had a mild altercation last night."

"I heard you arguing." Alex allowed Cass to seat her.

"Then you know we were arguing about Rider McCall."

Alex cast her son a look over her shoulder. "I wasn't eavesdropping, Cass. I just heard angry voices, and I heard you leave."

"I went to Colby's," Cass explained. "Bonnie ran into Rider at the races, and while they were talking, she inadvertently told him about the baby."

"Oh, Cass . . ."

"You know Bonnie. She still feels as if Rider is the abused one."

"I don't understand that girl at all," Leland grumbled.

"I let her know I didn't appreciate the way she lets him keep coming between us."

"Good grief, Cass," Alex chided, "you shouldn't still be fighting with Bonnie over something ten years old. It really has nothing to do with the two of you."

"I know, I know. Anyway, I went to Colby's I thought I should warn her in case Rider tried to contact her."

"Has he?" Leland asked.

"He called last night, but she wouldn't talk to him. I haven't been able to reach her all day."

"Rider may be many things, but I don't think he would do more than try to talk to her about it," Alex ventured.

"Don't give it a minute's thought," Leland said. "Rider McCall will be busier than a cranberry merchant the next few days. If we can keep him away from Colby until after the Derby, the son of a bitch will be too busy sweeping the streets to bother us."

Alex's suspicions began to nag at her. "For someone who could care less about the outcome of this race, you're awfully cocky."

Before Leland could answer, the maid spoke from the doorway. "Telephone, Mr. Cass."

"Maybe it's Bonnie," he said, scooting out his chair.

"I hope so."

After he abandoned the room to his parents, Alex countered Leland's challenging look with one of cool assessment. She hadn't lived with him for almost thirty-six years for nothing. "All right, what's going on?"

Leland lifted his Spode coffee cup. "What makes you think anything's going on?"

"I know you."

"Apparently not as well as you seem to think, my dear. Nothing's going on. Come on, Alex," he cajoled. "Stop seeing something nefarious in every innocent comment I make. You know as well as I do that the race is no contest. We—rather, you— have the superior horse, and Cass is the superior trainer."

"Don't underestimate Jock McCall."

Leland's smile turned mocking. "I never underestimate anyone. Particularly if his name is McCall. I just hedge my bets."

"I want you to stay out of this business between Colby and Rider. She'd a big girl, and she has to deal with her own problems."

"I'm her father. I have the right to offer her my advice on something as important as this."

"That's wonderful in theory, but you don't advise. You manipulate. Just as her divorce is between her and Kent, this is between her and Rider. If you'd stayed out of it before, none of this would have happened."

"If I'd stayed out of it, you'd have had Rider McCall for a son-in-law."

"I can think of worse things."

Her meaning wasn't lost on Leland. "If you didn't like having me for a husband, you could have done something about it."

"I know," she said, raising her Baccarat wine-glass. "You don't know how much I regret not being blessed with Colby's courage."

"Well, my dear, tomorrow's another day," Leland mocked. "Maybe you'll find it yet."

Alex downed the contents of the glass in an unladylike manner and set her glass on the damask-covered table with a muffled thud. "Maybe I will."

57

Springer Martindale took off his Stetson and crossed the dimly lighted club toward the woman who sat hidden away in the corner. She was blond and still beautiful despite the fine lines etched into her face. Not for the first time in all the years he'd known her, Springer wondered how Alexandra Creighton would be in bed. But he'd never tried to get her there. Their girls were close, and Cybill meant too much to him for him to lose her over an affair.

"Hello, Alex," he said, sliding into the leather booth across from her.

"Hello, Springer. I'm glad you came." She took

a quick puff of her cigarette and blew the smoke over her shoulder, away from him. "I hated to call you away from your family, but I really needed to talk."

"No problem."

Alex smiled and jabbed out the cigarette with sharp, staccato movements. "You may think I'm crazy for what I'm about to ask you, but it's very important that I know what's going on."

"Sure," Springer said, shrugging his massive shoulders. "What is it?"

"Did Leland buy that note of Jock McCall's you were telling us about?" Alex asked.

"Yeah. He offered me a nice profit, and I took it."

Alex leaned wearily against the table. "Damn!"

"What's the matter?"

"Everything. Did he say why he wanted to buy it?"

Springer smoothed his drooping mustache with his forefinger. "Leland said he knew Cass had the better horse, but that he started thinking about how great it would be to have both horses."

"I figured as much."

"What do you mean?"

"That isn't why he wanted the note, Springer. He wanted to get his hands on it because he hates Jock."

"What on earth could Leland possibly have against McCall?"

Alex tapped another cigarette against the table. "He suspects Jock and I had an affair years ago. And he's never forgotten or forgiven me."

Springer eyed her curiously; she met his gaze

with a steady one of her own. Alex wasn't one to kiss and tell, and what did it matter now, anyway?

He struck one of the club's matches and held it to the tip of her cigarette. "Hell, if that's the case, I've really screwed things up, haven't I?"

"You had no way of knowing what he was up to."

"What should we do?" Springer asked.

"I don't know. I'd hate for Jock to find out before the race. I imagine the pressure's pretty great right now. This would only add more."

"You're forgetting one thing."

"What's that?"

"Jock's colt's chances of winning are a lot better than average. I don't mean to put your colt down, but all this worrying might be for nothing."

"No one ever worries for nothing if my husband is concerned. It doesn't matter what Jock's Dream's chances are. Leland has an uncanny way of stacking the deck in his favor."

58

A sickle moon clad in wisps of cloud hung in the night sky. Rider pulled into his parking place at the apartment and turned off the engine. The glow of a security light illuminated the truck's interior.

Deep in thought, Colby was hardly aware that they had arrived. So much had happened. Too much. She still found it hard to believe her father had duped them all so easily, so completely. Oh, she knew he was a manipulator, but this—this was a masterpiece. Still, a big part of the blame for his success could be placed on her shoulders. If she hadn't gone to pieces and had to be kept drugged, maybe she would have had more presence of mind than to believe her father's lies about Rider. She'd played right into his hands. And there was nothing to be done about the lost years now.

Confused, and unsure what to do or say now that the explanations were over, Colby picked up a bottle of leg sweat, one of several bottles littering the seat, along with old racing forms, programs, and condition books.

"Your truck still looks like a garbage dump," she said, breaking the silence.

"It's a prerequisite of being a trainer."

His smile was as she remembered it, slow in coming and a little self-conscious. For the first time since he'd come back, the hurt receded, allowing a glimpse of the happier times they'd shared. He'd been worried about his truck the first time she'd ridden with him, the day their relationship had taken a turn for the better. "I still think it smells good."

"A prerequisite for being a breeder's daughter."

She smiled. "Maybe."

"Come on," he said. "I'll walk you to your car."

Colby nodded and got out of the truck. Rider was already a few steps ahead of her, and as she watched his loose, easy stride, she couldn't help wondering what had always made her more susceptible to a man in Levi's than one in a three-piece suit.

She realized suddenly that she didn't want to leave yet. She wanted to prolong her time with Rider. She wanted to savor the relative peace she was enjoying since they'd shared the truth and explore the unexpected awareness, an awareness that, despite everything that had happened between them, was growing.

For the first time in a long time, she wanted a man. This man. The man who had brought her more happiness in a few weeks than she'd known in a lifetime.

She didn't expect things to be the same, but after all they'd been through, didn't they deserve a bit of happiness, even if that happiness lasted only an hour?

"Rider?"

He turned. Lamplight lay along the rugged planes of his face. The lonesome song of a whippoorwill echoed through the darkness, and a gust of wind swirled a candy wrapper across the asphalt. Colby knew that the long, considering look he gave her registered every emotion she was feeling.

"What?" he asked at last.

"Ask me in for a cup of coffee."

"I don't think so, Colby," he said with a slow shake of his head.

She took a step closer. "Why not?"

"There's no future in it."

"How do you know?"

"There never was."

"I'm not asking you for anything you don't want to give."

His smile was lopsided and bittersweet. "Just a warm body, huh? You were never this easy before."

His cruelty snatched her breath, but the heated look in his eyes gave it back. Hadn't he always resorted to cutting remarks to keep her at arm's length?

She moved to within a foot of him. The breeze blew her hair into her eyes; she brushed it back. "I'm not easy now, either."

"Do you only proposition old lovers, then?"

"You're the only one I've had."

Rider laughed. "I may be a country boy, but I'm not naïve enough to believe that one."

"I didn't say there hadn't been other men, McCall. But I never considered them my lovers. They were just 'warm bodies,' as you called it, a way to try to keep the dreams at bay."

"What dreams?"

She closed her eyes and shook her head, as if denying not only the cryptic statement, but an explanation. She took his hand and carried it to her breast. "I don't want to talk about them," she said almost desperately. "I don't want to think about them. I don't want to remember. Not tonight. Tonight I want to fuck."

The ugly word stopped Rider in his tracks. The Colby he'd known never would have used that word to describe the incredible feelings they generated in each other. As his hand cupped her breast he said, "Don't you mean make love?"

"I don't make love anymore. Fucking is easier. It creates fewer problems." She tugged him toward the apartment. "Coming?"

Coming? How could he respond to the crudeness of her attitude with any tenderness when the loving memories of her lay shattered in the dust of his disillusionment? Yet, in spite of that disillusionment and against his better judgment, Rider knew he'd let her stay. While he unlocked the door, she was busy unzipping her dress. Inside, he watched as she kicked off her shoes and wriggled out of the Anne Klein original. Beneath it she wore ruby-red see-through lace undergarments that looked as out of place on the Colby he remembered as the smoldering look she turned on him. The old Colby had been innocent and funny when they'd made love. There hadn't been an ounce of calculation in her eyes or her actions.

Fighting a wave of bitterness at what should have been a dream come true, Rider watched her peel silk stockings down one shapely leg and then the other. She tossed aside the garter belt and crossed the room on bare feet. Looping her arms around his neck, she closed her eyes and nuzzled his throat, her open lips pressing damp kisses to his jaw. Slim and supple, she hung against him. "Kiss me," she whispered against his ear.

"Colby—"

She wound her fingers through his hair and pulled his head down, stopping his reply with her mouth. Rider shut his eyes tightly and fought the feelings building inside him. Like it or not, he was getting a hard-on, and under the circumstances he didn't like it one little bit. But he was no monk, and he'd been celibate longer than he ought to have been. Angry with her, furious at himself, he thrust her from him and headed for the bedroom, stripping off his shirt as he went.

"Where are you going?" she asked, following him.

He stopped just inside the bedroom door. Colby pressed her lips to his chest, her fingers already busy with the brads of his jeans.

Rider planted a row of rough, openmouthed kisses from her neck to her ear, growling a word between each kiss. "To . . . get . . . the . . . condoms."

Colby raised her head. "You never used condoms before."

He met her gaze steadily. "We made love before," he said, unfastening the front clasp of her bra. "When I fuck, I use condoms."

He left her standing there, a look of confusion on her face. When he entered the bedroom she was beneath the sheets. Wordlessly she held up one corner for him. Wordlessly he slipped beneath the cool percale. He eased one leg over her.

Colby sucked in her breath, and he moved his leg against her, loving the silky feel of her skin against his and remembering all the other times he'd felt her naked in his arms. He lowered his head and pressed his lips to the small mole that sat on the high rise of her cheekbone beneath her left eye. He had kissed the mole every time they were together. A tattered breath fluttered from her lips.

"We don't have to do this," he said, wanting it so badly he could hardly stand it but knowing it was wrong.

Her eyes flew open, and her hand found him. "Please. Yes. I do," she canted feverishly. "I have to see what it was like. I have to see what was so wonderful that I went crazy when I lost it."

Crazy. The whole thing was crazy. And he was crazy for letting her do this to him and to his memories of her, crazy with the need to know what it was like to have her just one more time.

She was desperate. He was hungry. She was skillful. He was impatient. She was rough. He was rougher. She wasn't the girl he had loved, but then he wasn't the same person she'd fallen in love with, either. They were ready for each other quickly, and Rider's breath hissed from him as he slid into her velvet warmth.

Frenzied, furious, it was over too soon, much too soon, a mating of flesh that had nothing to do with love and tenderness. Rider felt physically drained and emotionally empty. It was as wrong as anything he'd ever done.

He rolled away from her onto his back and flung his arm across his eyes, fighting the urge to cry for the innocence they'd lost, the innocence Leland Creighton had stolen.

59

Colby woke to the sound of a door closing. The place next to her was empty. She smoothed it with her hand and dragged the pillow against her face, breathing in the scent of some clean-smelling shampoo.

Sleeping with Rider hadn't been what she'd expected. But what had she expected, anyway? To recapture the heady rapture of young love? The sound of her bitter laughter filled the empty room. That was impossible. The rapture of young love required innocence, naïveté, and the ability to believe in impossible dreams. Once the realities of life robbed you of those childlike traits, it was never possible to recapture that feeling of young love again, as last night had proved all too well.

Colby's eyes filled with tears. After Rider rolled away from her, it had taken every ounce of willpower she possessed not to give in to the urge to throw up or scream, as the eight perfect half-moon shapes in her palms could testify.

What they'd shared hadn't been pretty at all. Or special. She'd felt strangely empty, used. Of course, if Rider had treated her more like a paid whore than the woman he had once claimed to love, she could take the blame for that. She'd wanted him without relinquishing any part of herself to him, assuming that if she kept all her emotions but the wanting locked up inside, he couldn't hurt her again.

Well, she'd had it her way, and now she knew. No matter what secret parts of herself she refused to give Rider, he would always have the power to hurt her. She rolled to a sitting position and buried her face in her hands. Lord, what did she do now? She'd hoped, prayed, that there would still be something between them. She'd needed to find some spark left, *some* reason to account for her inability to fall in love with someone else.

Giving a strangled cry, Colby threw the pillow across the room. Then she reached for the phone and dialed Pete Whitten's number. She didn't care that it was five in the morning. She needed to talk to him. Now.

Damn her father to an everlasting hell. She would never forgive him for what he'd done. Never.

60

Rider was watching a horse breeze, and Jock was helping Tomas give Jock's Dream a bath, when Springer strolled into the McCall shed row the next morning. The colt was kicking and playing and shaking his head against the fine spray directed at his face. He was feeling good, no doubt about it. Springer couldn't help noticing how good Jock looked, either—better than he'd looked in years. He sighed. Telling him about Leland wasn't going to be easy. Despite Alex's urgings, he'd decided it was the right thing to do.

"Mornin', Jock."

Jock looked up. Wariness replaced the pleasure in his eyes. "Good morning, Springer. What brings you out so early?"

Springer plunged his hands into the pockets of his tailored slacks. "I need to talk to you."

"I figured as much. Let me get finished here."

"Sure."

"There's fresh coffee in the tack room," Jock offered.

"Thanks."

Reading Jock's mind was easy. He thought the visit was to remind him that the note was due in a couple of days. Springer only wished the reason behind his visit was that simple. Dammit! How had he let himself get into such a mess?

The tack room was dim and cool and redolent of leather and coffee. The ancient plastic percolator sat on an equally ancient TV tray that had been spruced up with Con-Tact paper scattered with blue ducks and pink hearts. Covered jars held Cremora and sugar, and plastic spoons stood in a chipped I Love Horses mug. The tack room was orderly, and the cement floor was swept clean. The McCalls ran a tight ship, even if it was a small one.

Springer poured night-black coffee into a polystyrene cup and added two lumps of sugar. He sipped at the scalding brew and cursed when it burned his mouth.

"Did you find everything?" Jock spoke from the doorway.

Springer turned. "Yeah. Good coffee."

"I'm glad you think so. Tomas makes it, and I can hardly choke the stuff down."

They exchanged halfhearted smiles.

"The colt looks great."

"He's doing great," Jock said. "He'll give Runaway Again a run for his money on Saturday."

"I hope so."

"Look, Springer, if you're worried about the money, I—"

"I'm not," Springer interrupted. He drew a mono-grammed handkerchief from his hip pocket and wiped his forehead.

Jock frowned. "Then what is it?"

"Jesus, Jock, I don't know how to tell you. I've been such a fool, but I didn't know about you and Alex and—"

"What about me and Alex?" Jock's voice was sharp and defensive.

"She told me last night that Leland suspected that you'd . . . had an affair, and that he'd never let her forget it."

Like Alex, Jock refused to give away the truth. "What does that have to do with you and me?"

"If I'd known how Leland felt about you, I'd never have sold him the note."

The color drained from Jock's face. "You'd never have what?"

"Hell, I'm sorry. I mentioned that I'd bought your note, and Leland called me later and said he'd like to take a chance of getting the horse for Cass. He offered me a helluva profit. I never thought losing Jock's Dream would be a consideration, because you're so all-fired sure he'll win."

"I was," Jock said. "I am. So what happened to make you think otherwise? What scared you so bad that you had to come out here and warn me?"

"Alex."

"Alex?"

"She says Leland despises you and that he'll do whatever it takes to make you lose the race on Saturday."

"What do *you* think?"

"I think that after thirty-six years, Alexandra Creighton is bound to know her husband pretty well."

61

Rider could hardly keep his mind on the horses for thinking of Colby. He was ashamed of the way he'd treated her, and telling himself that she'd asked for it didn't ease his conscience. The lingering scent of her perfume wasn't helping his mood. Damn! What had he allowed to happen last night? And why?

Despite the sorrow he felt for what she'd gone through because of him, despite the great tenderness he had for her, he hadn't shown her any of it because it ticked him off that she'd come on to him like some two-hundred-dollar-a-pop call girl.

She'd felt good in his arms, and she'd remembered all the right buttons to push, which added to his dilemma. Where did they go from here? Was there anyplace *to* go? Or was last night the only culmination of a decade of regrets and wishes that weren't destined to come true? He had hoped there was more, but somehow happily-ever-after didn't fit the scenario. They needed to talk, but he didn't know what to feel, much less what to say.

Rider's black mood further deteriorated when he got back to the barn and found out Jock had left for the day.

"Oh, that's great," he said in disgust. "That's really great. Where the hell did he go?"

Tomas shrugged. "I don't know. Right after Mr. Springer left, Jock said he was sick. That he had to go home."

Rider swore roundly. Shit. Just what he needed.

62

Danny left the jocks' room at nine-thirty. He unlocked the Mercedes and slid inside its plush interior with a curse. It felt like a damn sweatbox. He started the engine, turned on the air, and put the car in gear. Then he noticed the piece of paper under the windshield wiper. For no reason he could put his finger on, his mouth grew dry and his heart started pounding. Frowning, fearful, he got out of the car and pulled the folded slip of paper from beneath the rubber blade. There was something heavy inside.

He unfolded the note and found that someone had taped a key inside. The address of a nearby apartment complex had been scribbled on the scrap of yellow legal paper. Danny didn't even have to ask himself what he'd find when he got to apartment 1021. Somehow, he knew. He tossed the key in his hand as if it were hot to the touch.

Solly Tobias's taunt about the diamond-and-emerald necklace had rung in his ears every waking minute for the last twenty-four hours. Fear and anger that what Solly said might be true had played seesaw with Danny's emotions. One minute he wanted to demand that Tracy produce the necklace and tell him where she got it. The next he was cursing himself for letting a slimebag like Tobias mess with his head. In the end Danny had kept silent, because he didn't really want to know if there was a man who'd given his wife a necklace. He didn't want what was left of his illusions destroyed.

But this . . . this was different. This demanded checking out, no matter what he found. His stomach tightened, and he got back into the car. Reaching over, he opened the glove compartment. The pistol gleamed a dull blue in the morning light.

Danny slammed the glove box shut and put the car in reverse. The apartment was only a few blocks away. He'd go there, use the key, and see for himself what was going on. Then he could figure out where to go from there.

The lock turned easily. Danny let himself in. A quick glance told him the apartment was nothing special, certainly not the kind of place where he'd expect to find Tracy. With the dining room straight ahead, he figured the hallway to his left would lead to the bedroom.

He had barely made it to the hall when he heard Tracy's voice, breathless and panting, urging some unknown man "deeper, deeper." Danny's stomach burned, but he continued to put one resolute foot in front of the other. He reached the open door and had to step inside to get a view of the bed. He wished to God he hadn't.

A young stud—there was no other word for the muscular college type—lay on his back, with Tracy astride him. Their eyes were closed, and Tracy held his hands to her breasts and urged him to a faster rhythm. It looked as if they were near the finish line.

Danny pulled the gun from the waistband of his jeans and gave the door a hard shove that sent it crashing into the wall. Tracy dismounted with a terrified curse, and when she saw who it was, her mouth fell open.

The sight of them scrambling apart would have been hilarious if it were someone besides Tracy doing the scrambling. The kid dragged a sheet over his lower body and tried to brazen it out. "Who the hell do you think you are?"

Danny had to give him a B for balls, considering he was looking down the barrel of a thirty-eight.

"Shit, Mark, who in sweet hell do you *think* he is?" Tracy cried. Not bothering to cover her nakedness, she went to Danny and put her hand on his arm. "Look, Danny, I can explain."

Danny regarded the face he'd fallen in love with. Tracy's eyes were dilated, and her nose was red. Obviously they'd indulged in a little recreational coke, too. He wanted to cry, to ask her what he'd done to deserve this. Hadn't he loved her enough? Instead he shook off her hand.

"I don't need any explanations, Tracy. It all looks pretty self-explanatory to me." He motioned the gun at Mark. "Get your clothes on and get out of here."

"Get out yourself. This is my apartment."

"Well, there's gonna be a vacancy in about thirty seconds if you don't get the hell out." Danny aimed the pistol at Mark's chest. His calm, controlled attitude must have gotten through. Mark got up and began pulling on his jeans.

"Get dressed, Tracy."

"Danny, I—"

"Get dressed."

"He doesn't mean anything to me!"

"Do they ever?"

She looked as if he'd slapped her.

Danny laughed. "Come on, Trace. Surely you aren't stupid enough to think I didn't suspect something like this was going on?"

Mark slipped his bare feet into leather loafers and grabbed a shirt. "I'm callin' the cops."

"Whatever," Danny said.

"I'm not stupid!" Tracy cried to the two men who were busy with their own conversation.

Mark flipped Danny the bird and disappeared down the hall. In a few seconds Danny heard the outer door slam shut. He grabbed Tracy, who was making no move to dress, and shoved her down on the bed. Instead of the fear he expected, she glared up at him.

"I am not stupid," she ground out. "I was smart enough to get you to marry me."

Danny ignored the burst of pain in his heart and placed the barrel of the gun between her perfect C-cup breasts. "Tell me about them, Tracy. Tell me who you've been sleeping with. I'm not riding today. I've got all afternoon."

"You self-righteous bastard," she said coldly.

"Self-righteousness has nothing to do with it. I'm pissed off. And I'm through letting you jerk me around. So let me lay it on the line for you." He stuck the gun back in the waistband of his jeans. "I'm not worried about lover boy. I know you well enough to know that he's nothing more than a means to scratch your particular itch. The only ones who concern me are the serious contenders. All you have to do is tell me who gave you the necklace, and I'm going to go blow his frickin' head off."

Surprise replaced the fury in her eyes. "Who told you about the necklace?"

Bitter laughter echoed through the room. "I thought you weren't stupid. If you were so smart, you'd have denied having the necklace, wouldn't you?"

Tracy surged up from the bed kicking and screaming. Danny grasped her wrists and used the force of his body to push her back down. Wisps of blond hair clung to the ripe fullness of her lips. Any other time it would have been a turn-on, but for the first time he could remember, Danny found no pleasure in the feel of her body beneath his. "Who gave you the necklace, Tracy?"

She shook her head and offered him a mocking, self-satisfied smile. "Someone who could buy and sell you a dozen times over. So how smart does that make me, Danny, huh?" She clamped her teeth over her bottom lip and laughed mirthlessly.

Danny wound his fingers through her hair and

jerked her head back. Her smile disappeared, and she groaned. "Who was it?"

They glared at each other for several seconds. The roar of the demons inside Danny kept time with the heavy beating of his heart.

"What the hell," Tracy said finally, as if she'd weighed her options and decided she had nothing to lose. "Leland Creighton gave me the necklace. For services rendered."

Leland Creighton. The name seeped into his mind and sapped the strength from his body. "But he's . . . old."

She smiled. "He's old, but he can still get it up, and he's loaded."

Leland Creighton. It hurt worse than finding her with ten Marks. There was something demeaning about knowing she preferred someone like Creighton over him, whatever the reason. Danny let her go and started toward the door.

"Hey! Where are you going?"

He heard panic in her voice. He turned. "Somewhere away from you."

63

Jock lifted the rapidly emptying bottle of Tul-lamore Dew to his lips, swiped the back of his hand across his mouth, and hummed a few unsteady bars of "José Cuervos," though God knew he didn't have anything to sing about. Springer's visit had pretty well ruined his day, not to mention what was left of his life.

Everything Jock had hoped for, dreamed of, was now going to hell in the proverbial hand basket. Not that he still didn't believe in the horse, but, like Springer and Alex, Jock believed Leland had ways of tipping the balances.

What would he tell Rider, after he'd interrupted his own life to come and help his no-account father run the Derby?

Nothing. He wouldn't tell Rider anything. Maybe there was a compassionate God who would let them win. Maybe Leland Creighton couldn't pay Him off.

Jock wanted to tell the bastard just what he thought of him. Damned if he didn't. He took another swig of the seven-year-old Irish whiskey and grimaced. He wasn't drunk. Not yet. When he was truly drunk, he couldn't feel the bite of the alcohol. All he felt was the numbness, the blessed, welcome numbness that blocked out the memories of all his failures.

He couldn't fail this time. He owed it to Rider to give it his best shot. Rider. Why did he owe Rider anything? He was Vicky's brat, most likely Creighton's spawn. Damn! Was it possible they were in this together? Jock shook his head. His thinking was getting worse than fuzzy, and his reasoning was eighty-proof blurred. Everything was getting mixed up, and that wasn't good, but it was . . . it was . . .

No. Rider wasn't in with Creighton. Rider wouldn't piss on Leland's guts if he was on fire. Maybe Leland Creighton ought to know that.

Jock reached for the telephone and dialed Information. In seconds the phone was ringing at Windwood.

64

Danny headed straight for the nearest liquor store, which he had trouble locating through the tears blinding him. He hadn't been drunk in ages, but under the circumstances he thought it was acceptable—maybe even mandatory—behavior.

He took the bottle home, where he could savor his misery in private. Then he stripped and got into the shower to wash away the lingering scent of Tracy's perfume. The bottle went with him. Too weary to stand, he leaned against the tiled wall and let the heat of the water wash away her fragrance, while the Scotch diluted the memory of what he'd found out.

Tracy and Leland Creighton. It was enough to make him want to puke. He wanted to take the gun and pump the trigger until every bullet was spent in Leland Creighton's black heart.

Danny hated the bastard, and he hated Tracy for all the men he knew she'd humped, but at the same time his heart was breaking into a million pieces.

God help him, he loved her.

He was halfway through the bottle when everything became crystal clear, as it can only be when you're three sheets to the wind. He had to have money, lots of money, to keep Tracy happy. And he wanted to keep Tracy happy.

What if she didn't want him back? What if she wanted Leland Creighton instead? That inner voice was back, asking those damnable questions.

She wouldn't want Creighton, would she? She'd be glad to come home. And if having her back meant throwing a race . . . no big deal. He was good. He could make it look good. It wasn't like somebody didn't do it every day.

You don't do it every day, Danny. So what? There was a first time for everything. He took another healthy swig of the Chivas to calm the murmurings of the demons.

It was all a matter of getting his priorities straight.

65

Alex was having lunch with Bonnie and Colby and listening to Colby's account of her conversation with Rider, when the maid called her to the phone. She excused herself and took the call in the library.

"Hello?"

"Alex? Let me talk to Leland."

The voice on the other end of the phone line was slurred but familiar nonetheless. "Jock? Is that you?"

"Damn straight."

Alex realized he was anything but, and her first thought was that Leland was somehow involved. "What's wrong? Why do you want to talk to Leland?"

"Springer tol' me 'bout the note. That bastard you're married to is boun' and determin' to ruin me. But he won't. I promise you that."

Damn! Springer had told Jock, even though she'd asked him not to put the added strain on him just now. Obviously she'd been right. It wasn't fair. Dear Lord, it wasn't fair that Leland could do this to people.

Alex thought of the way Jock had been when

she'd first met him—so strong and gentle and solid. She cradled the mouthpiece in her palms and swallowed the lump in her throat. "I know he won't, Jock. You're too strong for that."

"He thinks he's gonna win the race an' get my horse. Well, he isn't. Me and Rider are gonna win the Derby, and I'm gonna laugh my ass off. Know why?"

"No, Jock," she said. "Why?"

"I like your boy," Jock said, seeming to ignore her question. "I really do. He's a good-looking kid. Smart. A hard worker. A fine horseman."

Alex closed her eyes against an ancient pain. "Thank you, Jock. That means a lot to me."

"But I don't min' tellin' you that Rider's a damn good horseman, too. Damn good."

"I know."

"I jus' wanted to tell Leland that we inten' to win that race on Saturday. Nothing personal, you unnerstan'."

Alex smiled sadly. "No. Nothing personal."

"I just want the pleasure of knowing that I helped Leland Creighton's bastard beat his legi'mate son. Nothing personal. G'bye, Alex."

"Jock, wait!" The phone buzzed in her ear. She dialed Information and called him back. The busy signal beeped mockingly in her ear. Alex hung up the phone and rubbed her aching temples. This had gone on long enough. Too long. It was time to do what she should have done years ago.

Leland wouldn't be home for dinner tonight. It would be an excellent time to have Cass and Colby come out so that she could set the record straight. And if she could get in touch with him, she wanted Jock there, too. He obviously believed Rider was Leland's, but anyone who wasn't wearing blinders could see that the boy was exactly like a younger Jock McCall, just as anyone who was really looking could see that Cass was nothing like Leland.

Alex drew a shaky breath and retraced her steps to the dining room. It was time to set the record straight, even if it cost her Cass's love and respect.

Jock McCall deserved to know that Cass was his son.

66

Rider swore. He wasn't getting any response to his repeated knocking at Jock's door. He must be there, because his truck was parked outside. Rider tried to keep a rein on his anxieties. According to Tomas, Jock had left the track sick. Now that he wasn't coming to the door, visions of his father prostrate with a heart attack flitted through Rider's mind. Worry made him clumsy as he fumbled with the extra key and let himself in.

He was glancing around the small living room when a low groan emanated from the direction of the bedroom. Rider sprinted toward the partially opened door and saw Jock sprawled across his rumpled bed. His heart racing, Rider went to the bed and dragged a pillow beneath Jock's head. "Dad! Are you all right?"

Jock mumbled something unintelligible at the same time Rider got a whiff of whiskey and spied the empty bottle partially hidden in the folds of the bedspread. For a moment, he was so shocked he couldn't even be angry. He had expected this to happen every day since Jock had been released from rehab, but the more time that passed without Jock succumbing to temptation, the further away Rider imagined that temptation to be. Obviously he was wrong. Temptation was only a bad morning and a liquor store away.

Rider sat on the edge of the bed, rested his elbows on his knees, and buried his face in his hands. He was torn up inside by what had happened with Colby and justifiably concerned that something might happen to the colt before the race, which was only two days away. He didn't need this. Not now. How could Jock screw things up this late in the game?

He picked up the bottle and flung it across the room, where it splintered against the wall in a shower of iridescent slivers. Somehow, finding Jock in a drunken stupor was the crowning blow to his bitch of a day. "What else," he said to the empty room, "can possibly go wrong?"

He looked over his shoulder at his dad, who was snoring softly. What had set him off, anyway? He'd seemed in great spirits earlier, joking, laughing.

"After Mr. Springer left, Jock said he was sick. . . ." Tomas's comment surfaced from the turmoil of Rider's thoughts. Had Springer Martindale said something to upset Jock so much that he'd fallen off the wagon? If so, what could it possibly be?

Rider rose from the bed and scraped his hands through his hair. There wasn't anything he could do for Jock until he woke up, which might be hours. In the meantime he ought to look up Springer Martindale and see what the hell was going on.

Actually, Rider thought grimly as he let himself out of the apartment, it might be best if he stayed out of Jock's way until after the Derby. If he met him face to face, he might be tempted to kill him and put them both out of their misery.

67

Danny opened the door to Leland Creighton's office, the thirty-eight clutched in his hand. The secretary, a woman in her early twenties, looked up with a gasp and tried to shrink into the wall.

"I—I don't have any money," she stuttered, "j-just a few dollars in my purse. I—"

"I want to see Leland Creighton," Danny said, "and I want to see him now."

"Y—yes sir," the girl said, her eyes wide. "I'll just tell him . . . you're here."

"I'll tell him myself." Danny crossed the room and threw open the polished door of Leland's office.

The man he sought was ensconced behind a massive zebrawood desk that dominated the ebony-carpeted room. When the door crashed against the wall, Leland looked up from the papers he was reviewing. "It's all right, Cheryl," he said to the secretary, who stood behind Danny wringing her hands and making little distressed moans. "Go on back to work." To Danny he said, "Come in, Brewster. What can I do for you?"

Danny stepped inside and closed the door. "I thought it was what I could do for you."

Leland's lips stretched over his perfect white teeth, and one heavy eyebrow cocked upward in question. "Maybe you ought to explain that."

"I'm talking about the deal you had Solly Tobias offer me."

"Tobias?" Leland rubbed his index finger over his bottom lip.

"Don't bother denying it. I know you're the one behind all this. Tracy told me about the necklace."

Instead of the denial Danny expected, Leland looked thoughtful. "I was afraid she couldn't keep her mouth shut."

Danny had seen and heard too much to be surprised by this. "Then you admit you've been sleeping with her?"

Leland shrugged. "She's a very persuasive young lady."

Danny wanted to leap across the desk and pistol-whip the smug smile off the senator's face. Only the knowledge that Creighton would see him in jail—or worse—stopped him. Instead of rising to the bait, he said, "I came to make you a counteroffer."

"What do you have in mind?"

"You want me to see to it that Jock's Dream doesn't run first on Saturday. Okay, I'll do it. But I want two million."

"That's a lot of money, Danny."

"You can afford it."

Creighton nodded. "I suppose I can."

"And I want you to promise me that you'll leave Tracy alone."

"As I said, Tracy is very persuasive, but I'll agree to leave her alone if she'll leave me alone."

Danny spread his legs apart and, gripping the butt of the gun in both hands, leveled it at Leland's forehead. "You know, I used to be able to hit a target this close ten out of ten times."

"That's very impressive," Leland said coolly, but his smile had slipped somewhat.

"I hear you're pretty persuasive yourself, Senator. I think you can make her understand that you're through with her if you really want to. And I'd really want to if I were you."

Leland shrugged. "I do believe you hold all the aces this time, Danny. I'll tell her." He frowned. "The silly bitch was starting to get on my nerves anyway."

68

Tracy waited until she saw Danny leave the apartment before she sneaked in to pack some of her things. She didn't know where she would go, but she knew she needed to stay out of his way for a while. It hadn't been very smart of her to throw her affair with Leland in Danny's face, but it had been just a teeny bit upsetting for Danny to walk in on her and Mark that way. Talk about being caught with your pants down!

She still couldn't believe it had happened. How had Danny known where she was, anyway? Shaking her head, Tracy stripped down and got into the shower to wash away the scents of sweat and sex. She'd never seen Danny so mad. And where on earth had he gotten that gun? Tracy shuddered and turned off the water. Guns scared her. *Danny* had scared her.

She wondered how long he would stay mad at her this time. Poor Danny. He needed to loosen up a little and stop taking life so seriously. He should have known Mark didn't mean anything to her. Mark was nothing. She'd seen him at a department store a week before, he'd made a pass, and since he was quite a hunk, she'd thought, Why not? Now that she'd been caught with him, she was wondering *why*.

There were times—like now, when she was trying to juggle three men—that Tracy suspected she had a small problem saying no. But she liked men, and she liked sex, and she did practice safe sex, so why not? It was fun—more fun than shopping, even.

The doorbell rang, interrupting Tracy's thoughts. She hoped it wasn't Danny. She started to toss the towel aside and changed her mind. If it was Danny, it might be to her advantage to look her sexiest. She fluffed her damp hair and wrapped the towel around her, tucking it in above the swell of her breasts, before going to the door. A quick peek through the peephole revealed a thin, balding man.

She opened the door without a thought to modesty or possible mayhem.

The man smiled at her, a sort of greasy quirking of his thin lips that didn't reach the flat brown of his eyes. An uneasy feeling whispered through her.

"Hello, Tracy."

She frowned. "Do I know you?"

"I don't think so. I work for Mr. Creighton."

"Oh," Tracy said. "Is everything okay? Are we still on for tonight?"

"Actually, Mr. Creighton finds it necessary to cancel."

"Oh. Well, maybe tomorrow night, then," she said with a smile and a philosophical shrug.

"I don't think so."

Tracy frowned. "What's the matter?"

The man reached into the breast pocket of his Armani sport coat and drew out a legal-size envelope. He handed it to her. "This is from Mr. Creighton. He said you could consider it severance pay."

"Severance pay?" For a moment she looked puzzled, and then the meaning of what was happening dawned. "He can't do that!" she cried, stamping her bare foot. "He can't just dump me like yesterday's garbage."

"I beg your pardon, Mrs. Brewster, but I believe he just did." The man bestowed another arctic smile on her. "Have a nice life, Tracy, hear?"

Her mouth hanging open, Tracy watched Leland's goon leave. How dare that slimy pervert do this to her after everything he'd expected her to do for him?

"Hey, you son of a bitch, wait a minute!" Tracy yelled.

The man, who had already negotiated the steps, turned and looked up. "Tell your boss I might give it away, but I don't take payment for it."

She tossed the envelope at him, and hundred-dollar bills drifted to the ground. Tracy felt a momentary pang. Then she straightened her shoulders and pushed the regret aside. There were times in a girl's life when it was necessary to make little sacrifices, especially when it meant holding on to her values.

69

Thunder rumbled, and a jagged shaft of light-ning rent the Cimmerian darkness of the sky. The approaching storm was a reflection of Alex's stormy emotions. Nervous, angry, and fortified with three generous glasses of straight Stolichnaya Okhot-nichya, her favorite honey-and-fruit-flavored vodka, Alex paced the library and smoked one More after another, waiting for Colby and Cass.

Cass and Bonnie had called a temporary truce after she'd related the story Colby had told them at lunch. He had driven his wife in to Louisville to have dinner with her parents while the Creightons had their family discussion.

Though she'd tried steadily throughout the day, Alex had been unable to reach Jock to ask him to come and hear her confession. But she'd made up her mind that she wasn't going to let that keep her from telling Cass about Jock or from telling Leland the truth. Cass had a right to know that it wasn't wrong to feel about Leland as he did and that he got his love of horses from both his mother and his father.

Poor Jock. If he'd been uncertain about Rider's paternity all these years, he'd suffered enough at Leland's hand. And now Leland was doing his best to take away the only future Jock had. It was too much to allow, especially since Jock's call had interrupted Colby's horrible tale of what Leland had done to her and Rider.

Alex reached for another cigarette and gave the lighter a flick. The damned thing was empty. She hurled it across the room and dragged open the drawer of an Elizabethan secretary, her thoughts scrambling through her brain as her hands scrambled through the drawer's contents. There was India ink and a half dozen outdated fountain pens . . .

It was terrible to think that one man could manipulate lives so easily, so callously.

. . . paper clips, business cards, pencils . . .

Starting tonight, she intended to put stop to it.

. . . a small booklet of poems Colby had written in the second grade . . .

Alex had closed her eyes to her husband's shady dealings in the past, but she'd found out far too much today to let him continue playing God.

. . . some old coins way at the back, and . . . there it was! Right next to the derringer her grandfather had given her.

She couldn't let Leland hurt those she cared about anymore. Alex reached into the drawer and pulled out the cigarette lighter designed most convincingly like a small silver gun; it lay right beside the real one. She pulled the trigger, and flame shot out the muzzle. Alex put the cigarette to her lips and its tip into the flame, drawing in the smoke greedily. Outside, rain threw itself at the windows. She shivered. Lord, she would be glad when this was all over.

The front door closed, and Alex turned toward the sound. It must be Cass back from taking Bonnie into town or Colby arriving a bit early. Alex went to the library door, her mouth curved in greeting. The smile disintegrated when she saw Leland standing in the doorway, wiping the rain from his face with a monogrammed handkerchief.

He was still handsome, despite the heaviness of his jaw and the streak of white that divided his dark hair down the middle. He equated the streak with distinguished. Alex had another, less charitable, comparison in mind.

"I didn't think you were coming home for dinner."

He refolded the handkerchief. "I had a change of plans."

"I'll have Dulcie tell the cook." She started through the dining room to the kitchen, oblivious to the creamy damask cloth, the hundred-year-old silver, and the etched lead-crystal vase filled with spring flowers cut from the untamed gardens that bordered the woods.

"What are you drinking?"

His voice brought her up short. She turned. "Vodka."

"Straight?" he asked, tucking the handkerchief into his breast pocket.

"Yes, why?"

"Trying to bolster your courage, Alexandra?"

"I don't know what you mean."

"You only drink vodka when you're trying to screw up your nerve."

She looked thoughtful. "Perhaps you're right. Excuse me."

On her way to the kitchen Alex tried to figure out what she would say to Leland. Making up her mind to tell him the truth and doing it were two entirely different things.

When she reentered the dining room, Leland was pouring bourbon into a glass. Strange. Just as he knew she drank vodka when she was upset, she knew that he hardly ever drank, claiming that he preferred to be in control.

"Bad day?" she asked.

"A minor skirmish that was easily resolved." He indicated the table, set with the delicate Spode china her grandmother had bought at Staffordshire. "Are you expecting guests?"

"Colby and Cass."

"What about Bonnie?"

"She's having dinner with her parents."

"Hmm." Leland took a sip of his drink. "Sounds serious."

"What sounds serious?"

"A family dinner. No outsiders."

He was sharp. And he was right: he did know her well. "Bonnie is hardly an outsider."

"No?" Leland smiled. "Well, I hope I haven't ruined your plans."

Alex drew a faltering breath and brushed past him to top off her drink. Her hand shook the slightest bit as she poured the fortifying liquid. "Actually, what I have to tell them concerns you, too."

"Really?" He swept an arm toward the doorway. "Why don't we go into the study, and you can tell me what this is all about." From his patronizing tone, it was obvious that concern was at the bottom of his list, right below genuine interest in anything she might have to say.

She gulped a mouthful of her drink and preceded him to the room she'd just vacated. Leland settled himself in a capacious armchair; Alex elected to stand near the fireplace. "Colby was here today."

"How was she? I understand from Pete that she's been pretty upset over Rider McCall again."

How could he? Alex wondered in genuine amazement. How could he sit there and act as if he'd had nothing to do with ruining their daughter's life? The utter gall of his actions banished Alex's lingering doubts and put extra starch in her spine. "Actually, she's doing very well, considering what Rider told her last night."

On the surface, Leland looked as collected as ever. But Alex was familiar with the tic in his left eye, a sign that he wasn't as composed as he appeared. "Told her? She's seen him?"

"Yes." Alex fought to keep the smugness from her voice. "Last night, as a matter of fact. They talked at some length."

Leland rose and went to the decanter of brandy sitting on a nearby table and added a splash to his bourbon, unaware, or uncaring, that he was mixing his spirits. When he turned, his composure was in hand. He nailed her with a hard look. "Did the son of a bitch tell her why he deserted her?"

"As a matter of fact, he did. He also said you attempted to pay him off."

Leland laughed. "And she believed him?"

Lord, he was a consummate actor. No wonder he'd fooled so many people for so many years. The shame was that she hadn't done anything to stop him before now. Anger surged through her. Anger at him. At herself. Anger for all the wasted, lonely years. "Yes. She believed him."

"After everything he's put her through, I'd have thought Colby would be smarter than that."

Alex's glass thudded onto the mantel. "Stop it!" she cried. "Just stop it!"

"Stop what?"

"Stop the acting, dammit! It's over. It's all over. Rider told Colby the truth."

"The truth? His version of the truth, you mean?"

Alex tossed in her trump card. "He showed her the check."

"What check?"

"The check you gave him eleven years ago. He didn't cash it."

Leland paled.

"What's the matter? Did the infallible Leland Creighton let something slip by him?" Alex laughed. "You did, didn't you? Rider never cashed the check, and you forgot about it."

His blue eyes darkened with anger and something else, something she couldn't define. "You're drunk."

"No. Not drunk. Drinking." She scooped up her glass, pretended to toast him, and took another swallow of her vodka. "You know, you really ought to be strung up for hurting Colby and blackmailing Rider the way you did, not to mention what you've done to him and Jock this week."

"What have I done this week that's upset you so much?"

"I overheard your phone conversation with Springer, so I asked him what was going on. He told me about the note."

A haze of surprise clouded the confidence in Leland's eyes.

"You're a sorry excuse for a human being, Leland Creighton," Alex said softly, calling him by his first name for the first time in years. "You ought to be strung up from the nearest tree."

Leland dropped his nonchalance and let his true feelings surface. "Jackson McCall deserves everything I ever did to him."

Alex's mind raced. Dear God, what else had Leland done to Jock that no one knew about? "Why? Because you think I slept with him?"

Leland tossed back the remainder of his drink. "I know you did, but I've never been able to prove it."

"Well, what sort of proof do you need?" Alex quipped brazenly. "Dates? I'm sorry, but there was only one. May third, 1957."

70

Colby pulled into the driveway at Windwood and shut off the engine. She opened the door and, raising her umbrella, made a wild dash for the front door. Leaving the umbrella to drip on the wide porch, she stepped inside and closed the door behind her. Thunder rolled across the heavens, shaking the old house to its foundation.

She was about to call to her mother to let her know she'd arrived when she heard the sound of angry voices coming from the library.

"You admit it, then?" she heard her father say.

"Yes," Alex cried, "I admit it."

Colby froze. What was her mother admitting? What was going on?

"You slut."

You slut. The coldness of the two words rang through her mind. She could actually see the chilling hatred in her father's eyes, a curious sense of déjà vu that left her feeling sick and afraid.

"Spare me, please," her mother said. "You're hardly one to be calling me names."

"I don't owe you any apologies for anything I've done," Leland yelled.

"No? Well, I don't owe you a damned thing, either. I've given you thirty-six years, and that's more than enough."

Colby had never heard such finality in her mother's voice.

"What are you talking about, Alex? Divorce? What do you want to do? Start a life with that drunk?"

Drunk? Evidently Colby had missed some vital piece of information. Weak-kneed, she made her way down the hallway. Her head reeled with fragmented images and bit of conversation from the past, from the dream that wouldn't leave her alone. . . .

"Jock McCall has nothing to do with my decision," she heard her mother shout. "I can't go on living the way I have been. I don't want to live that way anymore."

Colby's head whirled in disbelief. Jock McCall and her mother?

"I can make things very hard for you and your father . . . very hard. . . ." Colby leaned against the wall in the hallway and clutched her head. Where had that come from? The words were as clear as if Leland had actually spoken them, but he hadn't. At least not just then. . . .

"I'll never let you divorce me." Like her mother's voice, her father's held a note of finality. "I'll see you dead first."

"Colby and I are getting married."

"Not as long as I'm alive."

"Well, maybe that can be arranged, too."

Echoes of Rider and her father arguing bounced off the fragile walls of her mind. Colby shook her head. She didn't want to remember. Not now. Please, God, not now.

She heard her mother cry out. Shaking off the memories, she took one hesitant step and then another until she stood near the open doorway of the library. Her father held her mother's upper arm. Alex looked tired but determined. Leland's face was contorted with fury.

"Dead? Do you think I care?" her mother said, jerking her arm free. "Anything is preferable to living with you. I'm tired of living a lie, tired of lying to my son."

"Cass?" Colby saw her father's hamlike hands close over her mother's slender shoulders. "What does Cass have to do with any of this?"

"Plenty."

Leland's fingers bit in. Colby cringed. Alex gave another small cry of pain, but she didn't back down.

"Didn't you ever wonder why the son you coveted was nothing at all like you?"

Leland grew still. The tic in his eye jumped. "What are you saying, damn you?" He shook Alex so hard that her hair came free of its ribbon and flew around her face.

Colby covered her mouth with one hand and grabbed the door frame with the other. She'd lived through all this before, somehow, but it had been Rider her father argued with, not her mother.

"You know what I'm saying." Triumph tinged her

mother's voice. "Cass is Jock McCall's son. Not yours."

Her father's face lost its ruddy color. "You're lying." Even as he said the words, Colby could see he didn't believe them.

"No."

Her father's cry of rage emanated from the depths of his soul. His fingers closed around her mother's throat. Horrified, Colby stood rooted to the polished floor, watching Alex claw at his wrists. Colby couldn't move, couldn't speak. All she could do was stand there, helpless to stop the door to the past that burst wide open, transporting her back to the day Leland had found her with Rider. . . .

Just as she remembered in the dream, they were making love. Everything was wonderful, perfect. She could almost feel the caress of the breeze. They were getting dressed, and Rider was kissing her, kissing her neck. It tickled, and she was laughing, and then everything went dark, and Colby began to tremble.

"What in the sweet hell do you think you're doing?"

She clutched her head. She didn't want to remember. She wanted to wake up, but this time there was no stopping the rush of memories she'd fought so hard to suppress.

Rider had stepped between her and her father. Colby was afraid, but she was her mother's daughter. She'd lifted her head. *"Nothing, now. We're done."*

"You slut!"

She moaned and shook her head. Who was her father talking to? Her or her mother? It was all so fuzzy, so . . .

A spear of lightning and a bolt of thunder cracked, jolting Colby from the spell of the past. She could see her parents across the room. Her father was still choking her mother, who looked limp, lifeless. Dear God! He was killing her, if he hadn't already.

"Mama!" she screamed.

Leland turned toward her, a look of surprise on his face. Colby launched herself at him with a maniacal shriek, her fingers curved into talons aimed for his eyes. He released Alex just in time to deflect the blow, and Colby's nails gouged four ragged lines in his cheek instead.

He swung his hand and caught her squarely across the face. Colby staggered back, and for a moment they stood there, just staring at each other, while the last veil of darkness lifted inch by agonizing inch.

Colby remembered hearing the sound of Rider's truck fade away into the distance and how she'd made an effort to rouse herself. She had lifted leaden eyelids and seen her father standing over her, a glazed look in his eyes, as if someone had put him under a spell. Afraid of the strangeness, she had tried to push herself to a sitting position. The grogginess that clung to her had made her clumsy.

"Stay where you are," he said sharply, the look in his eyes shifting to anger.

She did.

"That's better." He began to unbuckle his belt, and Colby's mouth grew as dry as Sahara sand. "You have to learn to obey me, Colby, and everything will be . . . just . . . fine." His voice was low, soothing, almost mesmerizing, like the downward glide of his zipper.

"Daddy—"

"I love you, Colby. My sweet little princess. I've always loved you. I've been waiting for you to grow up, and you have." His hand fumbled inside his clothing. "You're so beautiful," he said, exposing himself. "More beautiful than your cheating bitch of a mother. . . ."

Colby had screamed. And screamed. Just as she was screaming now. . . .

71

Cass was almost to the porch when he heard
Colby scream, a shrill, keening sound that was
clearly audible over the din of the rain. Taking the
shallow steps two at a time, he flung open the door
and raced down the polished plank floors, his wet
boots leaving puddles behind him.

By the time he reached the study door, Colby's
cries had mutated to rasping sobs. He stopped
cold, trying to make sense of what he saw. His
mother was lying on the floor. Colby, kicking and
screaming like a wild person, was attacking his father, who was trying to keep her at arm's length.

Leland looked up and saw him. "Help me, for
God's sake!"

The words freed Cass from the shock binding
him. He ran across the room and grabbed Colby
from behind, pinning her arms to her sides and
pulling her back against him. She fought him with
all her strength, harsh sobs clawing their way up her
throat as she tried to get at their father.

"Got her?" Leland asked, wiping his bleeding
face on the sleeve of his jacket. Cass nodded. "Hold

her tight." Leland opened a drawer and took out a small vial and a disposable syringe.

"Do you think that's necessary?" Cass asked, watching Leland break the seal and draw out the clear liquid.

Colby increased her struggles. "No!" she screamed. "No, Cass, no! He hurt us! He hurt all of us!"

"What do you think?" Leland said, tapping out the air bubbles and squirting a bit of the drug into the air.

Cass's heart broke. Colby was violent, incoherent. He nodded and held her still while Leland wrapped a piece of rubber around her upper arm and injected the tranquilizer into a pale blue vein with all the skill of a trained professional.

Colby glared at him, her eyes an abyss of hatred.

Leland didn't appear to notice. "There," he soothed. "You'll feel better in a minute."

She stopped struggling almost immediately, more as if she realized the futility of it than because she was feeling the effects of the drug. Cass loosened his grip; he had to be hurting her. "What's the matter with Mom?"

Leland went to Alex and lifted her to the sofa. "Colby . . ." he said, giving Cass a vague look.

"Is she all right?"

Leland smoothed Alex's hair away from her face. "She'll be fine."

Somewhat relieved that the situation was under control, Cass asked, "What the shit happened here?"

"Later," Leland said, going to the desk.

"Tell me now," Cass said, easing Colby's limp body into a wingback chair. When he turned he saw Leland filling another syringe. "What are you doing?"

Leland's bland gaze shifted from Cass to Alex. "She'll need this," he said, almost as if he were thinking aloud. "She'll be upset when she comes around."

"Cass . . ." Colby's voice sounded as if it were coming from the bottom of a very deep well. She reached out, and he took her cold hand in his. "Mama," she whispered. "Help Mama."

"Dad's helping her," Cass said, trying to soothe her fears. He watched the light in her eyes dim, flicker, and fade as the tranquilizer took effect. But before her eyelashes drifted down over her dull blue eyes, Cass could have sworn he saw condemnation there.

72

"Bonnie, honey, it's for you," Cybill said, holding out the phone to her daughter.

Bonnie looked up from the game of spades she was playing with Springer, who was more interested in the ten o'clock news.

"It's Cass. He sounds pretty upset."

Frowning, Bonnie laid down her cards and went to the phone. "Cass? What's the matter?"

"Everything."

"What?" For a moment Bonnie didn't hear anything but silence. When Cass spoke, his voice was thick with emotion.

"It's Colby. She's gone off the deep end again. Don't say anything to your parents until we can get our story straight, but she attacked Mom and made her hit her head or something. Then she started on Dad."

"Good Lord, Cass, what set her off?"

"I can't tell you over the phone, but I need you, baby. I need you with me."

"Where are you?"

"At the hospital. They're both still out, and Pete

Whitten thought it would be a good idea if they were both admitted, at least for day or two."

"I'll be there as soon as I can."

"What's the matter?" Cybill asked as Bonnie hung up the phone.

"There's been an accident at Cass's parents. I don't know any details."

"Oh, no!"

"Can I borrow your car?"

"Of course you can, sugar. Honey," Cybill called to Springer, "Bonnie needs to use the car."

"What's wrong?"

"An accident at Windwood. Cass needs me."

"Sure. Take the car." Springer shook his head. Bonnie couldn't help noticing he had a decidedly worried look. "Lots of bad things happening tonight. Must be a full moon or something."

"Why do you say that?"

"I just heard they found Luis Mendoza in an alley next to some bar."

"Mendoza? Isn't he Jock McCall's rider?"

Springer nodded and rubbed his mustache thoughtfully.

"What happened?" Cybill asked.

There was an almost frantic look in his eyes. "It looks like a mugging. His Rolex and his wallet were missing. He has a couple of busted ribs and a broken arm."

"Well, thank God it wasn't any worse. I wonder who Jock will put on the horse now?"

Springer shrugged. "I don't know. Not that it makes a whole helluva lot of difference."

73

Feeling strangely subdued, Leland stared out
the hospital window at the storm-swept night. It
had been a rough one, and it wasn't over yet. The
police would want to know what had happened at
Windwood. It was up to him to create a convincing
story, and imperative that he drill it into everyone's
head. One thing was certain. He couldn't tell them
what had really happened.

Alex, the cold, snotty bitch, had betrayed him. It
wasn't hard to believe, and her confession only cor-
roborated what he'd always known. What was hard
to believe was that she'd kept her secret so well,
and so long. He didn't know why the knowledge that
she'd slept with Jock McCall was such a thorn in his
side. Maybe it was all tied up with Vicky and the belief that Jock had screwed Alex as a way to get back
at him. Leland's jaw tightened. No one messed with
Leland Creighton. No one.

Knowing Cass was McCall's bastard cleared up a
lot of things that had bothered Leland through the
years—like why Cass had no discernible Creighton
drive. Jackson McCall had become Leland's hobby.

He knew more about the man than anyone could imagine. He should have realized how much like Alex's old lover Cass was. For his part, Cass could die a Creighton. Leland couldn't let his family suffer for Alex's sins, and he had no intention of letting anything ugly mar the Creighton name.

Ugly. The whole thing with Alex was ugly. Leland rubbed his bottom lip. He should have kept his cool, shouldn't have let her goad him the way she had. But that haze had come over him, that surreal feeling of being outside himself and watching someone else commit the acts he later realized he had committed himself. It hadn't happened often— a man in his position couldn't permit himself to lose control—but every time it had, he'd done something he was certain he never would have done otherwise.

Vicky was the first, a regrettable incident that had haunted him for more than thirty years. Then there was the time with Alex, the last time they'd slept together, when she'd refused to let him into her bed. But he could hardly regret that, when Colby had been the result. And now this. . . .

"Bonnie's on her way."

Leland turned toward the sound of Cass's voice. Funny that he'd never, not once in thirty-three years, noticed how much Cass looked like Jock McCall. But the resemblance was there, in the curve of his jaw and the shape of his eyes.

"Good."

"Dammit, Dad, what happened back there, anyway?" Cass said, crossing his arms and leaning against the wall.

Leland looked away, as if the telling were more than he could bear. He sighed. "Hell, I hate to be the one to break the news to you, but under the circumstances, I don't have any choice."

"You don't have any choice but to tell me what?"

"Colby overheard your mother telling me that Colby isn't my child."

"What!"

"I know, I know." Leland looked at the floor. "I . . . couldn't believe it myself. I never suspected."

"Who?"

Leland lifted innocent eyes to Cass's. "I don't know. Colby went totally beserk before Alex could tell me. She . . . attacked your mother. There's just no other word for it. I was trying to pull her off Alex when your mother lost her footing and hit her head on the hearth." Leland touched the scrapes on his face. "Thank God you came when you did."

Disbelief molded Cass's features. "Mom wanted me and Colby to come to dinner because she had something to tell us, but I never dreamed it would be anything like this."

Cass missed the flicker of surprise that crossed Leland's face. Alex had set things up perfectly. "I know. No wonder Colby took it so hard."

"Do you think she's going to be okay?"

"I don't know. I guess we'll have to wait and see what Pete thinks."

Cass swore. "I'm going downstairs to wait for Bonnie."

Leland nodded and watched as Cass disappeared around a corner. Cass had bought it. He'd bought every single lie. Now all that remained was to be sure he covered himself.

As Leland was congratulating himself, Peter Whitten appeared. Good. Time to put the plan in motion. "How are things?" he asked the psychiatrist.

Pete rubbed his balding head. "Fine for now. The injections you gave them will make them both sleep for a while."

"Good."

"What the hell happened?" Pete asked, his gaze glued to the scratches on Leland's cheek. "You didn't—"

"No." Leland interrupted the question he knew was coming. "It was a family squabble."

"Thank God."

"I want you to let Alex wake up, but keep Colby sedated, Pete."

"For God's sake, why?"

"Because I don't want her talking to anyone until I speak to Alex."

Pete couldn't hide his agitation. "I don't like this, Leland. I don't like it one little bit. And I'm telling you, I'm not going to put my reputation on the line for you."

"Why not? I did for you."

Pete grew a little pale, but rallied. "Whatever I owed you, I repaid the last time something like this happened. I don't intend to get mixed up in anything like I was before."

"I'm glad you remember that I helped you out of

a very sticky situation. And I won't ask for your long-term help unless it's absolutely necessary," Leland said in his most conciliatory tone. "But for the time being, I don't want Colby talking to anyone, especially her mother. You know McCall is back?" Pete nodded. "Well, he's making a nuisance of himself, and if we can just keep Colby out of his way until after the Derby, he'll be gone again. Believe me, I hate doing this to Colby as much as you do. But it's for her own good."

Pete nodded, but he was less than happy. "All right. I'll do that much for you."

"Thanks, Pete. You won't be sorry."

"I hope you're right." He didn't sound convinced, and he wanted to get away. "Look, I have another patient to see to. I'll talk to you later."

"Sure," Leland said with a benign smile. He'd told Whitten the truth. He felt a terrible sadness over what he was doing to Colby, but he couldn't bear to think of her turning on him the way she had. Hadn't he loved her? Worshiped her, even? Except for that one mistake so long ago, hadn't he given her all the best life had to offer?

A surge of self-righteous indignation pushed aside his sorrow. She shouldn't have talked back to him that day; she shouldn't have defied him the way she had, and she damn well shouldn't have let Rider McCall get in her pants. Leland straightened his shoulders. A father couldn't be blamed for setting his daughter straight, for wanting to be in control of the situation. If Colby weren't so headstrong, if she had obeyed him, it never would have happened.

Feeling better after rationalizing his actions, Leland turned his thoughts to the story he would tell the police. An intruder had overpowered Alex. Colby walked in on them, and he and Cass had arrived from town together and heard her screaming. The burglar had fled through the French doors as they entered the library. Leland lifted his hand to the still stinging scrapes adorning his cheek. Wild with fear for Alex, Colby had accidentally scratched him trying to get to her mother's side. If the cops wanted to know what the man looked like, Pete could tell them Colby wasn't able to give a statement.

It was simple. It should work, Leland thought with satisfaction. There had been burglaries in the area recently. The servants would corroborate the story if necessary; he had some minor indiscretion on each and every one of them. Cass would ultimately go along with it because he knew it was expected of him and he wouldn't want Colby and his mother to be the objects of any speculative publicity. Colby wouldn't be a problem. Pete could take care of her, indefinitely. And, despite her bravado earlier, Alex could be handled.

Leland had no qualms about lying to the police. Deceit was an integral part of his life. Lying—to himself and others—had made him the man he was.

74

Jock woke with a raging headache, a gut-deep guilt, and the sobering realization that he'd blown it. Jesus, what had possessed him to start drinking like that? Springer's news should have been a deterrent to drinking, not a signal to belly up to the bar. They'd brought the colt too far to screw up now.

Knowing that he had a rough day ahead, he headed for the shower. Showered, shaved, and with the horrible taste in his mouth brushed and gargled away, Jock downed three ibuprofen tablets and decided that he felt halfway like facing the day and whatever it had to bring, including Rider's wrath. Jock hated to think what Rider would have to say, but there was no delaying the confrontation.

Fortunately Jock was granted a brief reprieve. Rider was at the track with a horse when he reached the barn.

"Rider, he is not happy with you." Tomas gave a sad shake of his head.

"I'm not very happy with myself," Jock said, rolling a clean leg wrap.

"He's also pretty damn worried about Luis."

"What's wrong with Luis?" Jock asked sharply.

"You didn't hear?" Tomas asked. "They found him in a alley someplace. Busted ribs, broke arm. No wallet."

Jock tossed the wrap into a plastic clothes basket. "Shit!"

"That's what Rider says. 'Shit,' he says, 'what the fuck else can happen?' Then I told him what I heard on the news this morning about Miz Creighton, and he went loco, man. He was driving me crazy. I told him to take Big Guy to the track and get outa my face," Tomas rambled.

"Ms. Creighton?" Jock asked with a sinking heart. "Which Ms. Creighton?"

"Both," Tomas said with a nod. "Both of them are in the hospital. Somebody broke into their house and beat them up or somethin'."

Jock swore. He had a vague recollection of telephoning Alex the day before and telling her what he thought of her illustrious husband. He scraped a hand down his face and paced the length of a stall and back. Shit. She probably thought he was a real winner, calling her all drunked up like that. Now this. Beaten up by a burglar. Alex deserved better.

"Is she okay?" he asked Tomas.

The young groom shrugged and spit a stream of tobacco juice. "I don't know. The news lady didn't say."

Jock had to find out. "Look, Tomas, Rider is gonna be pissed off because I've skipped out on him again today, but I need to go to the hospital to see Mrs. Creighton."

"He won't be mad. He said he hoped he didn't have to see you today, or he'd knock shit outa you."

"Yeah, well, I don't blame him. Tell him I'm sober and I'm sorry and that I'll be here this afternoon at feed time."

"Okay."

"And tell him I swear on his mother's memory that it won't happen again."

75

Jock's Dream whickered softly as Rider approached his stall. Thank God the colt was healthy and fit. With everything in the world going to hell in a hand basket, he supposed he ought to be thankful for that.

He was upset over Jock and Luis and worried sick about Colby, but he couldn't go to the hospital to see about her or Luis until Jock showed up. *If* Jock showed up.

Top priority was winning the Derby tomorrow. He could worry about his personal problems after that.

So how was he going to win the Derby with his jockey in the hospital and his partner off on a drunk so they couldn't even discuss options?

"I'll do what I damn well please," Rider said aloud.

"You say somethin', Rider?" Tomas asked.

"Just talking to myself, Tomas."

"Loco," Tomas mumbled. "Oh, I forgot to tell you. Mister Jock came by. He said to tell you"—Thomas screwed up his face thoughtfully—"he's sober, he's sorry, and he swears by your mother's memory that it won't happen again."

"Yeah, sure. Where the hell is he now?"

"He went to the hospital to see Miz Alex, I think."

"Alex? Alexandra Creighton?"

"Yeah."

"Why would he go see Alex Creighton?"

Tomas shrugged and spit. "I don't know. He didn't say. But he left here runnin'."

Running? To see Alex Creighton? It didn't make sense. Rider knew Jock had worked for Alex before he was born, and he and Alex were polite when they did happen to run into each other, but they certainly hadn't been close during the time he'd run around with Cass and Colby. Why, Rider wondered, would Jock be going to see a Creighton when he'd been warned to stay away from them?

Something screwy was going on. First Springer had come by the barn and said something to cause Jock to hit the bottle. Rider had tried unsuccessfully to track down Springer Martindale all day the day before to find out what had happened.

Then, he'd been watching a TV movie when he

got the call about Luis. Now Jock had run off to see a woman he'd never given the time of day. Something weird was going on, and every time Rider thought nothing else could happen, it did.

"Hey, Rider!"

Rider turned and saw Danny walking down the shed row. His friend looked tired, strained. The way Rider felt.

"I was just getting ready to give you a call, Danny."

"Really? What's up?"

"I guess you heard about Mendoza."

"Yeah. Rotten luck."

"Or good, depending how you look at it. He could have been killed."

"You're right," Danny said with a nod. "He sure as hell could have."

"I'm in a bind, Danny. I want you to ride the colt tomorrow."

Danny offered him a world-weary smile. "That's why I came over. I was going to offer."

Rider smiled back. "You know you were my first choice."

"Yeah."

"I think we got a shot. A good shot."

"So do a lot of other people."

"So? What do you say?"

"Why not?" Danny said with a shrug and a small smile. "I got nothing better to do on a Saturday afternoon."

76

Jock pushed open the door to Alex's room.
She was awake, staring at the opposite wall. The
covers were pulled up to her chin, and an un-
touched breakfast tray sat near the bed. She turned
toward the sound of the opening door, and when
she saw him, her eyes filled with tears.

Alex held out her hand, and Jock went to her, taking it in both of his. The roughness of her hands
had always been a source of amazement to him.
They were so unlike the pampered, powdered rest
of her. His eyes searched her face for signs that she
was all right.

"I heard about the break-in when I got to the
track. Are you okay?"

Her eyes drifted shut, and she nodded, squeezing his hand tightly and carrying it to her cheek.

"Don't you think you ought to eat something?"

"I can't." The words were a raspy whisper.

"Don't tell me you're catching cold on top of everything else," he teased.

"No. Not a cold." Using her free hand to pull down
the blankets, she arched her neck back.

Jock swore. Blue-black bruises circled her throat.

"It hurts to even . . . drink." She tried to smile. "It hurts to . . . breathe."

"Who was it, Alex? Do you have any idea who the son of a bitch was who did this to you?"

She nodded. "It wasn't . . . a burglar, Jock. It was Leland."

"What!"

"I was waiting for Cass and Colby. I had . . . something to . . . tell them. I tried to call you . . . to tell you to come, too." She stopped and swallowed painfully.

"Don't talk. It doesn't matter."

"Yes, it does." Her thumb traced small concentric circles on the back of his hand. "Leland came home. I wasn't expecting him. We argued . . . about you."

"Me? Why?"

"He always . . . suspected that we slept together, but . . . he was never . . . sure," she croaked.

"And you decided to come clean thirty years after the fact?" Jock smiled briefly. "Admirable, Alex, but hardly necessary."

"I had to tell him. When I found out . . . that he used the note with Springer to hurt you, I made up my mind to put an end to the lies and the deceit . . . even my marriage."

"What lies?" Jock asked.

"Cass." Moisture gathered in her eyes again as she looked up at him.

"What about Cass?"

"Cass isn't Leland's son, Jock. He's . . . yours."

Jock was thankful there was a chair beside the bed. His knees gave way, and he sank onto the vinyl softness. "Are you sure?"

"Yes. Leland hadn't touched me in weeks. I guess he was too busy pursuing"—she started to say "Vicky" and thought better of it—"someone else. When I realized I'd missed a period, I made sure I . . . slept with him once, just so he wouldn't be . . . suspicious. It was the last time I let him touch me, willingly."

Jock stared across the room, trying to absorb what she was telling him. "Why didn't you tell me?" he asked at last.

"What would you have done? You made it very clear that you loved Vicky, and I . . . I wasn't brave enough to face the censure a divorce would bring."

Jock stood and paced the small room. "I just can't believe it."

"It's true. Cass is as much your son as Rider is. No. Don't say it. You called Rider Leland's bastard yesterday, but he isn't. I can promise you that."

"How can you be so sure? I never have been."

"I know because he's the spitting image of the man I fell in love with. The only man I've ever loved. If you hadn't been so busy looking for signs of Leland Creighton in him, you could have seen that he's just like you."

Jock could only stare at her. Deep down he'd known the truth for a long time, but he hadn't been able to admit it to himself. Admitting the truth would mean that he had to live with the knowledge that he'd punished Rider for no reason. Rider was his. And so was Cass. Jesus, how could he not have known? How could he ever make it up to her? "Alex, I—"

"Don't," she said with a wave of her hand. "You don't have to apologize for not . . . loving me. It isn't an emotion you can dictate. Vicky may have had you for twenty years, but I had one weekend that no one can take away from me." She sniffed and tried to smile. "I have no regrets, Jock. And you shouldn't, either. You have two sons, wonderful sons, instead of one."

He swallowed and passed his hand over his face. "I don't know what to say."

"You don't have to say anything."

"And you told Leland about Cass, and he—"

"Tried to kill me."

"Jesus!"

"I've known for a long time he was capable of violence."

"He's tried this before?"

"Not this, no." Alex brushed at a tear that slipped down her cheek. "After Cass was born, I wouldn't let him touch me. And one night, he . . . forced me."

"It was the last time I let him touch me, willingly." The meaning of the words she'd spoken moments before exploded in his mind.

"Forced you?" Jock echoed, disbelief whirling through his mind. "Do you mean he—raped you?"

Alex nodded. "When he was . . . finished, I told him that if he so much as stepped foot in my room, I would go to the police and the press and tell them exactly what a monster he was."

Monster didn't begin to describe Leland Creighton. Not only had he raped Vicky, he'd raped his own wife. No wonder Alex hardly spoke of him. Still, it was hard to believe that she and her husband hadn't made love in so many years.

"And he believed you?"

"Let's just say that . . . sex between us was never good enough that he'd want to risk everything he'd worked for to have it." Alex's mouth twisted into a bitter curve. "One good thing came out of it, though."

"What?" Jock asked, unable to imagine any good coming from that kind of violence.

"Colby."

"Colby?"

"There's more," Alex said, pushing herself into a sitting position. "A lot more."

Jock scrubbed at his face with his hands. "Shit, what else can there be?"

"About Colby—"

"She's here," he said. "Down the hall."

"I know."

"They said she saw the burglar hurting you and went at him. . . ." Jock's voice trailed away as he meshed that information with what Alex had just told him. "But if it wasn't a burglar, it must have been Leland she went for."

Alex nodded. "The last thing I heard before I lost consciousness was Colby screaming." All the talking had strained her bruised vocal cords, and her voice was a whisper, but Alex was determined to tell everything. "I don't know if she heard about Cass or not. I think seeing Leland choking me must have been what made her go to pieces again."

"Again? What do you mean, again?"

"Colby was in Forest Glade for a year, Jock."

"Forest Glade? Isn't that a psychiatric hospital?"

"Yes."

"Why?"

"If you believe Leland, which I guess I did until yesterday when Colby told me the truth, it was because Rider left her."

"Rider left her?" Jock held up a hand. "Whoa. Wait. What do you mean Rider left her? How could he leave her? She was in Chicago."

"They were seeing each other the summer Vicky died. I suspected she was interested in him because she was flying home so often, but I didn't really know until she came up pregnant at Forest Glade."

"Colby was pregnant? By Rider?" Jock needed a drink. Longed for one. Yesterday's problems were nothing compared to the Pandora's box he'd opened by coming to see Alex.

"Sit down, Jock, and I'll start at the beginning."

She told him Leland's version of what had happened the day he'd found Colby and Rider. Then she told him Rider's version. She omitted nothing. She told him about Colby's mental condition, about the abortion and how they'd all hated Rider. She told him about Colby's marriage to Kent, about her drinking and pills and how long it had taken her to put her life back together.

Alex explained that Leland had given Rider a

choice: he could leave, or be accused of rape and watch Leland ruin his father's business. When she finished, Jock was as white as the sheets she lay on.

"That's why Rider left so suddenly and didn't come back until now," Jock said with new insight.

"Leland can be pretty convincing, and Rider was hardly more than a kid. He loved you, Jock. He left for you and Colby."

Jock was bombarded with memories of all the hurtful things he'd said and done to Rider through the years. Guilt weighed him down. Jesus, what a mess he'd made of things.

"How could he possibly love me after the way I treated him?"

"I told you, love can't be dictated. You feel it or you don't. And you can't stop it just because life would be simpler without it."

Jock thought of Vicky. He'd tried to stop loving her, but he couldn't. At the time, his life would have been easier if he'd been able to turn that love off—or transfer it to the woman lying in the hospital bed beside him.

"You're right, Alex, it would be simpler that way. It may not mean anything after all this time, but I want you to know that if it hadn't been for Vicky, it would have been very easy to fall in love with you."

77

"Men!" There was a hint of desperation in Tracy's eyes as she outlined her lips with a rust-colored pencil. Just yesterday her life had been wonderful. She had been all set to spend some time with Leland when Danny had found her with Mark—what had she ever seen in *him* besides what he carried between his legs?—and everything had gone to shit.

After Leland's hired hand had picked up the money and left, she'd phoned Creighton at his office and, via his twit of a secretary, threatened him with full exposure if he didn't take her call. When she'd finally gotten him on the phone, she learned that Danny, the cocky little bastard, had forced his way into the office with a gun and demanded that Leland leave her alone, which, she decided, pursing her full lips, was sort of sweet, really.

Her husband might not be as big as Mark, but he had a lot more balls than that steroid-filled wimp and a lot more class than Leland Hotshot Creighton. *That* sorry slimebag had told her over the phone that even if Danny hadn't confronted him, he was getting sick of her tantrums and her greed. Leland was a fine one to talk about tantrums. Her mouth had been swollen for days after he'd slapped her that time.

Tracy decided it was time to be honest with herself. Even though she liked the expensive presents Leland bought her, she was sick of his little games. In spite of her claim to Danny, Leland had a hard time—Tracy smiled at her reflection in the mirror and brushed blush onto her cheeks—keeping it up unless she took off her makeup and dressed like a little girl, his little "princess."

He liked for her to sit on his lap and say "Yes, sir" to all his naughty suggestions. He liked to spank her, too—which might be okay for Breathless Mahoney but not for Tracy Brewster, who liked her sex frequent but straight, thank you very much. She sighed and rubbed the slightest bit of rouge on her nipples. Things were really screwed up, but thank goodness that creep was out of her life.

The sound of Danny's key turning in the lock brought a rush of panic. Tracy smeared some clear gel on her lips to make them shiny and shook her head to give the already jumbled curls a tousled look—the bed head, as Danny teasingly called it. She took a deep breath and spritzed some Opium over her body. She had one chance to turn this around, and it had to be good.

78

After Jock left, Alex called for a nurse and asked about Colby. Assured that she was fine, Alex slept. Deeply. She awoke to a feeling she hadn't experienced in years: peace. Confession was, indeed, good for the soul. She was reveling in the freedom she felt and savoring some apple juice when the door opened and Leland stepped into the room. He was carrying a sheaf of long-stemmed roses and wearing a smile.

Whatever bravado Alex had felt the night before vanished with the knowledge that this man, who was smiling like some benign philanthropist, had tried to kill her. Panic scurried through her, like rats through an empty building, seeking the dark corners of her psyche and hiding there in shivering apprehension.

He must have seen the fear in her eyes, because his smile made a subtle shift from joviality to sly consideration.

"Hello, Alex. How are you feeling?"

Alex fought the terror strangling her as surely as Leland's hands had the night before. Hundreds of confrontations had taught her that her husband had no respect for weakness in any form. If she didn't keep fighting, he would roll over her like some giant bulldozer crushing everything in its wake. She was the only thing standing between Leland and her children. She couldn't let them down now.

Before she could gather the courage to answer, a nurse with a stethoscope dangling from her neck came in.

"I see you have company," she said with a coy smile at Leland. "How are you, Senator?"

"Just fine, Ms. Collins," he said, reading the name from her badge.

"Oh, what lovely flowers," the woman crooned. "Aren't they gorgeous, Mrs. Creighton?"

Realizing that Leland could hardly try to harm her in the hospital, Alex found her voice and a trace of her spunk. "Roses have never been a favorite of mine." She let her eyes find Leland's. "They are beautiful, but all that beauty hides thorns," she said, her voice stronger but still raspy.

"Oh, but the florist dethorns them."

"I know, but sometimes they miss one, and just when you least expect it, it draws blood."

The nurse looked as if she thought Alex was being a bit paranoid, but Leland understood her perfectly. Nurse Collins took Alex's vital signs and left her alone with the man she'd promised to stay with until death parted them. It was beginning to look as if that was the only way they ever would be separated.

"What are you doing here?" Alex asked once the door had closed behind the R.N. "I'm sure you didn't come to inquire about my health."

"On the contrary, Alexandra, I'm sorrier than I can possibly say about that unfortunate incident last evening. I don't know what got into me."

"It's called evil, and you aren't wooing your constituents now, Senator, so you can stop dispensing all the shit." Alex reached for her cigarettes.

"Alex, Alex," Leland chided, swooping them up before she could. "How many times have I told you swearing is unladylike. I really must convince you to stop."

"You almost 'convinced' me last night."

"Yes, well, as I said, that was truly regrettable. I came to talk to you about it."

"What do you want,? My forgiveness?"

"No. I want your cooperation."

"My cooperation?"

"Yes. My son and I have already given the police our statements, and I wanted to make certain you understood what you're supposed to tell them."

Alex didn't miss the emphasis Leland place on the word *son*. He was saying that he had chosen not to tell Cass about Jock. And no wonder. The Creightons would come off looking less than perfect if the world found out their illustrious son had been cuckolded by a lowly horse trainer.

Well, she had no qualms about knocking her husband off his pedestal; she would enjoy it. She would see him in hell before she let him get by with trying to kill her. Cass would be told the truth, and then the lofty senator would see how long Cass lied for him. She wondered what kind of story Leland had told Cass that fooled him.

"I know what to tell the police, Leland. I'm telling them the truth. Where are they, anyway?"

"I had Pete see to it that they were detained."

Alex couldn't suppress the flicker of unease that spread through her. She knew that his contacts were far-reaching and powerful, but it was a shock when she confronted them herself. "Until you could get to me and we could get our stories straight, you mean?"

Leland's shoulders, impeccably covered in a custom-made black suit, rose in a negligent shrug. He shook out a cigarette, tore the filter off with careful deliberation, tossed both pieces into the wastebasket beside the bed, and picked up another. "I know you've been hearing the news reports about thefts in the area. Well, the burglar picked on us last night. When Colby saw him . . . hurting you, she went for him. He escaped through the French doors, even as Cass and I came into the house. We heard Colby screaming."

"Did Colby give you those scratches?"

"As a matter of fact, yes," Leland said. "When I was trying to get her off you to see what was the matter."

"No."

"No?"

"No." Her voice was a harsh whisper. "You tried to kill me, you bastard. I'm not going to lie about it to save your rotten hide."

"Alex, my dear," Leland said in a condescending voice that made her want to scream, "I don't think you fully understand your options. You do as I say, exactly as I say, or Pete Whitten will find it necessary to put Colby away again."

Alex felt the blood drain from her face. "You can't do that."

"You didn't see her. She was acting so . . . crazy, just the way she did before. It might be necessary, Alex. Really. But I sincerely hope not."

79

The hospital looked pretty much like any number of medical facilities Rider had seen through the years. But this time he had no business being there. The night he and Colby had spent together proved there was no recapturing what they'd felt in their youth, so why had he come?

He didn't know. Part of it was that he wanted to be far away from the barn at feed time, so he wouldn't have to face the possibility that Jock hadn't kept his promise to stay sober. The other part was that he was nervous about the race and had to keep busy. The real reason was that he couldn't stay away.

He stopped at the information desk for Colby's room number. When he was told that only family members were allowed, he lied, told the receptionist he was Cass, and prayed she wouldn't ask for an I.D. She didn't. Telling himself he was a fool, he got into the elevator. Within minutes he was standing at her bedside, feeling lost and helpless and a little like crying.

Colby, her hair reminding him of scattered skeins of black silk thread against the whiteness of the pillow, lay perfectly still. Her eyelashes cast fanlike shadows against her cheeks, which were as pale as the sheets.

There were faint lines radiating from the corners of her eyes, lines he hadn't seen the night she'd spent at his apartment. The kind of lines that came with age and the loss of innocence. He'd seen them take up residence around his own eyes.

Her mouth, relaxed in sleep, was full and innocently inviting, the way he remembered it. Ugly words should never come from a mouth like that. Colby's mouth was made to whisper all the sweet things he remembered, designed to worship a man's body and drive him to the brink of madness.

He knew, then, why he couldn't stay away.

He felt responsible. Loving him had cost Colby a year of her life, not to mention the time she'd spent dealing with drugs and booze. Even though Leland Creighton's machinations were behind her misery,

Rider couldn't help feeling it was somehow his fault things had gone so wrong.

Yet it was more than guilt and responsibility he felt.

It was a legion of memories, a summer of laughter, a decade of regrets, and the knowledge of one unborn baby that wouldn't loose their hold on him. And until he and Colby reached some sort of peace with that and each other, Rider knew he could never stay away from her.

80

Cass sat on the edge of the sofa in Bonnie's of-fice, his clasped hands dangling between his knees, staring off into space. It was the first time he'd been still for longer than two minutes since he'd arrived. Bonnie sat down on the plump paisley-print arm and kneaded the tight muscles of his shoulders. She'd left the hospital at midnight, but Cass had stayed the night, going straight from the hospital to the track. He'd stopped by her office for lunch but hadn't eaten a bite of the chicken Veronique she'd sent out for. All he'd done was pace and frown and curse.

"What's the matter, darlin'?" she asked, pressing a kiss to the back of his neck, where his hair grew too long and a bit curly. "Besides bein' at the hospital all night and trainin' all mornin', that is."

Cass covered one of her hands with his and tried to summon a smile. "Everything's going to shit, Bonnie Jean."

"What do you mean?"

"How would you feel if your dad told you your sister wasn't his, that your mom had gotten pregnant by some other dude?"

"I don't have a sister, but if my dad was your dad, I could see the wisdom of my mother's actions," Bonnie said, trying to make light of the situation.

Cass's wry smile cut at her heart. "Brilliant logic. Your hatred for my father knows no end, does it?"

"Ah, Cass, I don't hate him, but I hate what he does to people. He wants to control everythin' and everyone he comes into contact with, and that isn't right. I'm not sure it's even normal."

"So you think Mom was justified in getting pregnant by some other guy?"

"Who can blame her? You know your daddy's had his share of lady friends through the years, and your momma is hardly what I'd call promiscuous. She must have felt somethin' for this man, whoever he is." Bonnie looped her arms around his neck and laid her cheek against his back. "A body'll wither and die without love, darlin', and it's obvious that the senator just couldn't give her any."

Cass heaved a deep sigh. "Maybe. But I don't know what to say to her. I'm going to feel really uncomfortable."

"Why should you feel any differently about her just because you found out Colby isn't your father's child? She's still the same person, and so is your mother."

Cass looked thoughtful. "Yeah. I guess you're right. Jesus, I wonder what Colby will say?"

"She'll probably jump up and down with joy," Bonnie ventured. "I would. But more to the point, what was Leland's attitude?"

The question surprised Cass. He had been too wrapped up in his own concerns to be bothered with how his father had taken the news. Cass thought back over everything his dad had said and done. What *was* Leland's attitude? "He seemed . . . distracted more than anything. I don't know. Sad, maybe."

"Angry?"

"No. Not really."

"I rest my case." Bonnie didn't point out that Leland probably didn't care enough to be angry. Her concern was helping Cass. He pulled her around and onto his lap, holding her close. "I guess I ought to go see Mom this afternoon, huh?"

"She loves you very much. It'll break her heart if you turn your back on her."

"Dad would love it." The words came out of left field, out of nowhere. Their truth hung in the air.

"Mmm . . ." Bonnie said, her mind churning with a new possibility.

"What?"

"Nothing."

"I know that look. It doesn't mean nothing."

Bonnie smoothed his hair away from his forehead. "I don't know. I was just thinking."

"About Dad?"

"Uh-huh."

"And?"

"Do you think he's telling the truth about Colby or just trying to stir up another batch of trouble?"

"Why would he lie?"

"You said it. To drive a wedge between you and your mother."

"Why?"

"I don't *know* why. I don't know why your father does half the things he does. I do know that he's a master manipulator and a liar deluxe. I'm just saying it's possible, that's all."

81

Jock spent the rest of the morning worrying about Alex. He finally drifted off to sleep about noon and awoke at the ringing of the alarm, wanting a drink so badly he could have killed for it. The need to fall back into his old ways had been manageable until he took that first drink, but now the old craving was back, eating him up from the inside out.

He'd made a promise to Rider, though, and he owed it to him to keep that promise. He'd also promised Rider that they'd win the Derby, and that was top priority, especially since Springer had sold the note to Leland. There was no telling what Leland Creighton had in mind to stack the odds in his favor.

Jock clenched his fists and swore, willing away the need to take a drink. If he hoped to come out of this colossal mess with his integrity, the purse, and the horse, he had to keep his wits about him. Instead of the liquor his body craved, he downed three cups of warmed-over coffee, showered again, and, pulling on clean Levi's, left for the track. He'd told Tomas he'd be back at feed time, and it was getting close.

"Where's Rider?" he asked the groom, who was squirting vitamins into the grain-filled feed tubs.

"He said he thought he oughta stay outa your way. He was goin' to take some time off an' relax before the race."

"I changed my mind."

Jock and Tomas turned. Rider stood in the shed row, his thumbs hooked in the pockets of his jeans, the inevitable cigarette dangling from his fingertips. Tomas took one look at the two men and headed for the tack room.

Jock studied him closely, the boy he'd fought so hard to keep from loving, the boy who was a constant reminder of his and Vicky's failings, the boy who'd taken all the shit thrown at him and turned it into something good. As he had for thirty-three years, Jock looked for signs of Leland Creighton in Rider's face. All he saw was Vicky—from the touch of red in Rider's hair to the curve of his upper lip, nothing but traces of his dead wife. And a bone-deep weariness and disappointment. All because he had let him down. Guilt battled with the determination to make it all up to Rider.

"I'm sorry I let you down, son."

"Yeah, Dad. So am I."

"It won't happen again."

"I hope not. For your own good."

Jock realized Rider was going to let him off easy, and he didn't deserve it. Maybe the boy was like him—tired of fighting the demons of the past, just tired.

"I asked Danny to ride the colt tomorrow," Rider said. "I couldn't get hold of you after I heard about Luis, so I made the decision myself."

A subtle reminder that he hadn't kept up his end of their uneasy partnership, Jock thought. "Suits me. Danny knows the horse as well as anyone. I wanted to tell you that I think I'm gonna stay with the colt tonight."

"Do you think that's necessary?"

Jock knew he couldn't tell Rider about the note Leland held. He shrugged. "I don't have anything better to do. You never can tell. Tonight just might be the night the colt gets cast. At least I'd be there to help him up."

Rider thought of all the horses he'd seen cast in the past, horses that had lain down to roll too close to the wall and couldn't get their feet under them to get up again. They could kick in a wall, doing a lot of damage to those slender, fragile legs, just trying to stand. Sometimes they didn't manage at all. It was unlikely to happen tonight of all nights, but if Jock felt staying with the horse would redeem him, why not give him the satisfaction?

"Do whatever you think's best."

"I'll stay, then."

"Can I ask you something?" Rider asked.

"Sure."

He'd wanted to ask Jock why he'd started drinking but was afraid that bringing up the subject might begin the whole cycle again. Instead he asked the second question that was bothering him.

"Why did you go tearing off to the hospital this morning?"

"I, uh, needed to see how Alex was doing."

"Why? I thought you hated the Creightons."

"I never hated any of them except Leland," Jock hedged. "When I left Hastings' Meadows before you were born, Alex gave me a helluva recommendation. She's a classy lady, and I . . . I owe her."

He was thankful that Rider accepted the explanation without probing further. "What about you? I never knew you had a thing for Colby until Alex told me this morning."

Rider smiled bitterly. "Considering that you weren't crazy about my friendship with Cass, I figured you'd have a shit fit if you knew I was dating his sister. Besides, she didn't want her dad to find out, so the fewer people who knew about it, the better."

Rider didn't offer any information about Leland's blackmail or about Colby's pregnancy. Jock could hardly blame him. They'd never been close enough to share confidences before; it was a little late to expect it now. But later, after the race, he would sit down with Rider and tell him how sorry he was. For everything.

82

"Come on, baby," Tracy breathed huskily, caressing Danny through the soft-washed denim of his jeans. "Just a quickie. No all-night marathons."

"Not tonight, Trace," Danny said. He was already tired. Since he'd come home the day before and found her waiting for him, all abject apologies and sweet-smelling woman, hell-bent on worming her way back into his good graces and his pants, he'd accused her of trying to get rid of him a new way—death by orgasm. He wasn't stupid. He knew she wasn't as sorry as she seemed and that ninety percent of the reason she'd come back was that Creighton had given her the boot.

Danny also knew it wasn't very smart of him to let her stay, considering he knew she'd soon find someone else. The difference was, he had *no* illusions left. He knew her for what she was: shallow, self-centered, strangely shrewd, and oversexed. She wasn't what he wanted in a wife and never would be, but she was the closest thing he had, and he hadn't yet worked her out of his system.

"Why not?" she asked now, trying her damnedest to talk him around.

Danny couldn't tell her he was worried sick about what he was planning to do the next day. He couldn't tell her that because he was afraid to put the cash in the bank, he had hidden a wad of money big enough to choke a horse in the leather bag that housed his boots, helmet, and whip.

This was something he had to get through alone. He wished it were over. No, he wished he'd never agreed to it in the first place. It was his future he was putting on the line, and he was having second thoughts about whether or not Tracy was worth it. He moved her hand, which had already convinced the weaker part of him to do as she wanted.

"I've gotta rest for the race. I need to be thinking about it, not you."

She pursed her lips in a pout. Then she brightened. "I bought a new dress for tomorrow. Do you want me to try it on for you?"

Danny stood. "Not tonight. Surprise me."

"Where are you going?" she asked, following him to the door.

He turned, his palms upraised in a helpless gesture. "I don't know. Out. I feel restless."

"Will you be late?"

"I doubt it. Like I said, I want to get a good night's sleep."

"Okay." Tracy twisted a button of his shirt, looking up at him coyly from beneath her lashes. "Are you still mad at me?"

"No," he said, freeing himself and setting her away from him. "I'm not mad at you."

But he was furious at himself.

83

Jock sat on a bale of straw outside Jock's Dream's stall. The night sounds of the backside reminded him of the days when he'd foaled mares for Alex and spent a lot of time at the barn after dark. The peaceful ambience—horses blowing, snuffling, settling in for the night, an occasional whinny or the sound of pawing—was strangely at odds with the hectic pace of the day.

Across the way, faint sounds of M. C. Hammer proclaiming, "Can't touch this . . ." mingled with the lonely sound of Kenny G's sax. The music was punctuated with an occasional hoot of laughter or a string of curses. The grooms and stable hands who lived on the backside were no doubt engaged in a game of cards to pass the long spring evening, probably talking about their favorite horses and making bets among themselves about who would win tomorrow's race.

Jock sighed. He'd be glad when Saturday was over. He would be especially glad when this night was over. He couldn't shake the uneasy feeling that grew stronger with each passing hour. He didn't trust Leland Creighton. Never had, never would.

Jock wanted to win the race and then forget about horses long enough to get his life in order. He wanted to talk to both his boys and see where they stood. He'd even been toying with the idea that maybe when Alex left Leland, they could have a life together. They weren't spring chickens, but was it ever too late to look for happiness?

"How's it goin', Jocko?"

The scratchy voice pulled Jock out of the swirl of his thoughts. Danny, a brown paper bag in hand, stood a few feet away, a shadow in his eyes and a weary smile on his face.

"Fair, I guess," Jock said. "What're you doing here?"

"I dunno. I just felt sorta on edge."

"Don't we all?"

Danny sat on a bale of alfalfa and twisted the top off a bottle of sangria. "Want some?"

"No, thanks. I've got a Thermos of coffee."

"Are you okay, Jock? You look a little down."

"I could say the same about you."

"Marital problems." Danny took a swallow of the wine.

"They happen to the best of us." Jock hoped Danny wouldn't let his problems with Tracy interfere with his riding. "Rider said he named you on the colt."

Danny looked up sharply. "Yeah. I hope you don't care."

"Why would I?"

"You took me off him, remember?"

"You were riding like some green bug boy, Danny Wayne. You'd have done the same."

Danny thought about that. Jock was right. "I guess so."

"Like those bumper stickers say, Danny, 'Shit happens.' Life can make you or break you. I know. It just about did me in."

"The drinking?"

"Yeah, the drinking. It took me more than thirty years to realize I was wrong about some things. I was pissed off at the world in general, and it hurt my racing career. I also used someone close to me as my whipping boy."

As a kid, Danny had seen how tough Jock was on his son. "Rider?"

"Yeah, Rider. I took all my bitterness out on a kid who didn't do anything but try to please me. I was wrong, and the saddest thing about being wrong is that no matter how much you regret it, you can never take it back."

"No, sir," Danny said in a weak voice, thinking about his commitment to Leland Creighton.

Jock's voice grew thick with emotion. "God knows I'm sorry for the way I treated Rider. I might not be able to take it back, but I intend to spend the rest of my life making it up to him. And I'm going to start by winning the Derby tomorrow."

Danny took another gulp of the ruby-red wine.

"The colt is good, Danny. He's as good as we can get him. It's up to you, now. All you have to do is ride the hair off him."

"I can do that," Danny said, summoning a smile. The statement was like gall rising in his throat. He could do it all right. The only problem was, he'd been paid extremely well not to.

84

Cass opened the door to his mother's room quietly. Wearing a high-necked gown and a tailored rose-colored robe, she was sitting in a chair, staring at the television. Somehow he knew she wasn't seeing a thing.

"Hello, Mom."

She turned toward him, her eyes lighting up with pleasure. Cass couldn't stop the rush of relief that spread through him. He'd been so worried about her.

"Hello, Cass." She looked at the bouquet. "Are those for me?"

"Uh, yeah." His eyes swept the room, which was filled with every flower imaginable, giving it a sweet, florist's-shop smell. The small bouquet he'd bought at a nearby grocery store seemed inadequate and cheap amid the lush blooms. He thrust the tissue-wrapped blossoms at her. "They look a little out of place, though."

Alex touched the petals of a peppermint carnation. "They're beautiful."

She seemed quiet, he thought. Too quiet. "How are you feeling?"

"Better."

"Are you catching a cold?"

"No. Why?"

"Your voice sounds scratchy."

Alex laid his flowers in her lap and looked away. Her fingers toyed with the lace adorning the high collar of her gown.

"Mom . . . Dad told me what happened."

"And?" Leland might have blackmailed her into lying to the police about what had happened at Windwood, but she'd never promised not to tell Cass about Jock. She'd never said she would lie if Cass asked her.

"It was a surprise, of course, but Bonnie made me see that you were . . . justified."

She shook her head and met his gaze with as much bravery as she could muster. "I wasn't justified, Cass. Your father had hurt Jock by taking advantage of his wife, and the truth is, I'd fallen in love with him. But that didn't make it right."

"Jock? Jackson McCall?" Cass said in disbelief.

"Yes." Alex frowned. "Leland didn't tell you?"

"Jock!" Dumbfounded, Cass speared his fingers through his hair. "But this is . . . terrible."

"Why? Jock McCall is a much better man even as an alcoholic than Leland Creighton would ever be sober."

"I'm not talking about that. I'm talking about Colby and Rider. Didn't you think of that? Is that why you agreed to the abortion?"

Alex frowned. "What you talking about?"

"If Colby is Jock's, and Rider is Jock's . . ." Cass swallowed hard and let Alex's imagination fill in the rest.

As what Cass implied sank in, Alex realized what Leland had done. She lifted sorrowful eyes to Cass's. "It appears to me," she said at last, "that Leland has once again fabricated a tangled web of lies—to what end, I shudder to contemplate."

Cass's heart sank, and he was reminded of Bonnie's earlier observation. His Texas bride was a lot more savvy than he gave her credit for. "Lies? What did he lie about this time?"

Alex's eyes filled with tears. She unbuttoned the collar of her gown and bared her bruised throat to her son's gaze.

"Jesus, what happened?" His mind whirled. The burglar? But there was no burglar. Colby? Impossible. That left . . .

"Leland happened."

"Leland? Do you mean Dad did this to you?"

Alex nodded. "I have no idea why he said otherwise, but it isn't Colby who is Jock McCall's child."

"What?" Even as he voiced the shocked query, he read the truth in his mother's eyes.

"Jock isn't Colby's father, Cass. He's yours."

85

Alex held her tears until after Cass left. Then she cried for what seemed like an eternity. She wept for all the times she'd wanted to and wouldn't allow herself the luxury. Leland considered crying a sign of weakness, and Alex never gave him any weapons he might use against her. But she didn't give a damn what Leland used against her anymore. She was finished with the lies and half-truths. Finished.

There was no denying Cass had been shocked. She had told him the whole story, starting with Leland's pursuit of Vicky McCall and ending with the weekend she and Jock had spent together in May of 1957. In time, she felt, Cass would come to accept Jock as his father. She prayed he would.

Her tears spent, Alex blew her nose and wiped her eyes. Tossing out the soggy tissue, she stepped into the wide hospital hallway and headed for

Colby's room. She wanted to see for herself that her daughter was all right.

Nurses and visitors milled around, and patients garbed in gowns and robes were walking to build their strength. Alex admitted to trembling legs herself.

She pushed open the door to Colby's room and paused. Colby lay as still as death in the narrow bed. For one terrifying instant, Alex believed she was dead. But then she saw the shallow rise of Colby's chest as she drew a soft breath. For no apparent reason, the tears started again.

86

Pete Whitten was at the nurses' station, preparing to make his evening rounds, when he happened to glance up and see Alex Creighton leave her room. She looked weary and unsteady on her feet, and with her blond hair hanging in limp straggles around her face, she looked old. Pete had never considered Alexandra Creighton old.

He handed the chart he was holding to the nurse, picked up Colby's, and followed Alex. On the pretext of studying the chart, he stood outside the partially opened door and watched. Alex lowered the side of Colby's bed and pressed a kiss to her sleeping daughter's forehead.

"I'm sorry, baby," she whispered brokenly. "I'm so sorry. I should have known better than to believe him. I should have known your father was up to no good."

Alex stroked Colby's hand. "He tried to kill me, Colby."

Shocked, Pete took an involuntary step closer.

"He wants me to lie to the police about it, or he says he'll have Pete put you away again."

Pete's mouth drew into a tight line. The sorry, no-account bastard! Blabbing what they'd done all over the place. Pete knew that if the heat came down, Leland Creighton would make damn sure it didn't scorch him—which left Peter Whitten the scape-goat.

"I can't let that happen," Alex said fervently. "I won't let him do that to you again. I promise you that."

Nor, Pete thought, would he. Leland Creighton was a loose cannon, and someone had to stop him before he destroyed everyone who got in his way.

Alex swiped the back of a trembling hand across her eyes and smoothed the midnight blackness of Colby's hair away from her face. "I just want you to know that, whatever happens to me, I love you. I've always loved you, Colby, and I always will."

She turned away from the bed. By the time she got to the door, Pete was back at the nurses' station. He wrote on the chart and handed it to the R.N. in charge of medication.

"I want you to stop Ms. Creighton's injections," he said. "I don't think it's necessary that she be sedated any longer." He reached for Alex's chart and scribbled a notation on it as well. Leland Creighton had caused enough misery, and Pete Whitten wasn't going to be his accomplice anymore.

87

The security guard assigned to the stakes barn disappeared around the corner. Jock had just spent the better part of half an hour shooting the bull with him. Danny had left before ten, taking his wine and saying he was going home to get some rest. Jock was a little uncomfortable about Danny and the upcoming race. The boy was uptight. Depressed, even. And that didn't bode well for the outcome of the race. Still, Danny was one of the best, and if he got his mind right before tomorrow afternoon, he could pull it off.

He had to pull it off.

Yawning, Jock checked his watch. Eleven-ten. He

rose and stretched and sauntered over to Jock's Dream's stall. The colt was stretched out on his side, sleeping soundly, snoring. Jock smiled. He was resting well. That was good. One by one the radios had grown silent and the lights in the rooms occupied by the stable hands had gone out. Tomorrow was a big day, and like every other day at the track, it would start early.

There was a lot of night—too much night—left, and he was getting sleepy. Jock poured himself a cup of coffee from the Thermos. To keep from brooding over Leland Creighton's stranglehold, he turned his thoughts to Alex and Cass. It was hard to believe Cass was his son. No wonder Leland had never been able to get Cass into politics; the boy had horses born and bred into him on both sides.

Despite the pressure of the day ahead, Jock sighed in contentment, the first he'd known in years. If Alex was to be believed about Rider and Cass—and what would she have to gain by lying?— he had two sons. Two of the absolute best Thoroughbred trainers in the country, by damn. Jock permitted a satisfied smile to curve his lips. Whichever colt won, he could take satisfaction in knowing it was his flesh and blood who'd trained the winning horse. Like his determination to do right by Rider, Jock determined to get to know Cass, if the boy would let him.

A sudden yell from a barn across the way rent the stillness of the night. It was soon accompanied by the sounds of scuffling and a piercing scream. A light came on, and then another. Someone bellowed for security.

Jock climbed onto some bales of hay, straining to see what was going on. The security guard he'd been talking to rounded the corner of his barn in a dead run, his gun already in hand. While it happened rarely, a fight over a woman or a drug deal gone bad wasn't unheard of on any backside.

"Somebody call an ambulance!" The cry echoed through the night, along with the sound of doors opening and the pounding footfalls of the gathering crowd. It was almost like that morning in February when he'd come close to crossing the big chilly waters.

Without warning, Jock's legs buckled beneath him. A cry of surprise escaped him as he toppled off the hay onto the ground. He realized belatedly that his legs had given out because they'd been struck from behind. Before he could do more than register that fact, a wiry arm circled his throat, cutting off his oxygen supply. Retaliation was out of the question. The bastard, whoever he was, knew exactly what he was doing.

The assailant jerked Jock to his feet at the same time a white-hot pain pierced the area of his right kidney. A guttural grunt of satisfaction huffed into his ear. Jock managed to draw in enough air for a ragged gasp of pain as his back arched automatically away from the point of impact. He was no more prepared for the second searing onslaught than he had been for the first. By the time the blade found its mark the third time, Jock was hovering on the edge of consciousness.

He was released as quickly as he'd been grabbed, and the ground rushed up to meet him. Through the red haze of pain that engulfed him, Jock saw a new pair of high-priced running shoes. Rider had a pair like them, Jock thought before one of the shoes found his gut in a vicious kick that sent him rolling over to his back.

He managed to open his eyes wide enough to get a glimpse of a man dressed in black clothes with a stocking pulled over his face. He was breathing heavily. Before Jock's eyelids drifted shut, he could have sworn he saw the man smile.

There was the sound of a horse whickering and a scuffling in the stall. The bastard was going to hurt Jock's Dream! Jock wanted to get up and help the colt, but he couldn't find the strength. The last thing he heard was the forlorn sound of sirens screaming through the night and the rapid beating of his heart as it pumped out the life through the three holes in his back.

His last conscious thought was that he'd let Rider down . . . again.

88

Rider had plans for getting a good night's sleep, but the events of the past few days kept tumbling around inside his head like rocks in a polisher. But, unlike the smooth, pretty stones that came out of the tumbler, all that resulted from two hours of driving around thinking were more ugly questions and uglier answers.

He hadn't intended to check up on Jock at the barn when he'd left the apartment, but he was near the track, so what the hell. As touchy as his dad was these days, he hoped Jock wouldn't take his unexpected appearance the wrong way.

Rider pulled the truck to a stop at the stable gate. People were running around, and an ambulance eased its way through the gathering crowd. Somebody must have gotten into a hell of a fight.

The guard at the gate stopped him. "Hello, Mr. McCall."

"Hi, Cal." Rider jerked his head toward the departing ambulance. "What's going on?"

"Some guy found his chick with some other dude. One of them pulled a knife and cut up the other one a little. Nothing a few stitches won't fix. Just a lot of blood."

"Same ol' same ol', huh, Cal?" Rider said.

John Calhoun grinned. "Right."

"I'm going to check on my dad and the horse while I'm here."

"Sure thing."

Rider drove through the gate, parked his truck, and walked toward the stakes barn. The first thing he saw when he stepped into the shed row was the colt's head sticking out over the webbing. Where was Jock? Off checking out the fight? Jock's Dream whinnied nervously and pawed at the rubber mat beneath the straw.

Cursing, Rider scanned the area. He caught a glimpse of something on the ground and realized it was Jock, lying face up. Dammit! Rider thought, quickening his pace. Jock was out like a light. So much for his noble offer to stay with the horse.

Rider was a few feet away from Jock when he saw the irregular dark splotch beneath him. His anger vanished like a lingering scent in the wind, and a nebulous fear sprouted in its place. Dropping to one knee, he touched the wet dirt and lifted his finger to the light. Blood. Jock's blood.

His heartbeat quickened, and his hands shook as he tried to see what was wrong. The blood was coming from his back, so he wasn't vomiting it like before. There was no sign of a bullet's exit, which left a knife. Someone must have stabbed him. The same guy who'd been in the other fight? Rider's trembling fingers sought a pulse. It was weak, but there.

"What's the matter?"

Rider looked up. The guard Jock had been talking to earlier stood there, a questioning look on his face. "It's my dad. I think someone stabbed him."

"Holy shit!" the guard said. "What the hell's going on here tonight, anyway?"

"I don't know, man. Call for an ambulance and bring me a blanket, pronto."

"Sure thing." The man headed for the stable gate in a run.

Jock's Dream whinnied again. Damn! The horse! Knowing there was nothing he could do for Jock until he got the blanket, Rider gave Jock's shoulder a squeeze and went to check the horse. He ran his hand from the colt's silky nose to his forelock. "Whoa, now."

Jock's Dream slung his head and stilled beneath the soft influence of the familiar voice. Expecting the worst, Rider went into the stall and began to check the skittish animal from his feet to his knees. Why else, he wondered, running practiced hands over the horse's silky coat, would someone want to hurt Jock, unless it was to get to the colt? But Jock's Dream looked just . . .

Rider's thoughts came up short when his hand encountered a damp place on the colt's throat. When he examined his hand, there was a smear of blood on his fingertips. Someone had given the horse a shot, directly into the vein, and it didn't take a genius to figure out that that someone was the same person who'd knifed Jock. What they'd injected didn't matter. It could have been nothing more than Butazolidin, commonly used to reduce inflammation and pain. The problem was that if Jock's Dream won the Derby and an excessive amount of Bute was found in his system, the stewards would take away the purse.

It wasn't hard to figure out who had done the deed, either. Leland Creighton wanted him out of Colby's life, and he'd already proved he would go to any lengths to ruin the McCalls. He might never be able to prove Leland's connection to what had happened to his dad or the colt, but it didn't shake his convictions. He gave the horse's neck a pat and left the stall. Shit.

He knelt by Jock. His throat tightened. Hadn't Leland Creighton done enough harm? Wasn't it enough to ruin lives? Did he have to take them? Rider brushed a lock of Jock's hair off his forehead and felt again for his pulse. It seemed weaker than before.

"Hang on, Dad. Hang on."

Dammit! He couldn't lose Jock now. And he wasn't ready to lose the race by default, either. Jock wouldn't quit. Rider remembered the words he'd heard Jock say a hundred times in the past: "You can make the best of things, son, or you can lay down and let life run right over you. It's up to you."

Well, there was no way in hell Leland Creighton would get the best of him again. Jock's Dream would run the race, and if he won and they took away the purse, at least he and Jock would know what kind of horse they had. If the colt lost, no harm done.

He owed it to Jock.

89

Leland waited by the phone, smoking one of his rare cigarettes. He'd wanted one tonight. After all, it was a celebration of sorts. Tonight would see Jock McCall and his son out of the Creightons' lives forever. If anything went wrong and Jock's Dream won, the colt would be disqualified. And if the McCalls didn't get the purse, they couldn't pay the note. Jock McCall's penny-ante operation would slide on down the tubes. Leland smiled. It was the ultimate revenge for a thirty-year grudge against his whoring wife and her hired hand.

The phone rang, shattering the stillness of the library. Leland ground out the half-smoked Kool and reached for the receiver.

"Yes?"

"It's over."

"Any problems?"

"Not a one. The bitch didn't care who she

screwed, and those two would have let someone cut off their fingers for two grand."

"What about Mr. McCall?"

"He never knew what hit him. And with our little 'distraction,' no one else did, either."

"And the colt?"

"Taken care of."

"Very good. There will be a package for you in the post office box, as usual."

"Thanks. I'll talk to you soon."

"You can count on it," Leland said with a satisfied smile. He hung up the phone and reached for the cigarettes again.

Across town, Solly Tobias reached down and untied the laces of his new Nike Airs running shoes.

90

Rider rode in the ambulance to the hospital.
After showing the attending physicians a card with
his blood type, compliments of the Hot Springs
hospital, he donated blood for his dad, who was
sent straight to emergency surgery. Then he settled
in to wait.

Two hours later the operation was over, and the
surgeon, a man about Rider's age, assured him that
Jock had made it just fine.

Rider felt instant relief, as if he'd been holding his
breath for two hours and finally got a good lungful
of air.

"He's in pretty bad shape, and he's lost a lot of
blood. Whoever used the knife knew how and where
to do the most damage."

"Damn," Rider said.

The doctor gave an apologetic smile. "We'll just
have to see how the next few hours go. In the
meantime, you may as well go home. Your dad will
be in recovery for a while, and then in ICU, so
there's not a thing you can do for him here."

Rider knew the doctor was right, but he hated to leave Jock alone.

"Don't you have a horse in the Derby tomorrow?"

"Yeah."

The doctor gave Rider's shoulder a sympathetic squeeze. "Then go home and get some sleep. We'll call you if there's any change."

Rider finally agreed.

He didn't think he'd sleep at all, but too much had happened to him the last few days, and he was out as soon as his head hit the pillow.

The ringing of the phone woke him from a deep slumber. He groped for the receiver, dragged it to his ear, and glanced groggily at the clock. It was almost five in the morning. "Hello?"

"Mr. McCall?"

At the sound of the impersonal voice, a surge of fear gripped him. "Yeah?"

"This is the hospital. Dr. Avery asked me to call. I'm afraid your father has taken a turn for the worse."

91

Colby forced her leaden eyelids upward. Daylight poked skinny gray fingers through the cracks in the miniblinds covering the windows. But . . . her windows didn't have miniblinds. Panic swept through her. Where was she? She pushed herself to a sitting position, her eyes skimming the contents of the room.

A hospital.

Memories came rushing back with the force of a Gulf hurricane. Memories of her father choking her mother. Memories of her father forcing her to have sex with him that day he'd found her with Rider. . . .

Colby leaped from the hospital bed and lurched the few steps to the bathroom. Dry heaves shuddered through her, over and over, as if she were trying to rid herself of the ugly recollection by vomiting it out of her system.

Agonizing minutes later, she stood trembling before the bathroom mirror, staring at her pale reflection in the gloomy morning light. Dark circles ringed her eyes, and her hair was a rat's nest of tangled curls.

No wonder she'd gone crazy and had to be sedated. Her mind couldn't deal with the fact that the father who professed to adore her would do such a horrible thing. Colby raised a thin hand to the mirror and touched her reflection, as if to wipe away the misery she saw there. A single tear slipped over her lower lashes and trailed down her cheek.

The saddest part was that Rider had taken the blame for Leland's horrible transgression. But then, that was par. Her father always came out of his battles unscathed. But not this time. This time he'd gone too far. This time he'd hurt her mother, and Colby intended to see to it that he paid.

92

The soft blip . . . blip of the monitor kept time with Rider's own heartbeat. Blood dripped drop by life-giving drop into Jock's arm. The ICU nurse, busy with another patient, was within a few steps of the bedside. Her only comment was that Jock was a fighter. Rider had found that out in February, but it was cold comfort at the moment.

Dawn had stolen into the intensive care unit while

Rider stood beside Jock's bed, waiting and praying. He hadn't prayed in years—not since his mother died. He didn't even know where his rosary was. He wished he did. He wished—hell, he wished a lot of things, but mostly he wished his relationship with Jock had been different. Better.

He thought of people he'd grown up with and their relationships with their fathers. Danny and his dad were pretty close, but Danny had always felt the two were in competition. And Cass—well, Cass had no relationship at all with Leland, which was a blessing.

In comparison, maybe he and Jock hadn't been so far off base after all. Jock *had* come to visit him out in California. Even though they hadn't gotten along, Jock had made the effort. Funny. Until now, Rider never realized that maybe the visit had been as hard for Jock as it had been for him.

Rider wondered if he would ever get over feeling that he'd failed somehow. If only he'd been smarter, worked harder, something. Then maybe he would have heard his dad say those longed-for words: I love you, son.

A long beep startled Rider from his thoughts. His disbelieving eyes found the flat line stretching across Jock's monitor. Jumping to attention, the nurse called for a code, and within seconds the room was filled with medical personnel.

Surprisingly, no one seemed to notice Rider in the mayhem of trying to start Jock's heart again. Numbed by an overwhelming helplessness, Rider swallowed the lump of frozen tears lodged in his throat.

A few minutes later a doctor approached him with a long face and a sympathetic pat on the shoulder. He didn't even have to speak. Rider knew. He stared as the nurse drew the sheet up over Jock's head. Jock McCall left life the way he'd lived it . . . fighting.

And Rider would never hear him say those words.

93

She dressed in the same clothes she'd come to the hospital in, the same clothes she'd worn in anticipation of the family meeting. She was going home. When Pete Whitten had made his rounds he was quiet, withdrawn. She could hardly believe her ears when he'd told her he was releasing her.

Today was a perfect time to go to Windwood and start getting her life in order. It was Derby day, and everyone would leave early to get a start on all the excitement. The house would be empty.

Windwood was quiet, just the way she'd known it would be. As usual on Derby day, the servants had the day off. She bent and picked up the morning paper, which had been tossed into the dew-wet grass, and the rubber band holding it snapped, stinging her palm. The minor irritation drew a curse from her lips. She unlocked the front door and stepped inside, fighting the surreal feelings that surrounded her. It seemed like aeons instead of just two days since she'd been taken from the house to the hospital.

She was starving but afraid her churning stomach couldn't tolerate anything. Eager to get into fresh clothes, she tossed the paper onto the marble-topped table near the stairs. Leaning on the smooth banister, she started up the treads. She'd taken no more than a step when the bold headline snagged her attention:

TRAINER OF DERBY HOPEFUL INJURED

She backed down the step and snatched up the paper. The story was short, concise. Jackson "Jock" McCall had been with his horse when a fight had broken out on the backside. Some unknown person or persons had taken the opportunity to stab Mr. McCall, who had undergone emergency surgery. The police were still looking for suspects and had no motive for the incident.

The police might not have a motive, but she did. With trembling hands, she dialed the number of the hospital she'd just left.

"I'm calling to see how Jackson McCall is, please."

There was silence on the other line, as if the person were trying to find the information.

"I'm sorry, ma'am, but Mr. McCall expired about five-thirty this morning."

Dead! Impossible. Not Jock . . . not Jock. Leland had gone too far this time. There was no room for sadness in the sudden hardness of her heart.

"Thank you." Dry-eyed, she recradled the receiver and started up the stairs, where she changed into jeans and sneakers, cool deliberation in every move. Her mind whirled with half-formed plans and vows of vengeance as she went downstairs to the library and the gun she knew was there.

She reached inside the curved-front drawer and drew out the small silver derringer with the ivory-inlaid grip. It felt surprisingly compact, almost harmless in her hand. Stuffing it into her pocket, she left the house and headed for the track.

It would be over soon. Very soon. And Senator Leland Creighton would never hurt anyone again.

94

From its first running in 1875, the Kentucky Derby was a race of prestige and prominence, luring horses and patrons from every state. Every breeder wanted to breed a Derby winner, every trainer hoped to train one, and every jockey wanted to be on the horse that received the blanket of roses in the winner's circle.

Louisville on Derby day was one wild party. The wealthy started with a brunch of eggs Benedict and bloody bulls, then moved to the track for an afternoon of betting and sipping those famous Kentucky mint juleps. Spirits and attendance were high. As usual, the spectator overflow was directed to the infield.

Two exceptions to the high spirits were Rider and Cass. Rider was on his way to the paddock when Cass stopped him to offer his condolences. Cass looked as if he'd been dragged through a knothole backward, and Rider felt as if he had. He imagined that Alex and Colby being in the hospital was an added burden to Cass's load.

"Thanks, Cass," he said sincerely. "I appreciate it. How are Colby and your mother?"

"I haven't talked to them today, but they were fine when Bonnie called." Cass, looking more than a little uncomfortable, started to say something else and instead excused himself abruptly.

Rider didn't dwell on it. He had too much on his mind. He was sorry it had taken Jock's death to get his old friend to speak to him, but he was glad he finally had. Maybe after the race he could somehow set things straight with the Creightons who mattered.

Even Danny was subdued when he came to the paddock. "Hey, man, I'm sorry about your dad," he said, gripping Rider's hand.

"Thanks, Danny."

"I stopped by the barn last night and spent a little time with him."

"You did?" Rider said in surprise. "What time was that?"

"Probably around eight-thirty, quarter 'til nine, something like that. I left about ten."

"Did you notice anything unusual?"

"Do you mean, was he drinking? No. I offered him some wine, but he said he was on coffee."

Rider felt his load grow a little lighter.

"He had a lot on his mind."

"Yeah? Like what?"

"He told me he knew he hadn't treated you right, and he was sorry."

Rider had to look away to hide the moisture he felt gathering beneath his eyelids.

"He told me that he'd been pissed off at the world, and he'd taken it out on you." Danny paused and slapped at his boot with his whip. "He said that was wrong, and that he was going to spend the rest of his life making it up to you."

Rider knew Danny's explanation was as close to an "I love you" as he was ever going to get from Jock. It was enough, somehow. Maybe it was because he'd found out the last few days that things weren't always what they appeared on the surface. There were layers of truth, layers of feeling, layers of love.

"He wanted to win today more than anything," Danny said, drawing Rider's attention back. "He wanted it for you, not for himself."

"Danny!"

Both Rider and Danny turned toward the feminine voice. Tracy, dressed in a floral-print dress and a wide-brimmed straw hat, stood near the other railbirds, waving gaily. Rider had to admit she was a luscious-looking thing. As he watched, Tracy blew Danny a kiss and called, "Good luck!"

Then it was time to take the horses to the track for the post parade.

Rider gave Danny a leg up. "Thanks for telling me, Danny. And thanks for being such a good friend."

Danny turned beet red. "Sure. Any last-minute instructions?" he asked, changing the subject.

"You know the horse. You know the competition. Take your best hold."

95

Danny left Rider in the paddock and guided Jock's Dream onto the track. The crowd was singing "My Old Kentucky Home," and Danny felt a sudden surge of something he could only define as sorrow join the guilt eating away at his soul. He hadn't had a home since his mom left his dad when he was ten years old. Maybe that's why he'd tried so hard to overlook Tracy's faults. He wanted a home, and he didn't want to be a quitter like his mother.

Danny rode the horse through his prepost paces on automatic pilot, weighing his options, fighting his guilt, searching for a way out that would make everyone happy and knowing that was an impossibility. Was he being a quitter by taking the easy way out?

Tracy looks gorgeous, Danny boy. You know you'll do anything to keep her.

But Rider was an old friend, a valued friend. And Jock was a good guy, too.

You got half of Leland's money stashed away, and the rest will be delivered as soon as the race is over. Two million dollars is a lot of marital insurance.

Aw, hell! He couldn't go through with it.

You have to.

He'd never be able to pull it off.

Sure you can. It's a big field. With that many horses, anything can happen. Everyone knows you're replacing Mendoza. Hold the colt just enough that it looks good, and everyone will think you didn't know him well enough to give him the best ride.

The voices warred inside his head against the droning buzz of the crowd. God, he wished it was over.

Jock's Dream had an outside post and was one of the last horses to be loaded into the gate. Danny was hardly aware of the gate crew or of anything going on around him. He heard the bell and felt Jock's Dream shoot out of the gate. Danny gave him a little slack and moved him closer to the inside. The thunder of hooves was deafening as he maneuvered the colt to a better position.

Don't forget, you're doing it for Tracy, Danny.

As usual, there was a lot of speed in the race, and Danny let the speed horses set the pace, settling into a comfortable spot with the second cluster of horses as they passed the grandstand the first time. When they passed the clubhouse turn, they were still in an okay position. So far, so good.

It's a lot of money. A helluva lot of money.

As the horses strove into the backstretch, Danny was oblivious to everything but his next move. He couldn't have said who was beside him or ahead of him. All he was doing was calculating how much rein he should give the colt to make it look convincing. One by one, horses started passing him.

Not too many, Danny. You gotta make it look good. Tracy looks good.

Rider had to believe he'd given it his best.

Dammit! Rider was the best. And he'd looked so devastated over losing Jock. Jock had wanted the horse to win so badly. For Rider. And he was going to blow it all. For Tracy.

A picture of Tracy riding her young stud flashed through Danny's mind.

"He doesn't mean anything to me."

Then why did you do it, Tracy?

"Leland Creighton gave me the necklace, Danny. He's loaded."

Money. The root of all evil. Or maybe Leland Creighton was the root of all evil. Money might make the world go 'round, but it wasn't worth losing a good friend over. And, by God, he realized with a start, neither was Tracy.

The realization broke the spell binding Danny. Tears blinded him as he glanced around to see just where he stood in the race. He wasn't in a great position, but he was far from being last. Jock's Dream was live beneath him, just waiting to be let go.

Danny gave him his head and moved him around a horse on the outside. It was like getting a boost from a jet engine. The familiar exhilaration swept through him. He could still win this race. Jock's Dream could still win.

Danny began doing what had taken him to the top. He rode skillfully, brilliantly, and he took chances, some he shouldn't take.

A small spot opened up nearer the rail. Danny yelled into the colt's ear and guided him into it. One more move and he'd be in good shape. Just one more. A horse moved up in front of him, closing the narrow gap that would have put them in the clear. Making a split-second decision, Danny urged the horse to the outside, cutting in front of a bay colt that was making his move.

The next thing he knew, he felt suspended in space, in time. Then he realized that Jock's Dream was going down, and he was sailing over his head. Danny heard the cumulative gasp of thousands of fans. He was aware of nearby shouts and curses and felt the sting of flying hooves pelt his body. Then there was a sudden deprivation of oxygen as more than a thousand pounds rolled on top of him.

96

Rider saw Jock's Dream take a bad step—had he been clipped from behind?—go to his knees, and roll. Danny went flying through the air. Rider's heart sank to the pit of his burning stomach. He watched in horror as the jockey behind Jock's Dream tried to check his horse to keep from running over Danny and caused another colt to run into him, a perfect example of the domino effect.

Rider's heart leaped to his throat. The accident was one more in a series of catastrophes that had hounded his heels the last few days. Dear God, if this was some kind of bad joke, he wanted it to stop. He couldn't take any more. He blocked out the announcer's voice, blocked out the rumble of shocked voices around him. Pushing his way through the crowd, he started for the scene of the three-horse pile-up.

By the time he reached the track, security was trying to disperse the crowd that had gathered. The ambulance that was always on standby during the races had already reached the scene. All three horses were standing, but Rider could tell at a glance that one had a broken leg. It wasn't Jock's Dream, thank God. But Rider's top concern was the jockeys, especially Danny. One rider was upright, holding his ribs. Danny and another jock lay on the ground while paramedics worked over them.

By the time Rider elbowed his way to the ambulance, they were loading Danny onto the stretcher.

"How bad is he?"

"I'm sorry, sir," one of the paramedics said, "but we're not sure at this point. Excuse us."

Rider felt a curious helplessness as he watched Danny and the other jockey disappear inside the ambulance, which took off down the track with its lights flashing and its siren screaming. He was still staring after them when the track's horse ambulance pulled up. Jock's Dream, he thought suddenly. There was nothing to be done for Danny, but the colt still needed help.

"Rider."

Rider turned and saw Tomas, holding Jock's Dream's bridle, standing behind him.

"How is he?"

"He's got some cuts and a pretty damn bad limp, but I don't think anythin's broke. He'll be stove up pretty bad for a few days."

"Do you think we need the ambulance?"

Tomas shook his head. "Nah."

"I'll take him to the barn, then. You call the doc and tell him to meet us there as soon as he can. I imagine he's around somewhere."

"Sure." Tomas handed Rider the reins and disappeared into the crowd.

Slowly, taking his time, Rider led the limping colt to the backside and the familiarity of his stall, wondering when—if—the nightmare of the last few days would end and longing for the familiarity of the monotony he'd lived with for so long.

97

"What the shit?" When Leland saw Danny make his move on the horse, his self-satisfied smile turned sour. Damn the little pinhead, anyway. If he screwed up his part, he could forget about the two million. And if he'd developed a conscience and dared to double-cross Leland Creighton, he could expect to pay an even higher price.

Leland's furious thoughts were pulled up short when he saw Jock's Dream stumble and fall. After that, everything happened so fast he couldn't have said what transpired. All he knew was that when the rest of the pack thundered past, there were three horses and three jockeys left behind in the dirt.

Leland kept his eyes trained to the McCall stable silks as spectators surged onto the track. One by one the horses got to their feet. They were all shaken, all limping. One looked badly hurt. One of the jockeys rolled to his knees, and some man from the infield helped him to his feet. Danny stayed prone on the track.

As the scene unfolded before him, Leland's furrowed brow smoothed. Danny's accident hadn't changed anything. Actually, this was better than if he'd held the horse. The kid had a reputation for reckless riding, and no one would be the wiser. He should have known Danny wouldn't screw him around.

Leland looked at the tote board. Runaway Again hadn't even run in the money. No matter. Jock's Dream hadn't either. Smiling to himself and feeling for the papers in his breast pocket, Leland stood and made his way through the crowd.

As he got on the elevator, a roar went up from the crowd. The results of the one-hundred-and-sixteenth running of the Kentucky Derby were now official, and Unbridled made the coveted walk to the winner's circle.

98

The scent of fresh straw and alfalfa wafted
through the air as Rider led Jock's Dream into his
stall. He slipped the bridle over the colt's ears and
and gave him water, watching to see how much he
drank. The horse should have had ample time to
cool out on the slow trek from the track to the barn,
but Rider didn't want to take a chance of foundering
him on top of everything else. Satisfied that Jock's
Dream wasn't going to drink the bucket dry, Rider
left it in the stall. There was nothing to do now but
wait for the vet and see what damage showed up
on the X-rays.

Rider unlocked the tack room and flipped on the
bare sixty-watt bulb. How, he wondered as he carried the bridle inside, could so many things go so
wrong in such a short time? Hell, he'd barely had
time to call Farley about Jock and stop by the funeral home to make arrangements for the crema-
tion. There had been no time to grieve, and now
this. Rider poured a cup of stale coffee into a mug
and stuck it into the small microwave Tomas used
to warm up his honey buns every morning.

"Rider."

Startled, he turned toward the doorway. Colby stood silhouetted in the afternoon sunlight, wearing a windbreaker over her turtleneck and jeans.

"What are you doing here?" he asked with a frown. "Shouldn't you still be at the hospital?"

"I saw the race," she said, changing the subject and stepping into the room. "I hope Jock's Dream is okay."

"So do I."

She looked exhausted, he thought, but there was more than weariness in her eyes. A look of quiet desperation lurked in their blue depths that even the dim light of the room couldn't hide. Where was the joy, he wondered? Where was her sass? Rider felt like crying for their loss and for the loss of the old Colby . . . his Colby. "I heard about the burglar. Are you all right?"

"There was no burglar, Rider."

Rider was surprised to see that his system could still register disbelief. "What do you mean, there was no burglar? Then what happened, for God's sake?"

Colby paced the width of the small room and turned. "I don't know what happened between my parents before I got there, but when I walked into the library, my father was trying to kill my mother."

"What!"

There was a distant look in her eyes, as if she could see it all over again in her mind. "He was choking her. And when I saw him doing that, I remembered everything that happened." Colby

winced and raised a trembling hand to her forehead, as if the memories were more painful than
she could bear. She pinned him with a steady gaze.
"That day he found us and I went a little crazy—it
wasn't because of you, Rider. It was—"

"What are you doing here, Colby?"

Rider turned toward the newcomer. Leland
Creighton's broad body filled the doorway, blocking
out the light. Rider had the distinct impression that
Leland was surprised to see his daughter. Shocked,
even.

Rider glanced at Colby, who thrust her hands into
her pockets and took a step closer to him. On the
surface, she looked calm. Then he saw her eyes.
She was staring at her father with a hatred so deep
it sent a shiver racing down Rider's spine. A sense
of foreboding crept through him. Something was
definitely not right here.

"What do you want, Creighton?" he asked, hoping to get rid of Leland before he found himself in
the middle of a major shitstorm between him and
Colby. His stress level was already on overload.

Leland dragged his gaze from his daughter and
sauntered into the room as though he didn't have
a care in the world. "I came to collect on Jock's
debt."

Rider's first thought was that his dad wasn't even
cold and the vultures were already circling. His second was, no way would Jock ever allow himself to
become indebted to Leland Creighton.

"Thank you for your condolences, Senator," Rider
said. "Your concern about my father's death is really

appreciated. Now, if you'll get the hell out of my tack room, I have a horse to take care of."

Leland cast a glance at Colby. "The horse is the reason I'm here, McCall. He's mine, and I came to get him."

Rider felt the air leave his lungs. The senator was too confident to be blowing smoke, so what the hell was going on? "Jock's Dream isn't going anywhere."

"I beg your pardon, son," Leland said, reaching into the breast pocket of his navy blue serge suit and drawing out some papers, "but I'm afraid he is." With a hint of a smile, he held them out to Rider.

Rider unfolded the legal-looking documents and gave them a quick perusal. Cold seeped into his bones. He'd been right about one thing: Jock hadn't originally been indebted to Leland. For some reason Rider couldn't fathom, Springer Martindale had sold Creighton a note Rider hadn't even known existed.

Rider stared at the papers, trying to make some sense of what was happening. Jock had pinned his dreams on the colt, and Leland Creighton's web of deceit was about to enmesh Jock's Dream. He handed the documents back.

"If it's all the same to you, I'll take the colt now and let our veterinarian look at him." Leland reached for a leather lead shank hanging on the wall and started for the door.

"Did you have to have him killed?" Rider asked.

Leland turned slowly. "What are you talking about?"

"You know damn well what I'm talking about. Someone knifed my dad last night, then gave the horse something to make sure we wouldn't get any part of the purse if we won. Don't you think that's a little coincidental, considering you hold that note?"

"I hope you aren't insinuating I had anything to do with that unfortunate accident."

"Unfortunate accident." Rider pretended to consider the words. "Now, that's an unusual way to describe murder, but that's exactly what I'm insinuating, you sorry bastard," he said through clenched teeth. "And if I can't help the police prove it, I'll personally accompany you to hell."

"And I'll help him. Gladly."

Leland looked toward his daughter. So did Rider. She'd been so quiet, he'd almost forgotten she was there. There was no ignoring her now, though. She held a small silver gun in her trembling hand, and the barrel was pointed squarely at her father's wide chest.

"Tear up the papers, Daddy."

A bit of color had drained from Leland's florid face. "Put the gun away, Colby."

"Not until you tear up those papers and forget you ever made that deal."

"I can't do that, baby."

"Don't call me that!" she screamed. She made a visible effort to get her emotions back under control, but she was shaking as if she had a chill. "I'm offering you a good trade-off, actually. You tear up the papers, and maybe I'll keep my mouth shut about what you did to Mama the other night. I'll even," she said in a quavering voice, "keep my mouth shut about what you did to me."

Leland looked as if she'd struck him a blow in the face.

"Colby—" Rider began, taking a step nearer.

"Shut up, Rider! Just shut up!" she shouted in a feverish voice. "This is between me and my *daddy*. I remember now, Daddy. When I saw you with Mama, I remembered everything, every sickening thing that happened."

"You're getting all worked up, Colby," Leland said in that soothing, mesmerizing voice that had three-quarters of the state fooled. "Let's go see Pete and get you some medicine."

She laughed, a low, bitter sound that seemed to emanate from her very soul. "Oh, you'd like that, wouldn't you? You'd like to have me put away again. You'd like to send me to Forest Glade to cover up your sins, just like you did before."

He took a step closer to her, a beseeching look on his face.

Colby raised the derringer higher. "I wouldn't, if I were you. I have absolutely no qualms about putting a hole in your black heart."

She was serious. Rider could see it in her eyes. "Colby, let me have the gun," he pleaded.

"No! He's through playing God. And he's through hurting people. We loved each other, Rider, and he cost us eleven years of happiness. He cost us our baby."

"There's no way I would have let you have his

baby," Leland said, unable to keep his hate for the McCalls at bay.

"That's the whole point. You weren't sure it was Rider's baby, were you? There was a chance it could have been yours."

Rider felt as if someone had just delivered a hard right hook to his gut. Leland, his white face now suffusing with hectic color, actually staggered back a step.

"You raped me after Rider left. *That's* why I went crazy. That was nice and convenient for you, wasn't it, Daddy? It made it easier for you to put me away so no one would be the wiser."

"That's a damn lie!" Leland said, but there was no conviction in his voice.

Colby continued as if he hadn't interrupted her. "When you found out I was pregnant, you made me have an abortion, just in case. But it was Rider's baby. I was just waiting for the right time to tell him."

Leland lunged toward her, his face twisted with rage and grief. Two sudden, loud pops filled the room. For an instant he froze, a look of wide-eyed bewilderment on his face. Then he took a single, faltering step and collapsed facedown on the tack room floor.

From outside came a sudden flurry of shouts.

Rider cut his gaze from the two small holes in Leland's back to Colby, who stood pale and trembling, her head moving from side to side in denial. With a strangled cry, she dropped the gun.

Rider tried to deal with this newest shock. How

had Leland Creighton lived with himself? He'd taken a life and ruined God only knew how many others. He had raped his own daughter, destroyed the woman Rider had loved, and left nothing but this beautiful, empty shell who was capable of killing her own flesh and blood.

Colby must have seen the horror in his eyes. Her steps faltered for a second, and then her arms were around his waist and she was clinging to him, seeking a comfort he wasn't sure he could give.

He gripped her arms to put her away from him, when a movement in the doorway caught his attention. Alex stood there, holding a gun similar to the one Colby had used to threaten Leland. Her hair hung in limp blond strings around her pale face, and there were dark smudges beneath pale blue eyes that gleamed with a fierce exultation.

Rider looked at Leland's body with sudden understanding. Alex, not Colby, had shot Leland.

Feeling the sudden tenseness in Rider, Colby raised her head. "Mama?" she said. "What are you doing here?"

Instead of answering Colby, Alex walked to Leland's still body. "I told you I wouldn't let you hurt Colby again," she said in a flat voice. "And now you can't."

"Hold it, lady."

The curt voice drew Colby and Rider's attention. Alex kept staring at Leland. One of the track security men, his gun on Alex, entered the room. "Don't anybody move." He held out his hand. "Give me the gun, ma'am. Butt out."

Alex just stood there.

"Mama?" Colby said, her voice thick with tears. "Mama, listen to the man."

Alex looked up. "Colby. What are you doing here?"

"I . . . came to see Rider. Give the man the gun, Mama. Please."

"Gun?" Alex looked down at the small derringer in her hand as if surprised to see it. Wordlessly she handed it to the guard, who rolled Leland's body over.

"My God! It's Senator Creighton."

"Yes," Alex said in a soft voice. "Senator Creighton. My husband. He killed Jock McCall, and he tried to kill me. I had to stop him before he hurt someone else."

"Is it true?" the guard asked.

Colby nodded. "I saw him."

The guard shook his head and took Alex's arm. "Come on, Mrs. Creighton. Let's get you to the station. They'll help us straighten this all out."

The sound of approaching sirens mocked the sudden stillness in the room, mocked life.

"Life has a way of bringing you to your knees, Rider. It's up to you to decide what happens when it does. You can get up and make the best of things, or you can lay down and let it run right over you. But remember this, son. Life either makes you or breaks you."

"Rider?"

Colby looked up at him, her eyes awash with

tears. She seemed to be asking "What next? Where do we go from here?"

Rider didn't know. He didn't know if they could learn to love the people they had become or if Leland had robbed them of all hope of happiness.

But he knew he'd never forgive himself if he didn't give it a try. They'd already lost a decade. Drawing a deep, fortifying breath, he wrapped his arms around Colby and drew her close. It was a closeness she'd needed for eleven endless years. A closeness that broke the dam of emotion binding her. She began to cry, harsh, bone-jarring sobs to purge the hate and sorrow from the depths of her soul.

Rider blinked back his own tears. He hoped that, at last, they were finished with hurting each other.

99

It was still dark when Rider approached the stall, a paper sack in his arms. Jock's Dream whinnied a soft welcome, as if to say that the nightmare weekend was over and a new day, a new week, a new beginning, was at hand. The problem was, Rider wasn't sure if the new beginning was anything more than a continuation of the nightmare.

The X-rays showed that Jock's Dream had sustained a hairline fracture to the cannon bone. Not good news, but, considering the severity of the accident, it could have been worse. Cass had agreed to ship the horse to Hastings' Meadows for a lengthy recuperation.

The hospital had confirmed yesterday that Danny's reckless riding had grounded him for good. Chances were slim the jockey would ever walk again.

Fortunately or unfortunately, depending on whom you talked to, Leland hadn't died from the .22-caliber slugs Alex had pumped into him. The bullets had been dug out, and as soon as Leland was well enough, he would face charges for his part in Jock's death.

Rider unlocked the tack room and went inside. The small room was cool and smelled of leather and Murphy's oil soap and leg sweat. He set down his burden and filled the coffeepot, even though he wasn't sure of the measurements. Hell, he wasn't sure of anything. His life felt more unsettled than it had when he'd first agreed to stay and run the colt.

With Jock gone, there was no reason to stay in Kentucky. Except Colby. And he wasn't sure there was anything to salvage of what they felt for each other. So much had changed. So many things had happened, things like finding out about his mother and Leland Creighton. Things like learning Cass was his half brother.

Cass had broken the news to him after the paramedics had taken Leland and Colby to the hospital, and the police had taken Alex to the police station. As he'd listened to the long, convoluted tale of double infidelity that had fed one man's pain and another's revenge, he finally understood why Jock had been so hostile to the Creightons and so hard on him and his mother.

Looking back, Rider realized there were limits to how much a person could take. Jock had found comfort and forgetfulness in a river of Irish whiskey. Colby had succumbed almost immediately. Alex had withstood more than thirty years. The jury was still out on his own tolerance level. *"Life makes you or breaks you . . ."*

The aroma of perking coffee mingled with the scent of leather and soap, taking Rider back to the days when his mother had carried him to the barn in the early-morning darkness and he had awakened in his makeshift lawn-chair bed.

"He's a good man, Rider. He doesn't mean to be so hard. He's just trying to teach you right."

The sound of his mother's voice was so clear that, for an instant, Rider fully expected to see her standing there in her jeans and flannel shirt. He understood, finally, what she had meant. And for the first time, he believed it.

Rider opened the paper sack, lifted out the handsome urn that held Jock's ashes, and started out the door. The track would be empty, and he'd be able to say his good-bye in peace.

When he got to the end of the barn, Cass was waiting there, his hands in the pockets of his bomber jacket, a solemn look on his face as he eyed the urn.

"I'm going to the track," Rider said.

"I'd like to go with you."

"Sure."

Side by side they walked to the oval that had shaped each of their lives. So different, so much the same. Rider took off the lid and stuck it in the pocket of his windbreaker. The stables were black silhouettes against the drab gray of dawn, and he heard the sounds of the backside as it woke to a new day. Then the red lip of the sun edged up over the horizon, and a light breeze sprang up, riffling Rider's hair. He imagined he could smell the scent of hay and manure and sweaty horseflesh. In spite of everything, the familiarity brought a certain peace.

"It gets in your blood, boy. There's something about the smell of manure and the sight of an animal doing what it's bred to do that just flat gets in your blood."

Rider didn't try to check the tears that ran unashamedly down his cheeks as he sprinkled the ashes onto the sandy soil of the track. The lighter the urn grew, the less he felt of the bitterness and hurt that had been his companions for most of a lifetime.

"He's a good man, Rider. He's just trying to teach you right."

A deeper understanding stole over him like the softness of the morning breeze.

Life wasn't about getting rich or becoming famous or breeding and running the best horse in the country. It was about meeting whatever the day threw at you with as much dignity and honor as you could muster, as his mother and Alex had. It was about doing the best you could day after day, no matter what, as Jock and Colby and tens of thousands of other people did every waking moment.

Rider emptied the urn and looked at Cass, who was having a hard time controlling his own tears. Cass was hurting too, for the same reasons and for different ones. All the Creighton money couldn't stop heartache. Rider gave his new brother a fierce, one-armed embrace, and Cass lost the battle with his tears. Together they started toward the back-side.

When they reached the gap, they passed a trio of horses kicking and high-stepping in the cool morning air.

"Hey, Rider. I'm sorry to hear about your dad," one of the exercise boys said in passing.

"Thanks."

"What are you going to do with the horses?"

"It gets in your blood, boy. It gets in your blood."

Rider surprised himself by saying, "Run them, I guess." Farley Pennington would understand.

"Life has a way of bringing you to your knees, Rider. You can get up and make the best of things, or you can lay down and let it run right over you."

Some days you weren't up to the challenge, and you fell. Some days you just didn't feel particularly honorable or dignified. All you could do was hold on to the dream and hope that tomorrow would be different.

EPILOGUE

Rider was accustomed to the drive to Forest Glade. He'd been making it once a week for the last six months. Colby was better. He could see it in her eyes and hear it in her voice. Peter Whitten had been dismissed, and Forest Glade's new head psychiatrist had encouraged them all to talk—about everything, and often. They had. This time Rider knew Colby's improvement was for good.

He and Cass had grown closer every day, and it felt right, lasting, the way it was meant to be.

Leland had been indicted on two separate charges: conspiracy to commit murder—Jock's— and assault with intent to kill—Alex. In typical Leland Creighton fashion he had cut a deal to save what he could of his hide. He had agreed to drop the aggravated assault charges he'd leveled against Alex—provided she delayed divorce proceedings until his trial was over, so that she couldn't be called to testify against him.

Rider thought it was poetic justice that yesterday's paper had also linked the illustrious senator to a twelve-year-old scandal involving Peter Whitten. Whitten had once been accused of using hypnosis and drugs to cover up his own misconduct with a minor who had come to him for help. Evidently his friend Leland Creighton had offered the victim's family a large sum of money to keep their suspicions to themselves. Even then Leland had known the value of having the goods on someone.

When Leland realized what he'd done to Colby in a moment of blind fury, it was only natural that he had taken her straight to Whitten. After all, Pete owed him, and Pete knew exactly what to do. Unfortunately it had taken more than a decade for their sins to catch up with them.

The trial had started a week ago, and the newspapers didn't think he or Solly Tobias stood a chance of beating the charges, especially after Danny Brewster's damning testimony the day before.

The last half year had been hell for Danny. News that he might never walk again had sent Tracy to the nearest divorce lawyer. Though Danny was hurt to the quick, he and everyone else agreed he was better off without her. His progress had been agonizingly slow, and he was still able to walk only with the help of a walker, but he *was* walking, and Rider had no doubt that one day he'd walk alone.

The other jockeys injured in the race were all back riding. One horse had had to be destroyed. Neither Runaway Again nor Jock's Dream had made it to the Preakness or the Belmont, leaving Summer Squall and Go and Go to garner the second and third jewels of the Triple Crown. Rider knew Jock would be disappointed but philosophical.

"Don't worry about what you can't change."

It was a motto they were all trying hard to live by. They were taking life one day at a time, and working through their problems.

Colby was almost like the old Colby. Almost. They'd both changed, and Rider knew they couldn't turn back the clock, but for the first time he felt good about tomorrow.

She stood alone, away from the buildings and the carefully manicured lawns bordered with blooming chrysanthemums. The garden, set amid trees blazing with riotous autumn colors, was her sanctuary away from the "guests" of Forest Glade.

Her gaze was fixed on the cement drive winding around curves and climbing the slight hills, while her fingers stripped the bark from a supple twig.

Rising on tiptoe, she tilted her head, listening intently and trying to sort out the sounds around her—voices, laughter, the chattering of an angry squirrel, the ragged beating of her heart—trying to pick out the distinctive sound of Rider's truck.

For the tenth time in as many minutes, she glanced down at the platinum watch circling her wrist. He was late. Her stomach churned.

Then she heard it—the roar and rattle of a bad tailpipe. A smile blossomed on her lips, and she raced to the parking area, grinning from ear to ear.

She saw him get out of the truck and light a cigarette. She stopped on the sidewalk, caught in a feeling of love so deep she felt like crying. It might be true that you could never recapture the innocence of young love, but Colby was beginning to believe that if you were lucky enough to get a second chance, that second chance was better, more precious.

He looked up and saw her, and a slow smile spread across his face. His lazy, easy gait brought him to her side. "Well?"

"Praise the Lord!" she said dramatically. "I'm cured." She grinned. "Michael said only to come back if I want to talk."

"That's great. I'm getting a little tired of this drive."

"And I'm getting a little tired of your complaining," she quipped.

Rider was glad to see her spunk and her sharp tongue return. The shadows were fading. He ground out his cigarette and planted his hands on his Levi's-clad hips. "You're really feeling your Cheerios, aren't you?"

"I'd feel a whole lot better if you'd take me home to bed."

Rider feigned shock. "Bed? Do you mean to tell me you haven't gotten enough rest up here?"

Colby threw her arms around his neck and looked up at him with shining eyes. "I want to go home to bed, Rider. I want to make love."

Penny Richards is the bestselling author of fourteen romance novels under both her real name and her pseudonym, Bay Matthews. She has won a number of awards, among them the *Romantic Times* Lifetime Achievement Award. Her books appear regularly on the Waldenbooks bestseller list. She lives in Louisiana.